Ali-A Adventures

GAME ON!

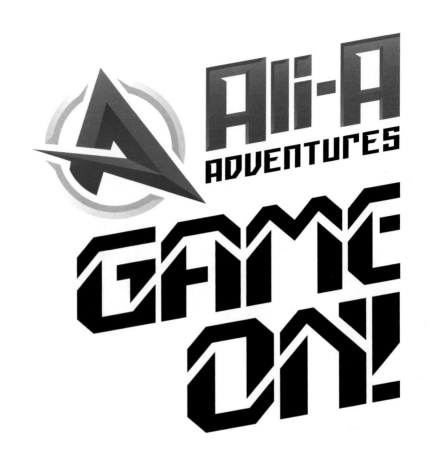

PRESS START

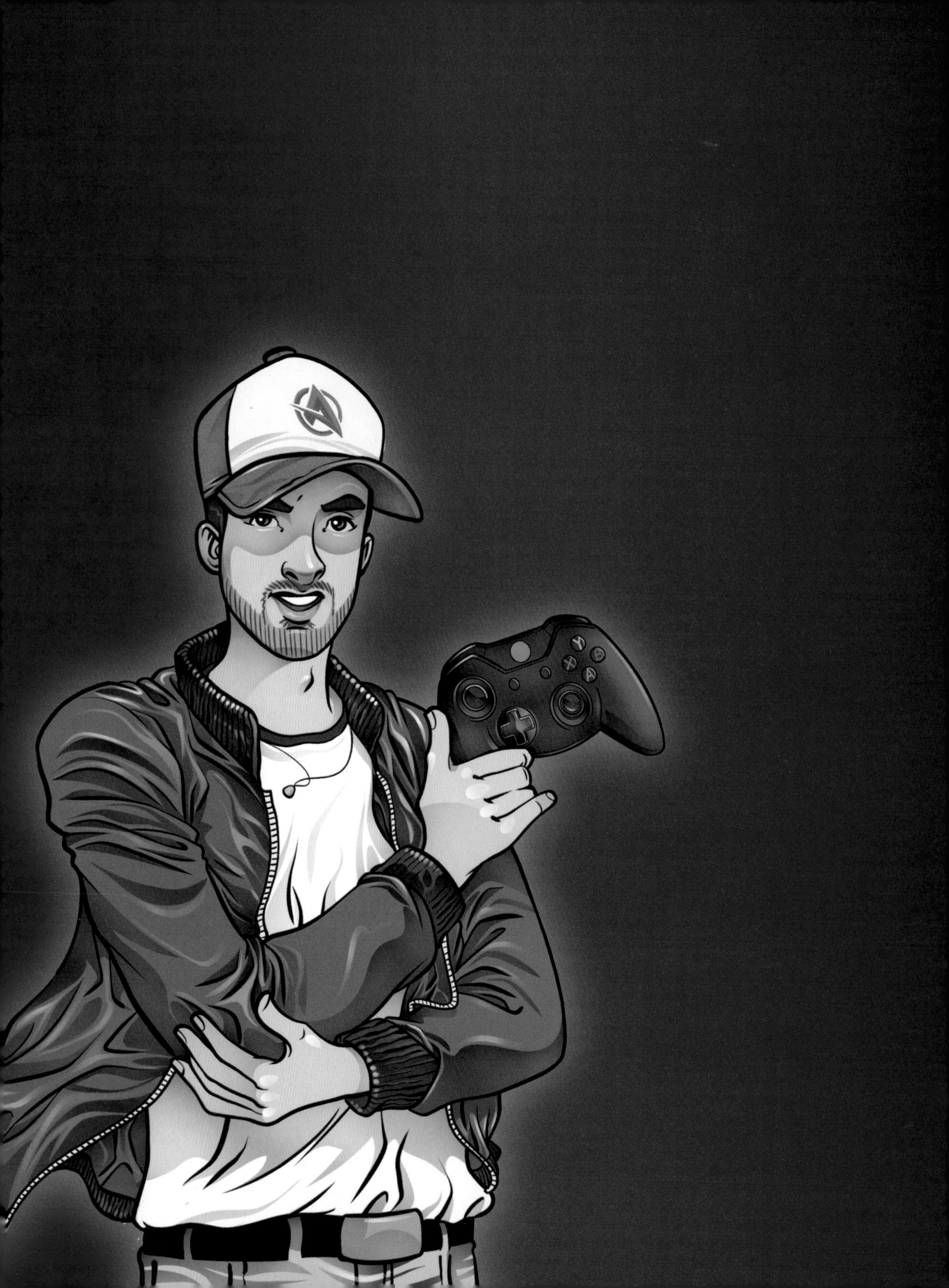

THANK YOU FOR PICKING UP MY VERY FIRST BOOK--
ALI-A ADVENTURES: GAME ON!

JOIN ME AND CLARE (AND EEVEE, OF COURSE!)
AS WE GO ON OUR FIRST BIG ADVENTURE TO SAVE
THE WORLD.

I REALLY HOPE YOU ENJOY THE BOOK AS MUCH
AS I ENJOYED WORKING ON IT!

ALI-A

Originally published in Great Britain by Puffin Books, a division of Penguin Random House Ltd., London, in 2017.

Random House and the colophon are registered trademarks of Penguin Random House LLC.

Visit us on the Web! rhcbooks.com

Educators and librarians, for a variety of teaching tools, visit us at RHTeachersLibrarians.com

Library of Congress Cataloging-in-Publication Data is available upon request.

ISBN 978-1-5247-7095-2 (trade) — ISBN 978-1-5247-7096-9 (lib. bdg.) — ISBN 978-1-5247-7097-6 (ebook)

Written by Alastair Aiken and Cavan Scott
Lead artist: Aleksandar Sotirovski

Printed in the United States of America
10 9 8 7 6 5 4 3 2 1
First American Edition

Random House Children's Books supports the First Amendment and celebrates the right to read.

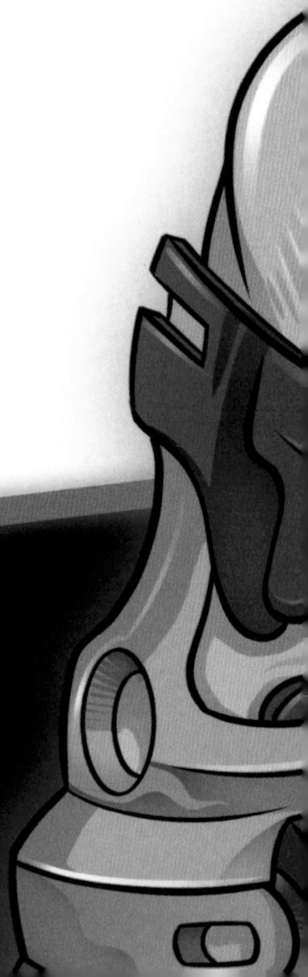

Ali-A Adventures

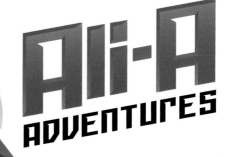

Game On!

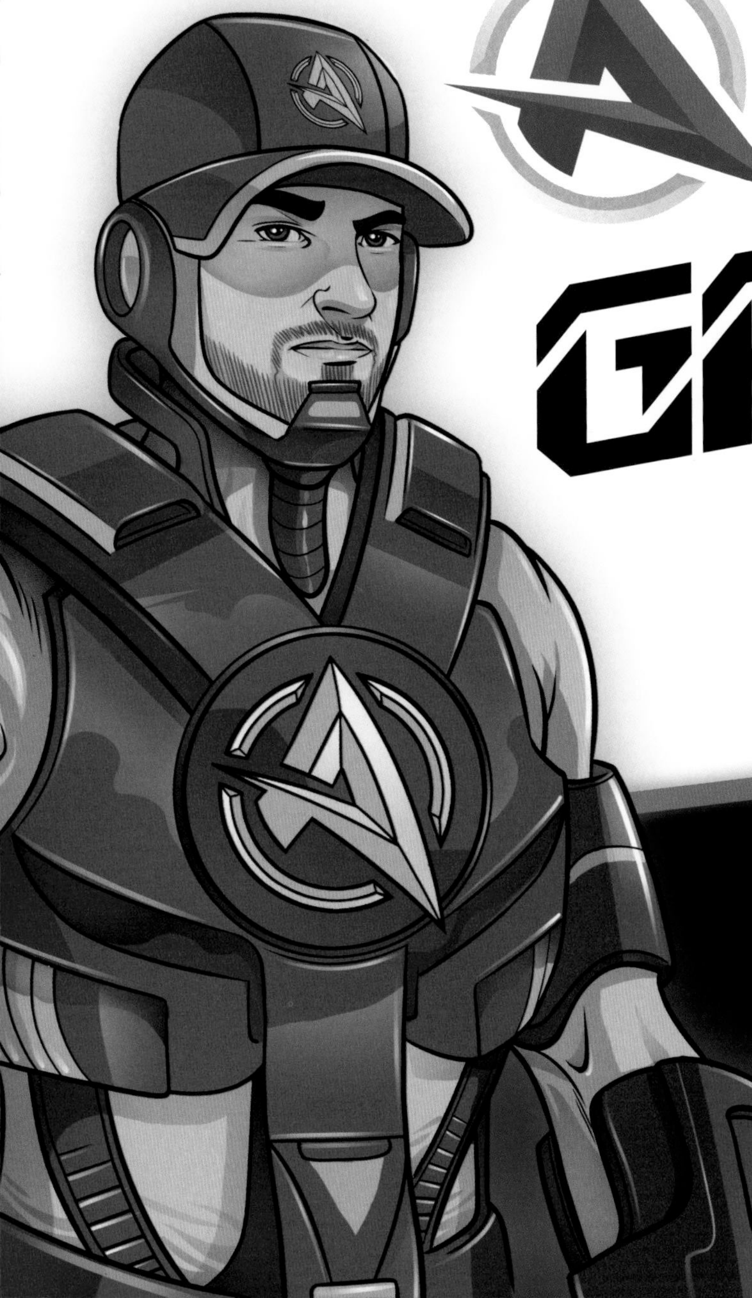

Random House
New York

MEET THE HEROES

EEVEE
ALI AND CLARE'S
FOUR-LEGGED FRIEND
IS NO ORDINARY PUP!

ALI-A
HE'S CONQUERED THE
GAMING WORLD--NOW
HE'S HERE TO SAVE THE
REST OF IT.

CLARE
SHE'S AN ACE GAMER
AND AN AWESOME
ADVENTURER.

LEVEL ONE

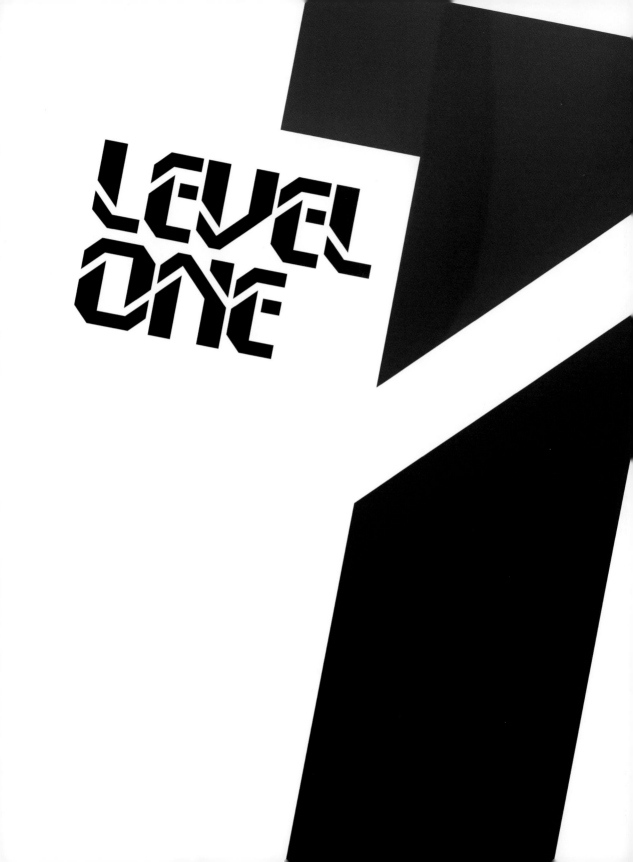

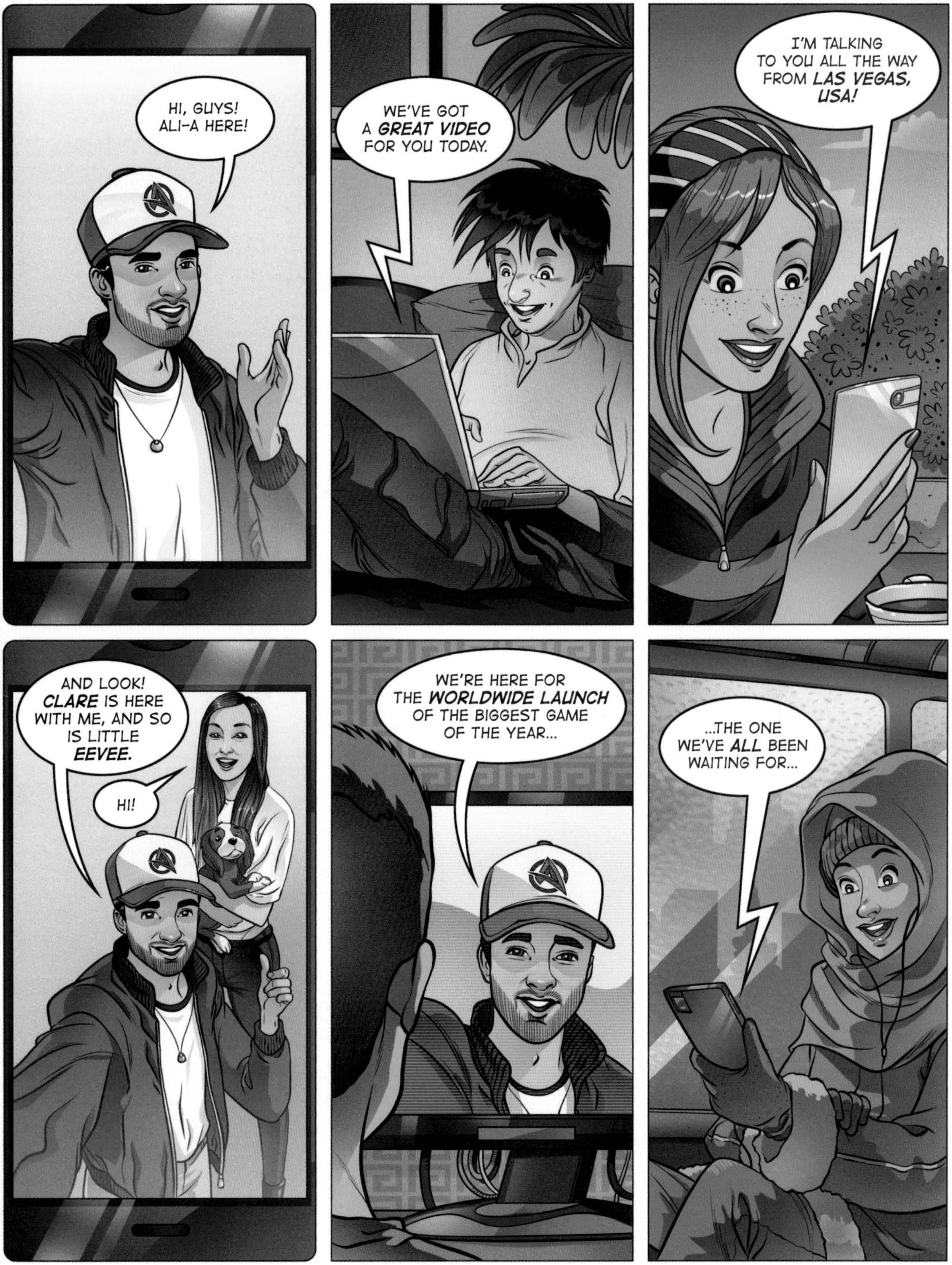
HI, GUYS! ALI-A HERE!
WE'VE GOT A **GREAT VIDEO** FOR YOU TODAY.
I'M TALKING TO YOU ALL THE WAY FROM **LAS VEGAS, USA!**
AND LOOK! **CLARE** IS HERE WITH ME, AND SO IS LITTLE **EEVEE.**
HI!
WE'RE HERE FOR THE **WORLDWIDE LAUNCH** OF THE BIGGEST GAME OF THE YEAR...
...THE ONE WE'VE **ALL** BEEN WAITING FOR...

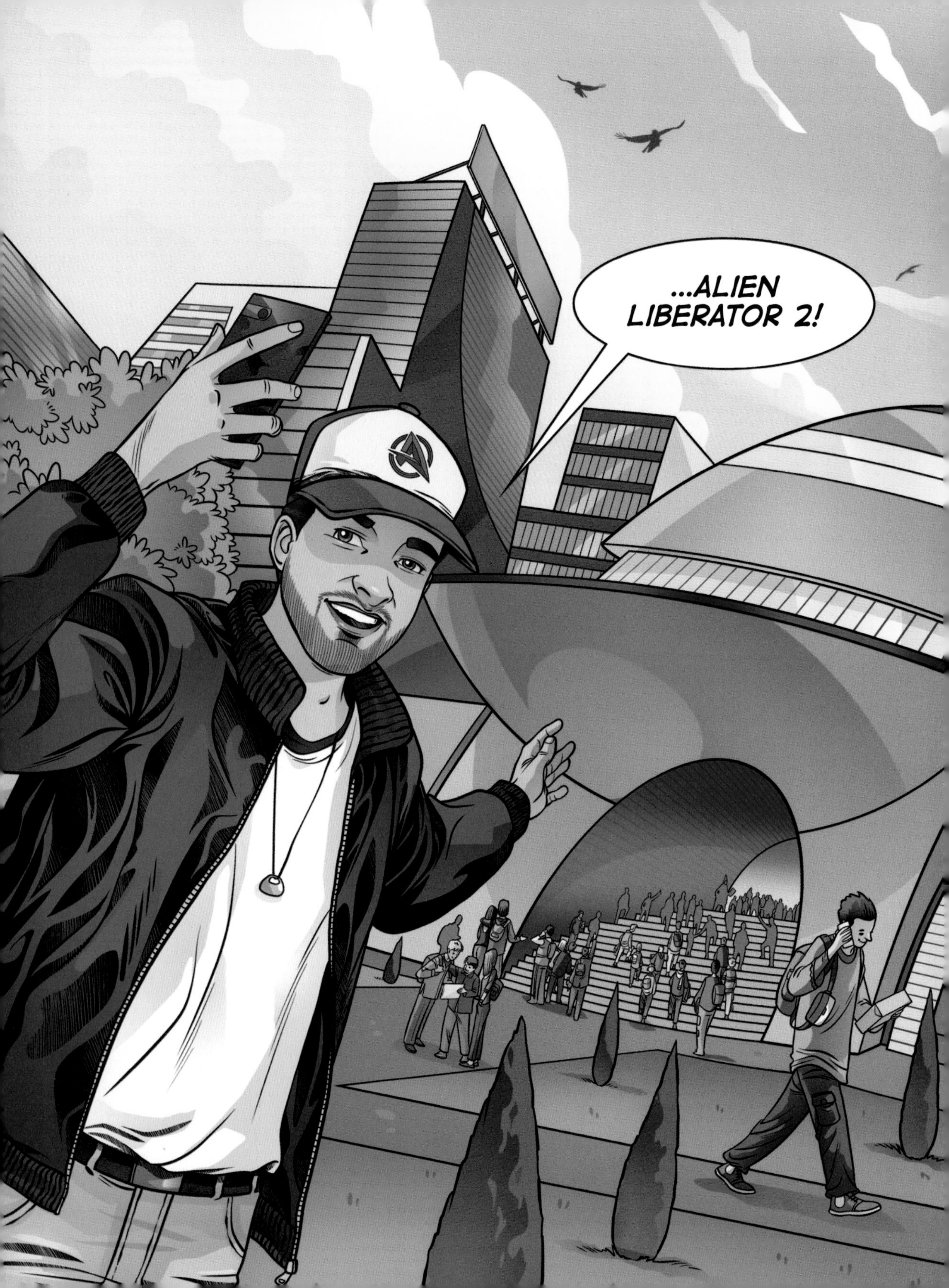
...ALIEN LIBERATOR 2!

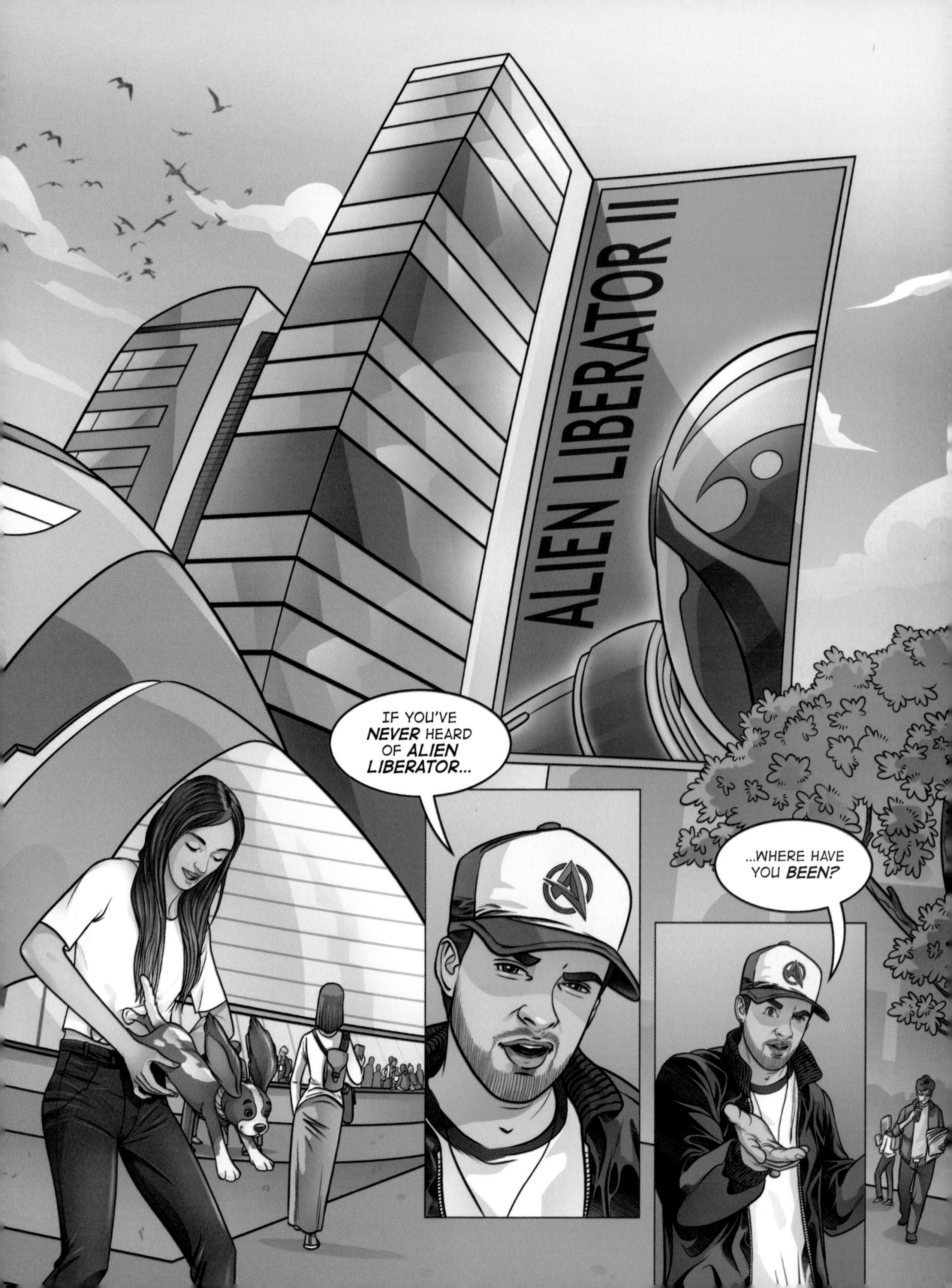
ALIEN LIBERATOR II
IF YOU'VE NEVER HEARD OF ALIEN LIBERATOR...
...WHERE HAVE YOU BEEN?

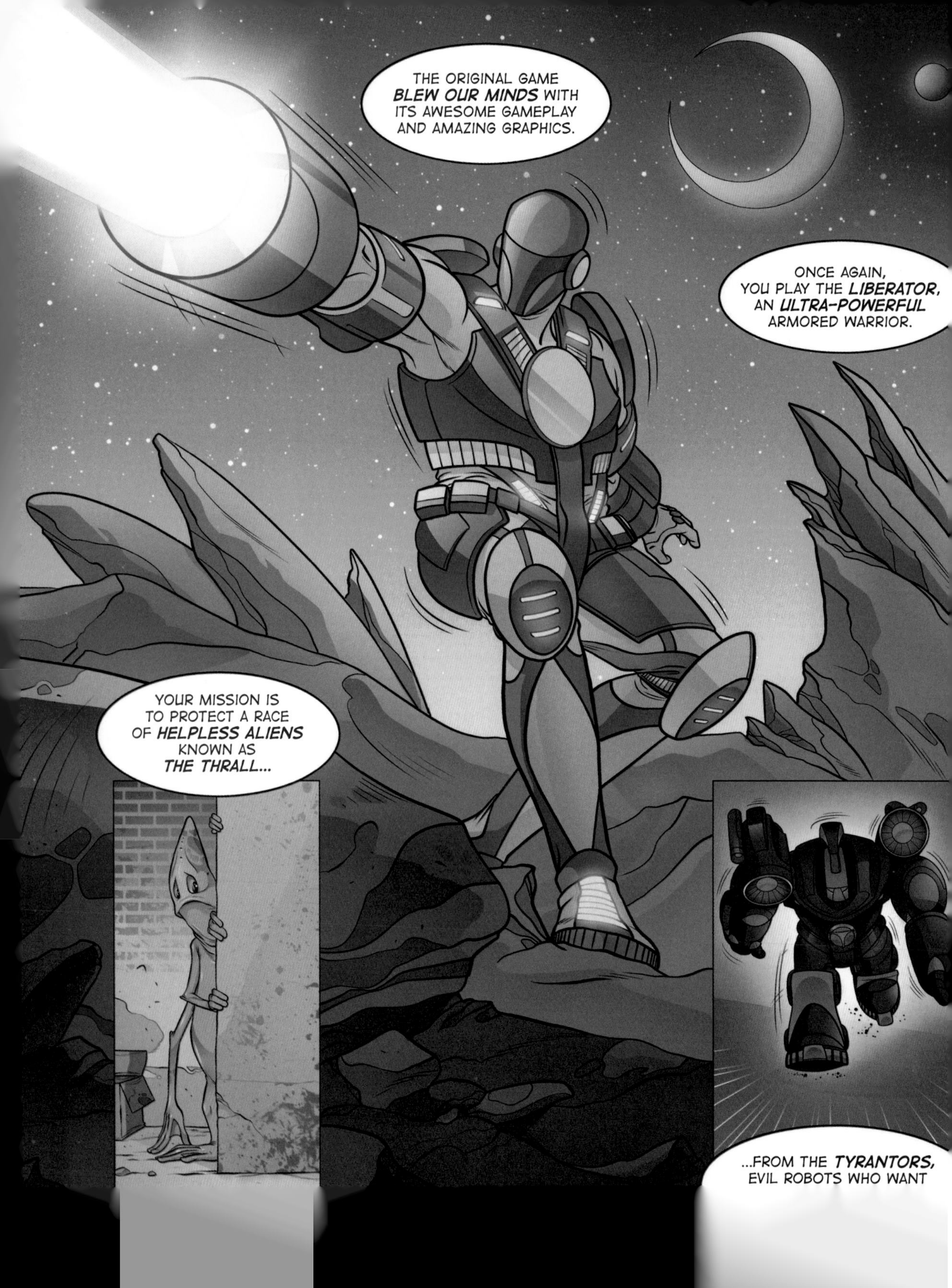
THE ORIGINAL GAME BLEW OUR MINDS WITH ITS AWESOME GAMEPLAY AND AMAZING GRAPHICS.
ONCE AGAIN, YOU PLAY THE LIBERATOR, AN ULTRA-POWERFUL ARMORED WARRIOR.
YOUR MISSION IS TO PROTECT A RACE OF HELPLESS ALIENS KNOWN AS THE THRALL...
...FROM THE TYRANTORS, EVIL ROBOTS WHO WANT

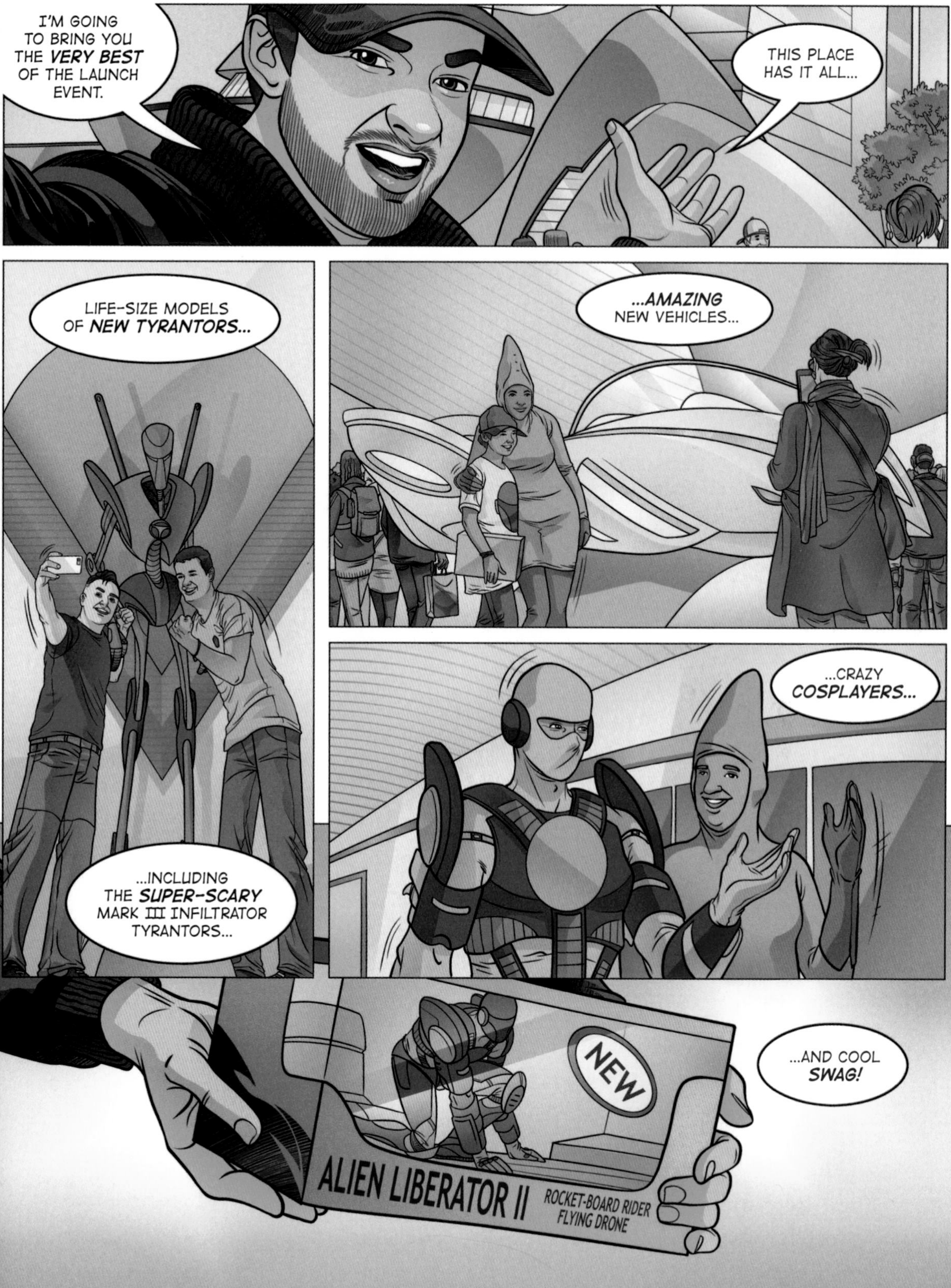
I'M GOING TO BRING YOU THE VERY BEST OF THE LAUNCH EVENT.
THIS PLACE HAS IT ALL...
LIFE-SIZE MODELS OF NEW TYRANTORS...
...INCLUDING THE SUPER-SCARY MARK III INFILTRATOR TYRANTORS...
...AMAZING NEW VEHICLES...
...CRAZY COSPLAYERS...
NEW
ALIEN LIBERATOR II
ROCKET-BOARD RIDER FLYING DRONE
...AND COOL SWAG!

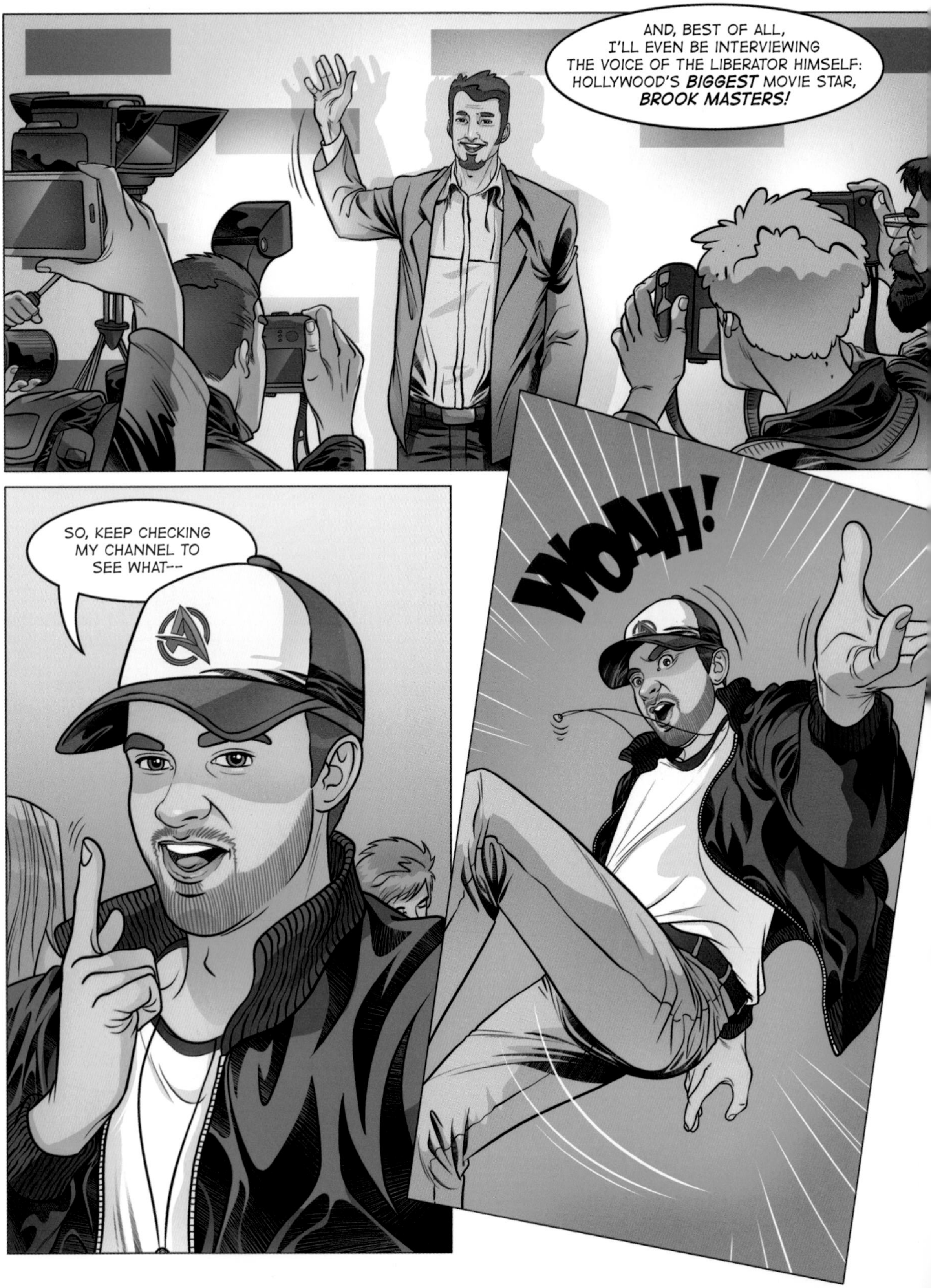
AND, BEST OF ALL, I'LL EVEN BE INTERVIEWING THE VOICE OF THE LIBERATOR HIMSELF: HOLLYWOOD'S BIGGEST MOVIE STAR, BROOK MASTERS!
SO, KEEP CHECKING MY CHANNEL TO SEE WHAT--
WOAH!

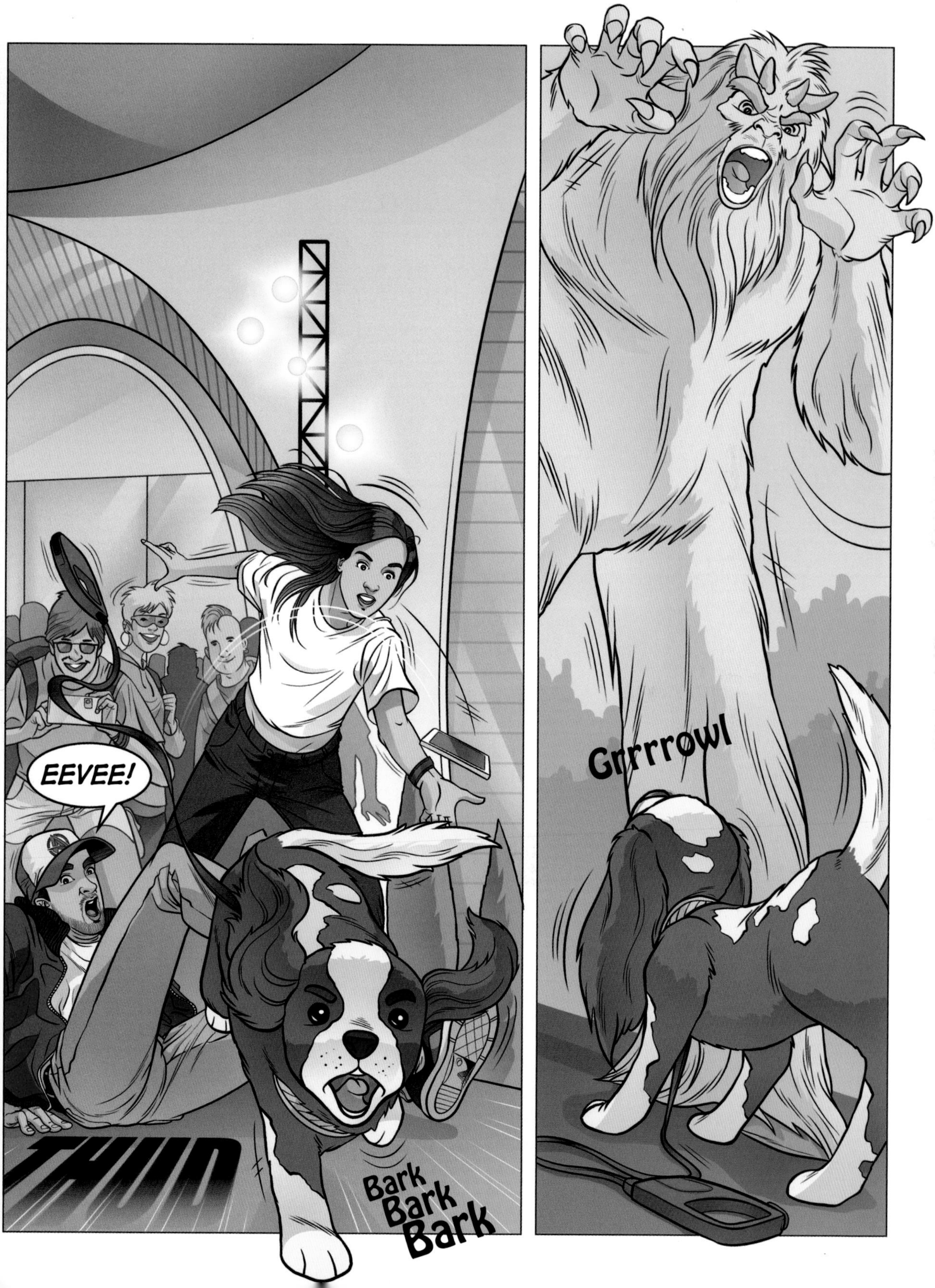
EEVEE!
THUD
Bark
Bark
Bark
Grrrrowl

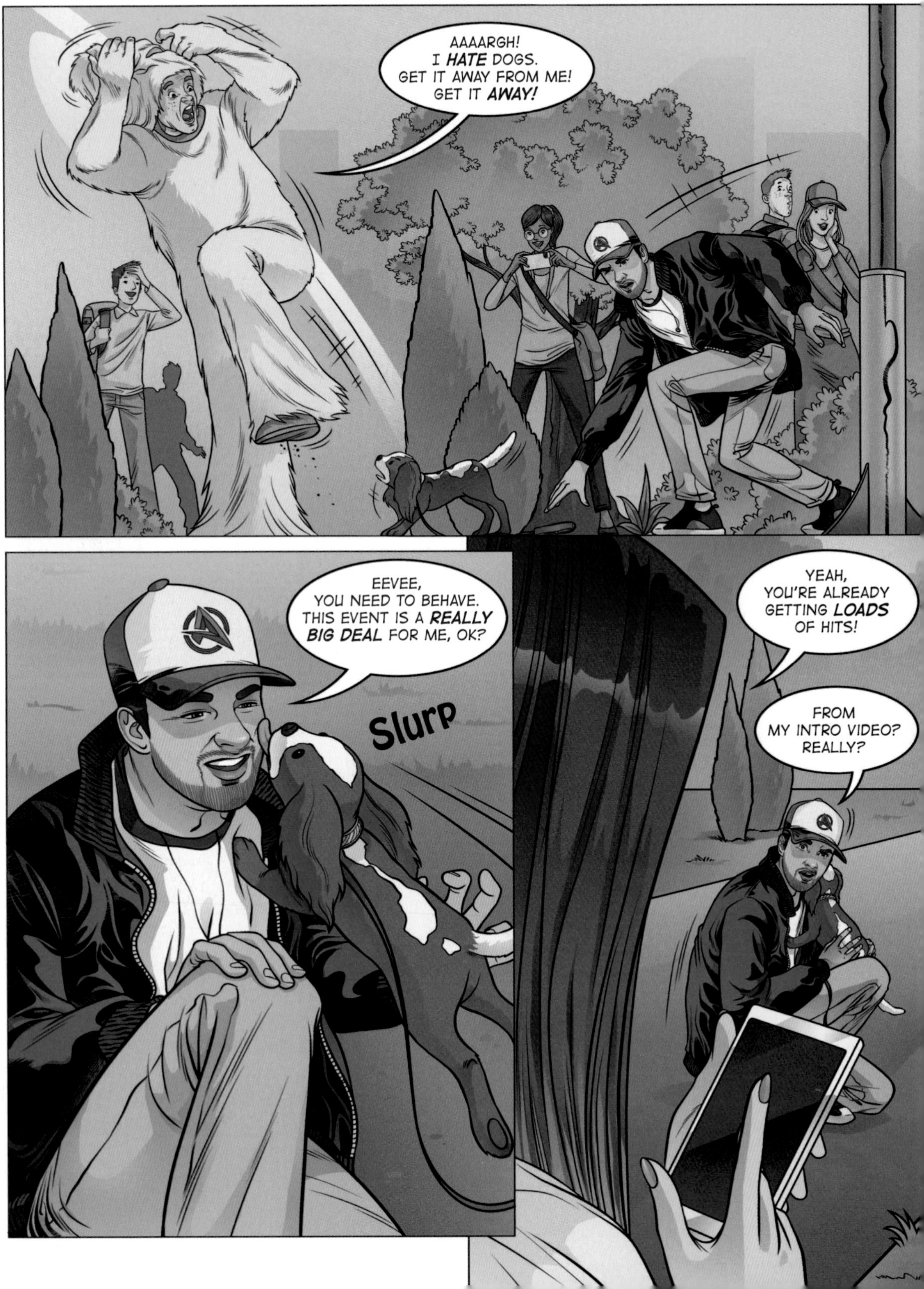
AAAARGH! I HATE DOGS. GET IT AWAY FROM ME! GET IT AWAY!
EEVEE, YOU NEED TO BEHAVE. THIS EVENT IS A REALLY BIG DEAL FOR ME, OK?
Slurp
YEAH, YOU'RE ALREADY GETTING LOADS OF HITS!
FROM MY INTRO VIDEO? REALLY?

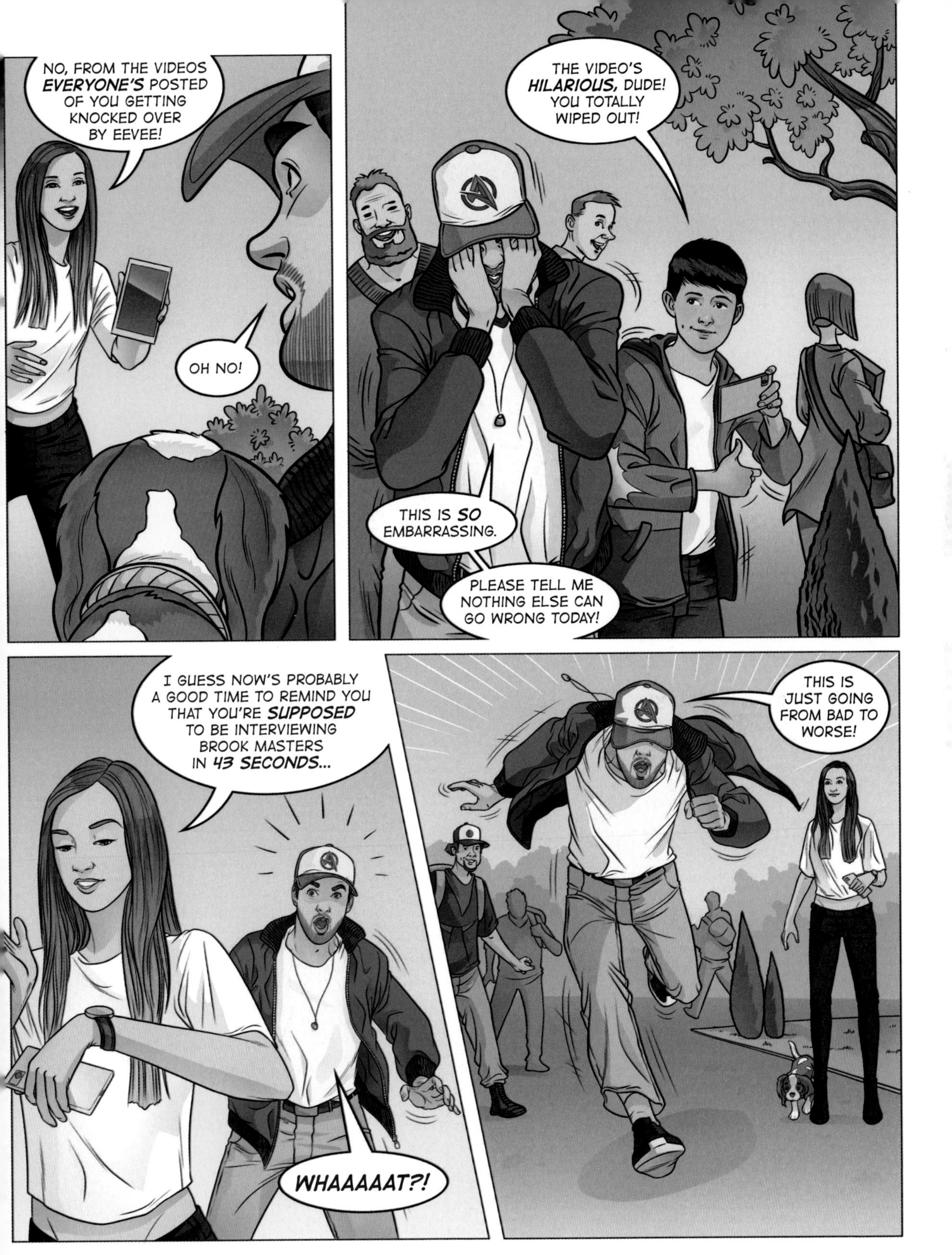
NO, FROM THE VIDEOS EVERYONE'S POSTED OF YOU GETTING KNOCKED OVER BY EEVEE!
OH NO!
THE VIDEO'S HILARIOUS, DUDE! YOU TOTALLY WIPED OUT!
THIS IS SO EMBARRASSING.
PLEASE TELL ME NOTHING ELSE CAN GO WRONG TODAY!
I GUESS NOW'S PROBABLY A GOOD TIME TO REMIND YOU THAT YOU'RE SUPPOSED TO BE INTERVIEWING BROOK MASTERS IN 43 SECONDS...
WHAAAAAT?!
THIS IS JUST GOING FROM BAD TO WORSE!

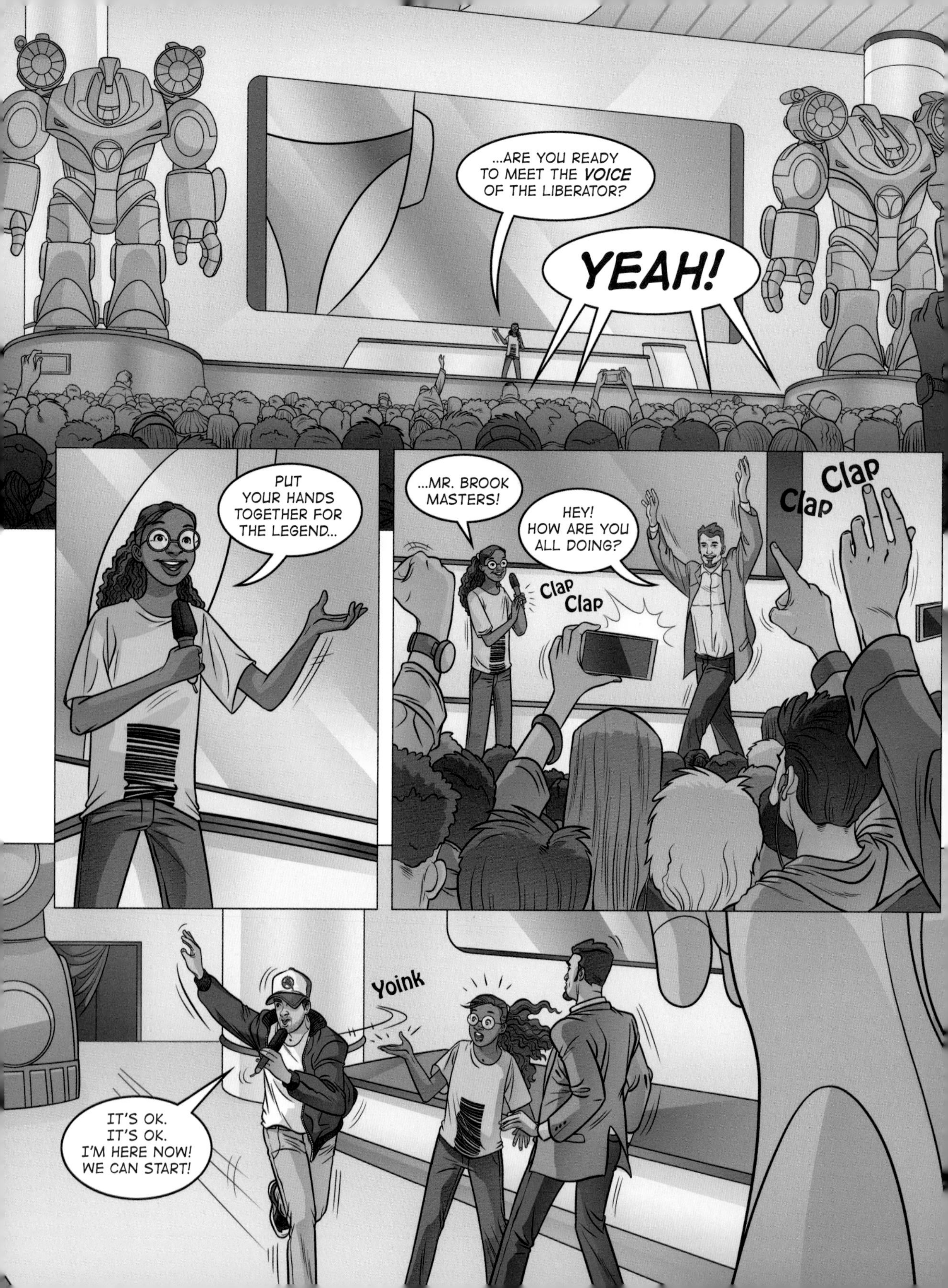
...ARE YOU READY TO MEET THE *VOICE* OF THE LIBERATOR?
YEAH!
PUT YOUR HANDS TOGETHER FOR THE LEGEND...
...MR. BROOK MASTERS!
HEY! HOW ARE YOU ALL DOING?
Clap Clap
Clap Clap
Yoink
IT'S OK. IT'S OK. I'M HERE NOW! WE CAN START!

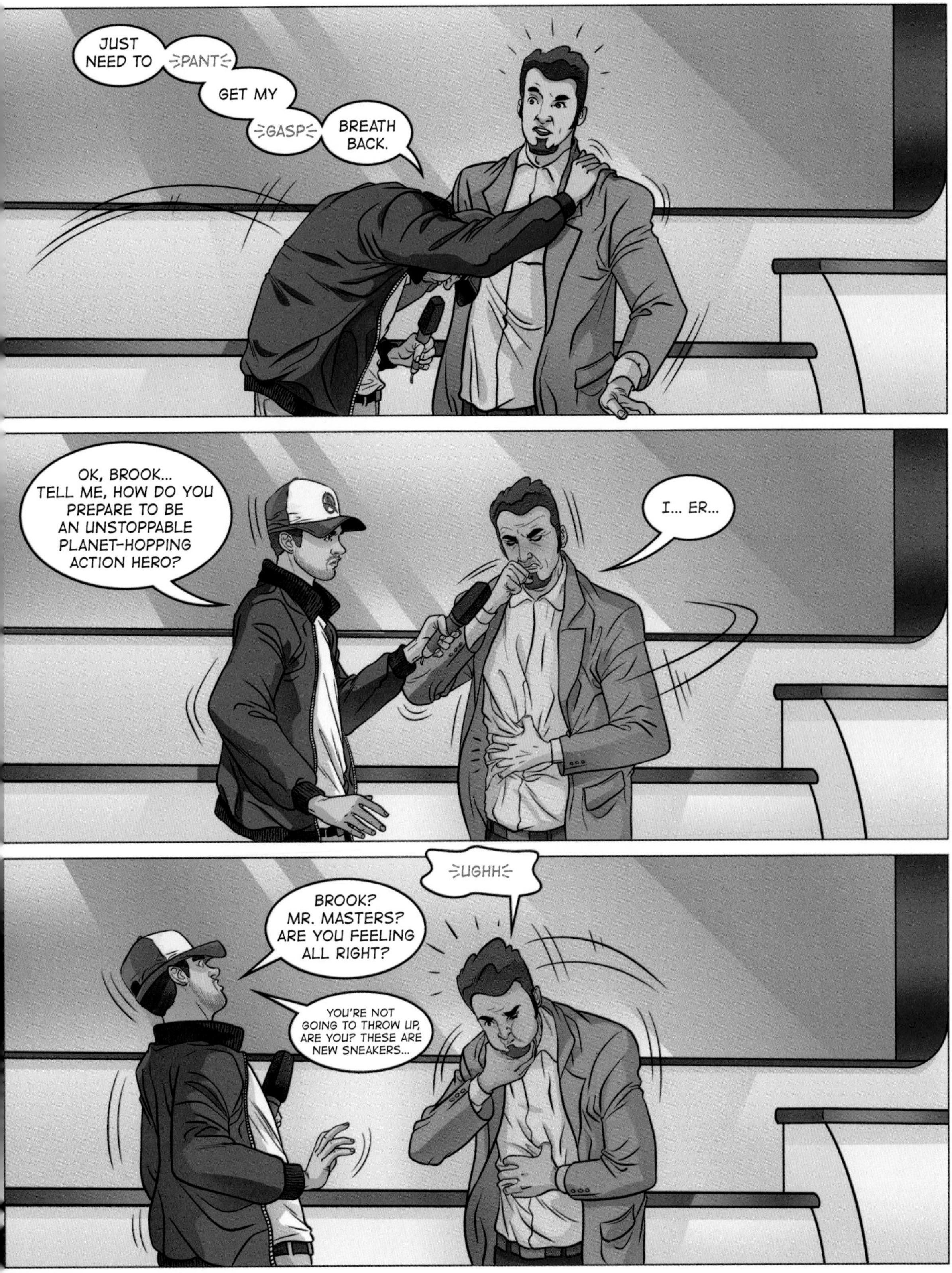
JUST NEED TO
PANT
GET MY
GASP
BREATH BACK.
OK, BROOK... TELL ME, HOW DO YOU PREPARE TO BE AN UNSTOPPABLE PLANET-HOPPING ACTION HERO?
I... ER...
UGHH
BROOK? MR. MASTERS? ARE YOU FEELING ALL RIGHT?
YOU'RE NOT GOING TO THROW UP, ARE YOU? THESE ARE NEW SNEAKERS...

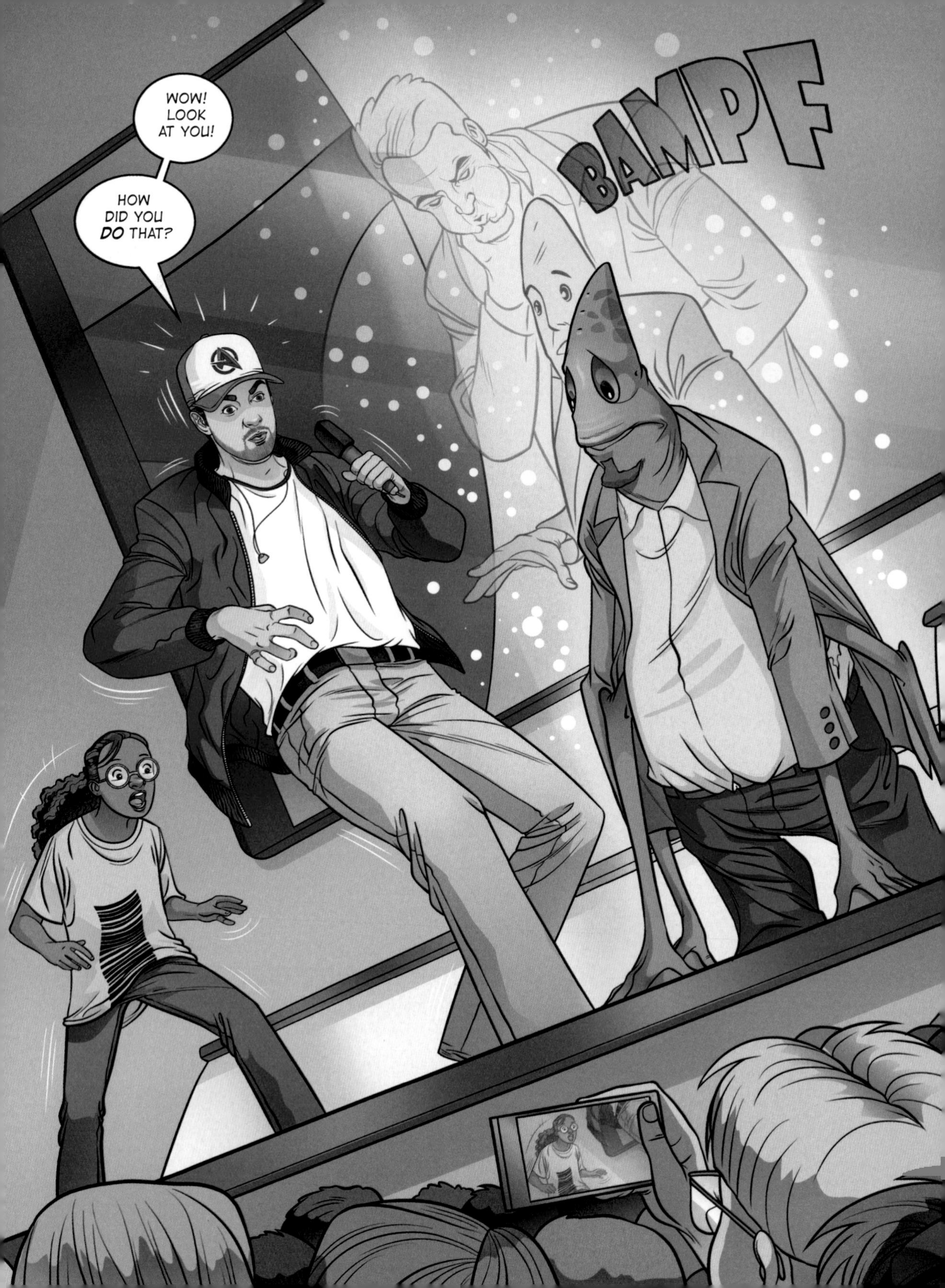
WOW! LOOK AT YOU!
HOW DID YOU DO THAT?
BAMPF

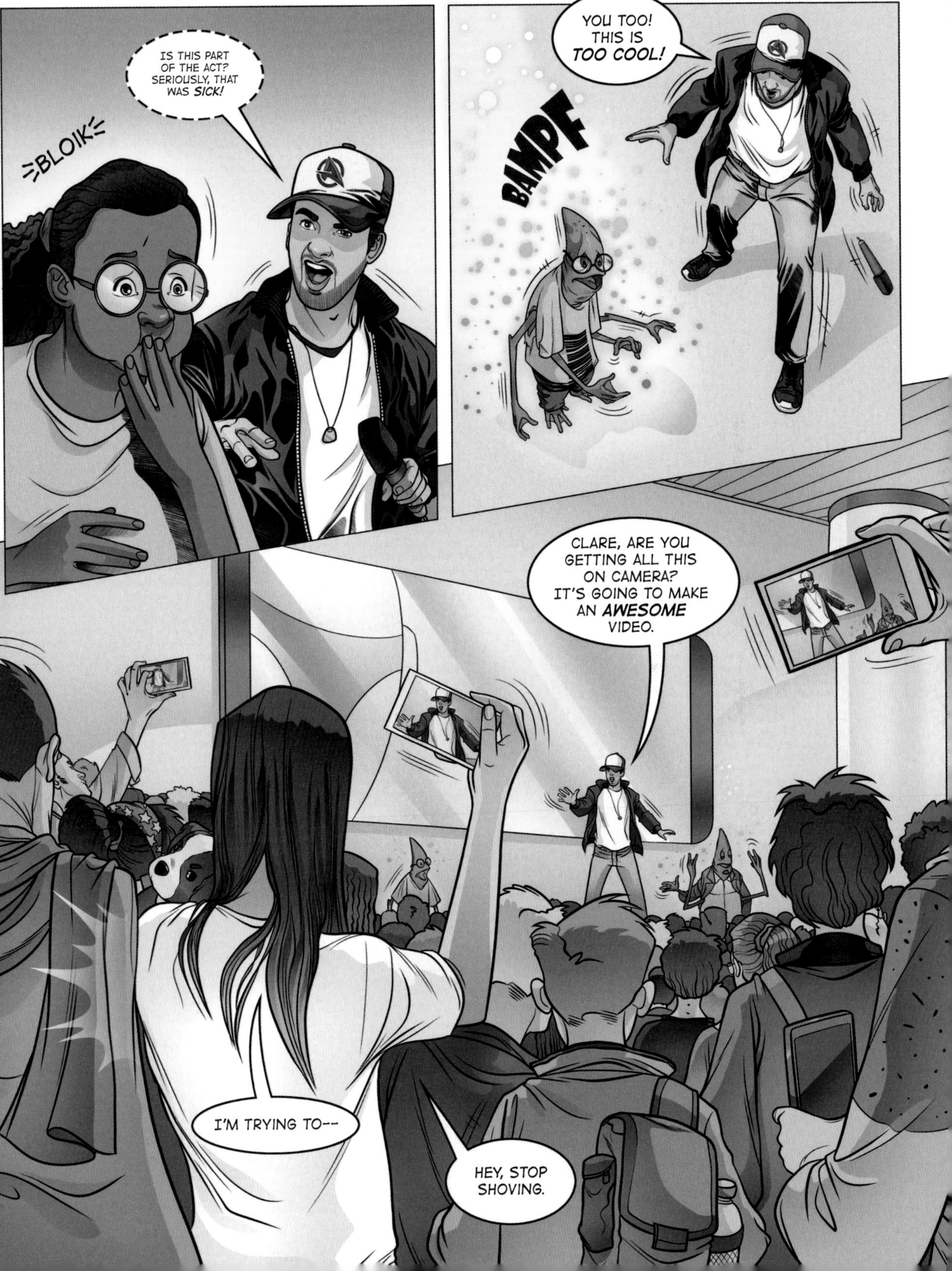
BLOIK
IS THIS PART OF THE ACT? SERIOUSLY, THAT WAS *SICK!*
YOU TOO! THIS IS *TOO COOL!*
BAMPF
CLARE, ARE YOU GETTING ALL THIS ON CAMERA? IT'S GOING TO MAKE AN ***AWESOME*** VIDEO.
I'M TRYING TO--
HEY, STOP SHOVING.

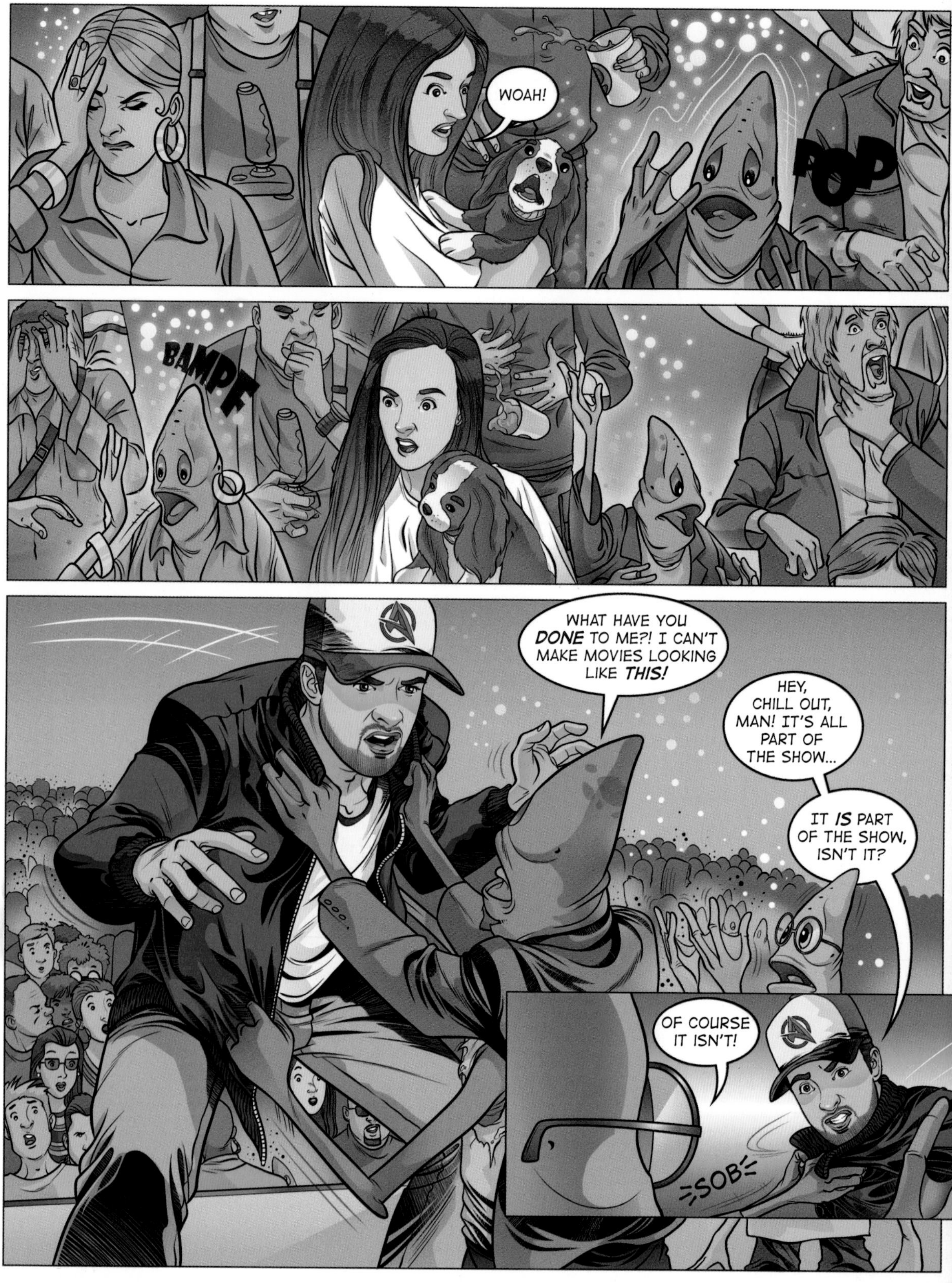
WOAH!
POP
BAMPF
WHAT HAVE YOU DONE TO ME?! I CAN'T MAKE MOVIES LOOKING LIKE THIS!
HEY, CHILL OUT, MAN! IT'S ALL PART OF THE SHOW...
IT IS PART OF THE SHOW, ISN'T IT?
OF COURSE IT ISN'T!
SOB

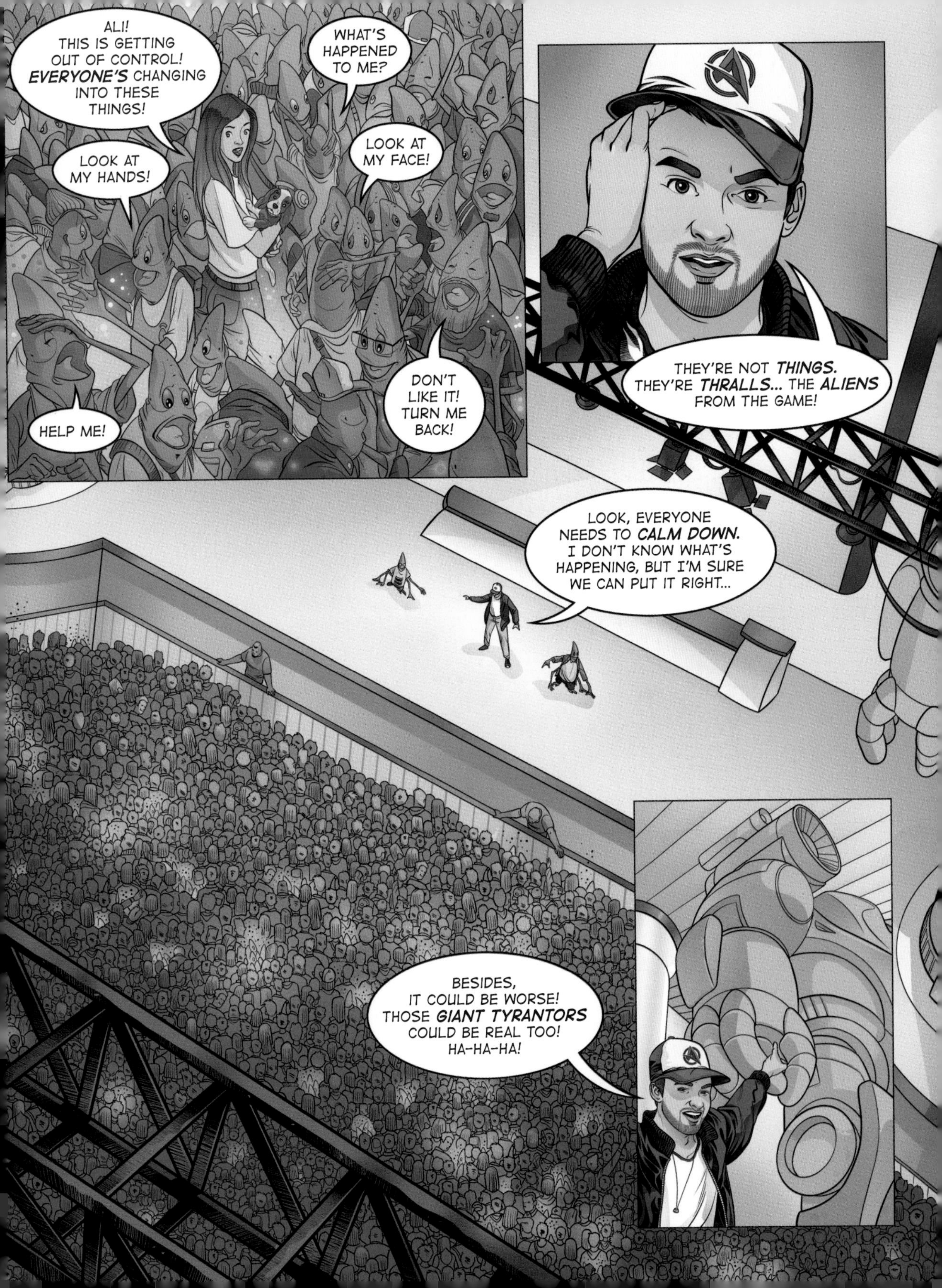
ALI! THIS IS GETTING OUT OF CONTROL! EVERYONE'S CHANGING INTO THESE THINGS!
WHAT'S HAPPENED TO ME?
LOOK AT MY HANDS!
LOOK AT MY FACE!
HELP ME!
DON'T LIKE IT! TURN ME BACK!
THEY'RE NOT THINGS. THEY'RE THRALLS... THE ALIENS FROM THE GAME!
LOOK, EVERYONE NEEDS TO CALM DOWN. I DON'T KNOW WHAT'S HAPPENING, BUT I'M SURE WE CAN PUT IT RIGHT...
BESIDES, IT COULD BE WORSE! THOSE GIANT TYRANTORS COULD BE REAL TOO! HA-HA-HA!

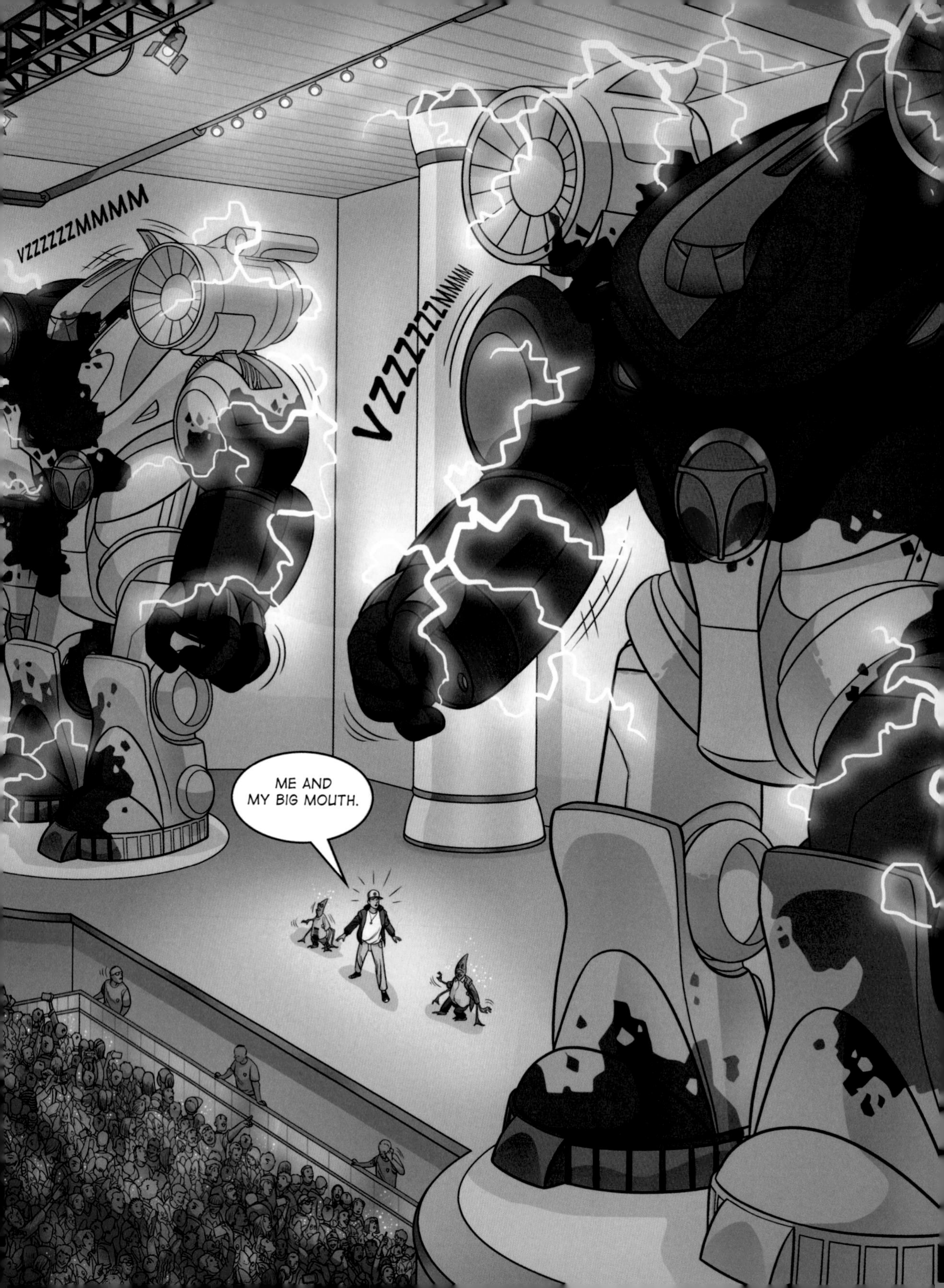
VZZZZZZMMMM
VZZZZZZMMMM
ME AND MY BIG MOUTH.

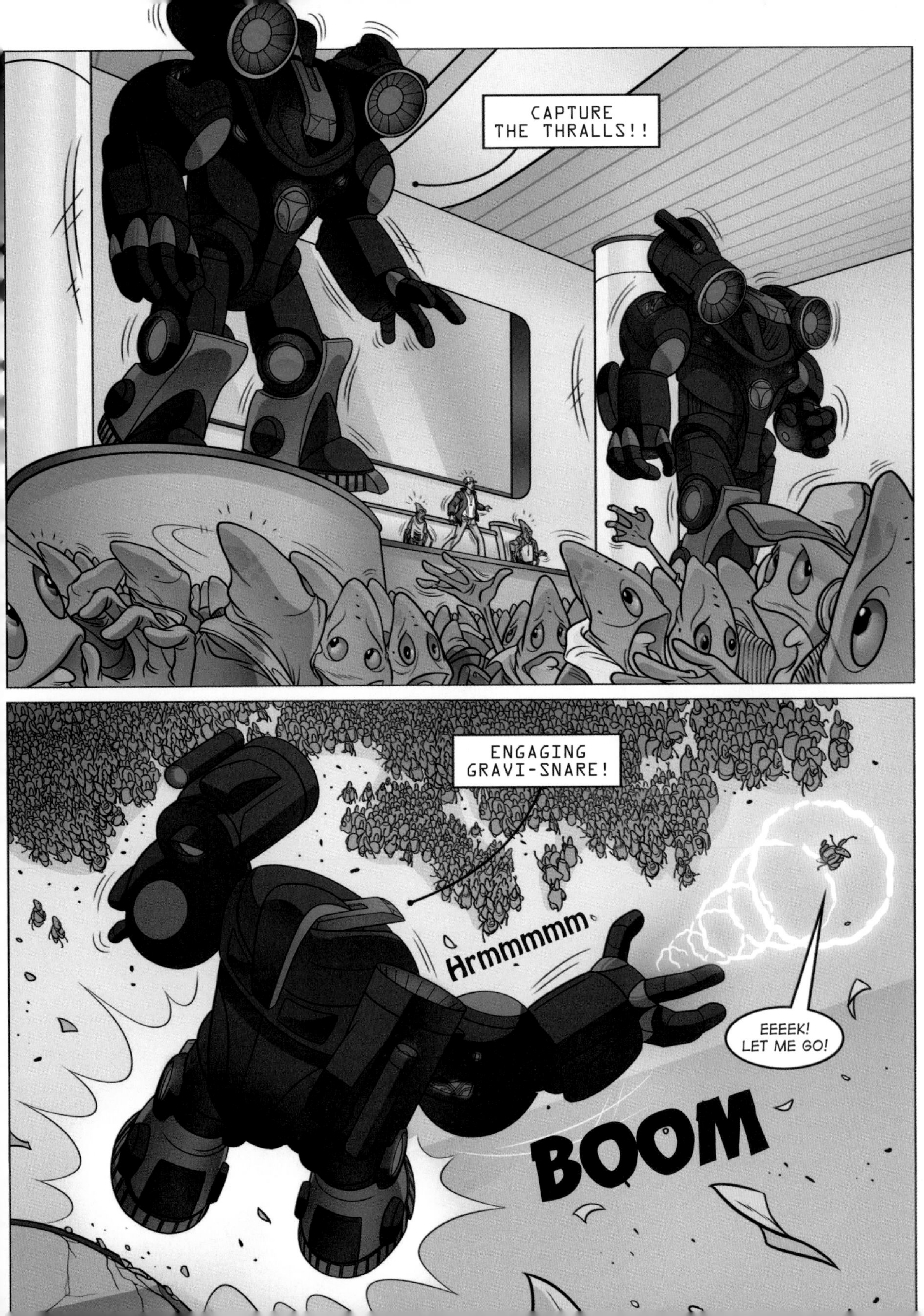
CAPTURE THE THRALLS!!
ENGAGING GRAVI-SNARE!
Hrmmmmm
EEEEK! LET ME GO!
BOOM

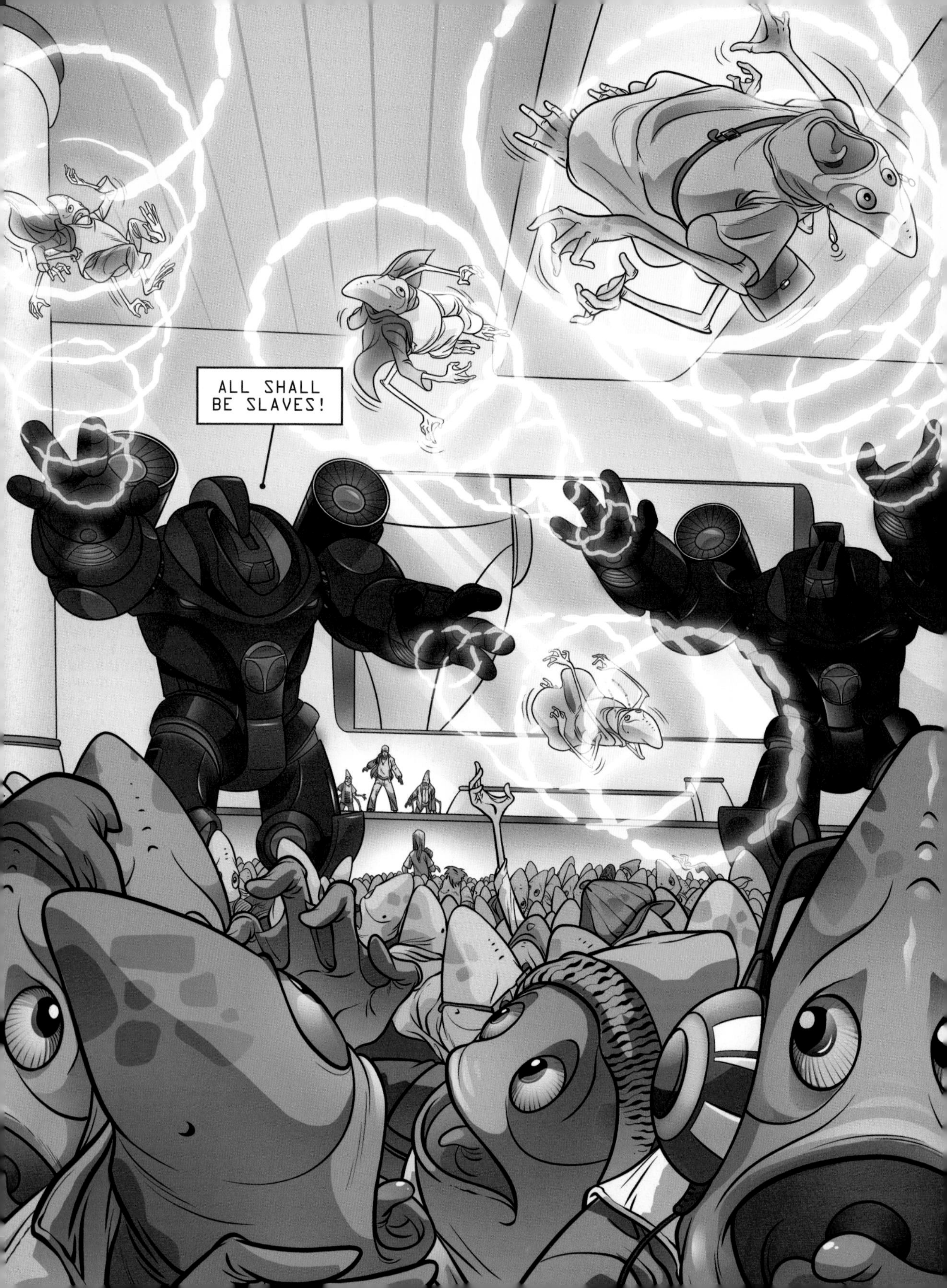
ALL SHALL BE SLAVES!

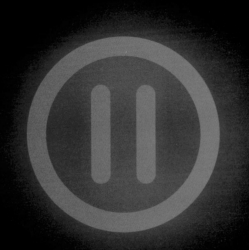

LEVEL TWO

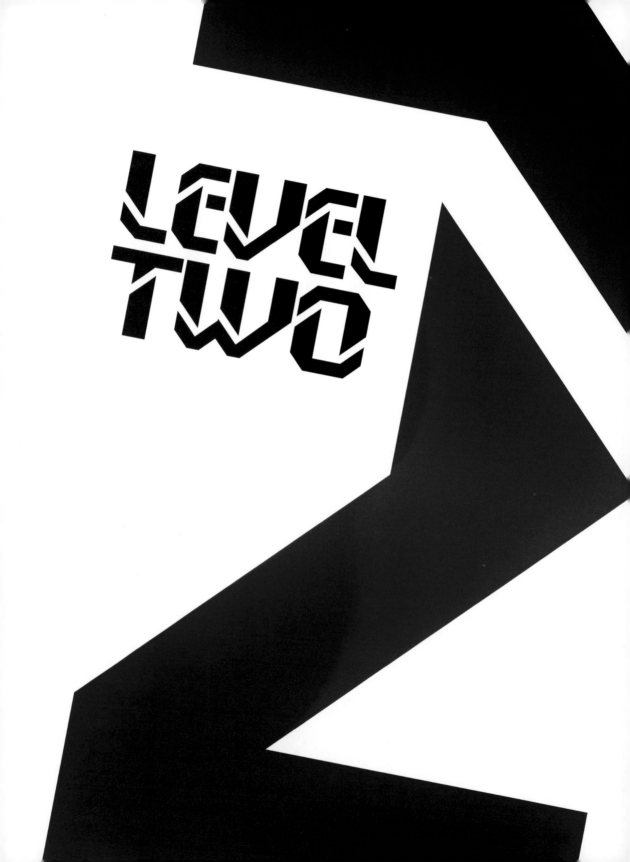

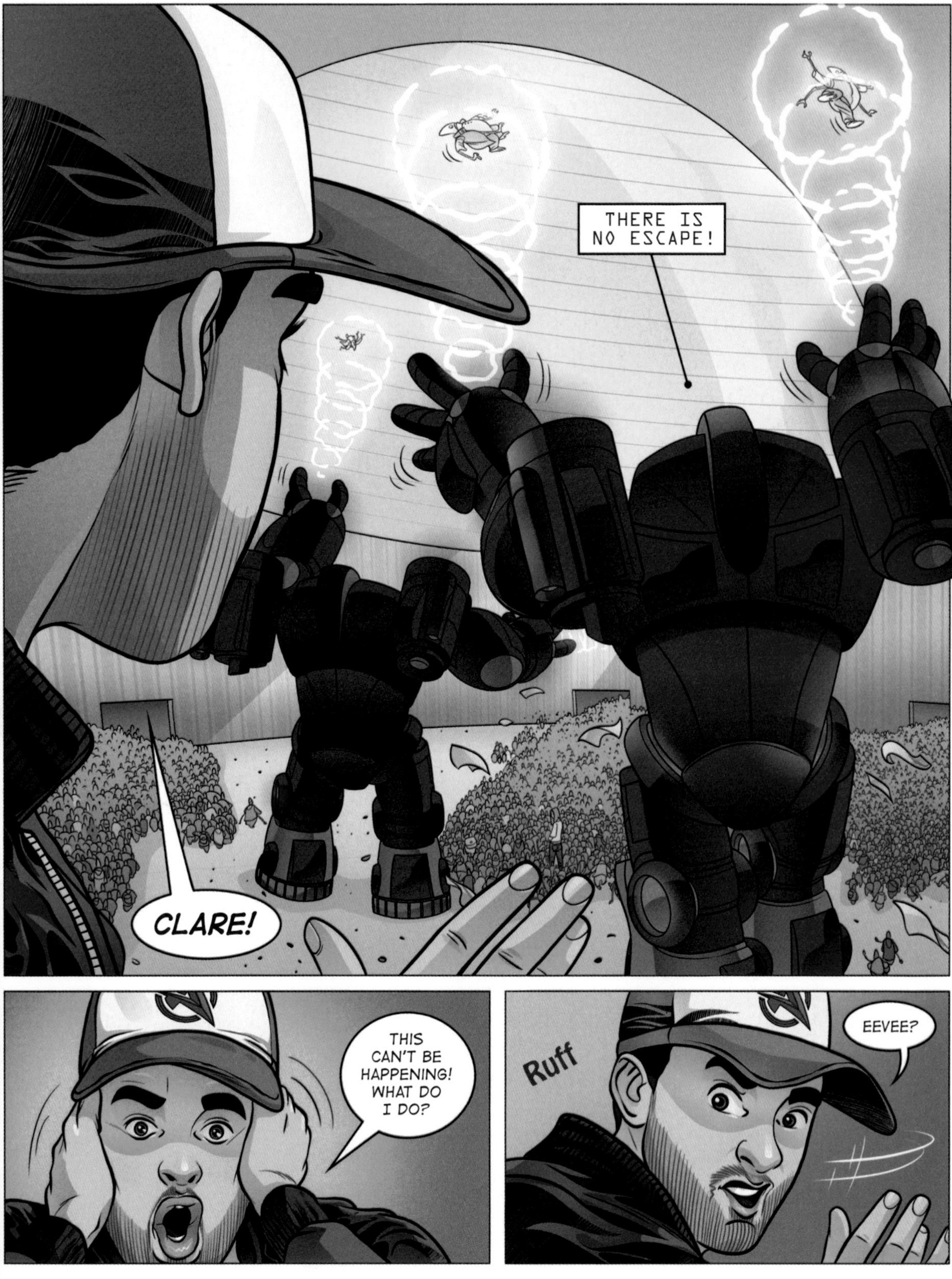
THERE IS NO ESCAPE!
CLARE!
THIS CAN'T BE HAPPENING! WHAT DO I DO?
Ruff
EEVEE?

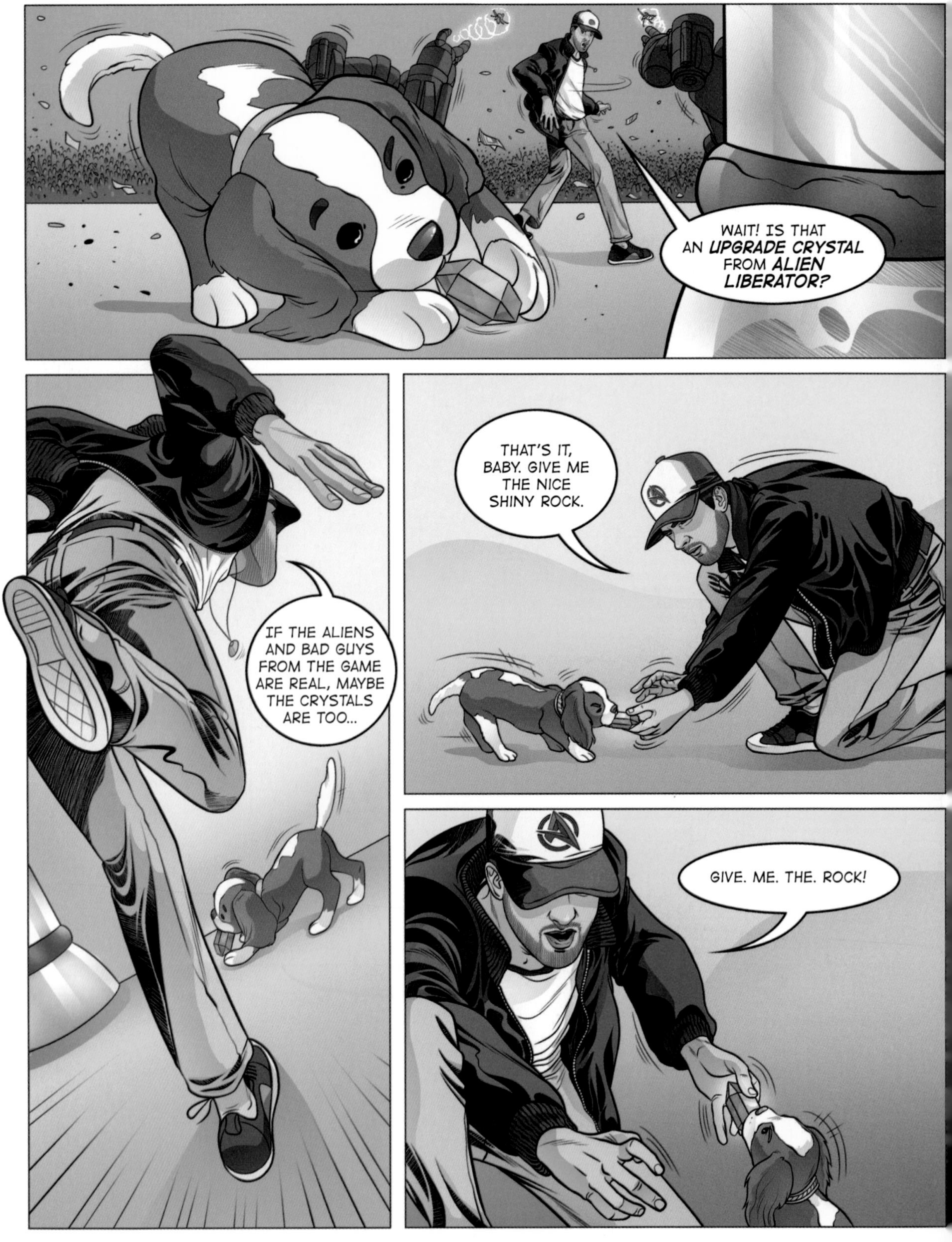
WAIT! IS THAT AN UPGRADE CRYSTAL FROM ALIEN LIBERATOR?
IF THE ALIENS AND BAD GUYS FROM THE GAME ARE REAL, MAYBE THE CRYSTALS ARE TOO...
THAT'S IT, BABY. GIVE ME THE NICE SHINY ROCK.
GIVE. ME. THE. ROCK!

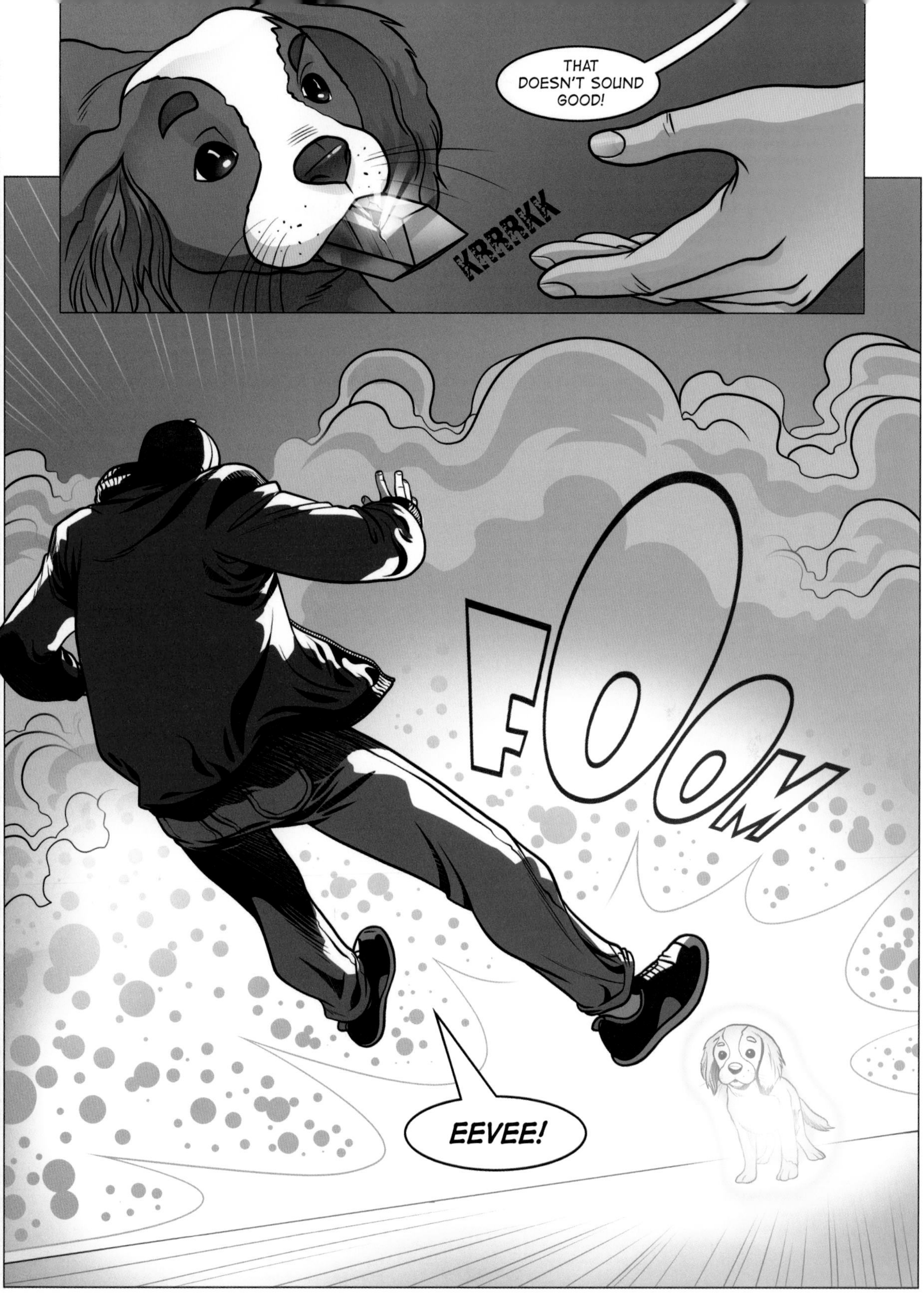
THAT DOESN'T SOUND GOOD!
KRRRKK
FOOOM
EEVEE!

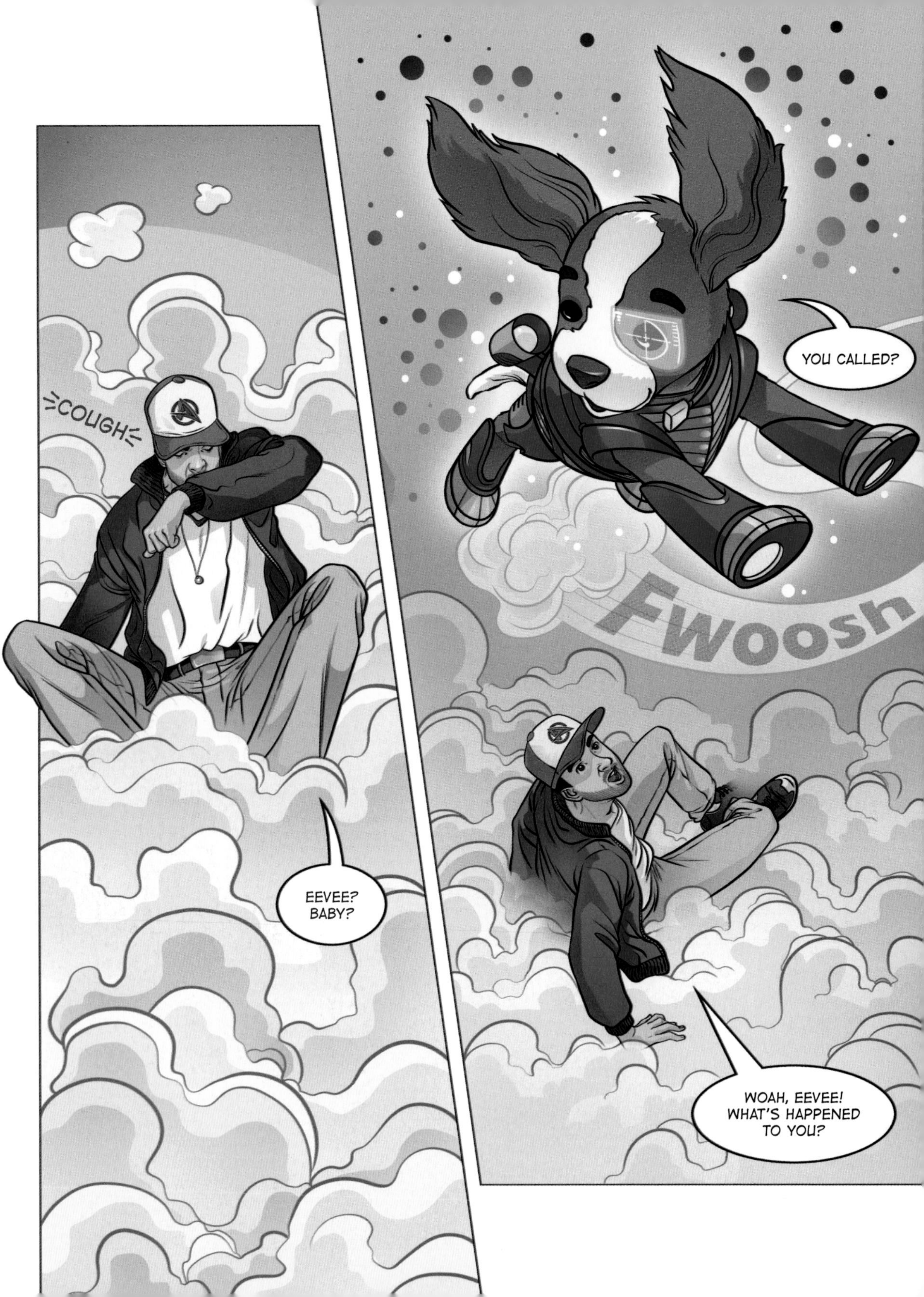
COUGH
EEVEE? BABY?
YOU CALLED?
FWOOSH
WOAH, EEVEE! WHAT'S HAPPENED TO YOU?

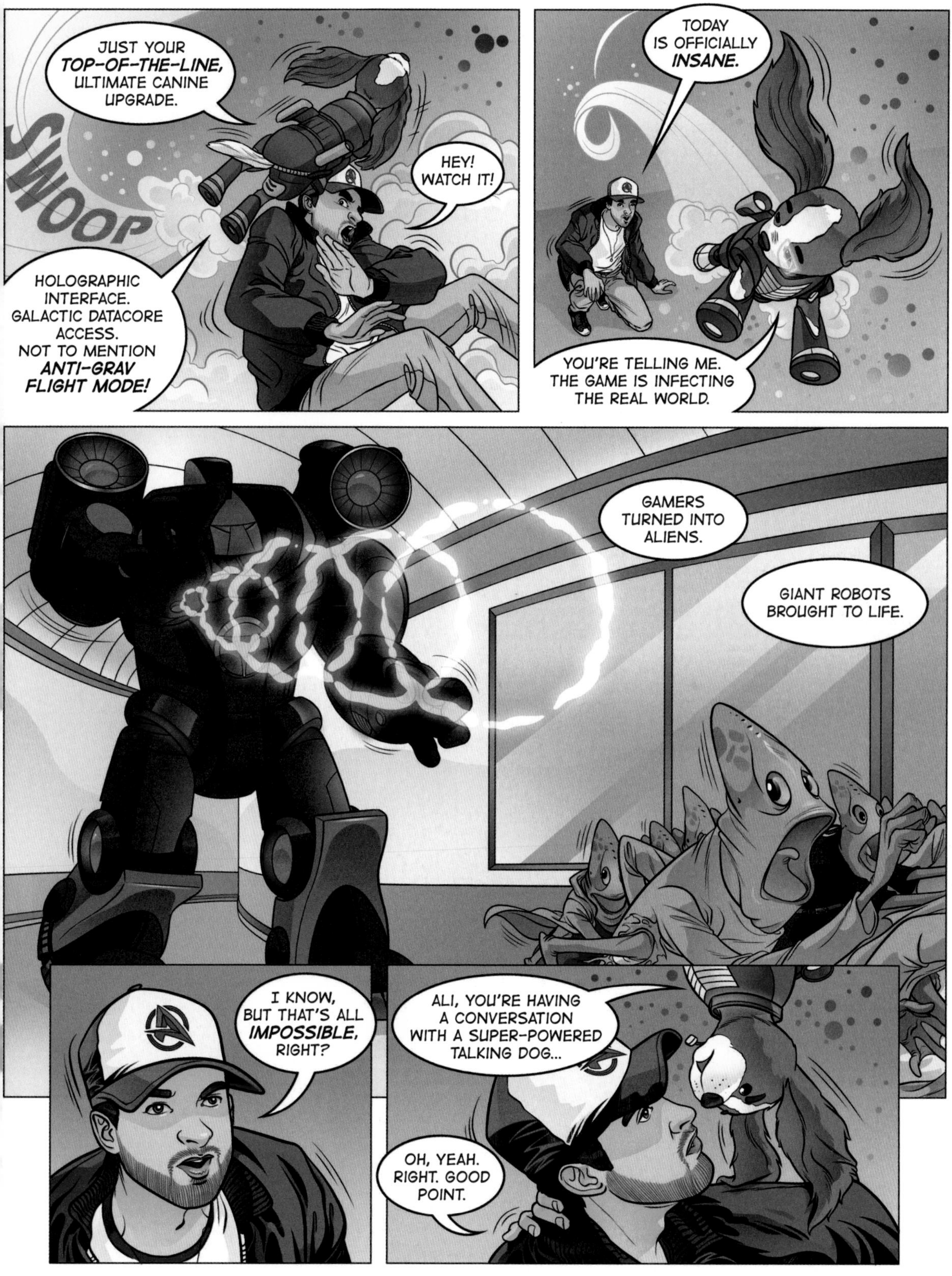

JUST YOUR TOP-OF-THE-LINE, ULTIMATE CANINE UPGRADE.
SWOOP
HEY! WATCH IT!
HOLOGRAPHIC INTERFACE. GALACTIC DATACORE ACCESS. NOT TO MENTION ANTI-GRAV FLIGHT MODE!
TODAY IS OFFICIALLY INSANE.
YOU'RE TELLING ME. THE GAME IS INFECTING THE REAL WORLD.
GAMERS TURNED INTO ALIENS.
GIANT ROBOTS BROUGHT TO LIFE.
I KNOW, BUT THAT'S ALL IMPOSSIBLE, RIGHT?
ALI, YOU'RE HAVING A CONVERSATION WITH A SUPER-POWERED TALKING DOG...
OH, YEAH. RIGHT. GOOD POINT.

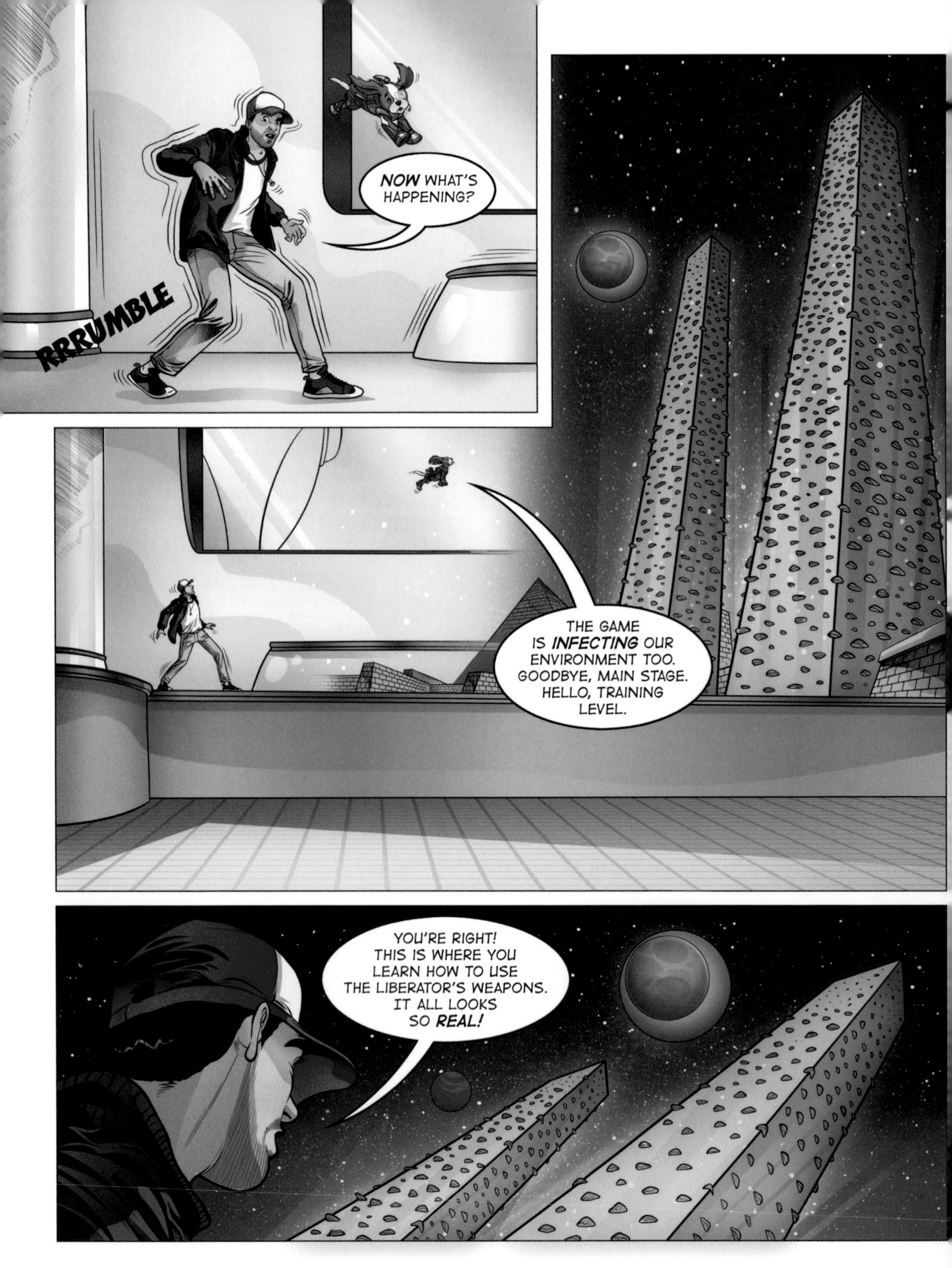
NOW WHAT'S HAPPENING?
RRRUMBLE
THE GAME IS INFECTING OUR ENVIRONMENT TOO. GOODBYE, MAIN STAGE. HELLO, TRAINING LEVEL.
YOU'RE RIGHT! THIS IS WHERE YOU LEARN HOW TO USE THE LIBERATOR'S WEAPONS. IT ALL LOOKS SO REAL!

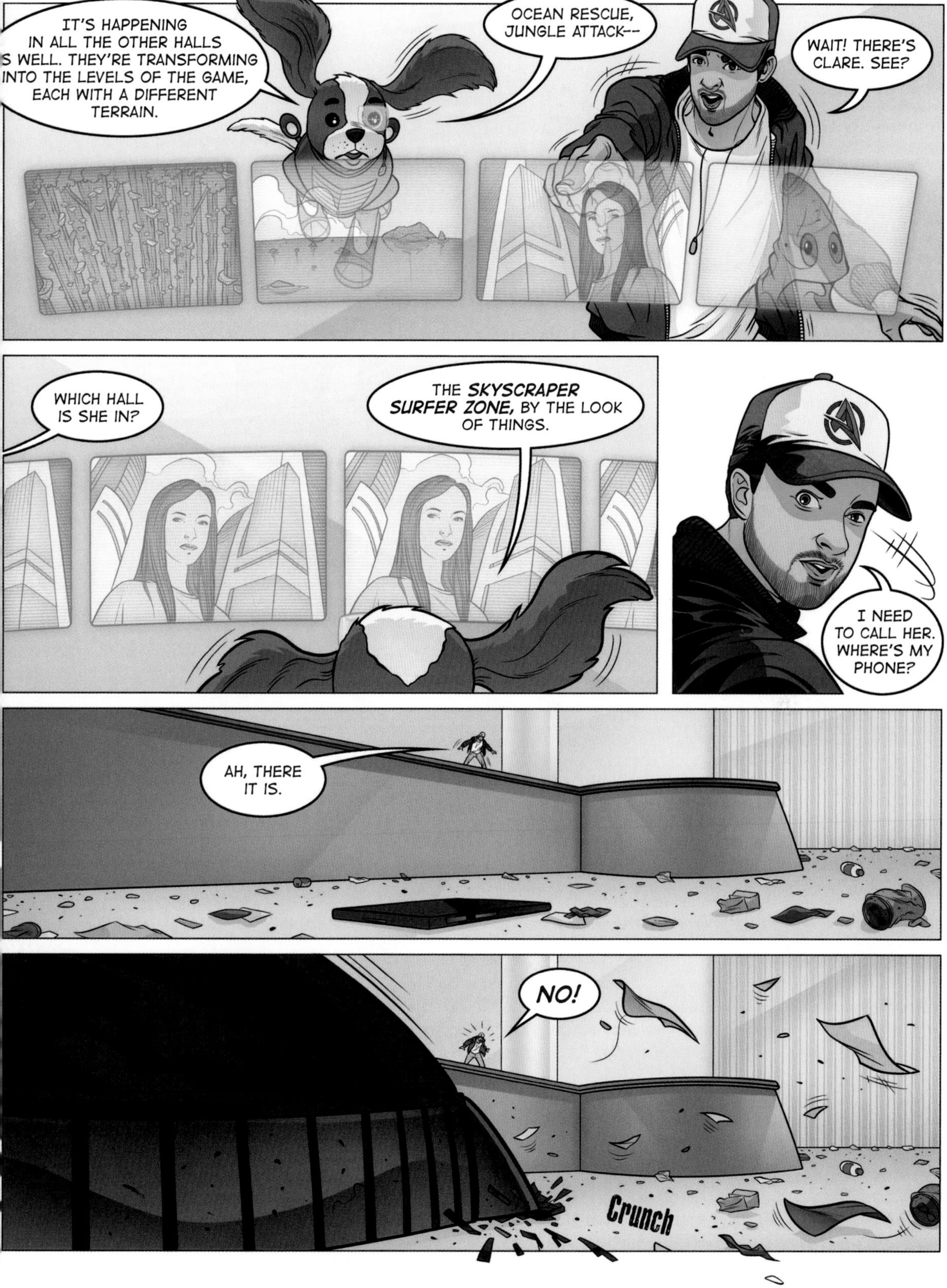
IT'S HAPPENING IN ALL THE OTHER HALLS S WELL. THEY'RE TRANSFORMING INTO THE LEVELS OF THE GAME, EACH WITH A DIFFERENT TERRAIN.
OCEAN RESCUE, JUNGLE ATTACK--
WAIT! THERE'S CLARE. SEE?
WHICH HALL IS SHE IN?
THE SKYSCRAPER SURFER ZONE, BY THE LOOK OF THINGS.
I NEED TO CALL HER. WHERE'S MY PHONE?
AH, THERE IT IS.
NO!
Crunch

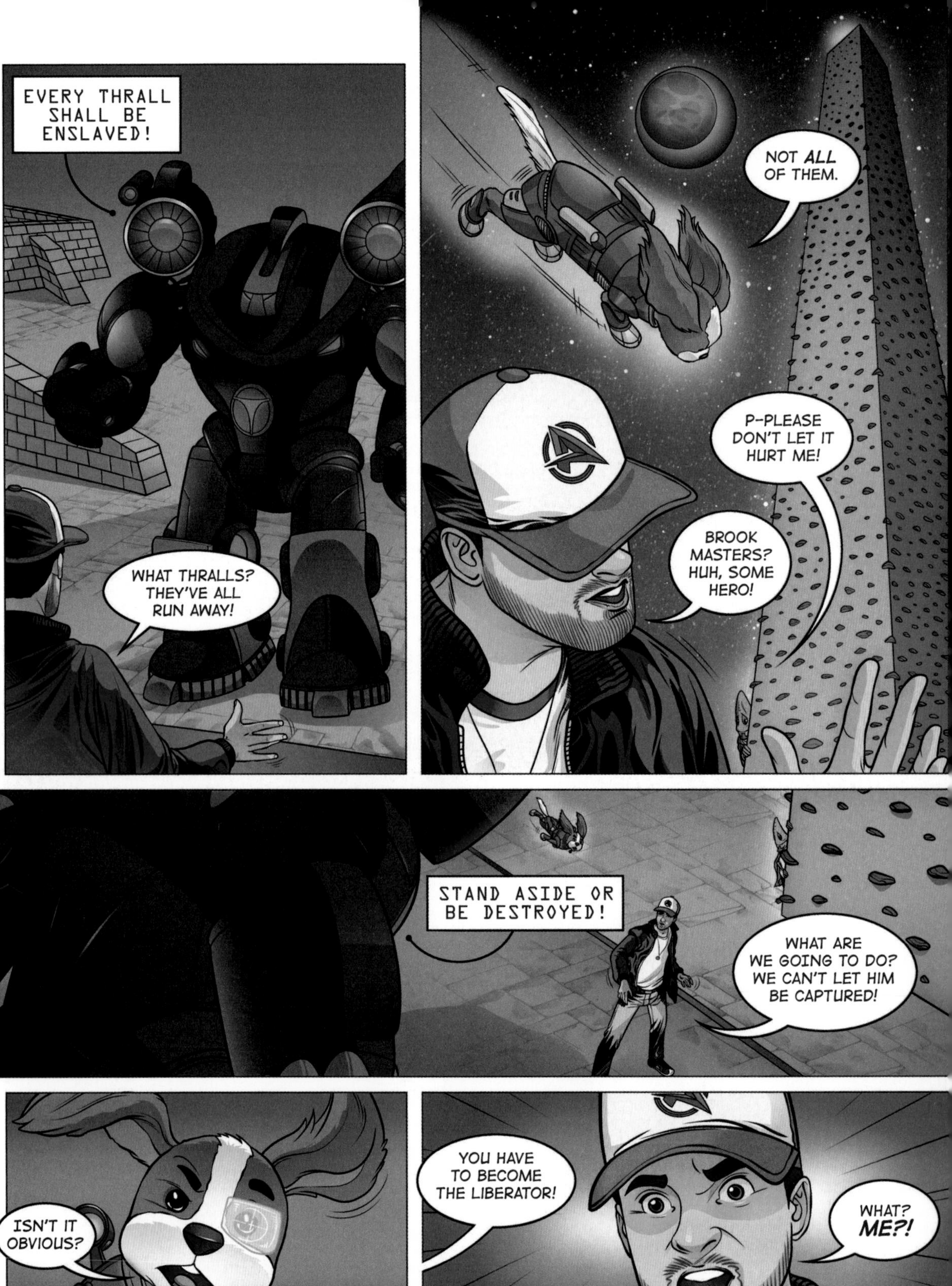
EVERY THRALL SHALL BE ENSLAVED!
WHAT THRALLS? THEY'VE ALL RUN AWAY!
NOT ALL OF THEM.
P-PLEASE DON'T LET IT HURT ME!
BROOK MASTERS? HUH, SOME HERO!
STAND ASIDE OR BE DESTROYED!
WHAT ARE WE GOING TO DO? WE CAN'T LET HIM BE CAPTURED!
ISN'T IT OBVIOUS?
YOU HAVE TO BECOME THE LIBERATOR!
WHAT? ME?!

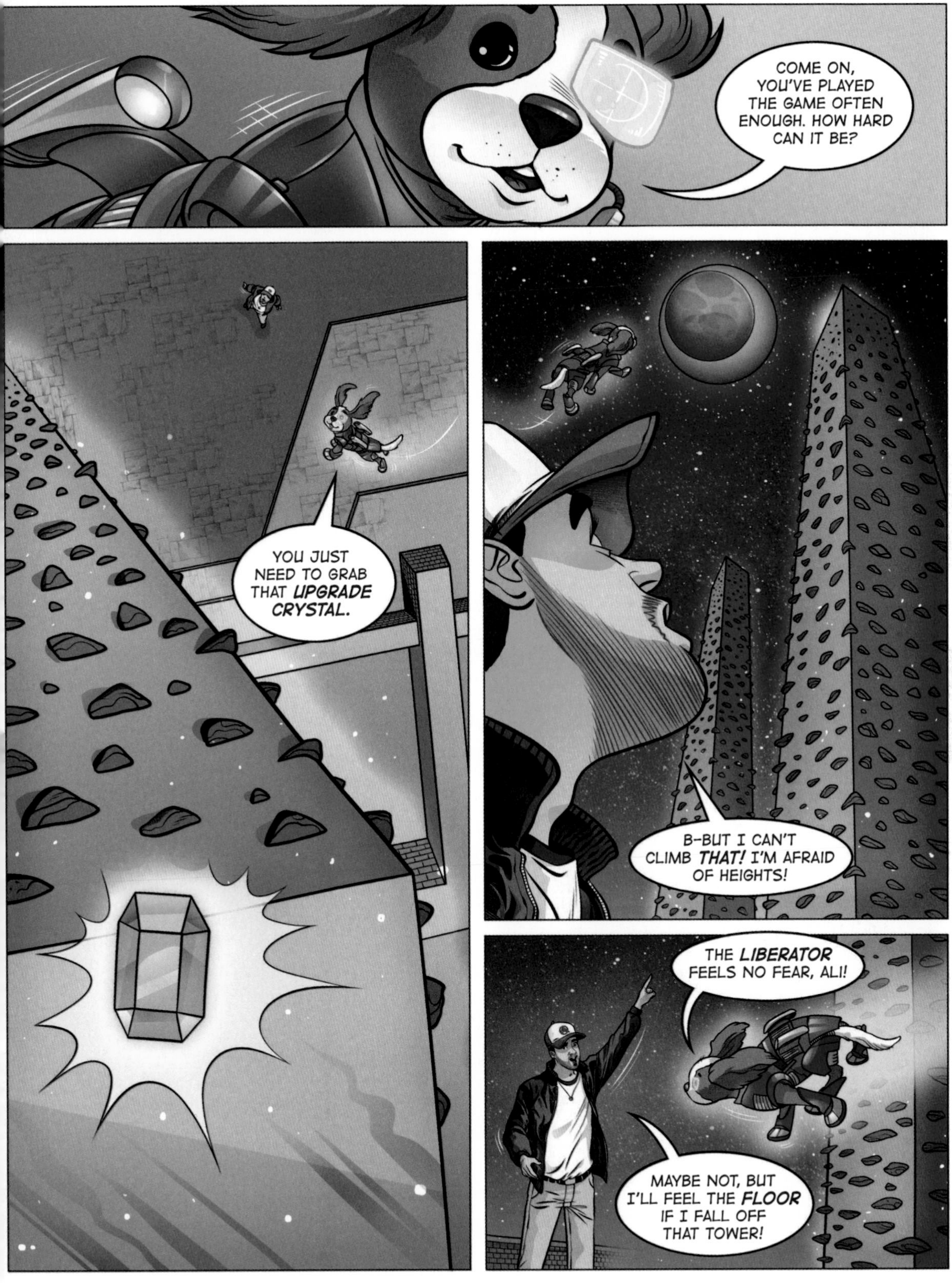

COME ON, YOU'VE PLAYED THE GAME OFTEN ENOUGH. HOW HARD CAN IT BE?
YOU JUST NEED TO GRAB THAT *UPGRADE CRYSTAL.*
B-BUT I CAN'T CLIMB ***THAT!*** I'M AFRAID OF HEIGHTS!
THE ***LIBERATOR*** FEELS NO FEAR, ALI!
MAYBE NOT, BUT I'LL FEEL THE ***FLOOR*** IF I FALL OFF THAT TOWER!

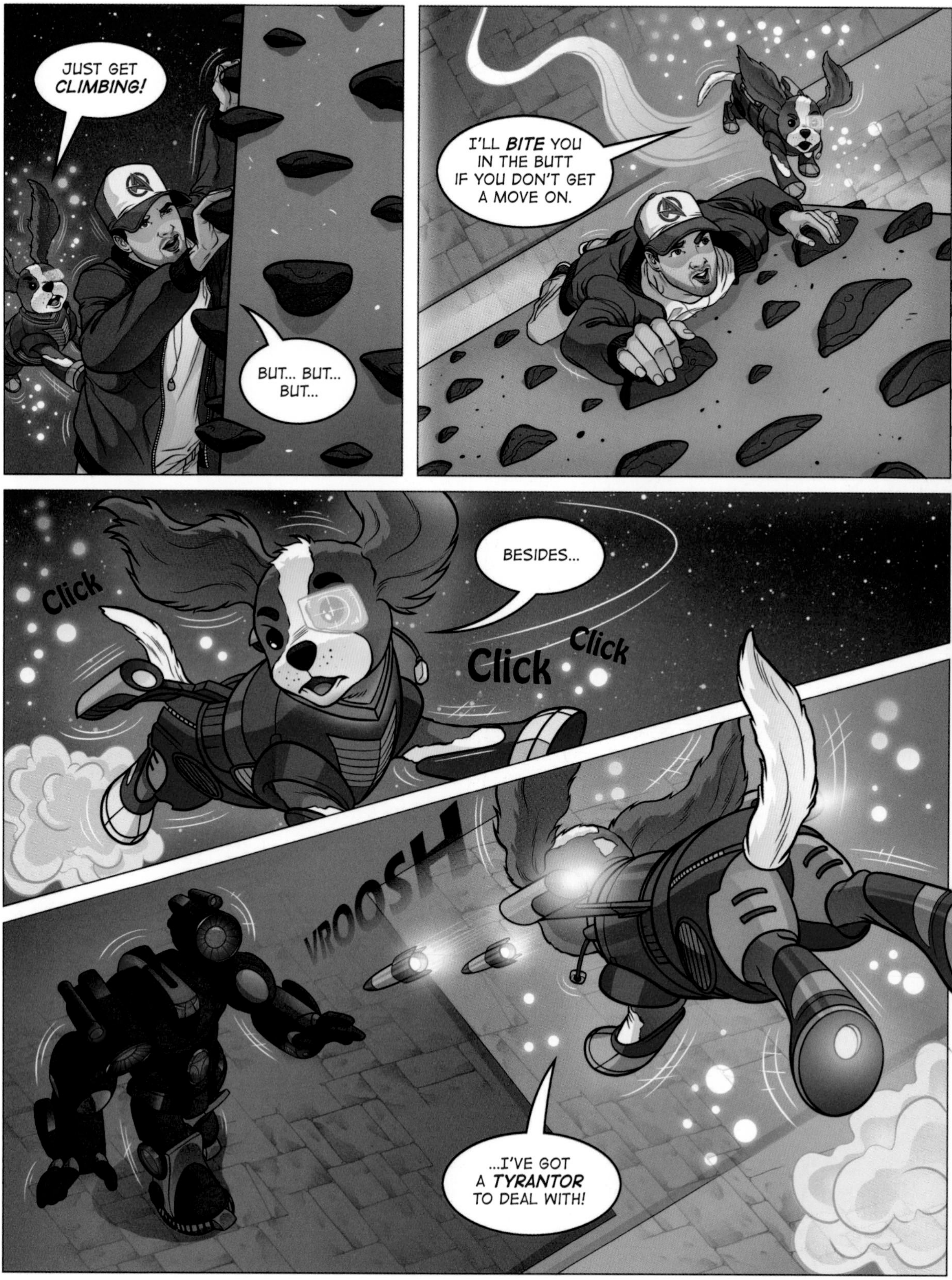
JUST GET CLIMBING!
BUT... BUT... BUT...
I'LL BITE YOU IN THE BUTT IF YOU DON'T GET A MOVE ON.
BESIDES...
Click
Click
Click
VROOSH
...I'VE GOT A TYRANTOR TO DEAL WITH!

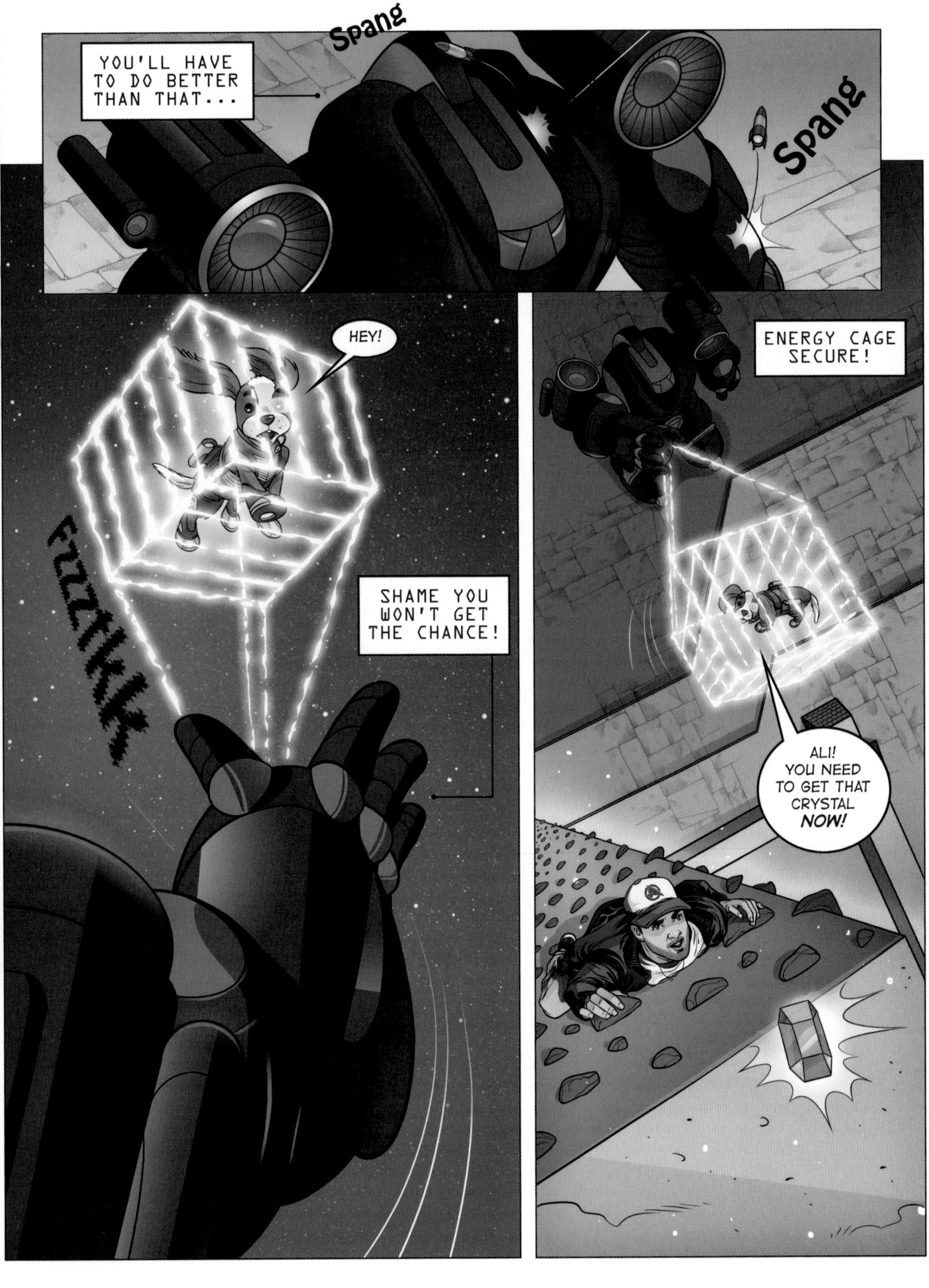
Spang
YOU'LL HAVE TO DO BETTER THAN THAT...
Spang
HEY!
FZZZTKKK
SHAME YOU WON'T GET THE CHANCE!
ENERGY CAGE SECURE!
ALI! YOU NEED TO GET THAT CRYSTAL NOW!

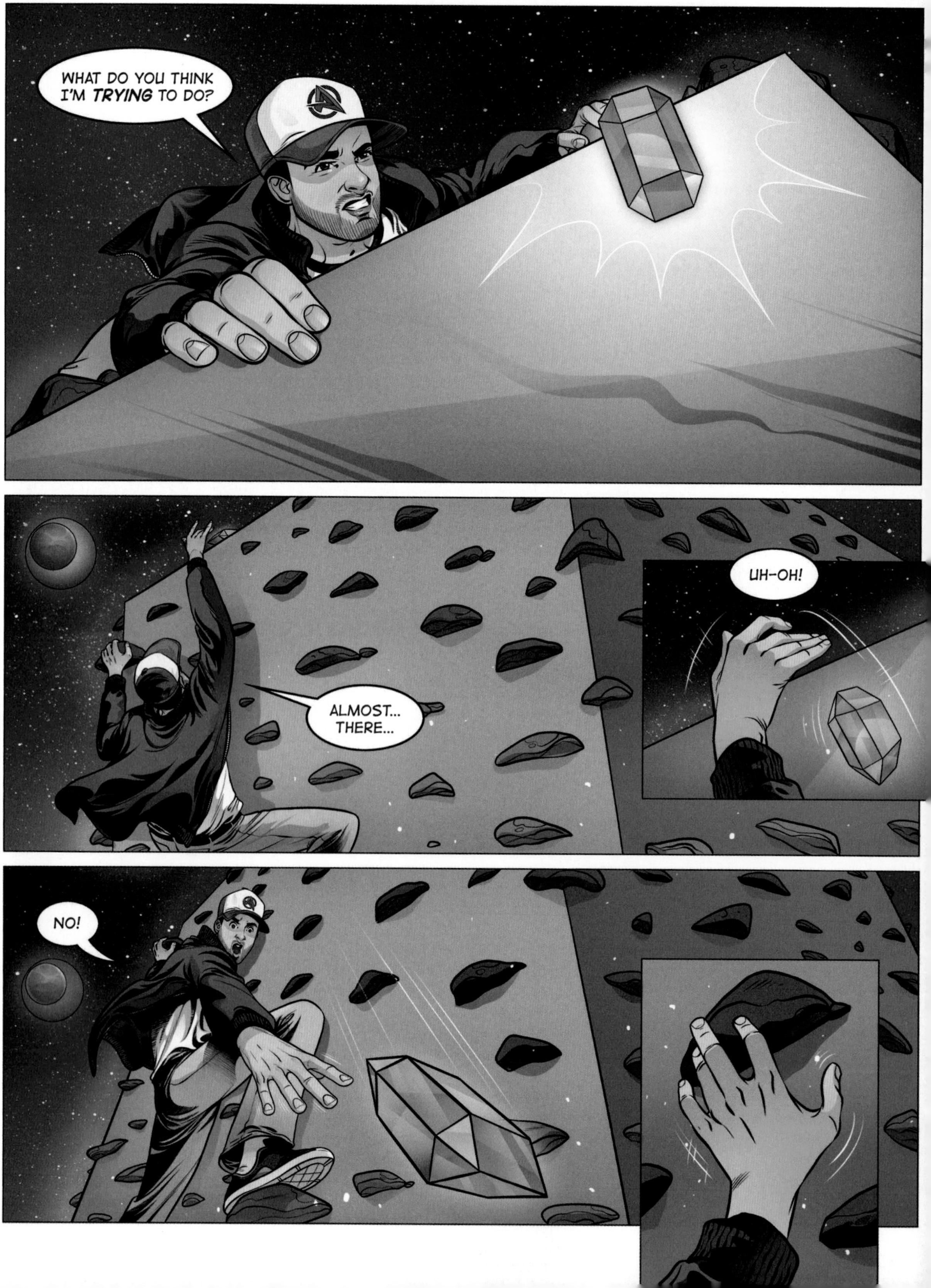
WHAT DO YOU THINK I'M *TRYING* TO DO?
ALMOST... THERE...
UH-OH!
NO!

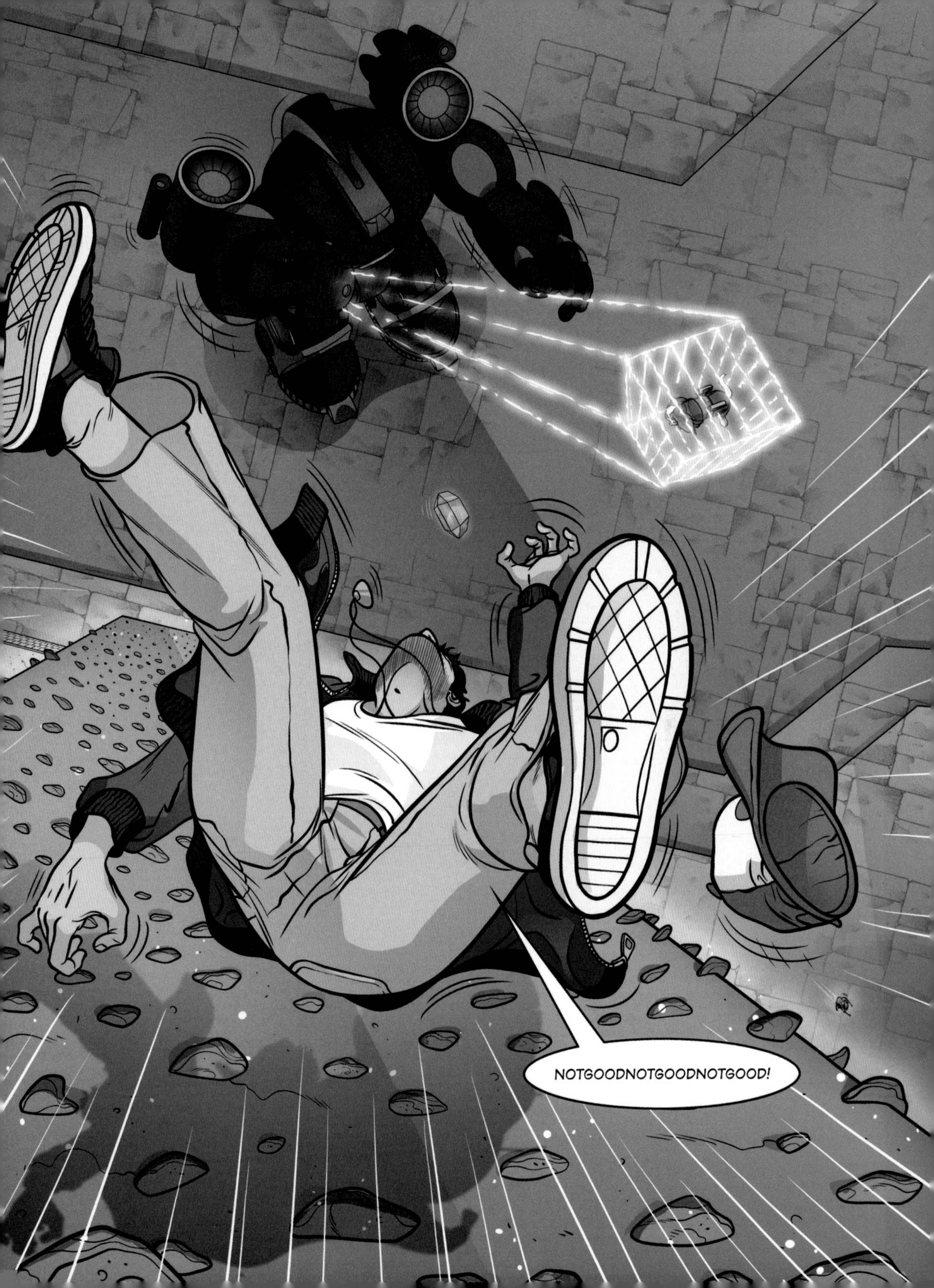
NOTGOODNOTGOODNOTGOOD!

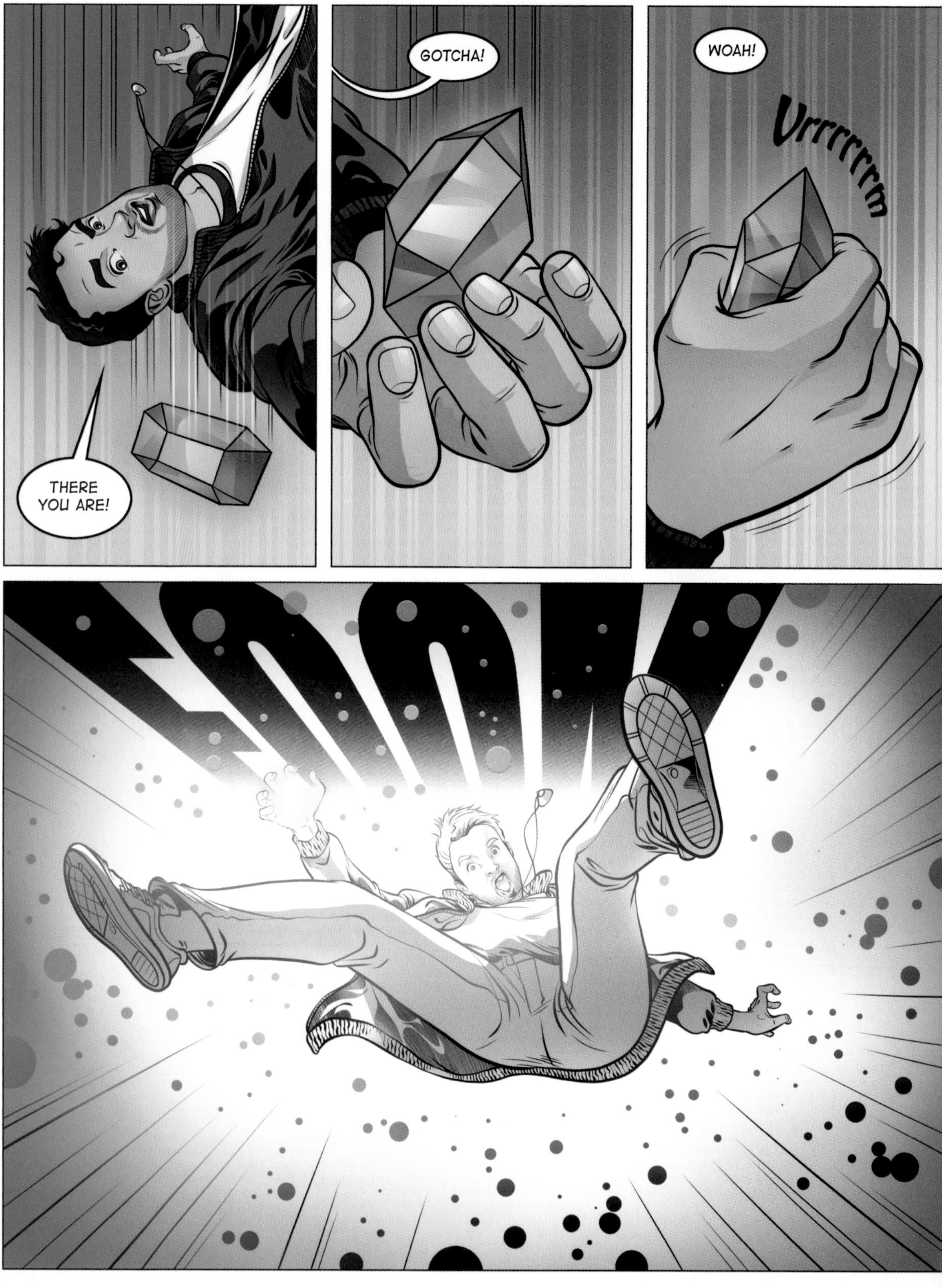
THERE YOU ARE!
GOTCHA!
WOAH!
Urrrrrrm

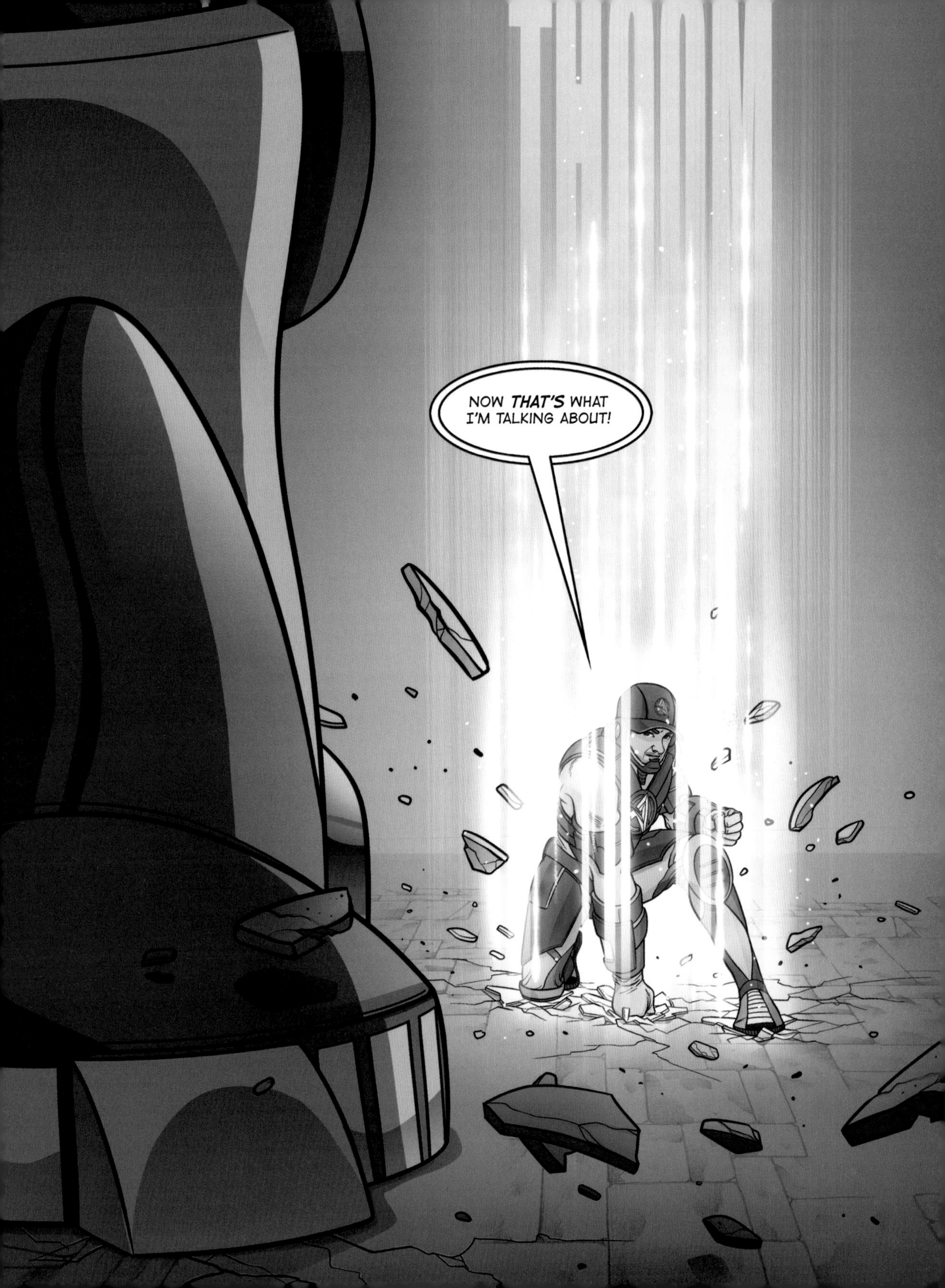
THOOOM
NOW *THAT'S* WHAT I'M TALKING ABOUT!

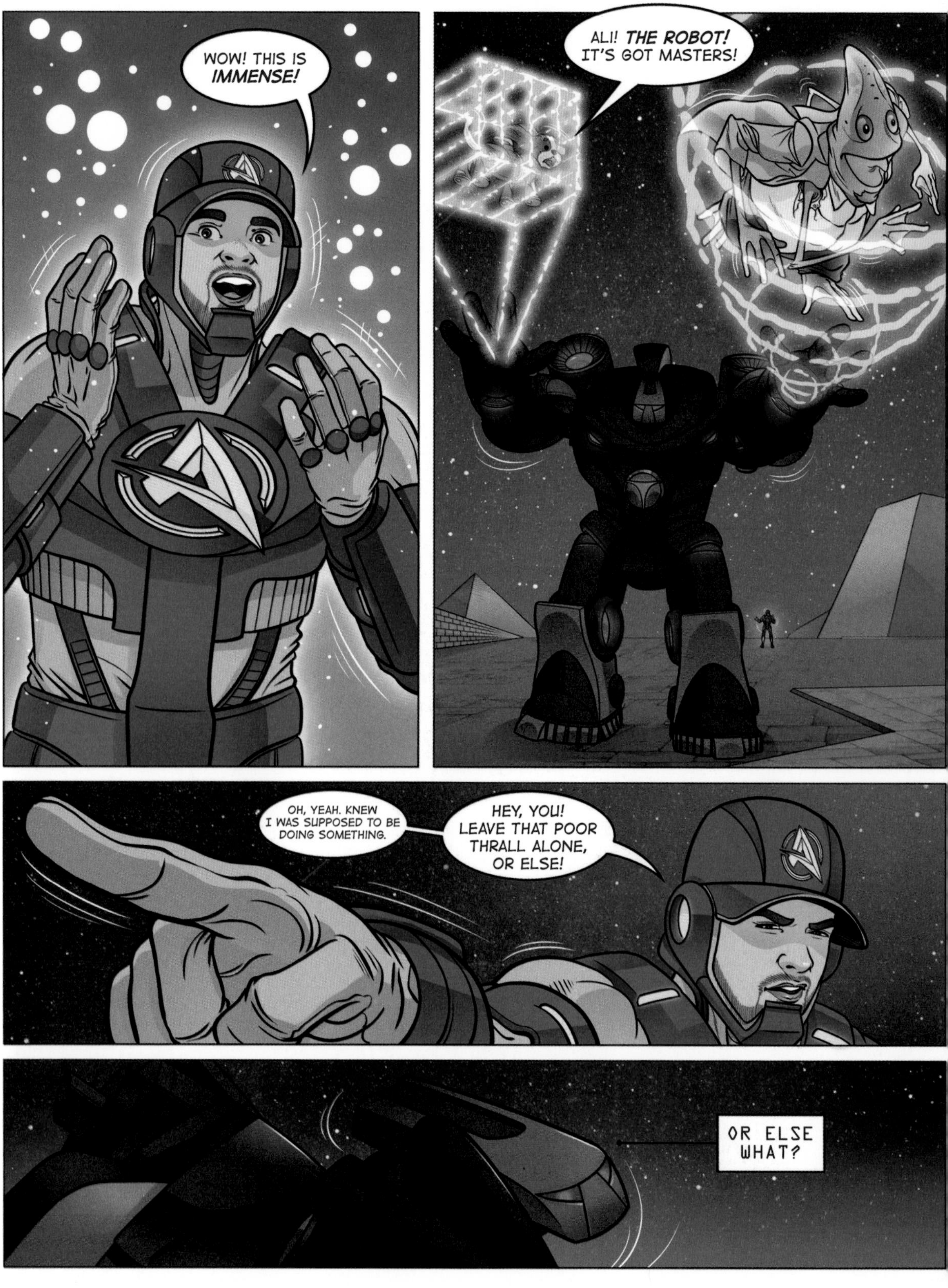
WOW! THIS IS IMMENSE!
ALI! THE ROBOT! IT'S GOT MASTERS!
HEY, YOU! LEAVE THAT POOR THRALL ALONE, OR ELSE!
OH, YEAH. KNEW I WAS SUPPOSED TO BE DOING SOMETHING.
OR ELSE WHAT?

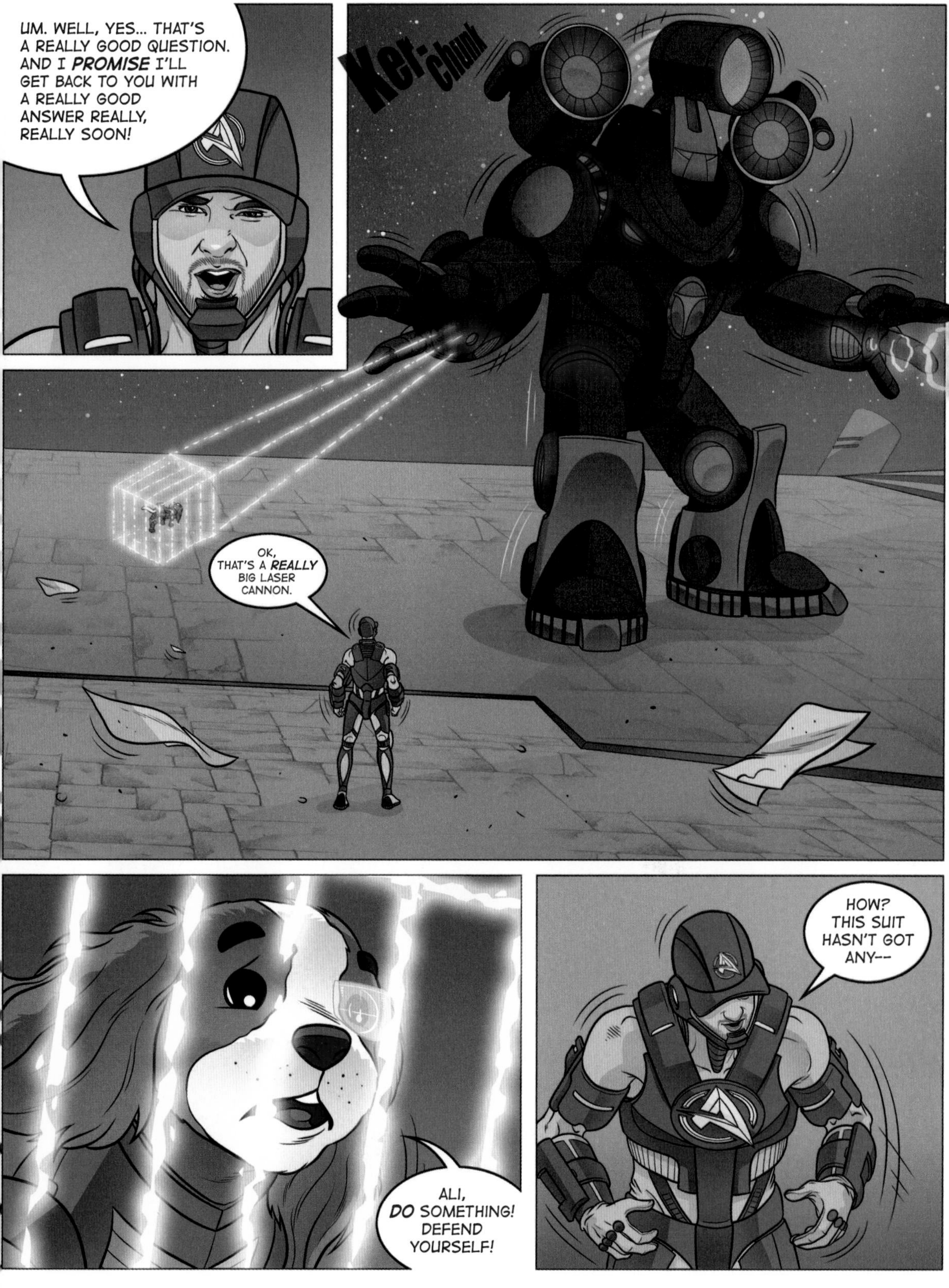
UM. WELL, YES... THAT'S A REALLY GOOD QUESTION. AND I PROMISE I'LL GET BACK TO YOU WITH A REALLY GOOD ANSWER REALLY, REALLY SOON!
KER-CHUNK
OK, THAT'S A REALLY BIG LASER CANNON.
ALI, DO SOMETHING! DEFEND YOURSELF!
HOW? THIS SUIT HASN'T GOT ANY--

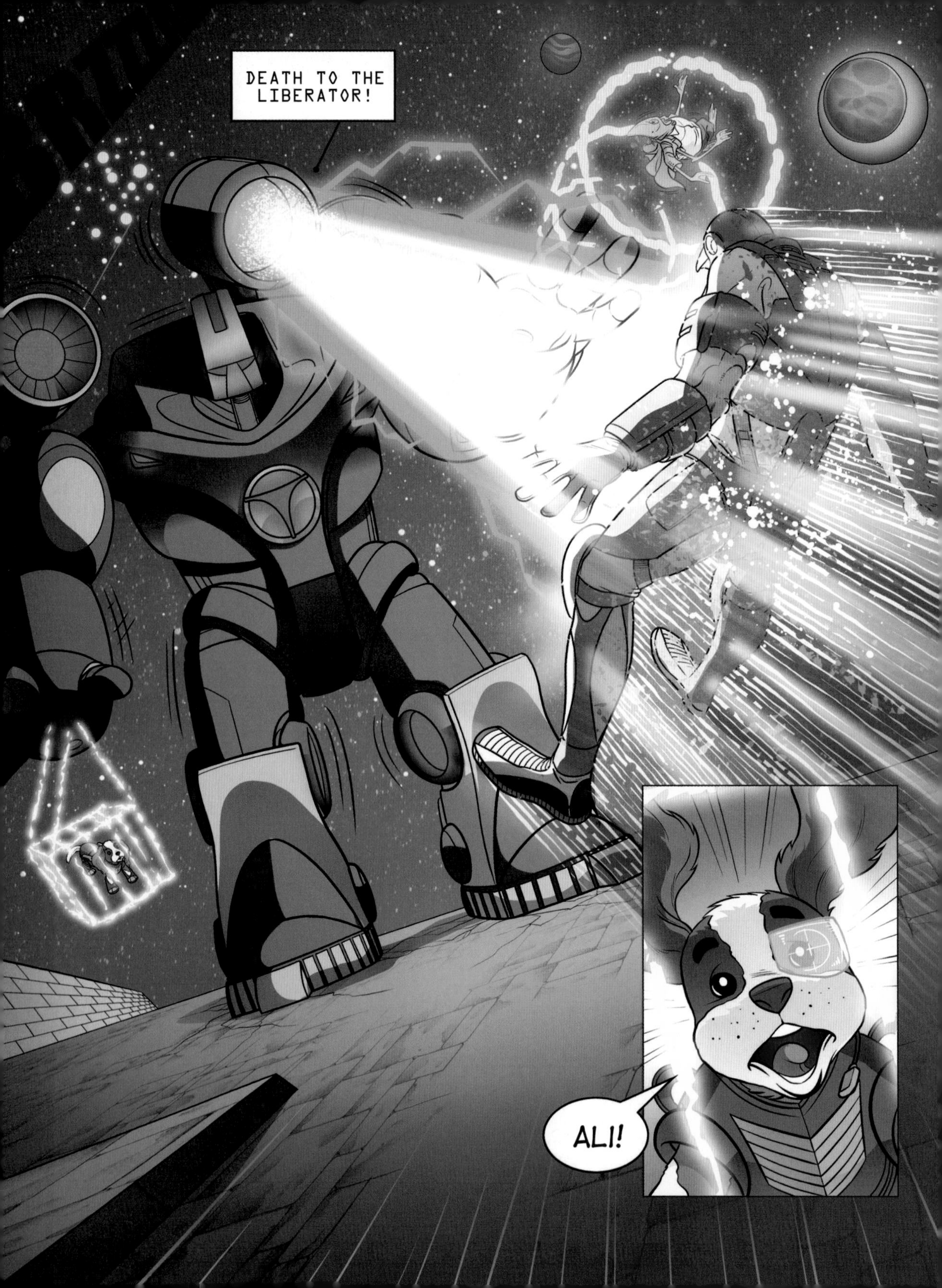
DEATH TO THE LIBERATOR!
ALI!

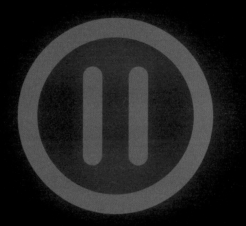

LEVEL THREE

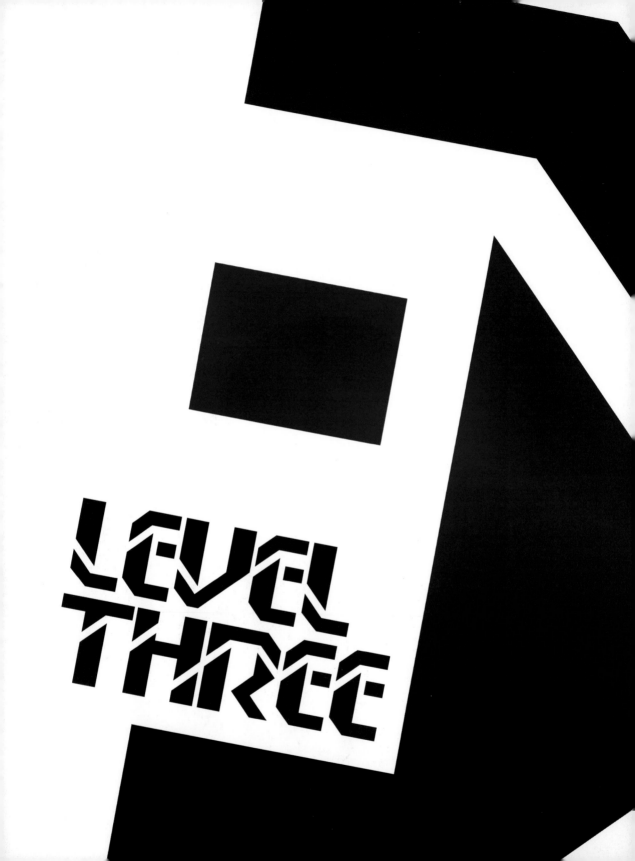

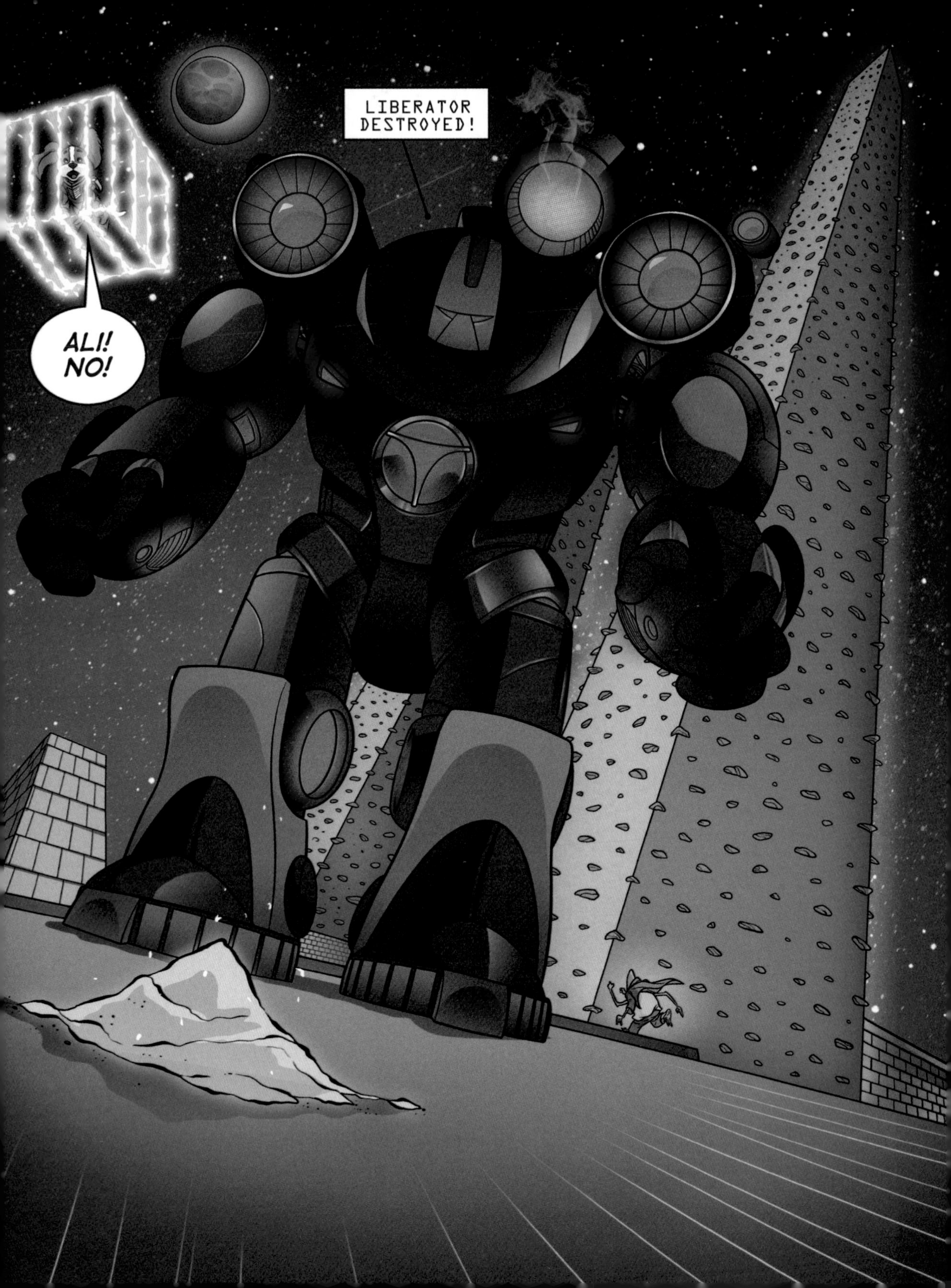
LIBERATOR DESTROYED!
ALI! NO!

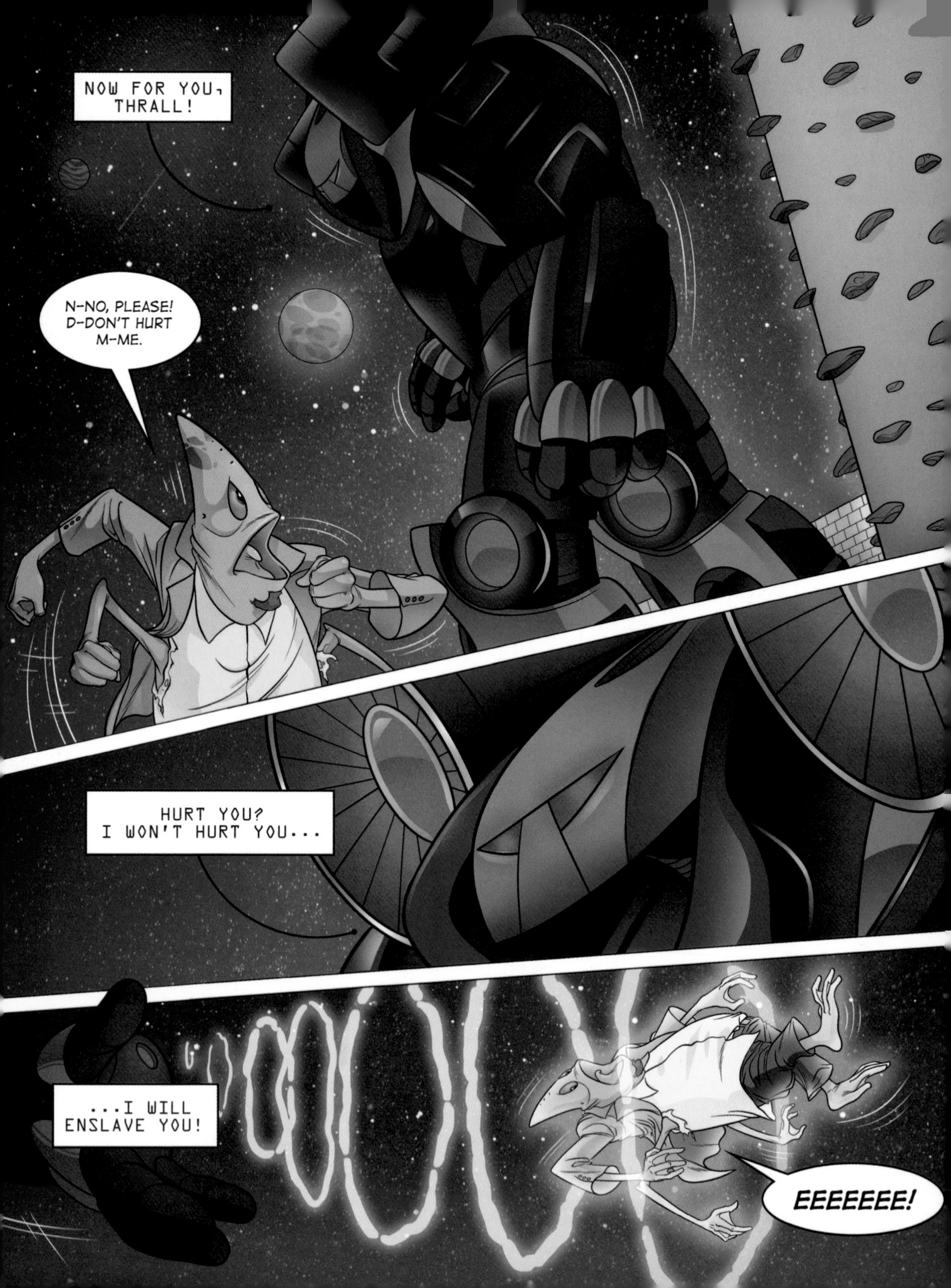
NOW FOR YOU, THRALL!
N-NO, PLEASE! D-DON'T HURT M-ME.
HURT YOU? I WON'T HURT YOU...
...I WILL ENSLAVE YOU!
EEEEEEE!

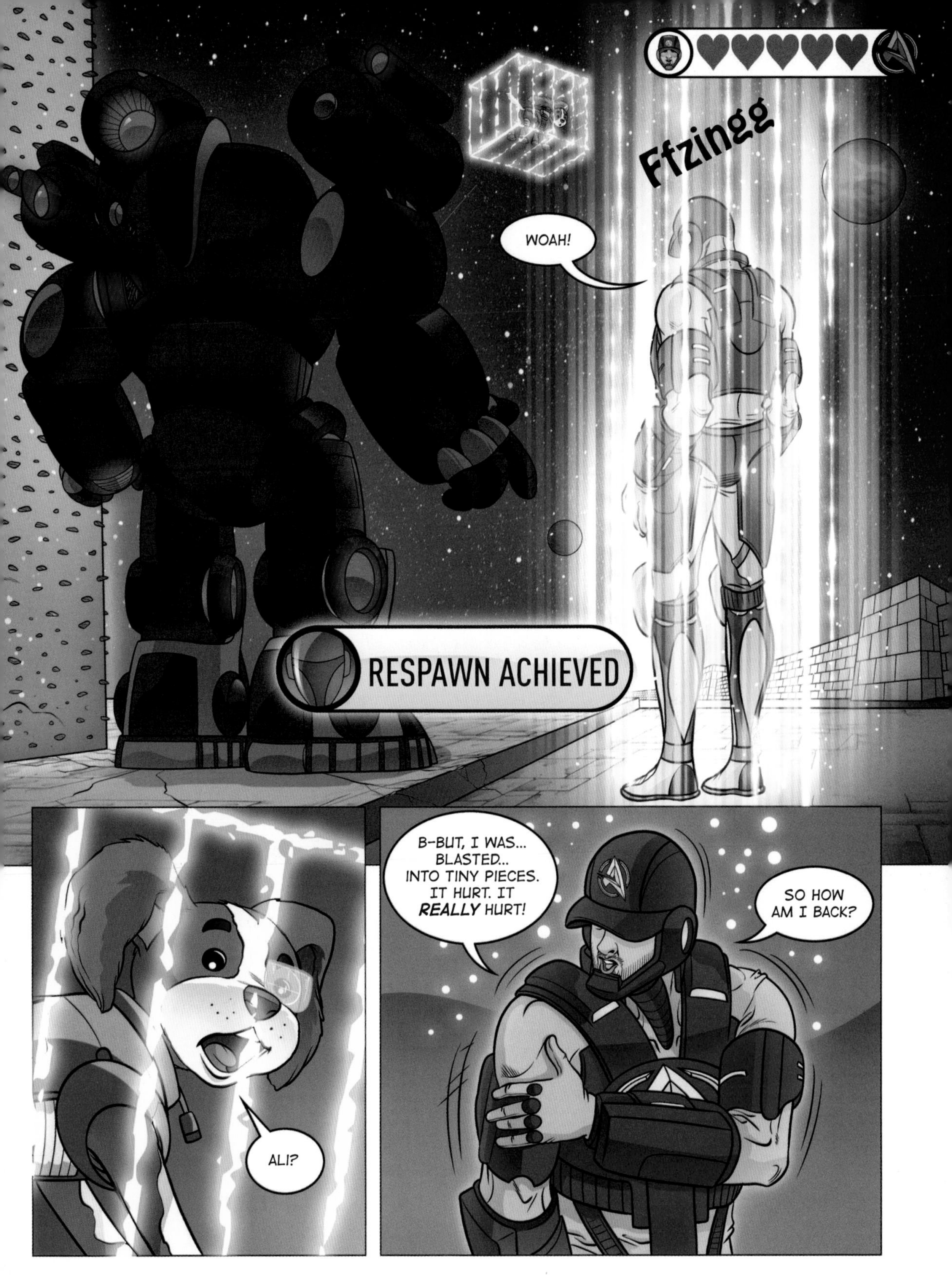
Ffzingg
WOAH!
RESPAWN ACHIEVED
ALI?
B-BUT, I WAS... BLASTED... INTO TINY PIECES. IT HURT. IT *REALLY* HURT!
SO HOW AM I BACK?

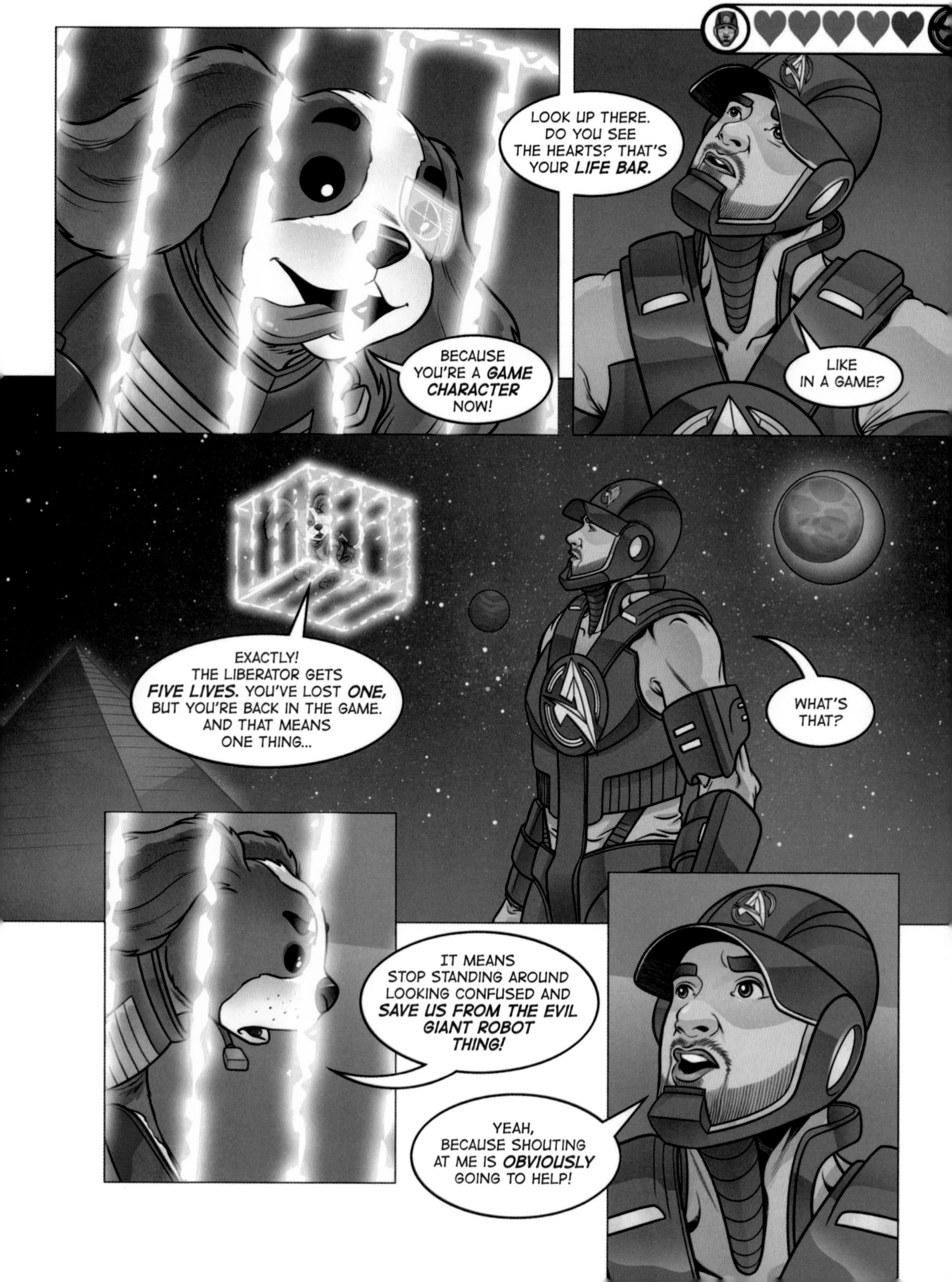
LOOK UP THERE. DO YOU SEE THE HEARTS? THAT'S YOUR LIFE BAR.
LIKE IN A GAME?
BECAUSE YOU'RE A GAME CHARACTER NOW!
EXACTLY! THE LIBERATOR GETS FIVE LIVES. YOU'VE LOST ONE, BUT YOU'RE BACK IN THE GAME. AND THAT MEANS ONE THING...
WHAT'S THAT?
IT MEANS STOP STANDING AROUND LOOKING CONFUSED AND SAVE US FROM THE EVIL GIANT ROBOT THING!
YEAH, BECAUSE SHOUTING AT ME IS OBVIOUSLY GOING TO HELP!

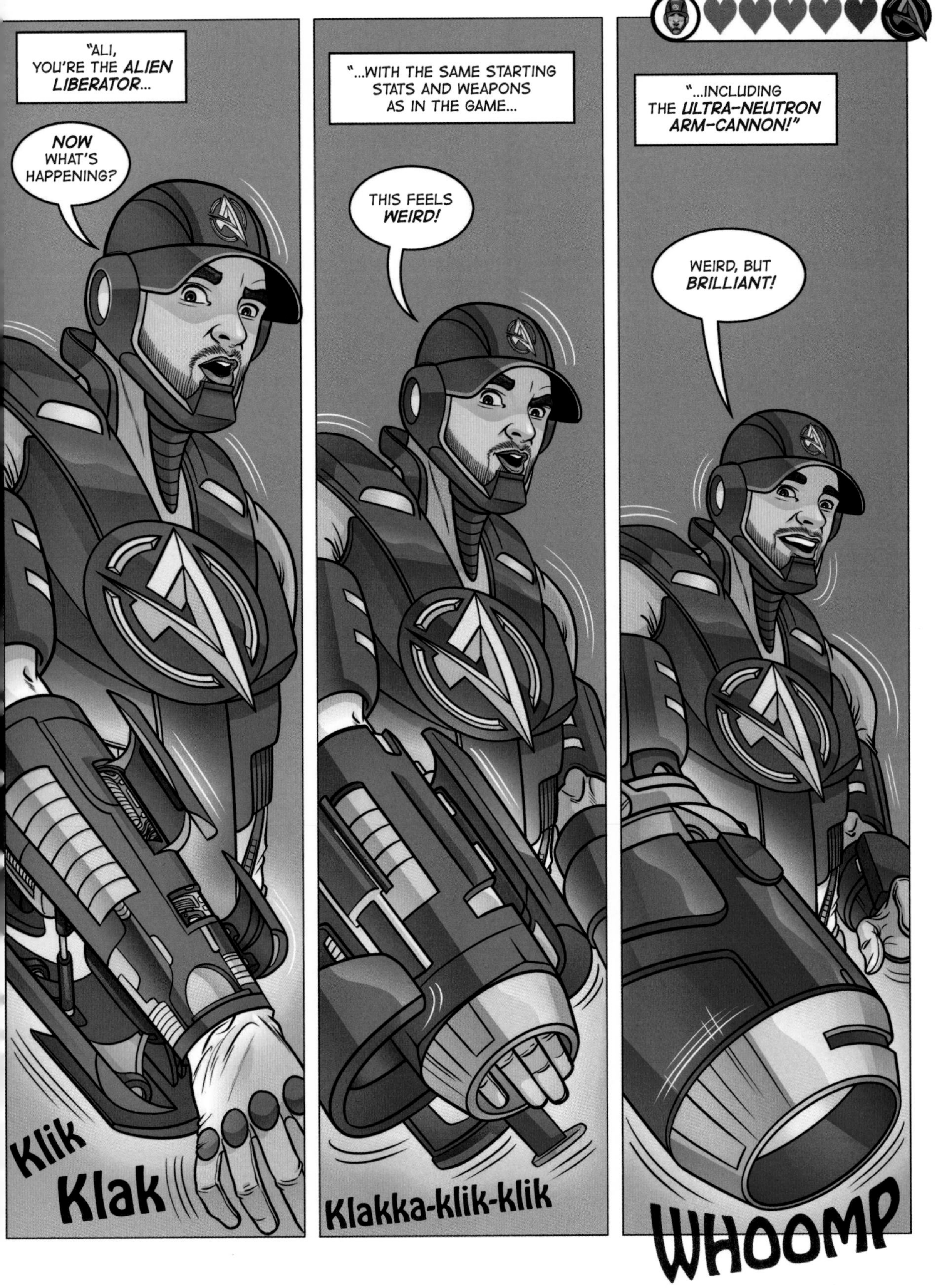
"ALI, YOU'RE THE ALIEN LIBERATOR...
NOW WHAT'S HAPPENING?
Klik
Klak
"...WITH THE SAME STARTING STATS AND WEAPONS AS IN THE GAME...
THIS FEELS WEIRD!
Klakka-klik-klik
"...INCLUDING THE ULTRA-NEUTRON ARM-CANNON!"
WEIRD, BUT BRILLIANT!
WHOOMP

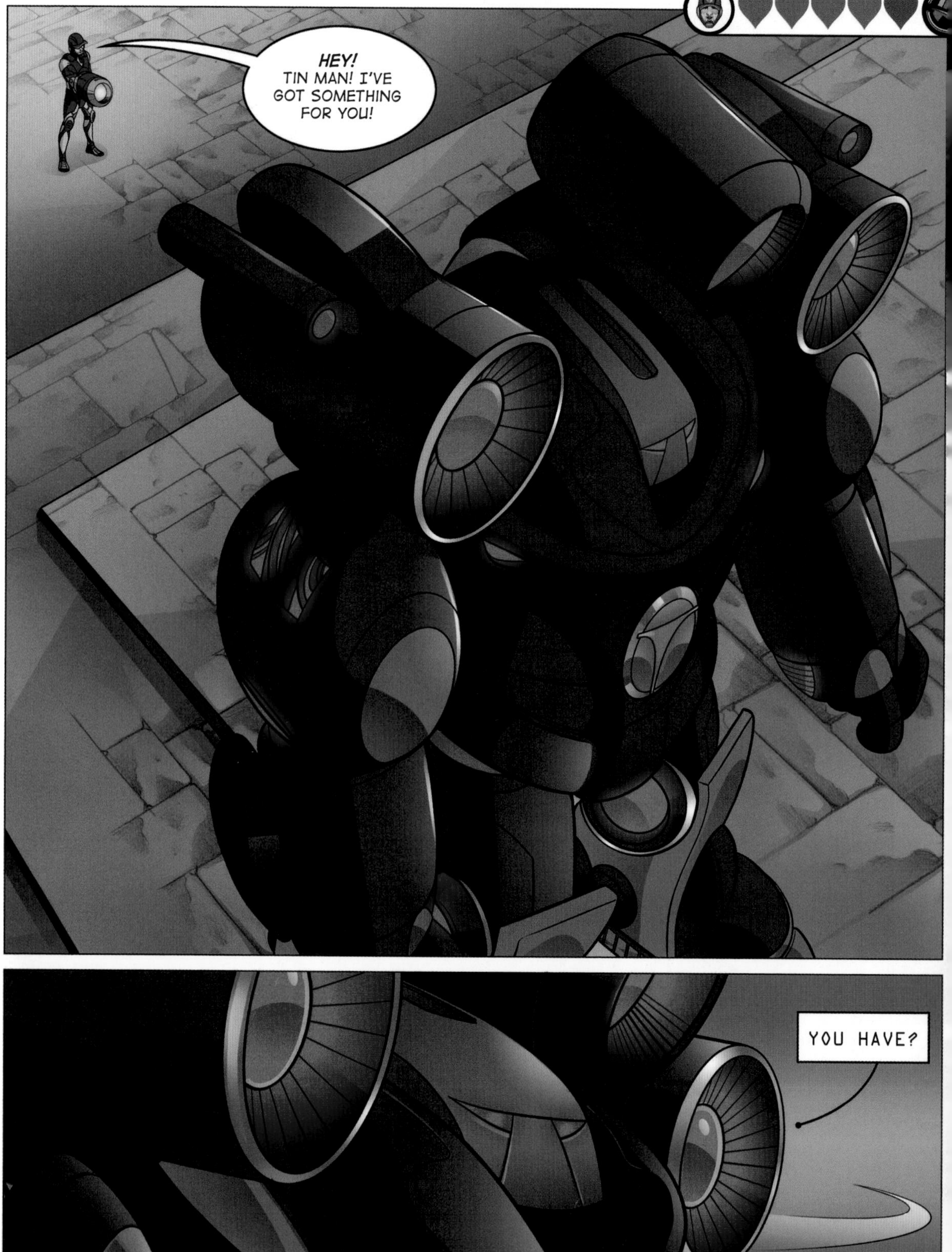
HEY!
TIN MAN! I'VE GOT SOMETHING FOR YOU!
YOU HAVE?

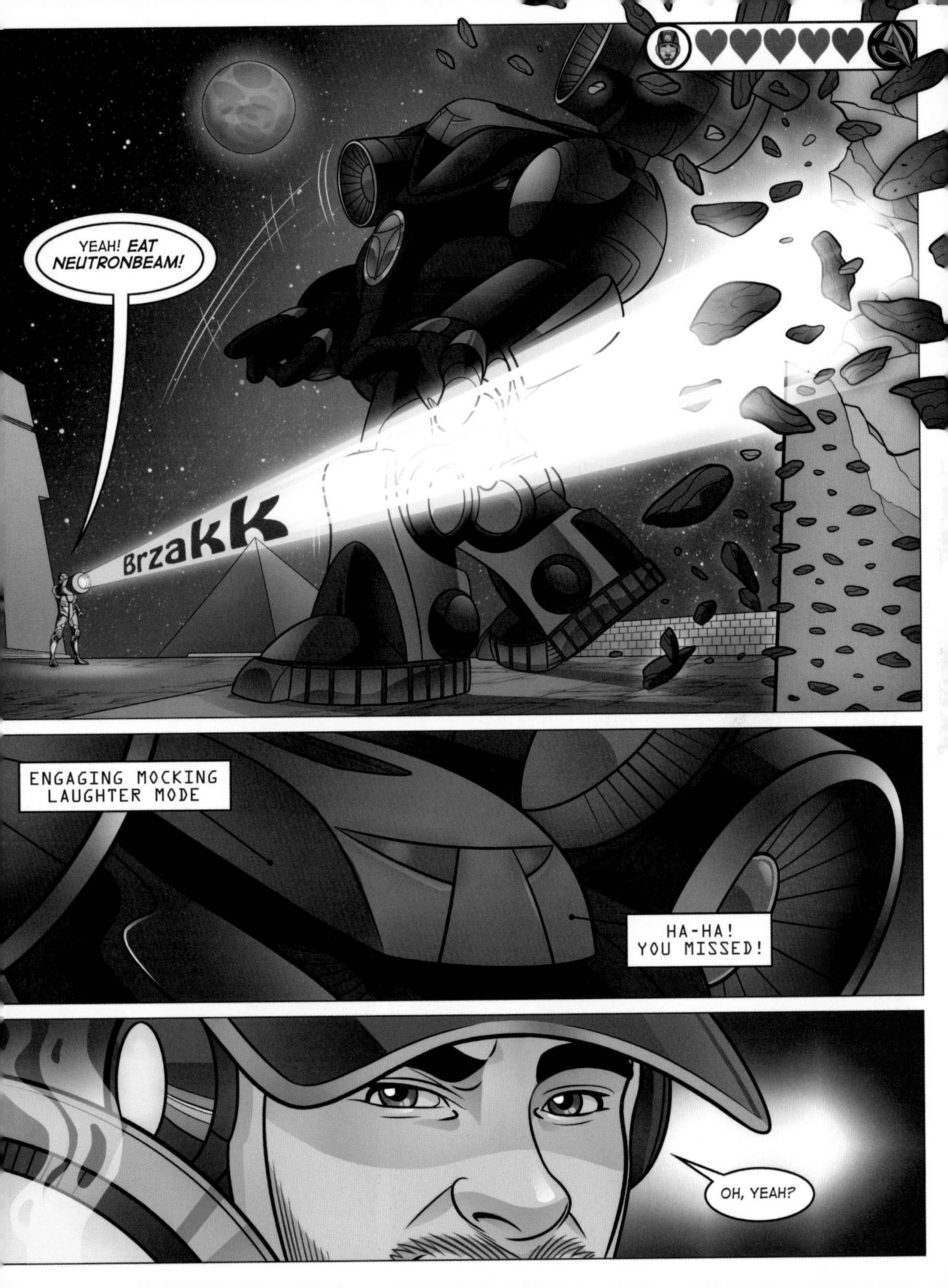
YEAH! EAT NEUTRONBEAM!
BrzakK
ENGAGING MOCKING LAUGHTER MODE
HA-HA! YOU MISSED!
OH, YEAH?

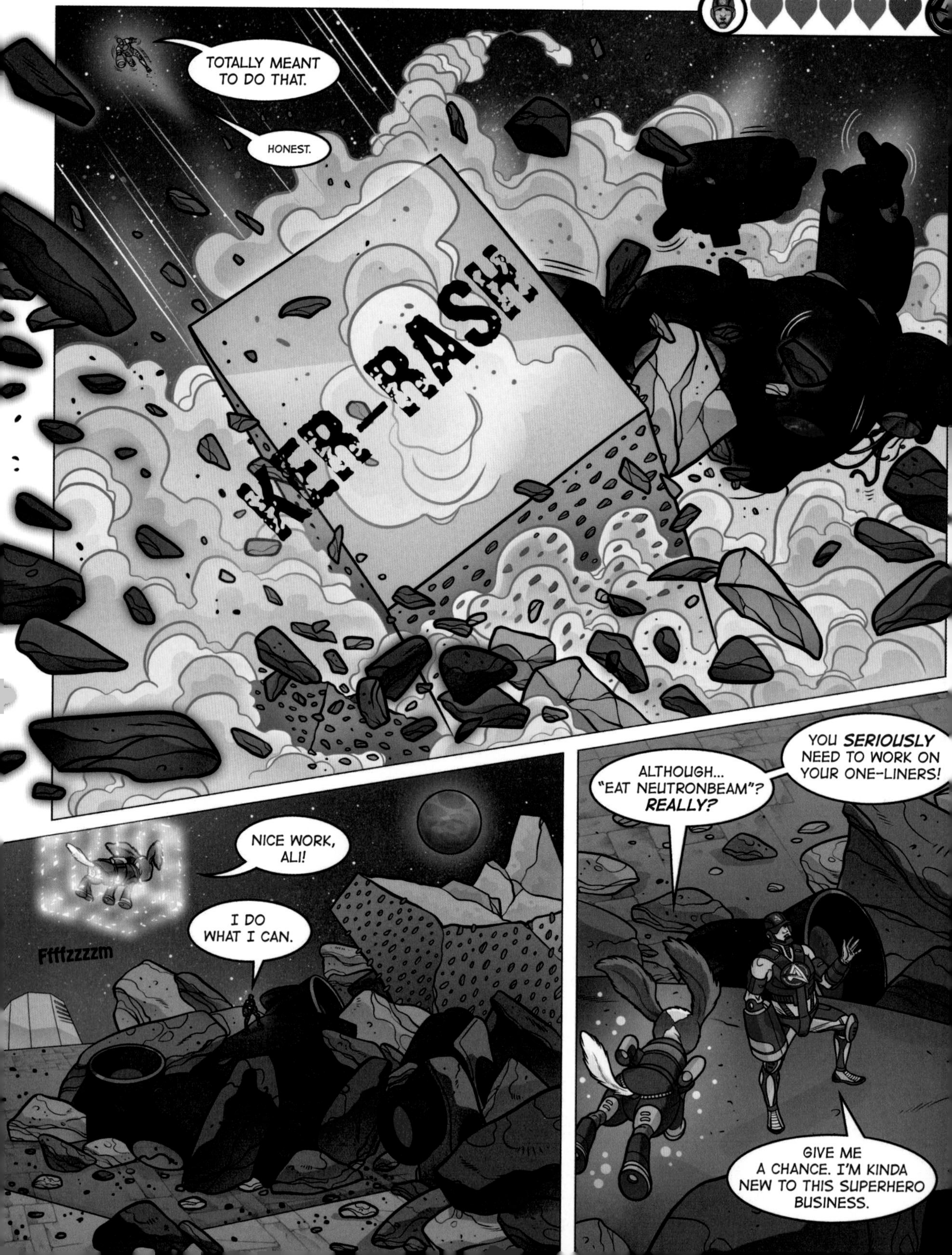
TOTALLY MEANT TO DO THAT.
HONEST.
KER-RASH
NICE WORK, ALI!
I DO WHAT I CAN.
Ffffzzzzm
ALTHOUGH... "EAT NEUTRONBEAM"? *REALLY?*
YOU *SERIOUSLY* NEED TO WORK ON YOUR ONE-LINERS!
GIVE ME A CHANCE. I'M KINDA NEW TO THIS SUPERHERO BUSINESS.

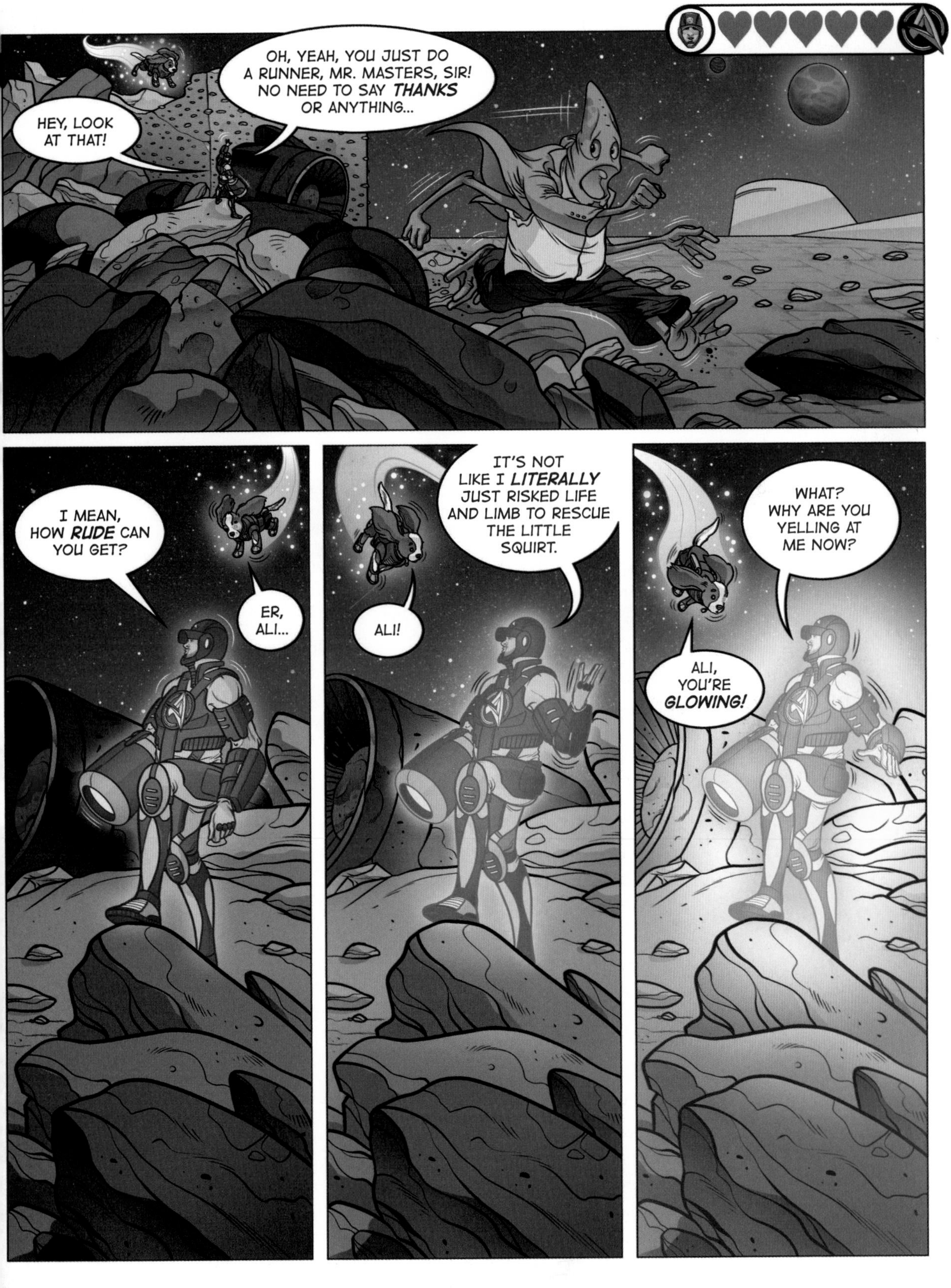
OH, YEAH, YOU JUST DO A RUNNER, MR. MASTERS, SIR! NO NEED TO SAY THANKS OR ANYTHING...
HEY, LOOK AT THAT!
I MEAN, HOW RUDE CAN YOU GET?
ER, ALI...
IT'S NOT LIKE I LITERALLY JUST RISKED LIFE AND LIMB TO RESCUE THE LITTLE SQUIRT.
ALI!
WHAT? WHY ARE YOU YELLING AT ME NOW?
ALI, YOU'RE GLOWING!

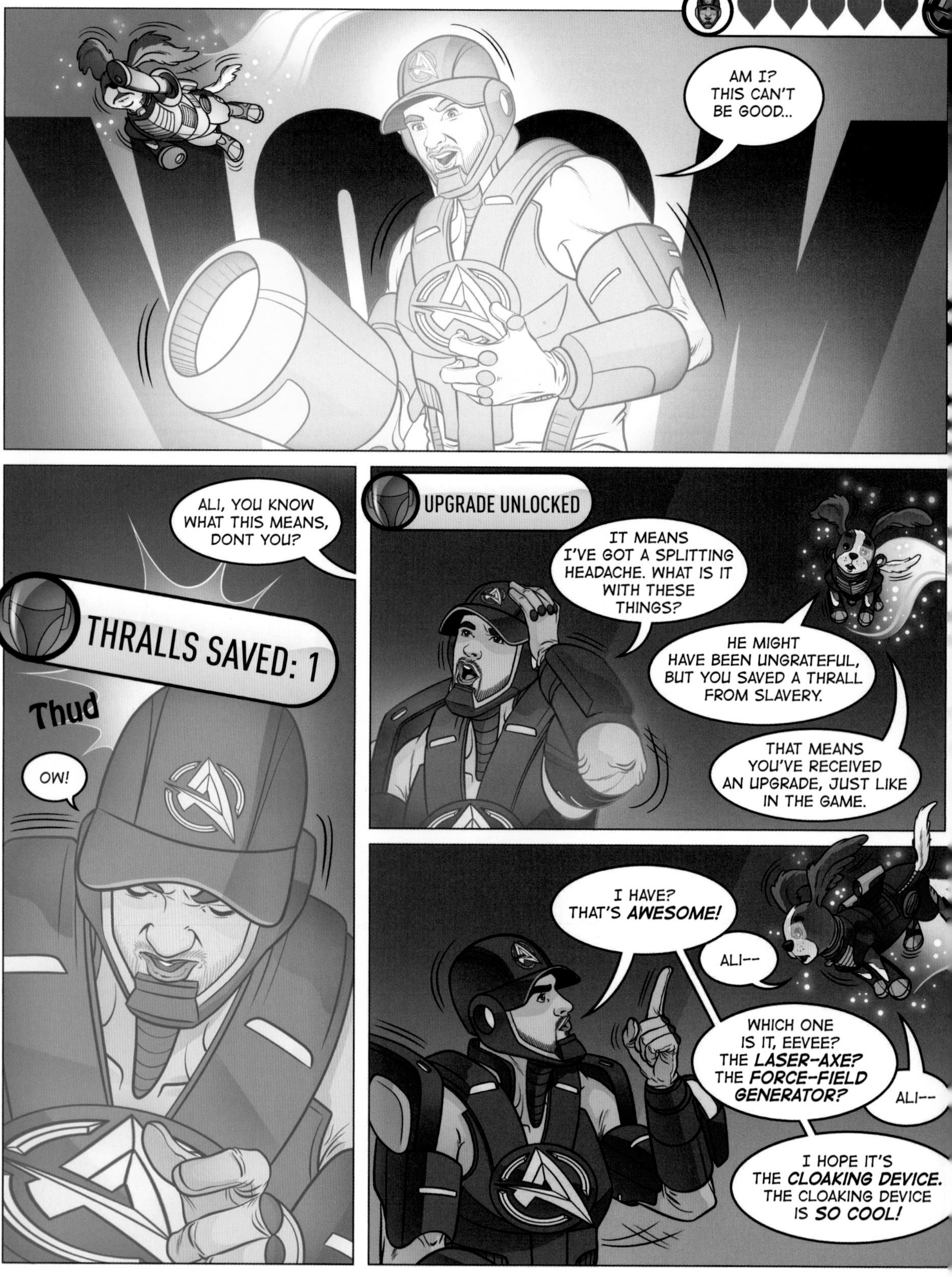

AM I? THIS CAN'T BE GOOD...
ALI, YOU KNOW WHAT THIS MEANS, DONT YOU?
THRALLS SAVED: 1
Thud
OW!
UPGRADE UNLOCKED
IT MEANS I'VE GOT A SPLITTING HEADACHE. WHAT IS IT WITH THESE THINGS?
HE MIGHT HAVE BEEN UNGRATEFUL, BUT YOU SAVED A THRALL FROM SLAVERY.
THAT MEANS YOU'VE RECEIVED AN UPGRADE, JUST LIKE IN THE GAME.
I HAVE? THAT'S **AWESOME!**
ALI--
WHICH ONE IS IT, EEVEE? THE ***LASER-AXE?*** THE ***FORCE-FIELD GENERATOR?***
ALI--
I HOPE IT'S THE ***CLOAKING DEVICE.*** THE CLOAKING DEVICE IS ***SO COOL!***

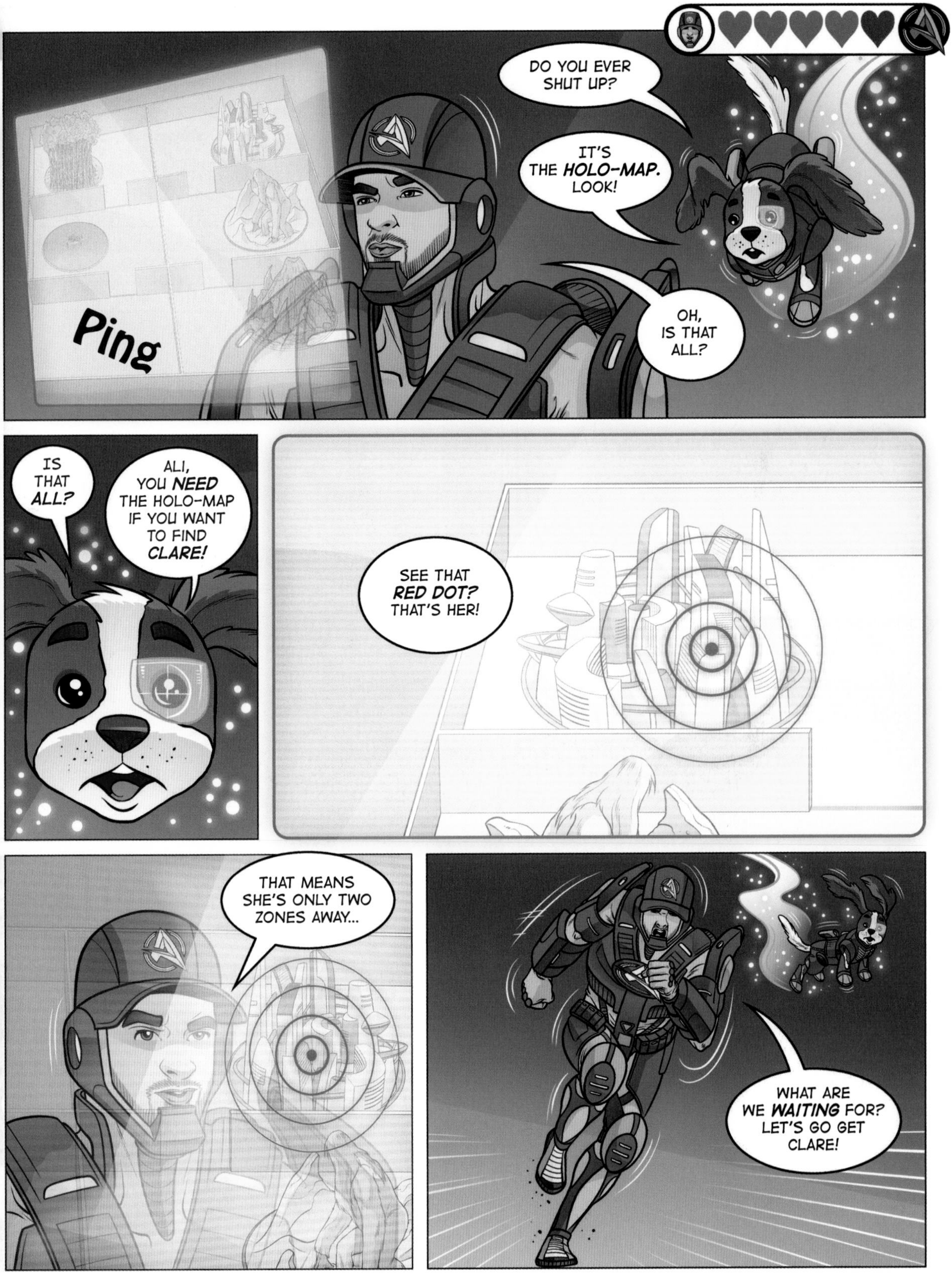
Ping
DO YOU EVER SHUT UP?
IT'S THE HOLO-MAP. LOOK!
OH, IS THAT ALL?
IS THAT ALL?
ALI, YOU NEED THE HOLO-MAP IF YOU WANT TO FIND CLARE!
SEE THAT RED DOT? THAT'S HER!
THAT MEANS SHE'S ONLY TWO ZONES AWAY...
WHAT ARE WE WAITING FOR? LET'S GO GET CLARE!

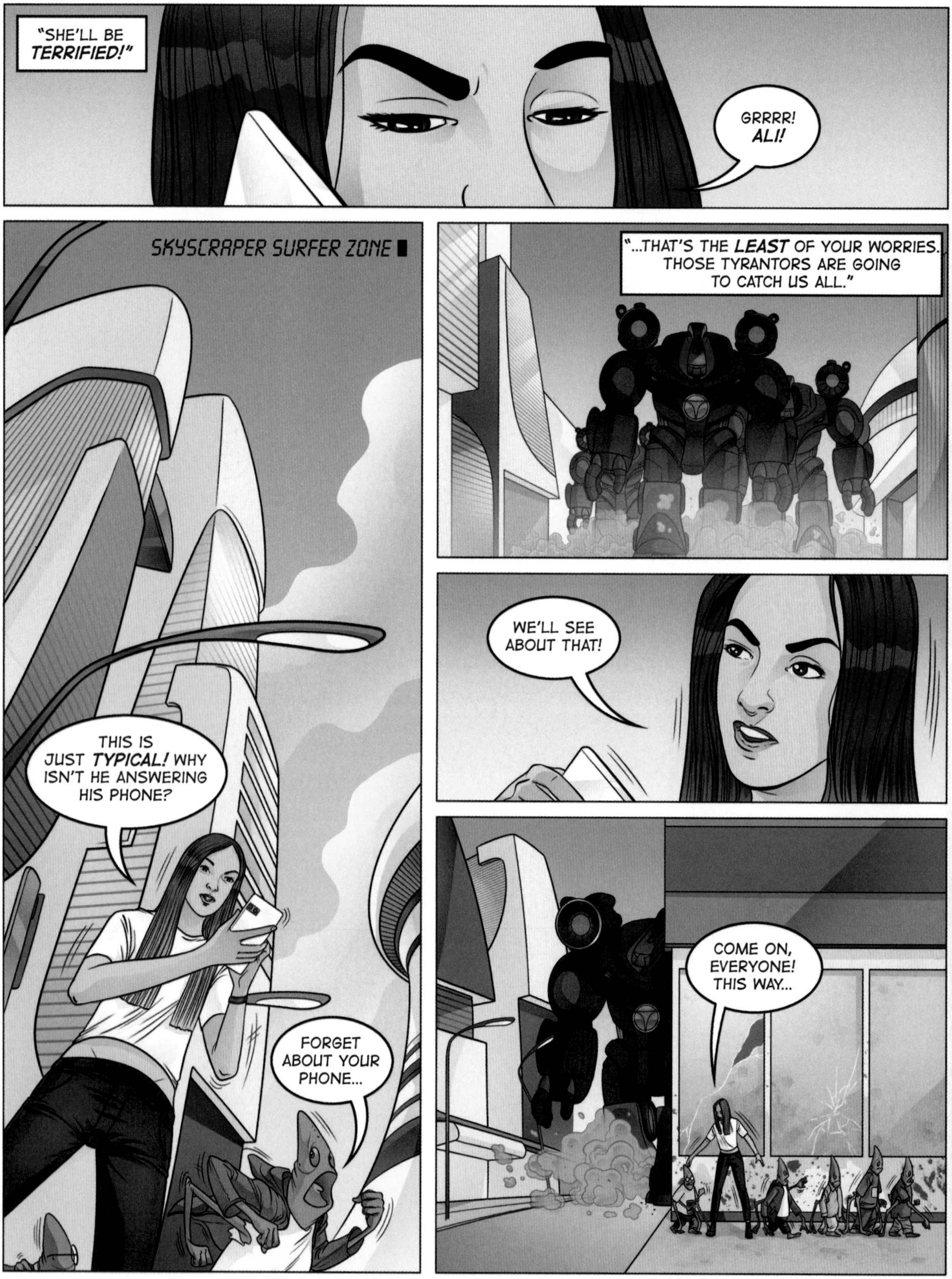
"SHE'LL BE TERRIFIED!"
GRRRR! ALI!
SKYSCRAPER SURFER ZONE
THIS IS JUST TYPICAL! WHY ISN'T HE ANSWERING HIS PHONE?
FORGET ABOUT YOUR PHONE...
"...THAT'S THE LEAST OF YOUR WORRIES. THOSE TYRANTORS ARE GOING TO CATCH US ALL."
WE'LL SEE ABOUT THAT!
COME ON, EVERYONE! THIS WAY...

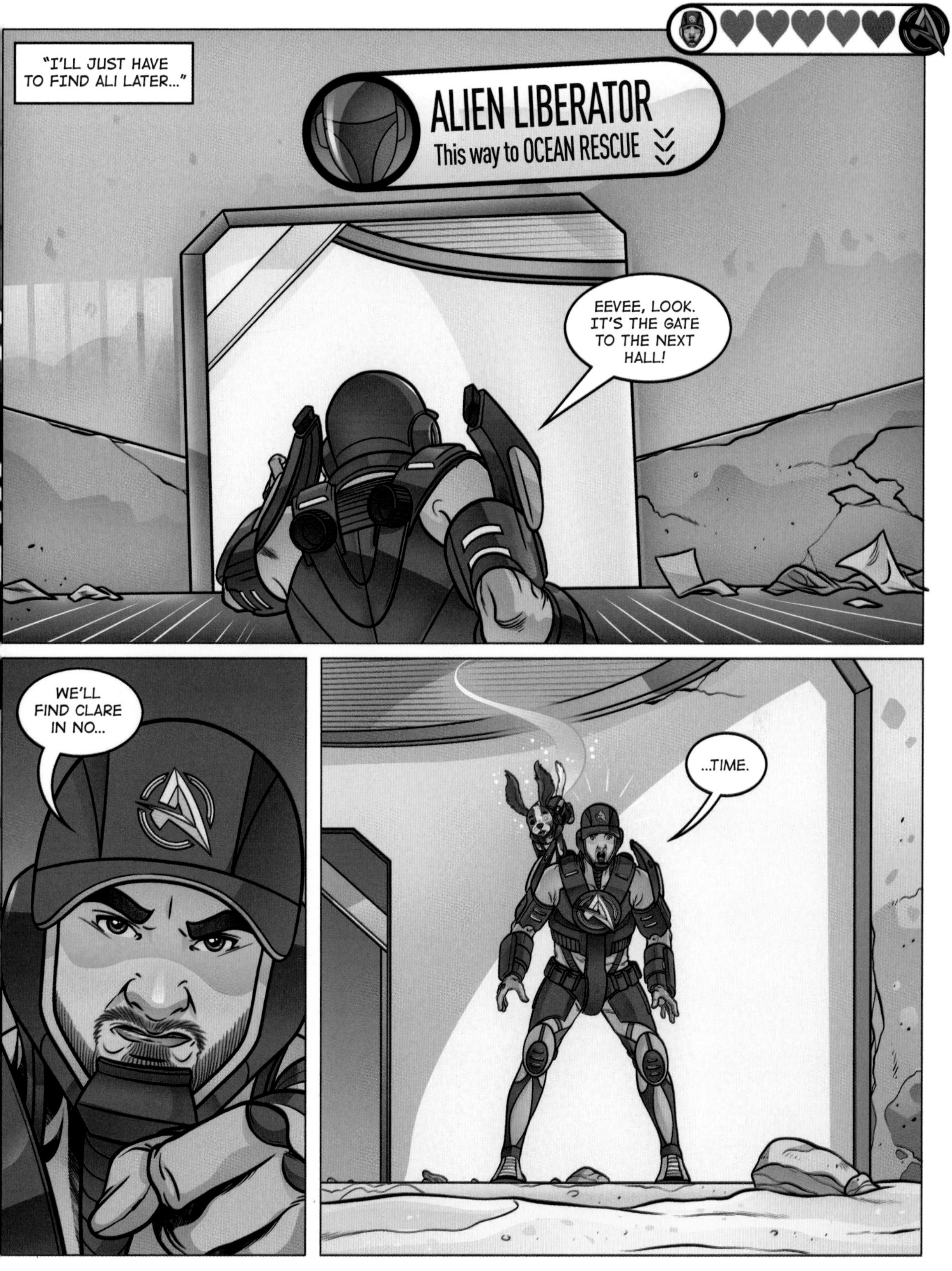
"I'LL JUST HAVE TO FIND ALI LATER..."
ALIEN LIBERATOR
This way to OCEAN RESCUE
EEVEE, LOOK. IT'S THE GATE TO THE NEXT HALL!
WE'LL FIND CLARE IN NO...
...TIME.

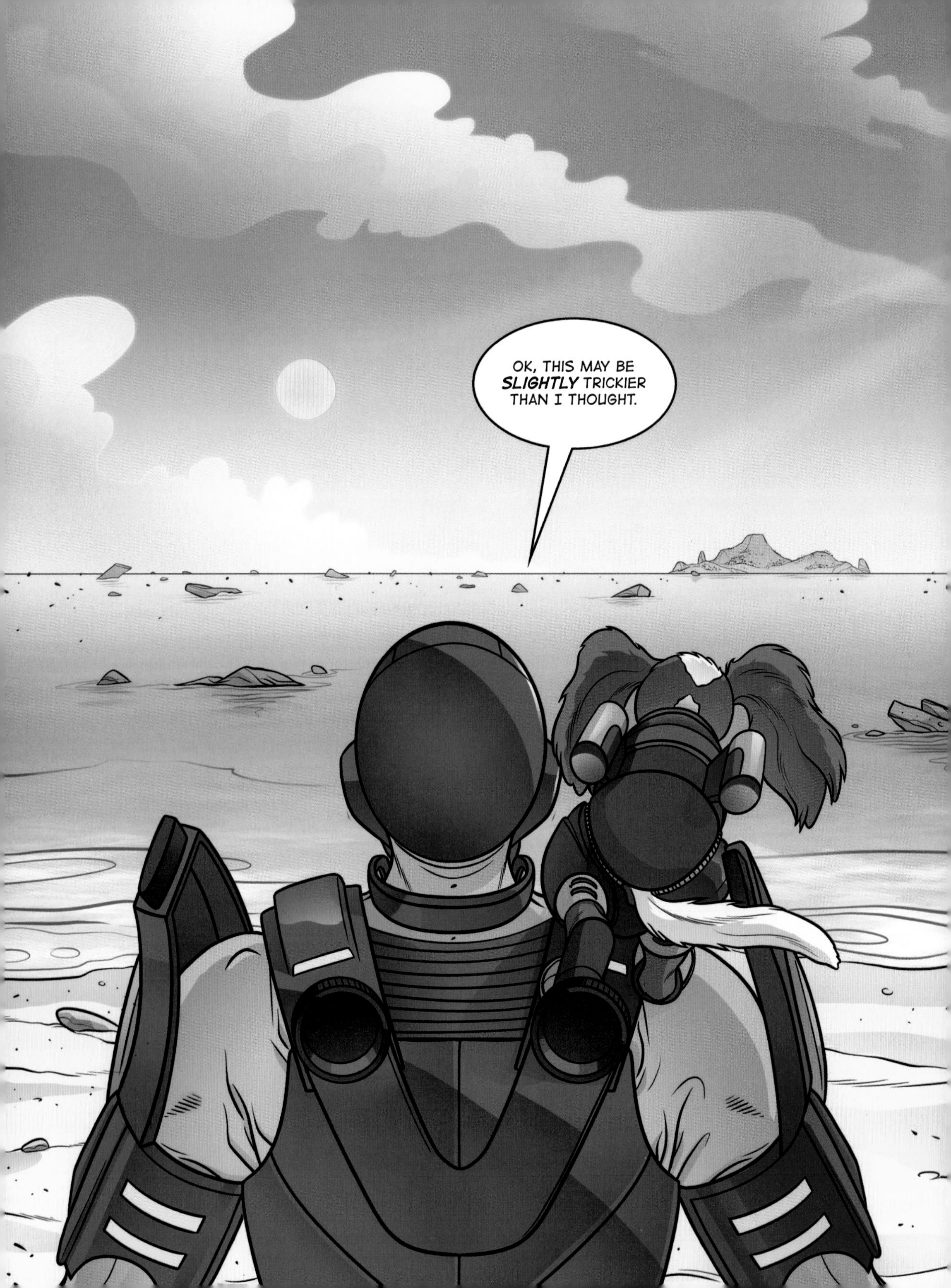
OK, THIS MAY BE SLIGHTLY TRICKIER THAN I THOUGHT.

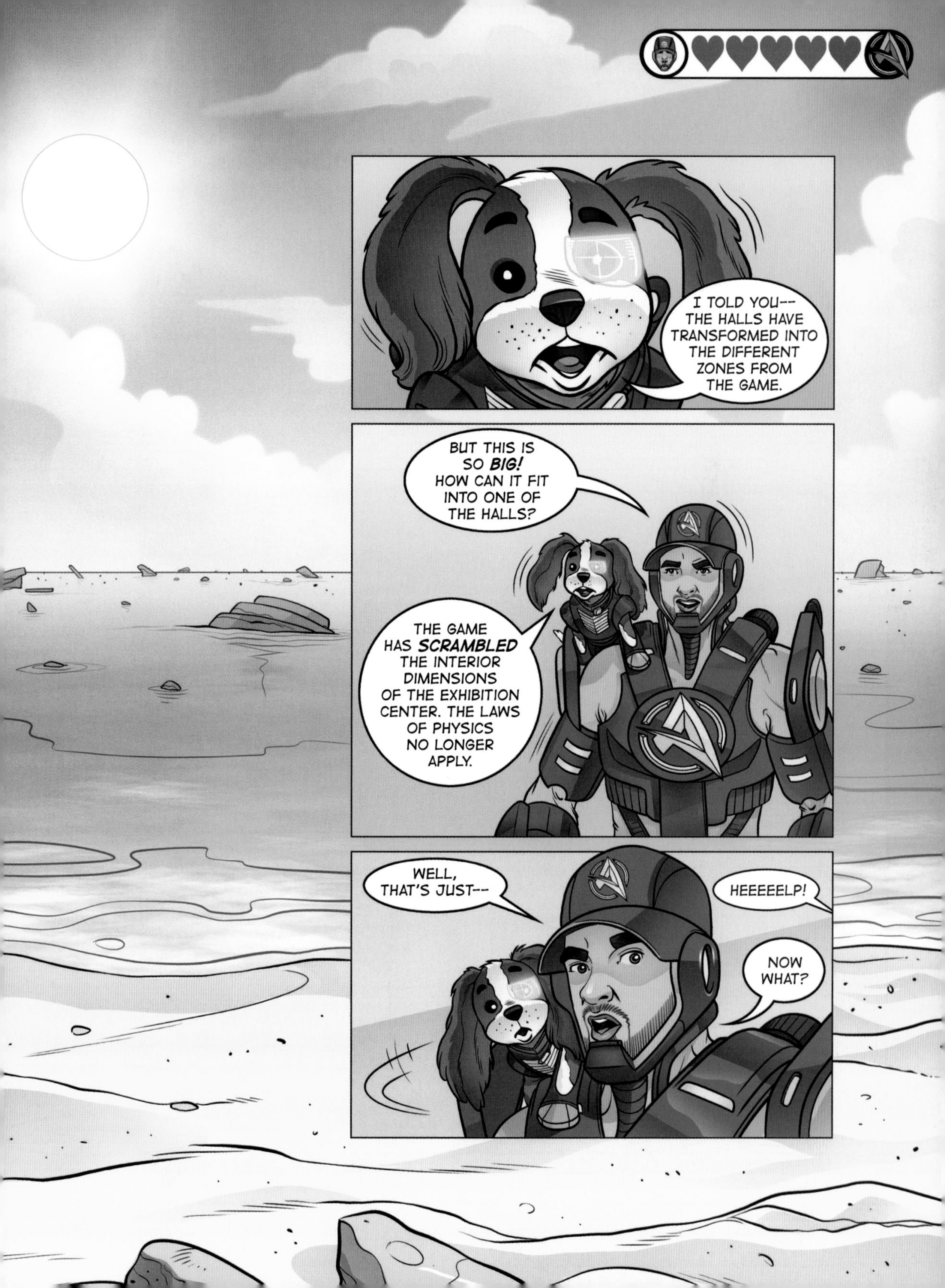
I TOLD YOU-- THE HALLS HAVE TRANSFORMED INTO THE DIFFERENT ZONES FROM THE GAME.
BUT THIS IS SO BIG! HOW CAN IT FIT INTO ONE OF THE HALLS?
THE GAME HAS SCRAMBLED THE INTERIOR DIMENSIONS OF THE EXHIBITION CENTER. THE LAWS OF PHYSICS NO LONGER APPLY.
WELL, THAT'S JUST--
HEEEEELP!
NOW WHAT?

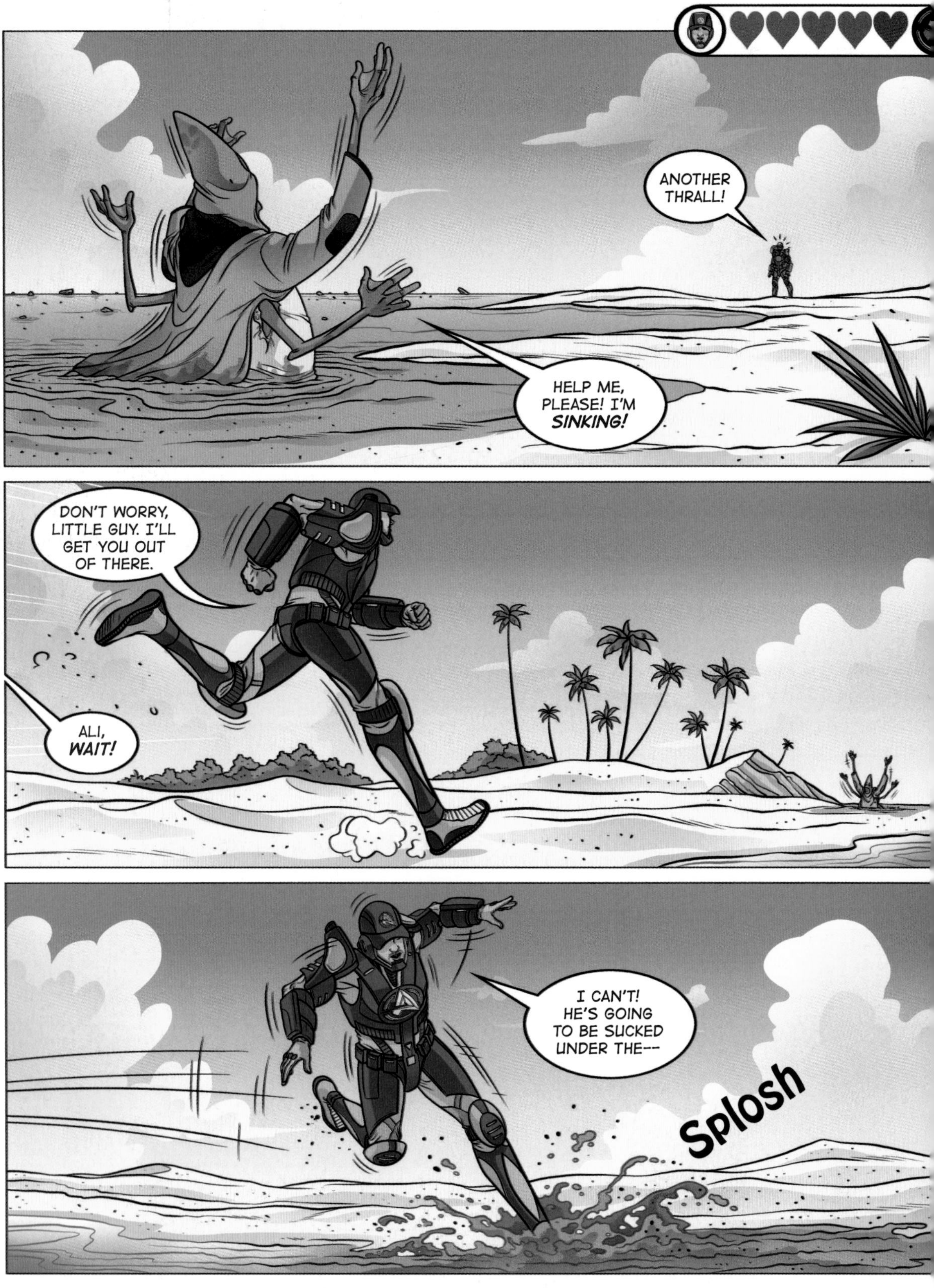
ANOTHER THRALL!
HELP ME, PLEASE! I'M *SINKING!*
DON'T WORRY, LITTLE GUY. I'LL GET YOU OUT OF THERE.
ALI, *WAIT!*
I CAN'T! HE'S GOING TO BE SUCKED UNDER THE--
Splosh

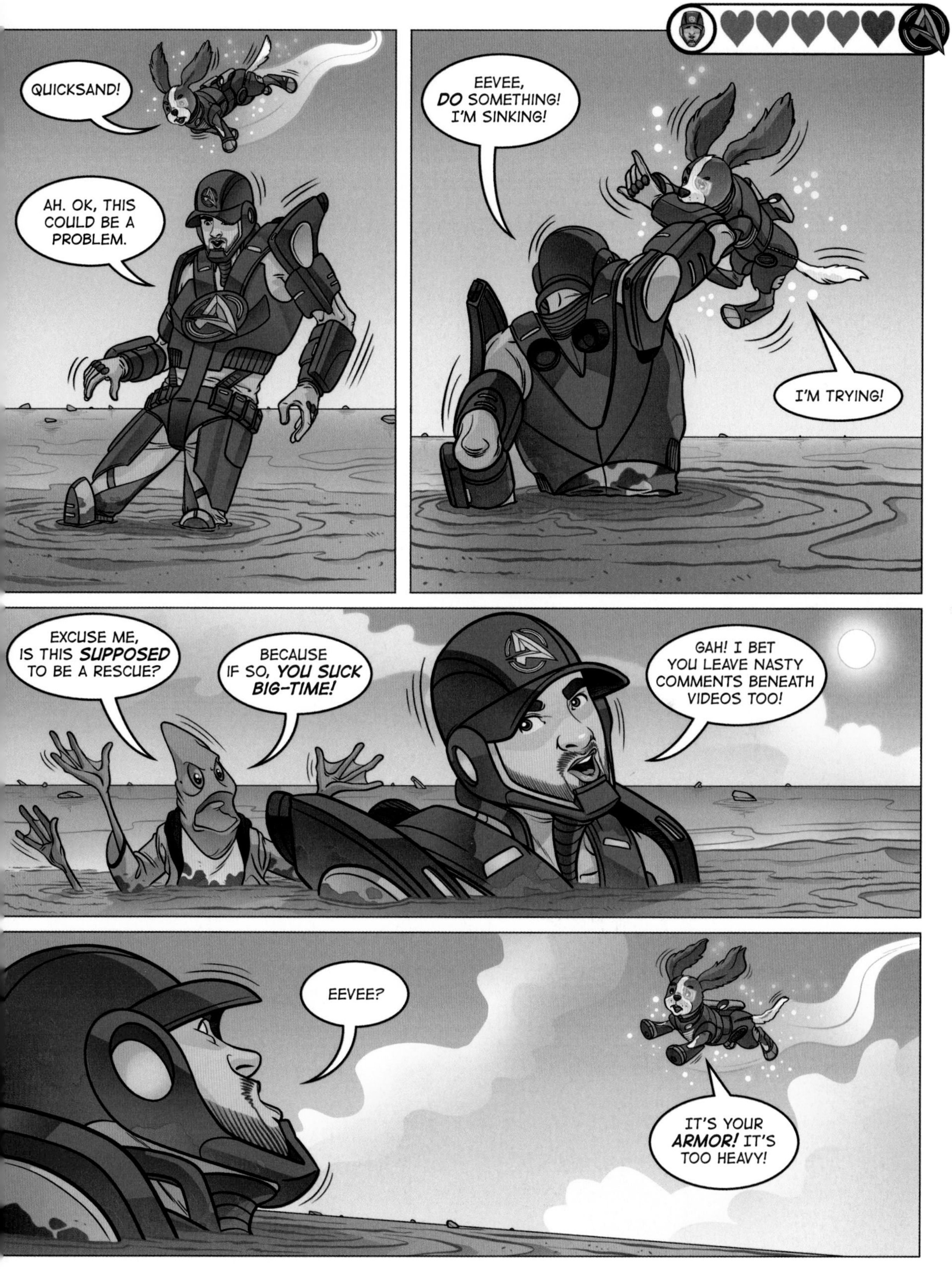
QUICKSAND!
AH. OK, THIS COULD BE A PROBLEM.
EEVEE, DO SOMETHING! I'M SINKING!
I'M TRYING!
EXCUSE ME, IS THIS SUPPOSED TO BE A RESCUE?
BECAUSE IF SO, YOU SUCK BIG-TIME!
GAH! I BET YOU LEAVE NASTY COMMENTS BENEATH VIDEOS TOO!
EEVEE?
IT'S YOUR ARMOR! IT'S TOO HEAVY!

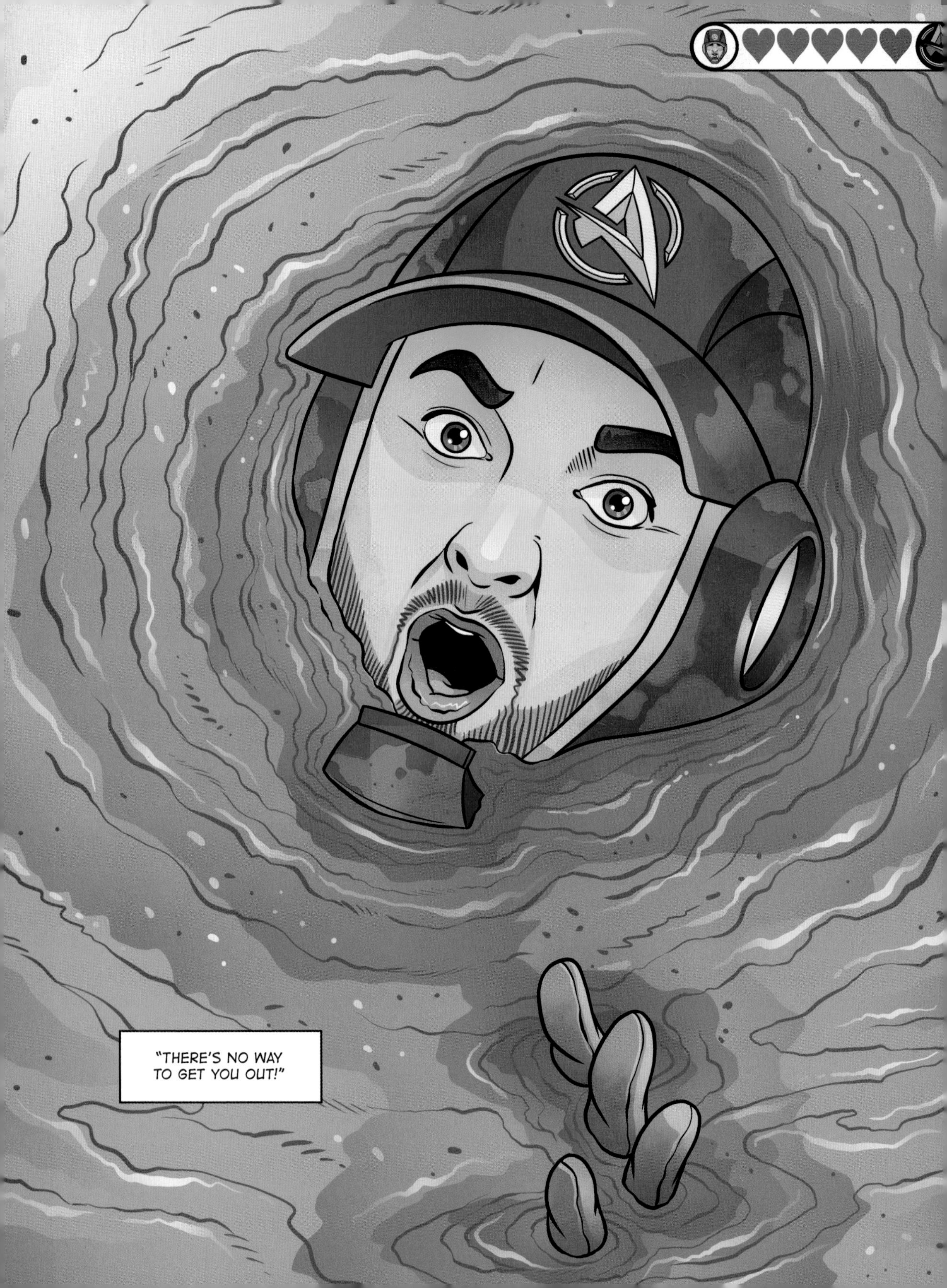
"THERE'S NO WAY TO GET YOU OUT!"

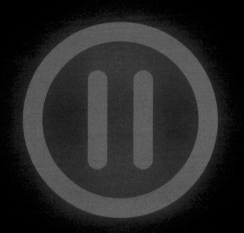

LEVEL FOUR

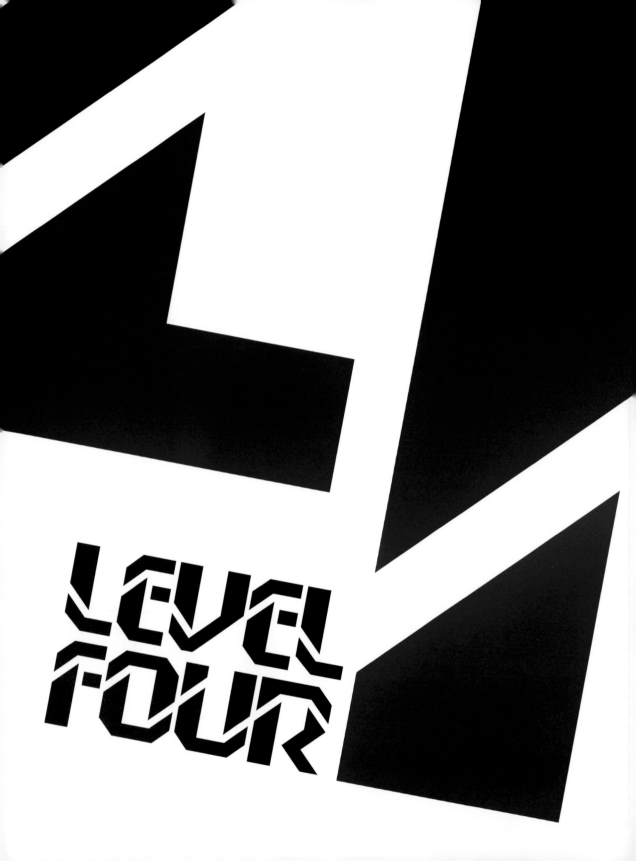

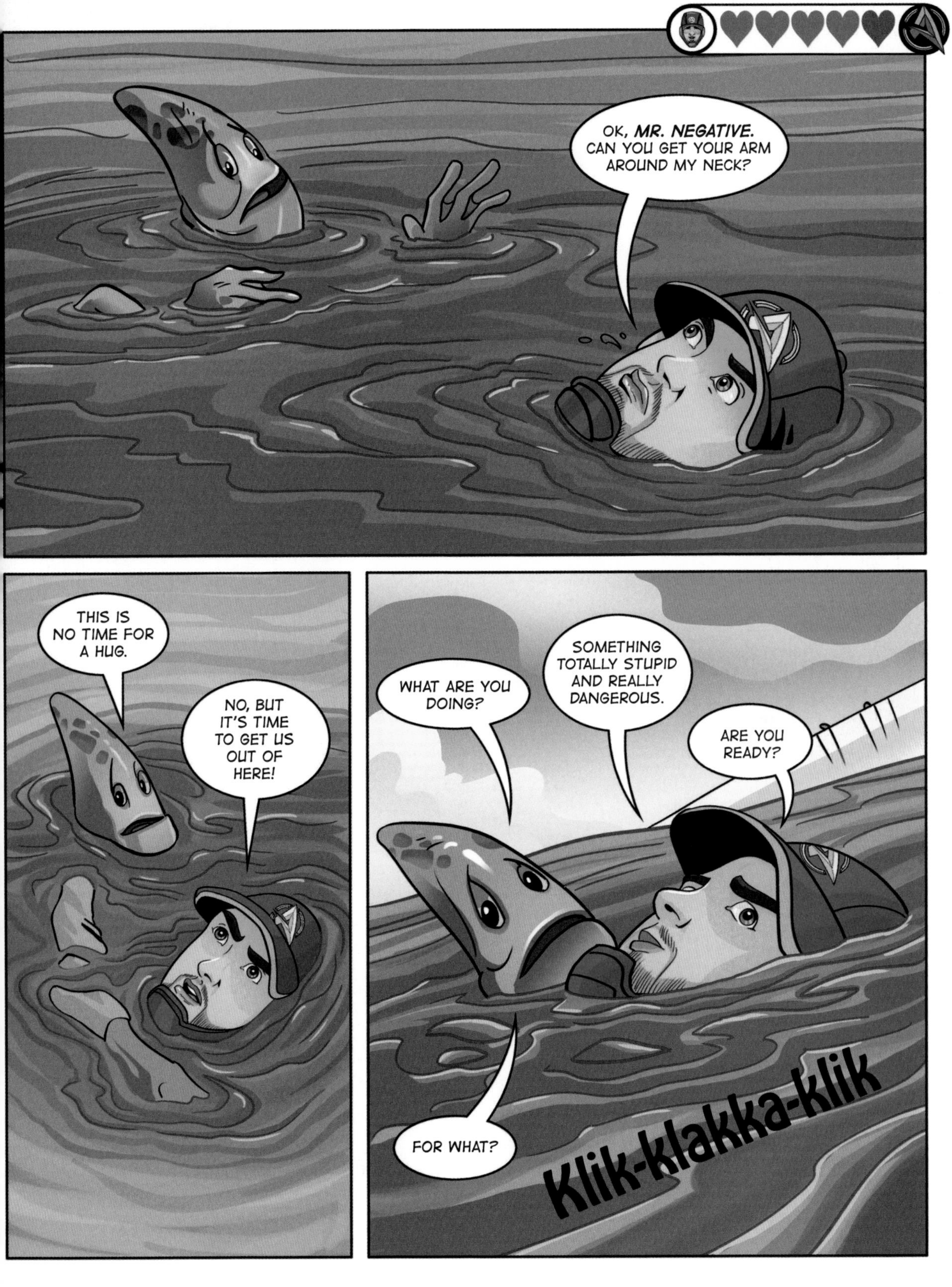
OK, MR. NEGATIVE. CAN YOU GET YOUR ARM AROUND MY NECK?
THIS IS NO TIME FOR A HUG.
NO, BUT IT'S TIME TO GET US OUT OF HERE!
WHAT ARE YOU DOING?
SOMETHING TOTALLY STUPID AND REALLY DANGEROUS.
ARE YOU READY?
FOR WHAT?
Klik-klakka-klik

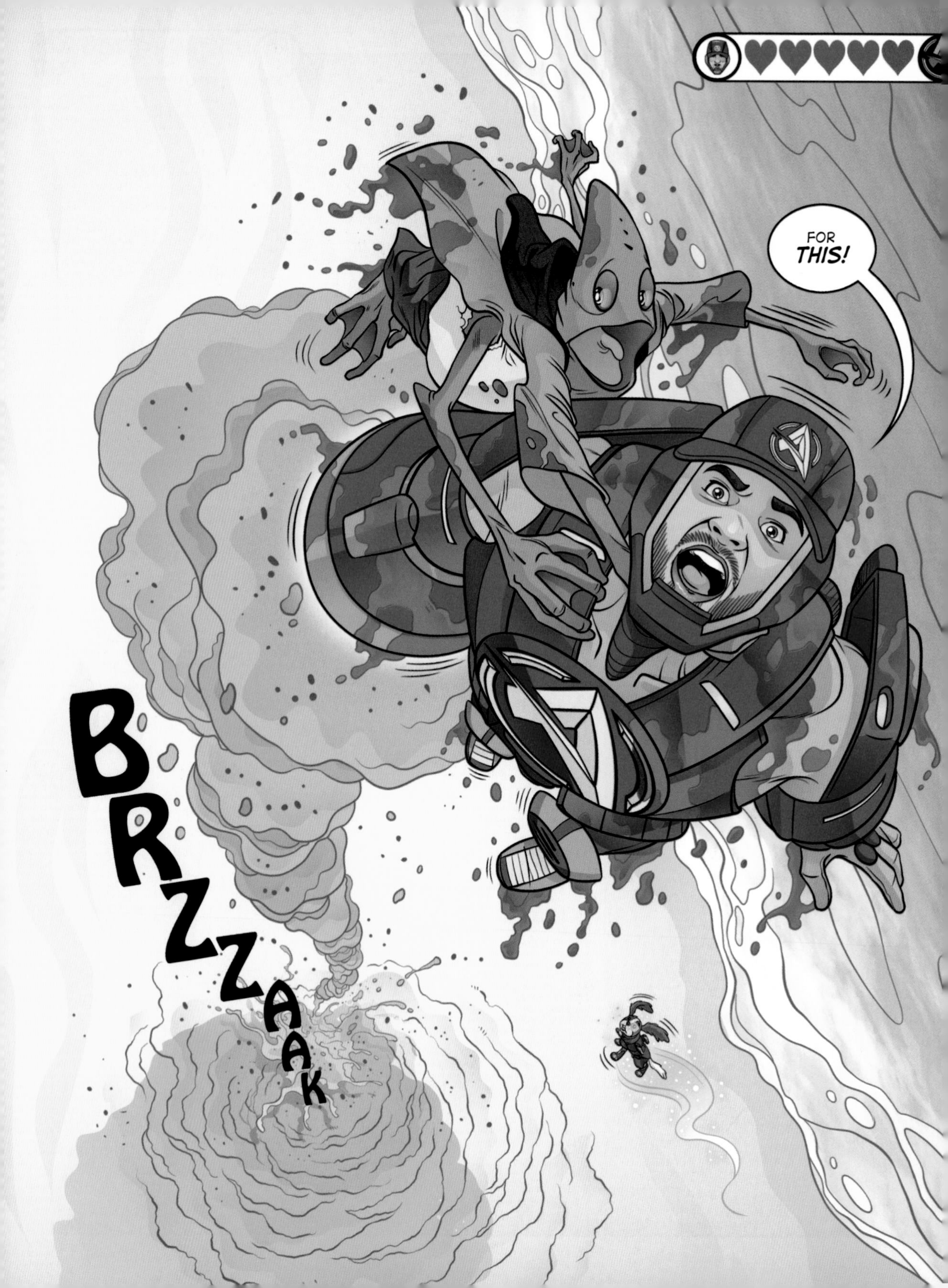
FOR THIS!
BRZZAAK

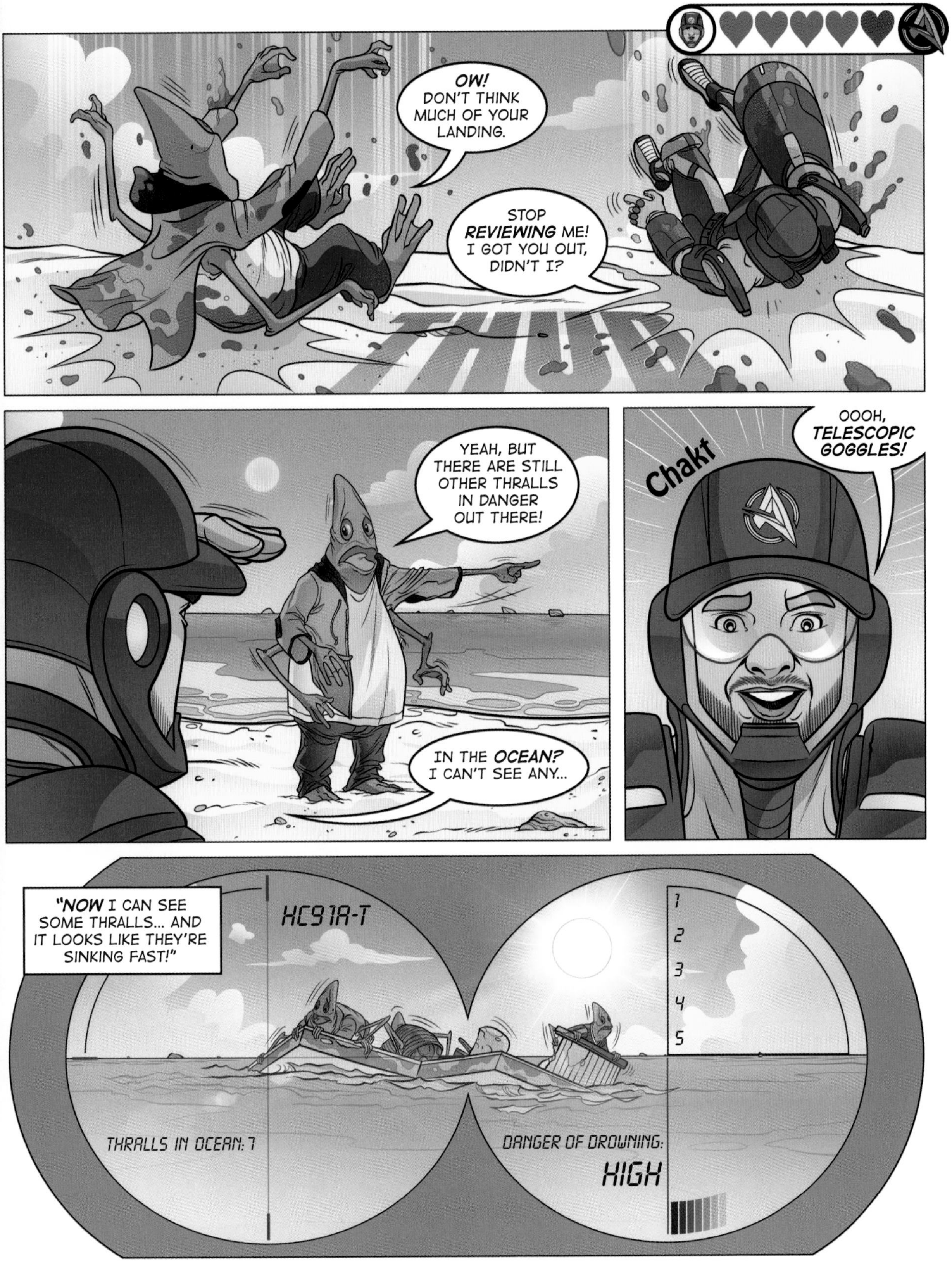
OW! DON'T THINK MUCH OF YOUR LANDING.
STOP REVIEWING ME! I GOT YOU OUT, DIDN'T I?
THUD
YEAH, BUT THERE ARE STILL OTHER THRALLS IN DANGER OUT THERE!
IN THE OCEAN? I CAN'T SEE ANY...
Chakt
OOOH, TELESCOPIC GOGGLES!
"NOW I CAN SEE SOME THRALLS... AND IT LOOKS LIKE THEY'RE SINKING FAST!"
HC91A-T
1
2
3
4
5
THRALLS IN OCEAN: 7
DANGER OF DROWNING:
HIGH

REMEMBER, ALI, THE MORE THRALLS YOU *SAVE,* THE MORE ENERGY YOU'LL *GET* AND THE MORE ENERGY YOU GET--

THE MORE *UPGRADES* I'LL RECEIVE. YEAH, I KNOW. ANYTHING TO HELP ME FIND CLARE.

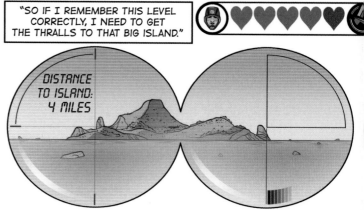

"SO IF I REMEMBER THIS LEVEL CORRECTLY, I NEED TO GET THE THRALLS TO THAT BIG ISLAND."

DISTANCE TO ISLAND: 4 MILES

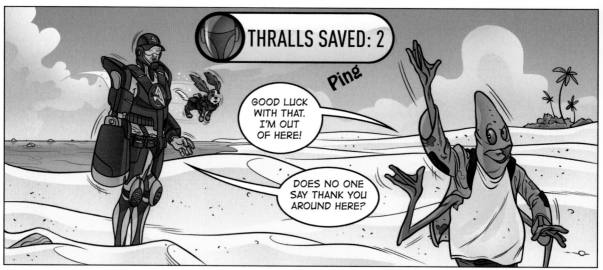

THRALLS SAVED: 2

Ping

GOOD LUCK WITH THAT. I'M OUT OF HERE!

DOES NO ONE SAY THANK YOU AROUND HERE?

ALI, FOCUS!

OK, OK, OK...

PLAYERS CAN TRADE LIVES FOR EMERGENCY VEHICLES IN THE GAME, RIGHT?

HMMM... I'M NOT SURE THAT'S A GOOD IDEA.

Clik

WHAT CHOICE DO I HAVE? LET'S DO THIS!

tschh

Ping

SELF-SACRIFICE TROPHY

UPGRADE UNLOCKED

Ping

THIS IS MORE LIKE IT! LET'S SEE WHAT WE'VE GOT.

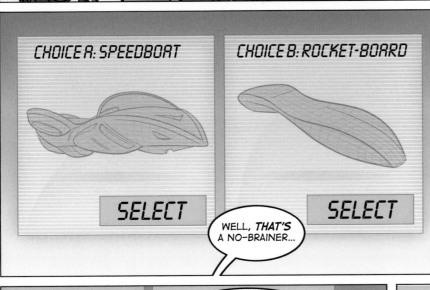

CHOICE A: SPEEDBOAT

SELECT

CHOICE B: ROCKET-BOARD

SELECT

WELL, THAT'S A NO-BRAINER...

RIGHT-- THE ROCKET-BOARD. YOU CAN FLY THE THRALLS TO SAFETY!

THE ROCKET-BOARD? NO WAY! NOT NOW. NOT EVER.

WHY?

YOU'RE NOT GETTING ME BACK IN THE SKY, NOT AFTER CLIMBING THAT TOWER.

NO. MORE. HEIGHTS. OK?

BESIDES...

SELECT

Beep

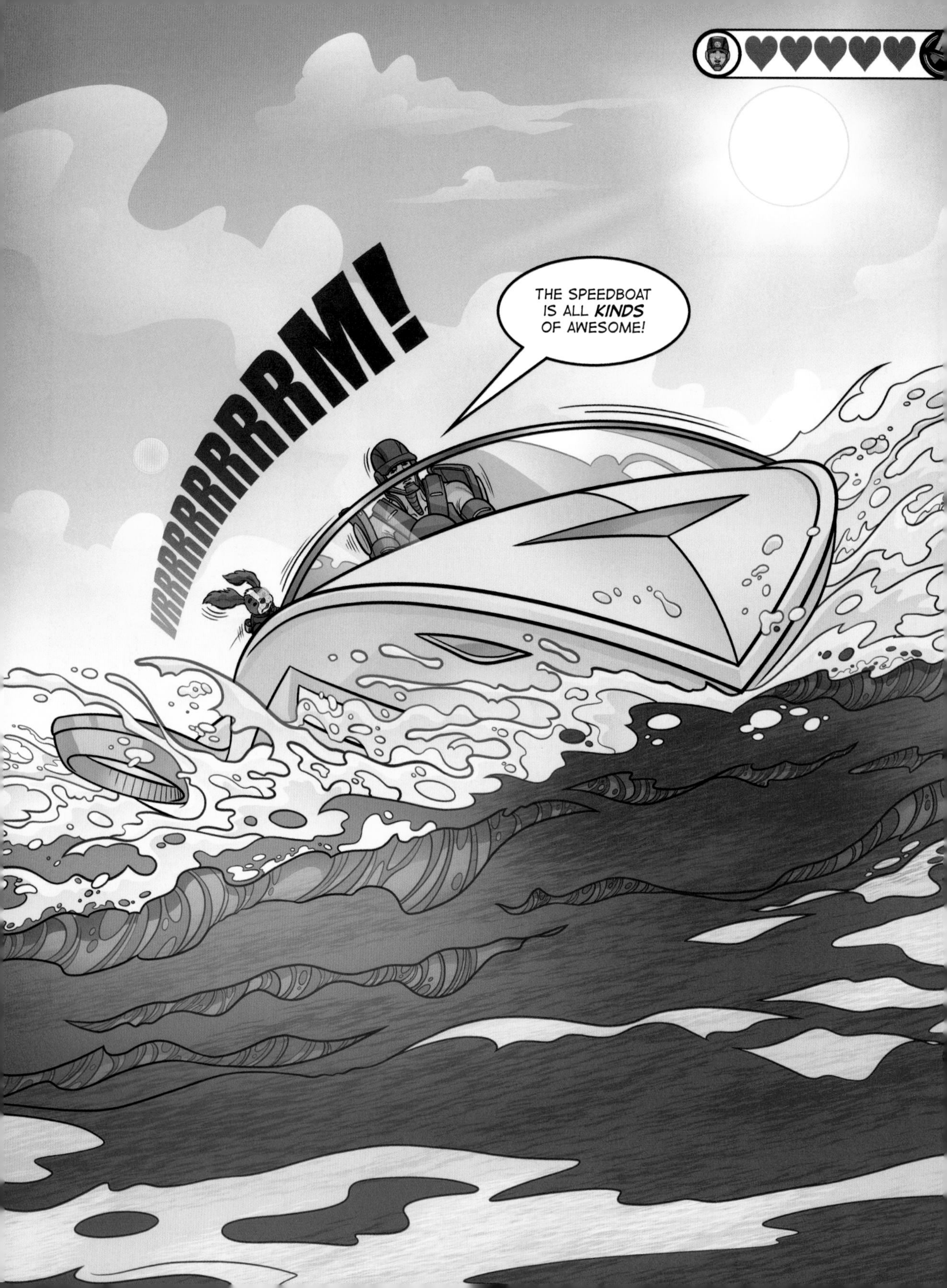
VRRRRRRRRRRRRM!
THE SPEEDBOAT IS ALL *KINDS* OF AWESOME!

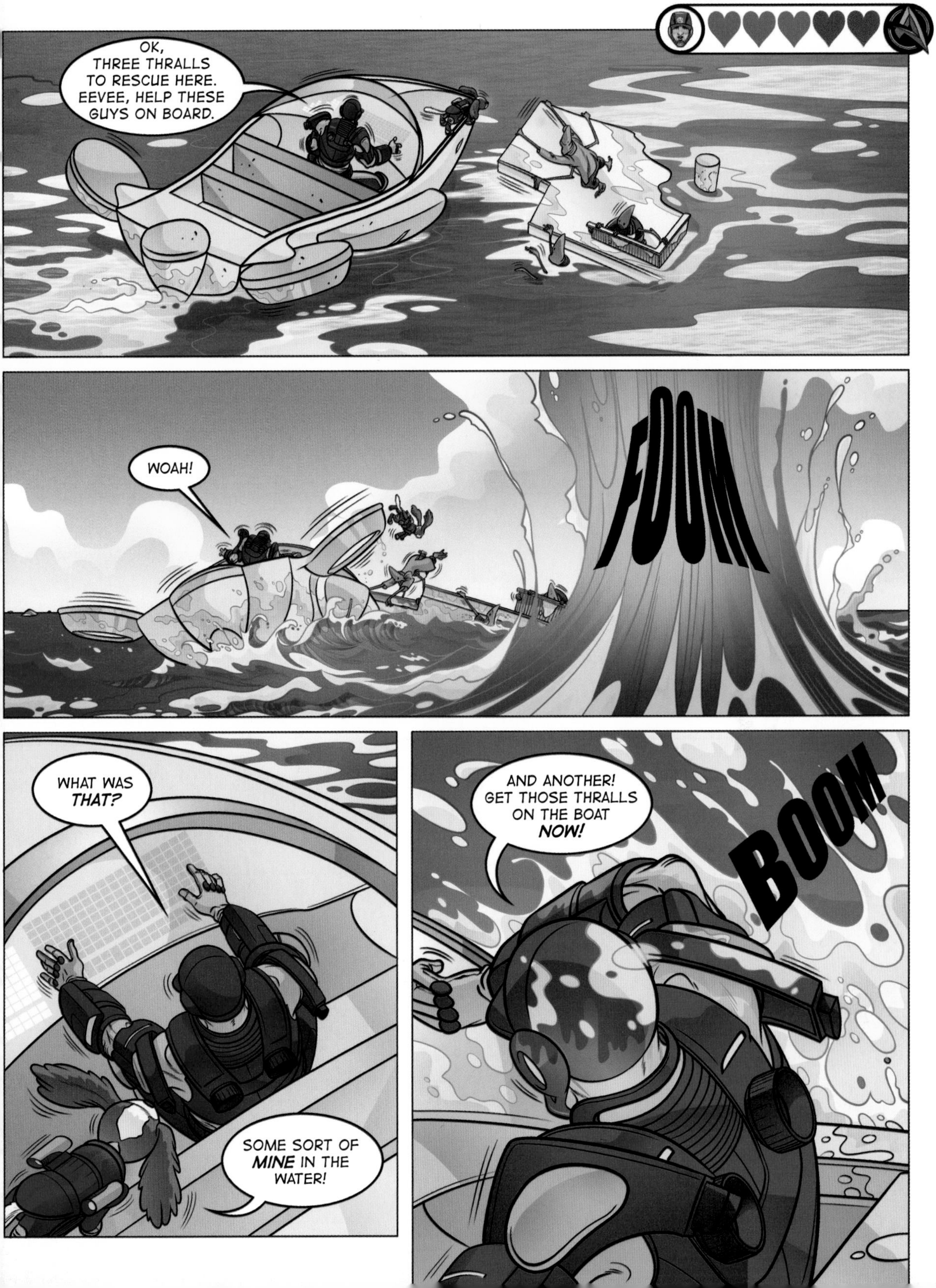
OK, THREE THRALLS TO RESCUE HERE. EEVEE, HELP THESE GUYS ON BOARD.
WOAH!
FOOM
WHAT WAS *THAT?*
SOME SORT OF ***MINE*** IN THE WATER!
AND ANOTHER! GET THOSE THRALLS ON THE BOAT ***NOW!***
BOOM

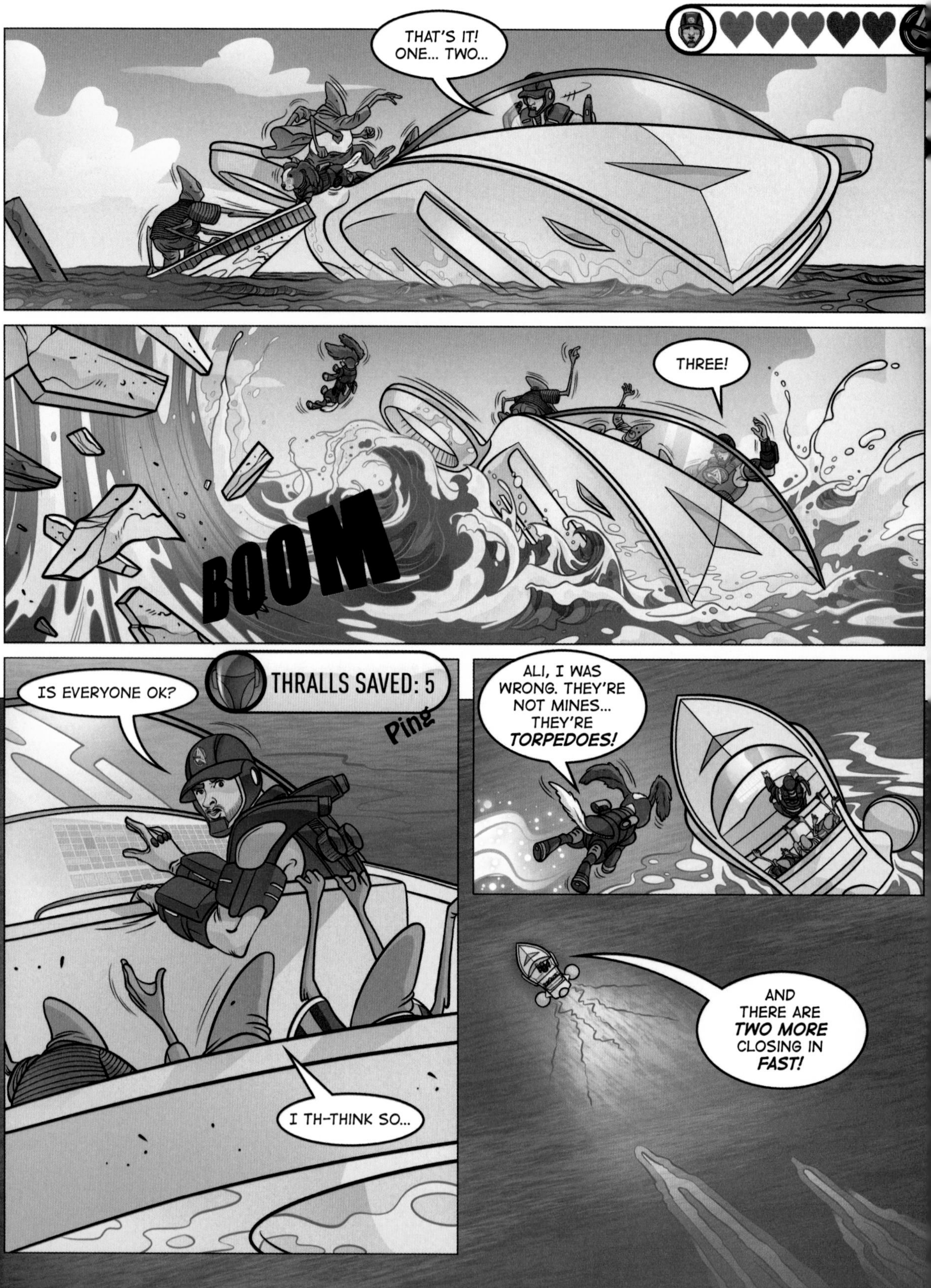
THAT'S IT! ONE... TWO...
THREE!
BOOM
THRALLS SAVED: 5
IS EVERYONE OK?
Ping
I TH-THINK SO...
ALI, I WAS WRONG. THEY'RE NOT MINES... THEY'RE TORPEDOES!
AND THERE ARE TWO MORE CLOSING IN FAST!

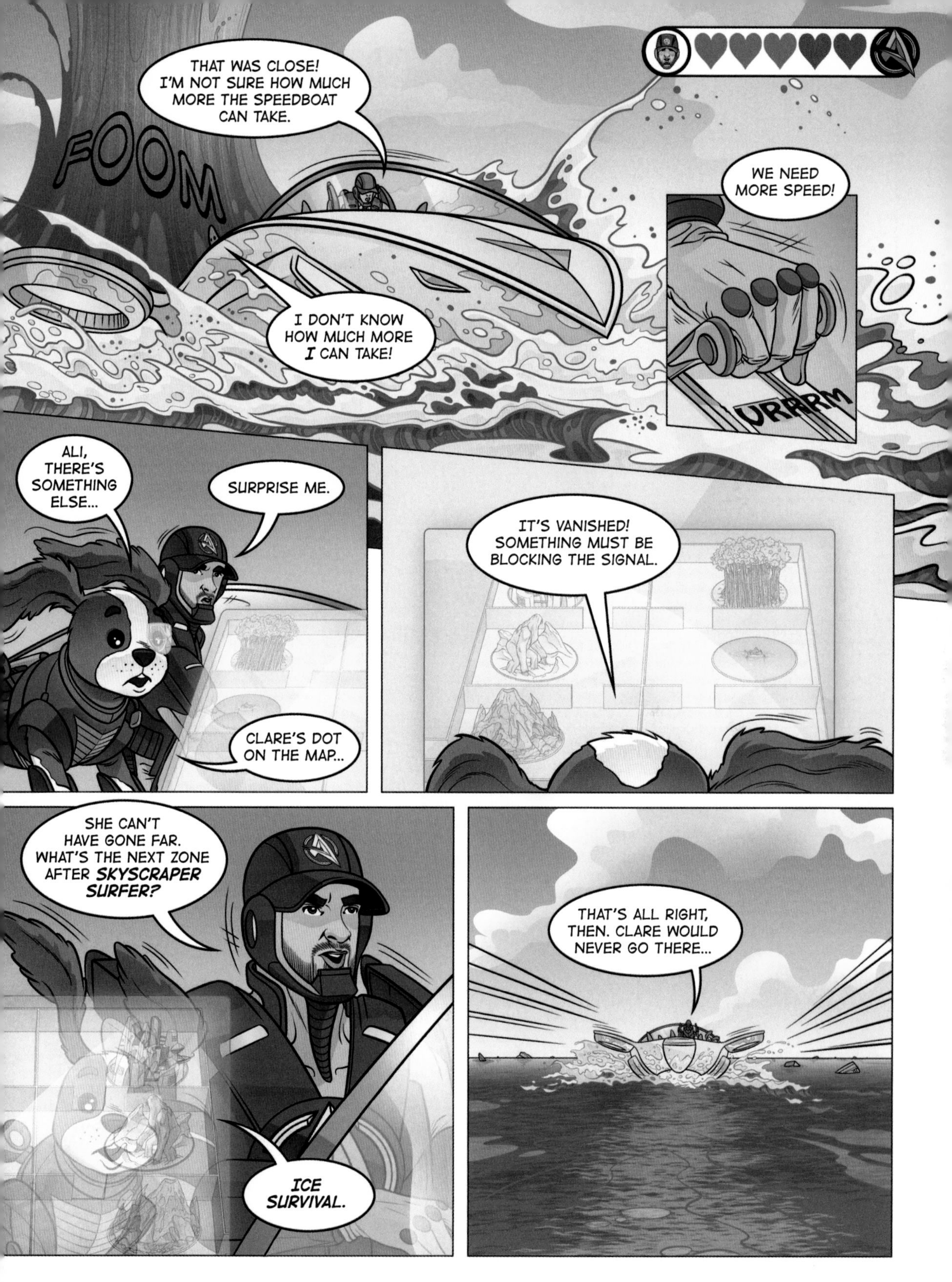
THAT WAS CLOSE! I'M NOT SURE HOW MUCH MORE THE SPEEDBOAT CAN TAKE.
FOOM
I DON'T KNOW HOW MUCH MORE *I* CAN TAKE!
WE NEED MORE SPEED!
URRRM
ALI, THERE'S SOMETHING ELSE...
SURPRISE ME.
CLARE'S DOT ON THE MAP...
IT'S VANISHED! SOMETHING MUST BE BLOCKING THE SIGNAL.
SHE CAN'T HAVE GONE FAR. WHAT'S THE NEXT ZONE AFTER ***SKYSCRAPER SURFER?***
ICE SURVIVAL.
THAT'S ALL RIGHT, THEN. CLARE WOULD NEVER GO THERE...

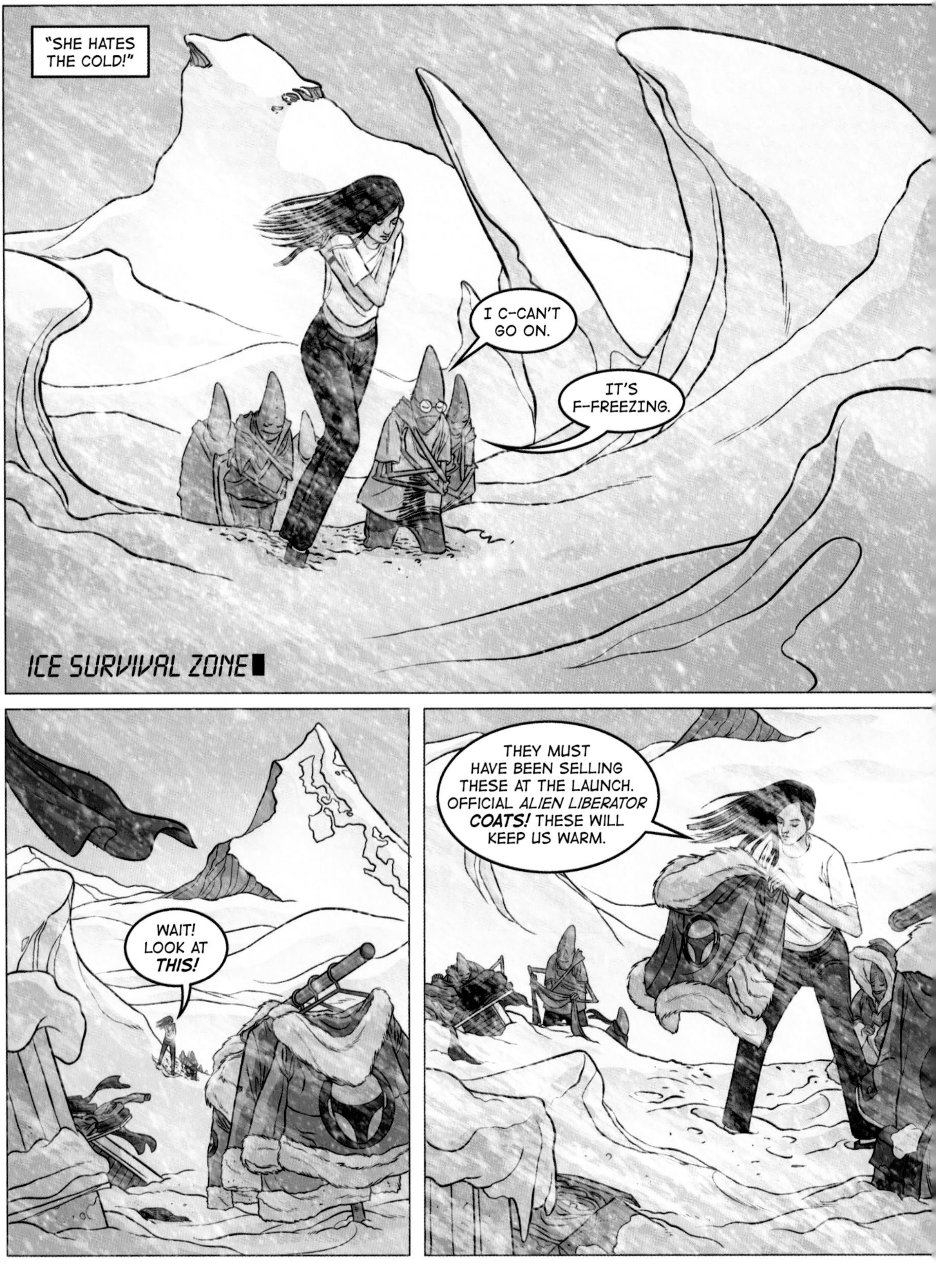
"SHE HATES THE COLD!"
I C-CAN'T GO ON.
IT'S F-FREEZING.
ICE SURVIVAL ZONE
WAIT! LOOK AT ***THIS!***
THEY MUST HAVE BEEN SELLING THESE AT THE LAUNCH. OFFICIAL *ALIEN LIBERATOR* ***COATS!*** THESE WILL KEEP US WARM.

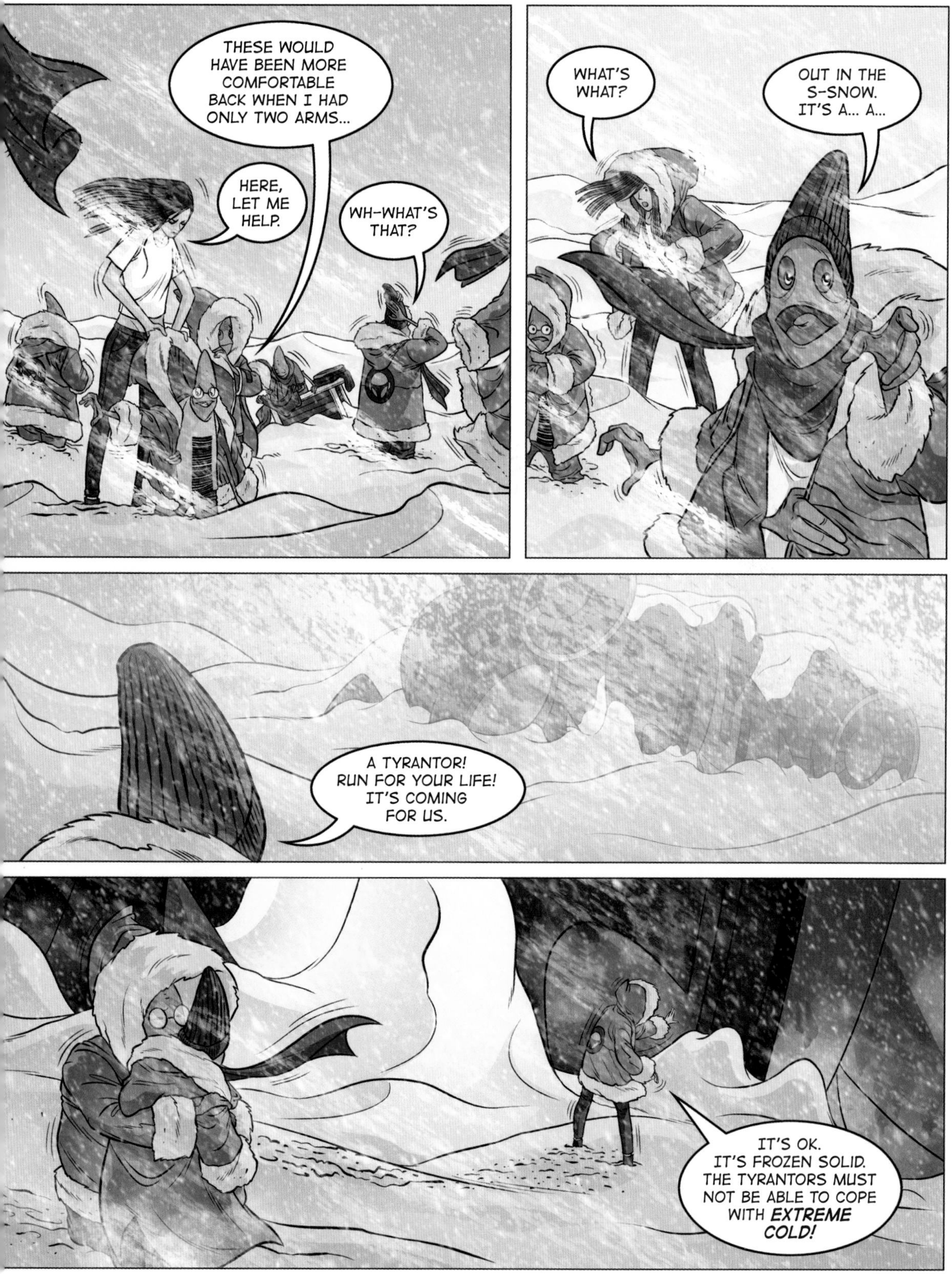
THESE WOULD HAVE BEEN MORE COMFORTABLE BACK WHEN I HAD ONLY TWO ARMS...
HERE, LET ME HELP.
WH-WHAT'S THAT?
WHAT'S WHAT?
OUT IN THE S-SNOW. IT'S A... A...
A TYRANTOR! RUN FOR YOUR LIFE! IT'S COMING FOR US.
IT'S OK. IT'S FROZEN SOLID. THE TYRANTORS MUST NOT BE ABLE TO COPE WITH **EXTREME COLD!**

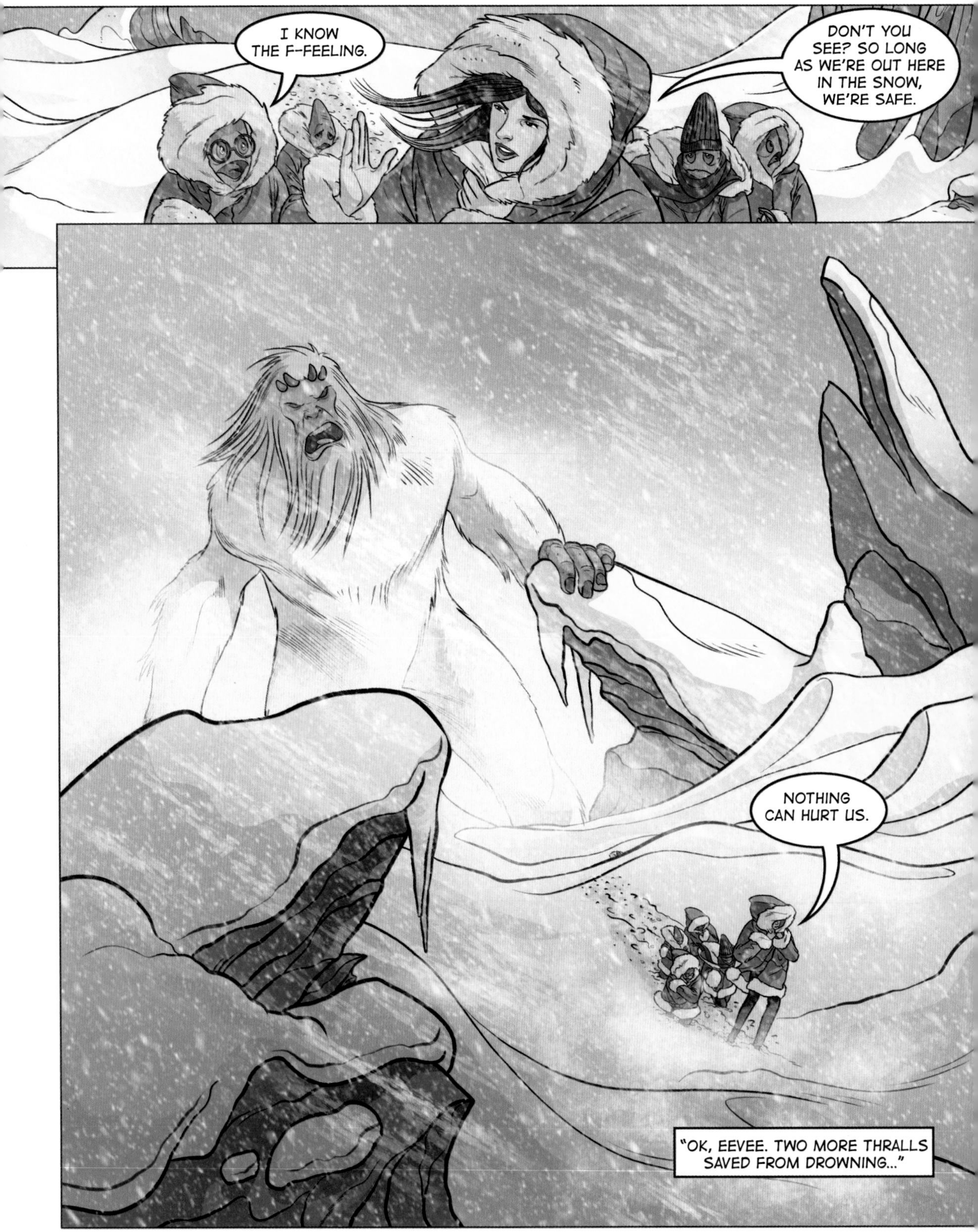
I KNOW THE F--FEELING.
DON'T YOU SEE? SO LONG AS WE'RE OUT HERE IN THE SNOW, WE'RE SAFE.
NOTHING CAN HURT US.
"OK, EEVEE. TWO MORE THRALLS SAVED FROM DROWNING..."

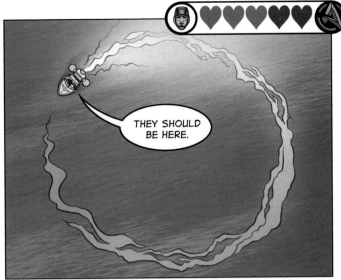

Ping

VRRRRM

...TWO MORE TO GO. WHERE *ARE* THEY?

I DON'T KNOW.

THEY SHOULD BE HERE.

OVER HERE! HELP!

THERE'S ONE!

=GASP=

DON'T WORRY. WE'VE GOT YOU.

TH-THE BOOTH WE WERE ON... IT *S-SANK.*

MY F-FRIEND WAS STILL ON IT.

YOUR FRIEND WENT DOWN WITH THE WRECKAGE?

YOU HAVE TO *HELP* HER! SHE CAN'T SWIM!

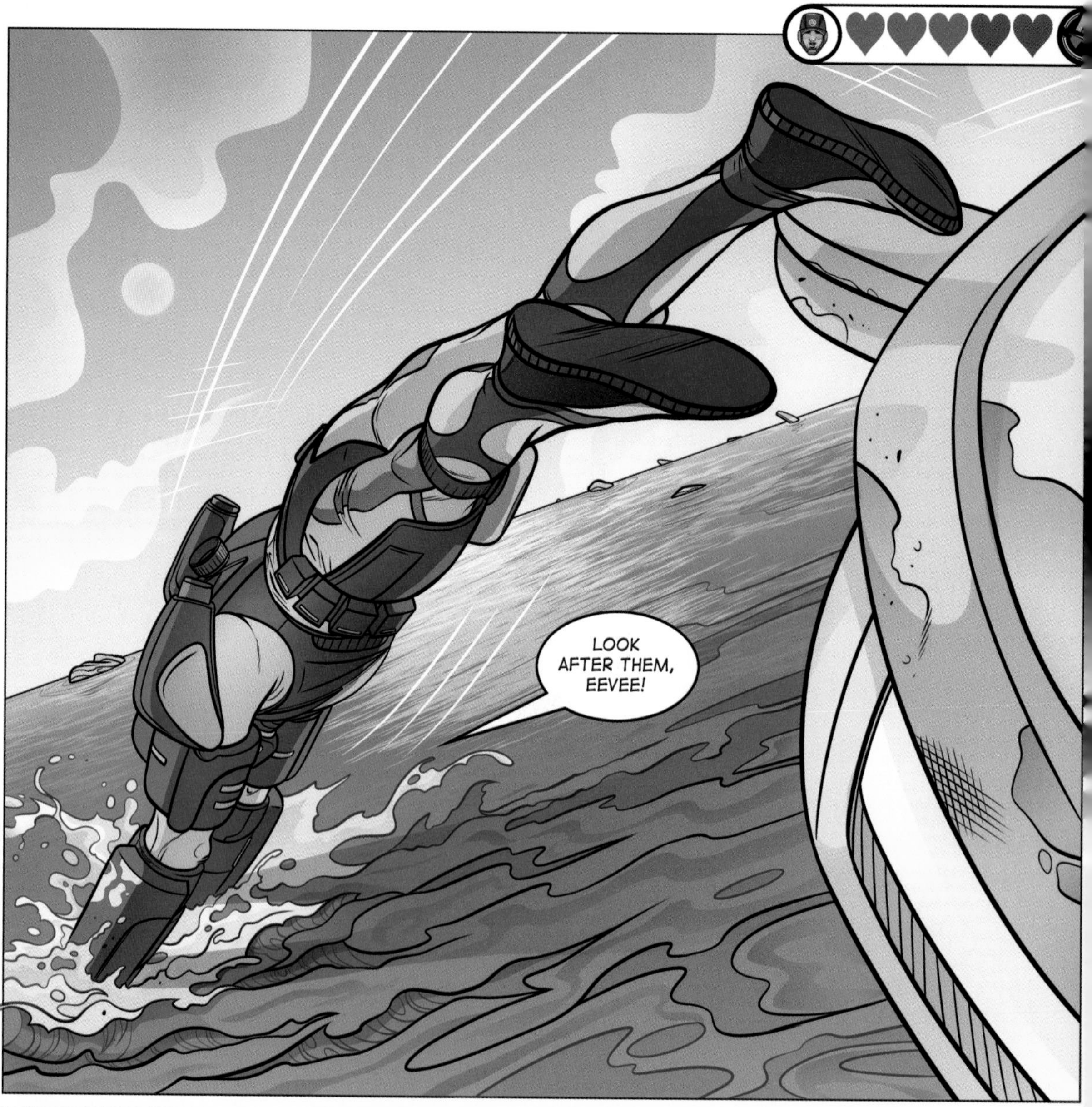
LOOK AFTER THEM, EEVEE!

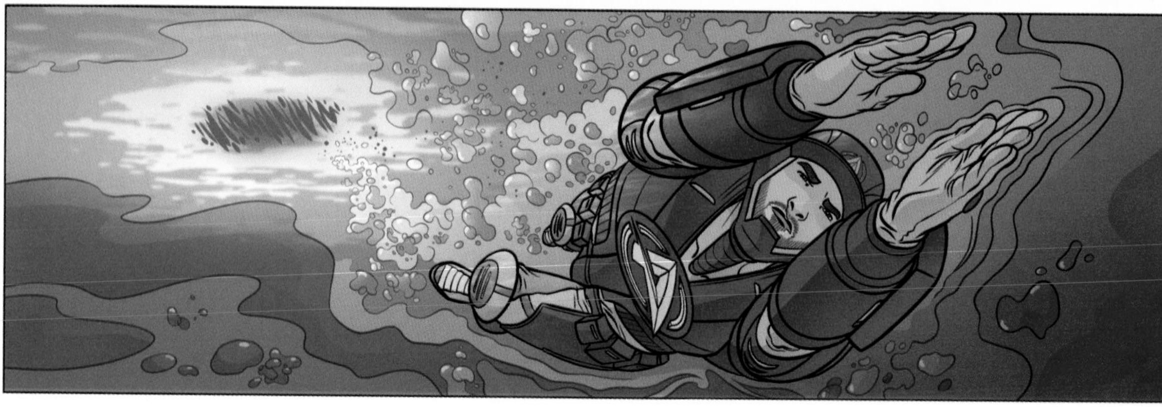

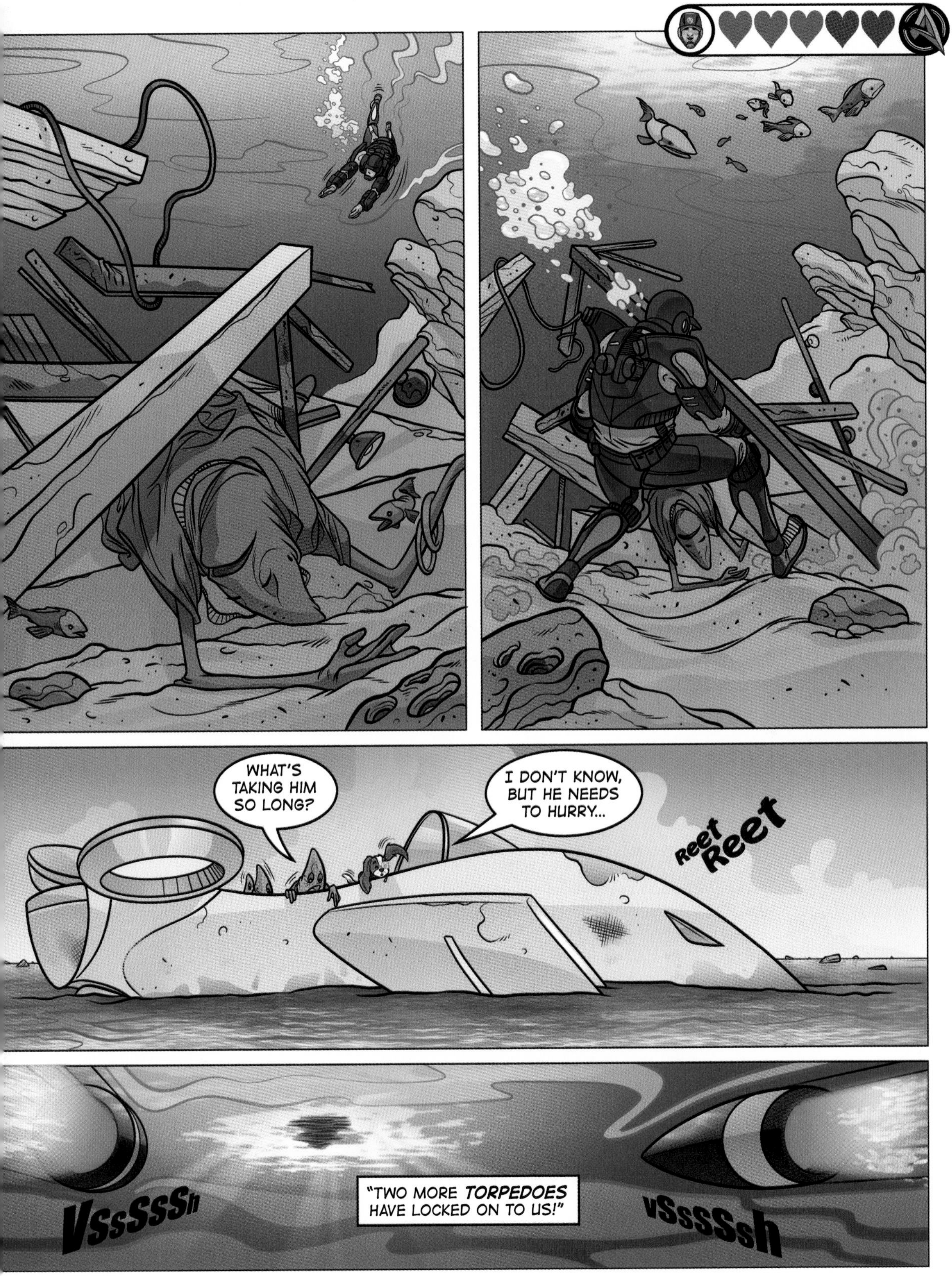
WHAT'S TAKING HIM SO LONG?
I DON'T KNOW, BUT HE NEEDS TO HURRY...
Reet Reet
"TWO MORE TORPEDOES HAVE LOCKED ON TO US!"
VsSsSSh
vSsSSSsh

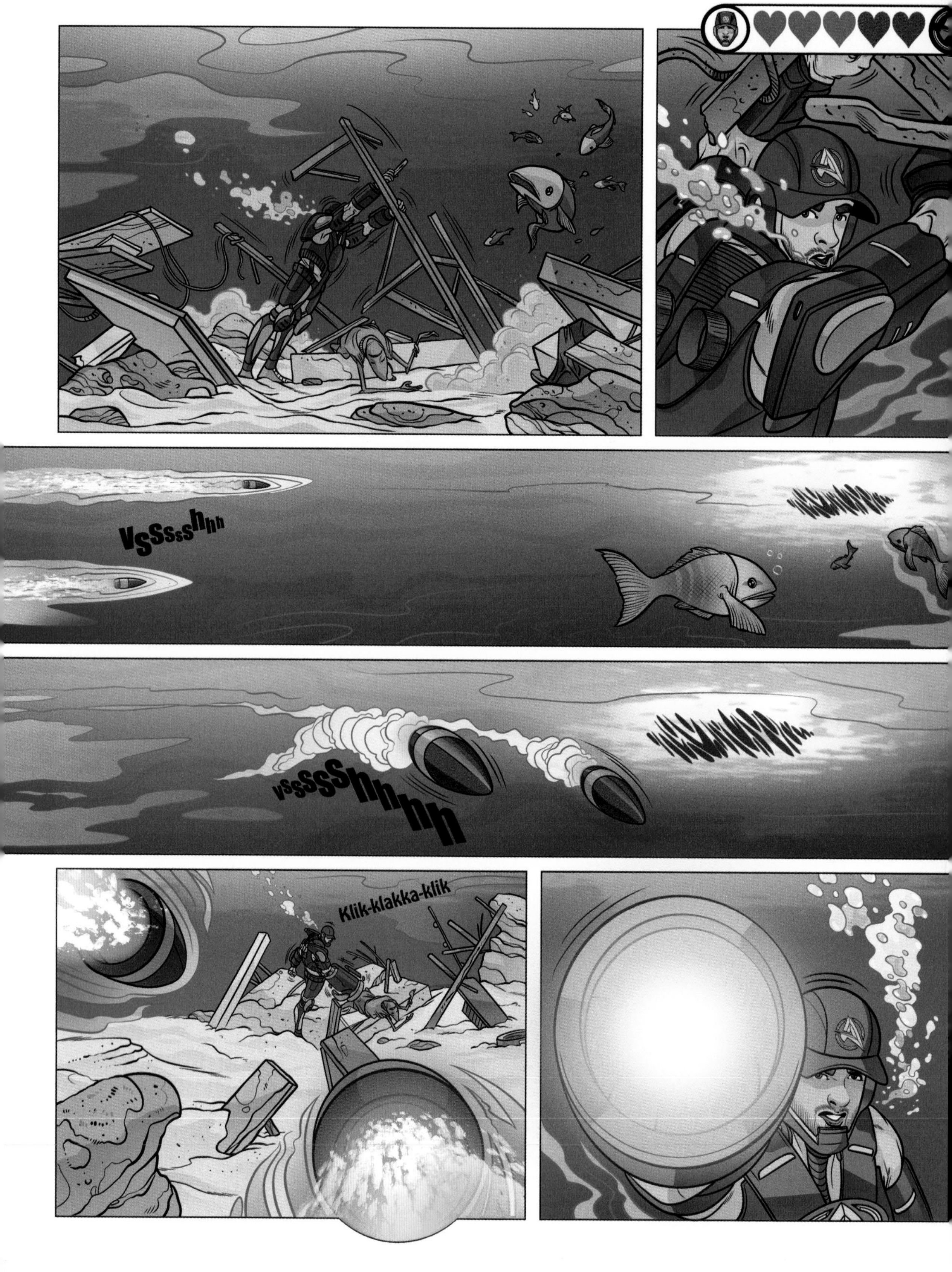

Vssssshhh
vsssSShhhhh
Klik-klakka-klik

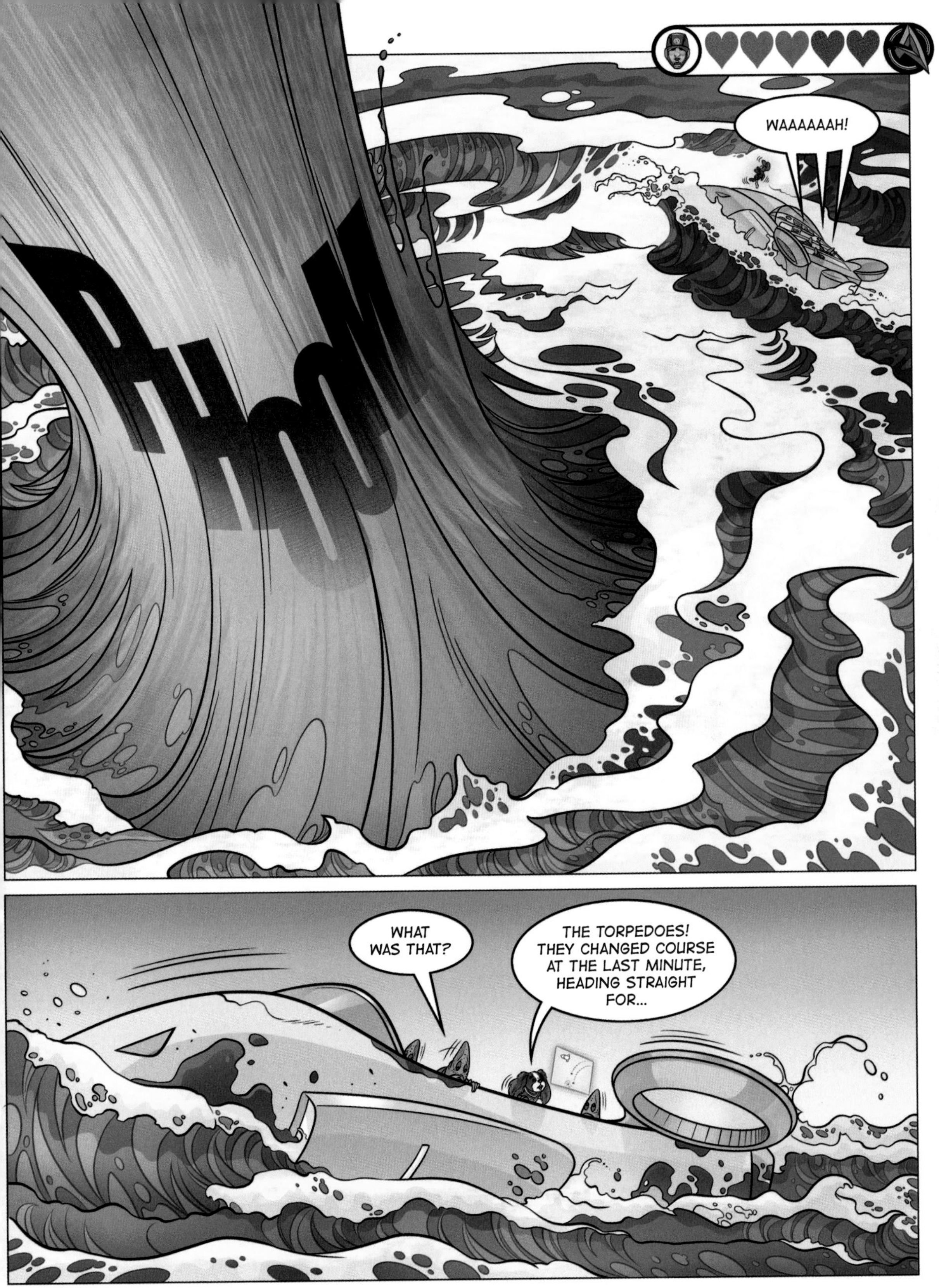
WAAAAAAH!
WHAT WAS THAT?
THE TORPEDOES! THEY CHANGED COURSE AT THE LAST MINUTE, HEADING STRAIGHT FOR...

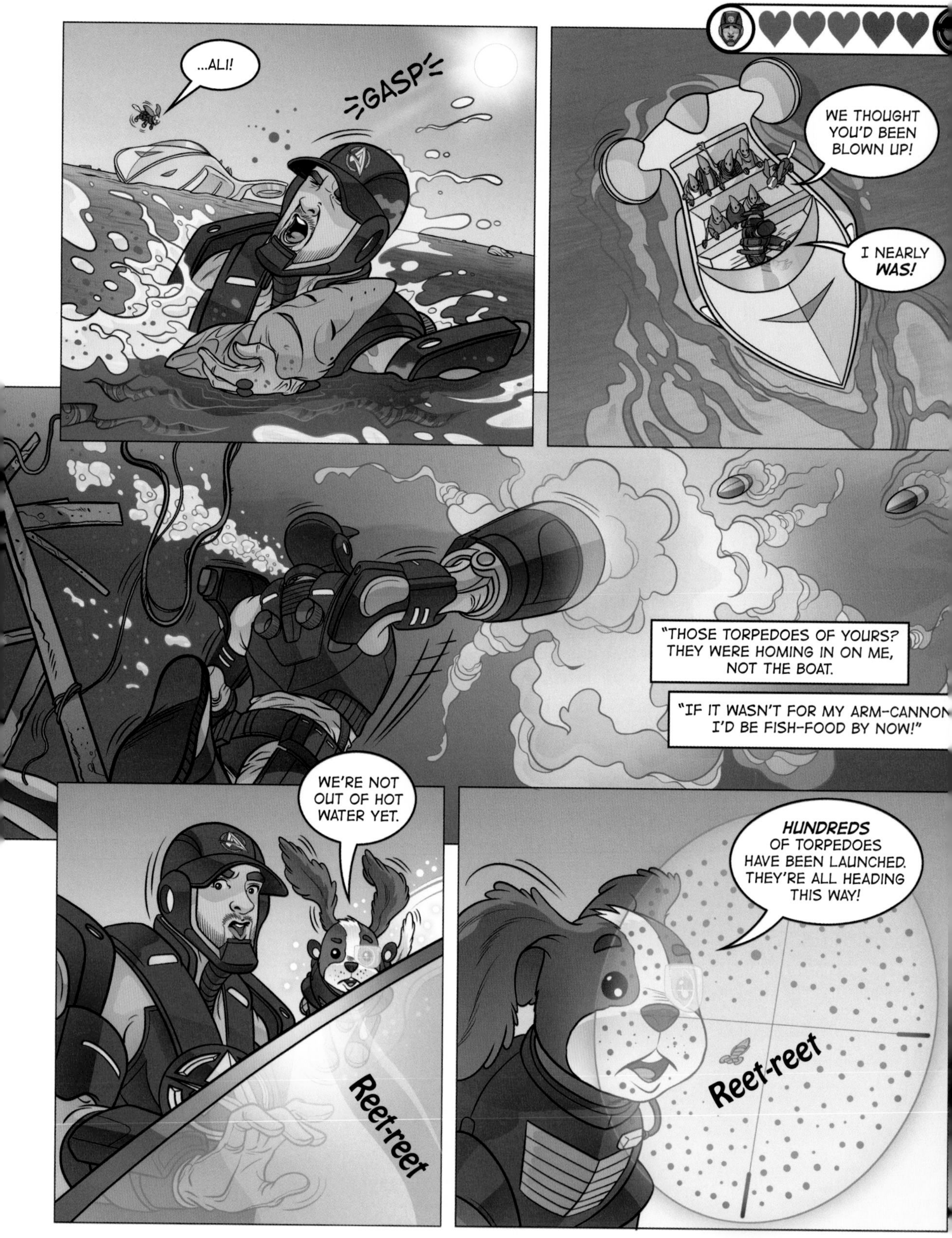
...ALI!
GASP
WE THOUGHT YOU'D BEEN BLOWN UP!
I NEARLY WAS!
"THOSE TORPEDOES OF YOURS? THEY WERE HOMING IN ON ME, NOT THE BOAT.
"IF IT WASN'T FOR MY ARM-CANNON I'D BE FISH-FOOD BY NOW!"
WE'RE NOT OUT OF HOT WATER YET.
Reet-reet
HUNDREDS OF TORPEDOES HAVE BEEN LAUNCHED. THEY'RE ALL HEADING THIS WAY!
Reet-reet

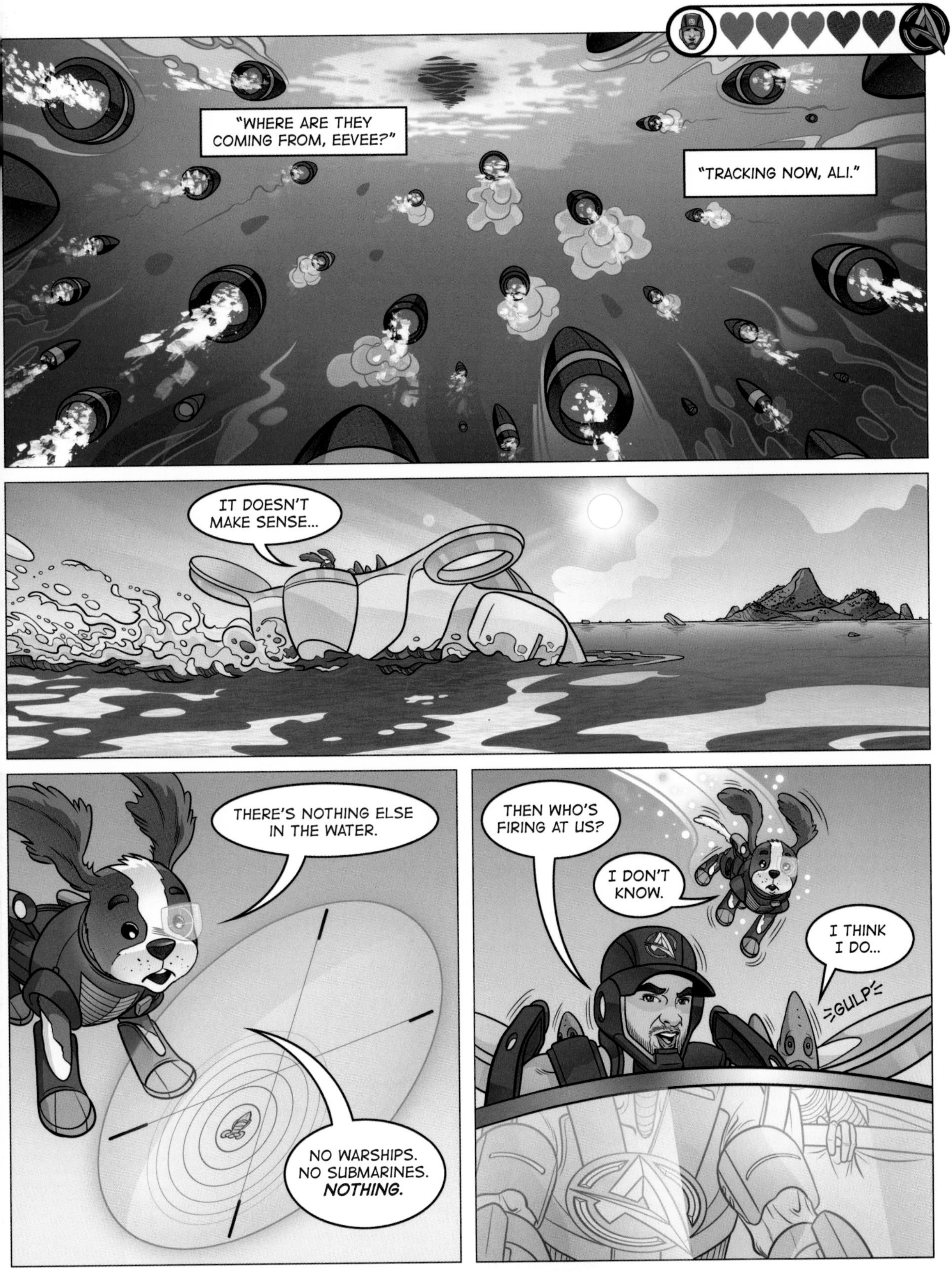
"WHERE ARE THEY COMING FROM, EEVEE?"
"TRACKING NOW, ALI."
IT DOESN'T MAKE SENSE...
THERE'S NOTHING ELSE IN THE WATER.
NO WARSHIPS. NO SUBMARINES. *NOTHING.*
THEN WHO'S FIRING AT US?
I DON'T KNOW.
I THINK I DO...
GULP

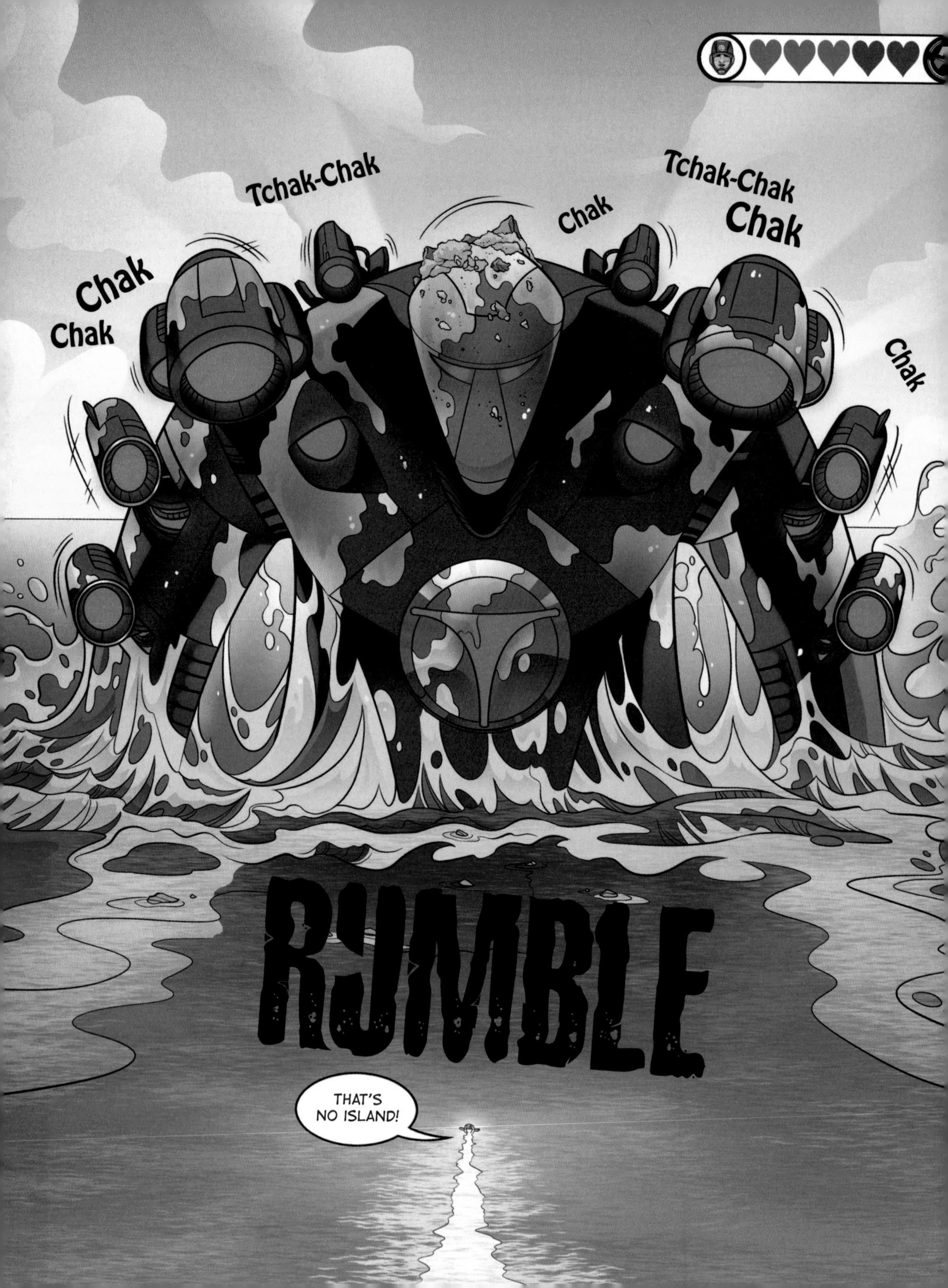
Chak
Chak
Tchak-Chak
Chak
Tchak-Chak
Chak
Chak
RUMBLE
THAT'S NO ISLAND!

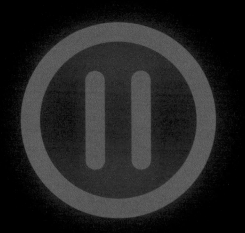

LEVEL FIVE

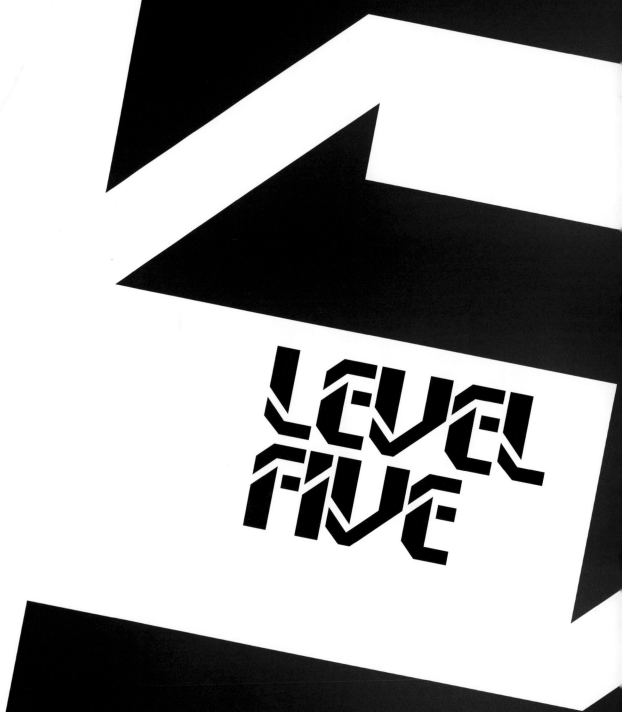

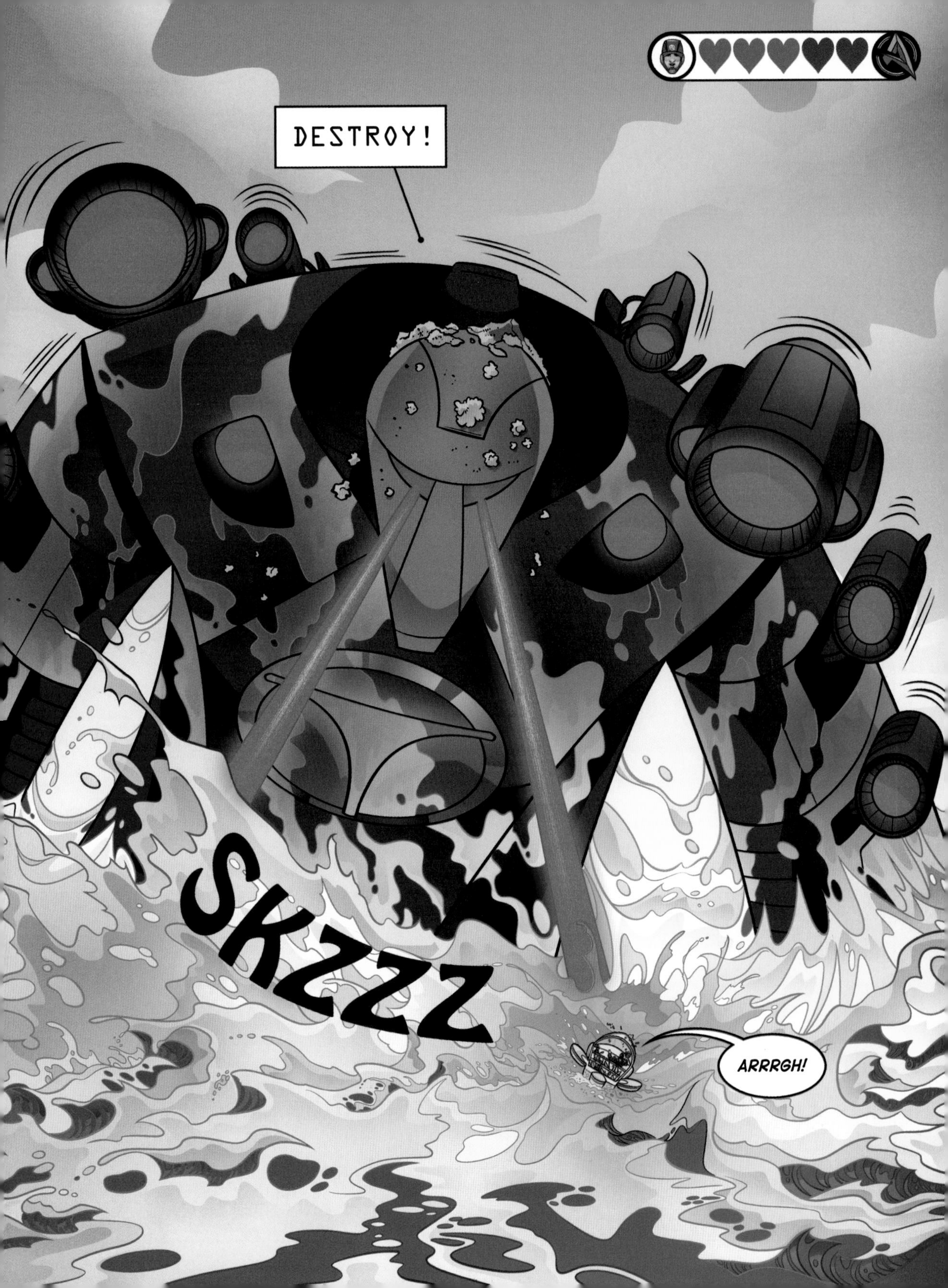
DESTROY!
SKZZZ
ARRRGH!

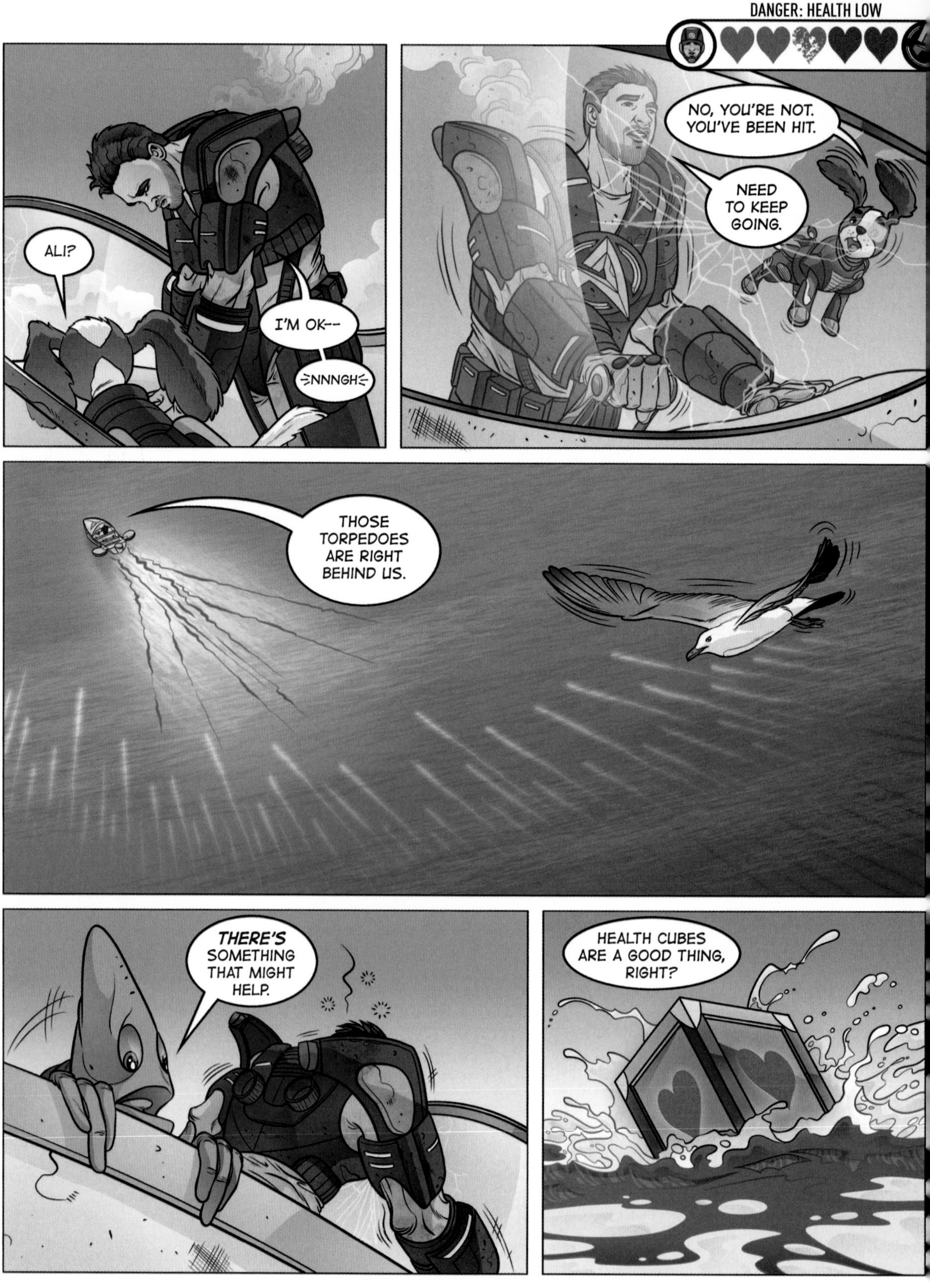
DANGER: HEALTH LOW
ALI?
I'M OK--
NNNGH
NO, YOU'RE NOT. YOU'VE BEEN HIT.
NEED TO KEEP GOING.
THOSE TORPEDOES ARE RIGHT BEHIND US.
THERE'S SOMETHING THAT MIGHT HELP.
HEALTH CUBES ARE A GOOD THING, RIGHT?

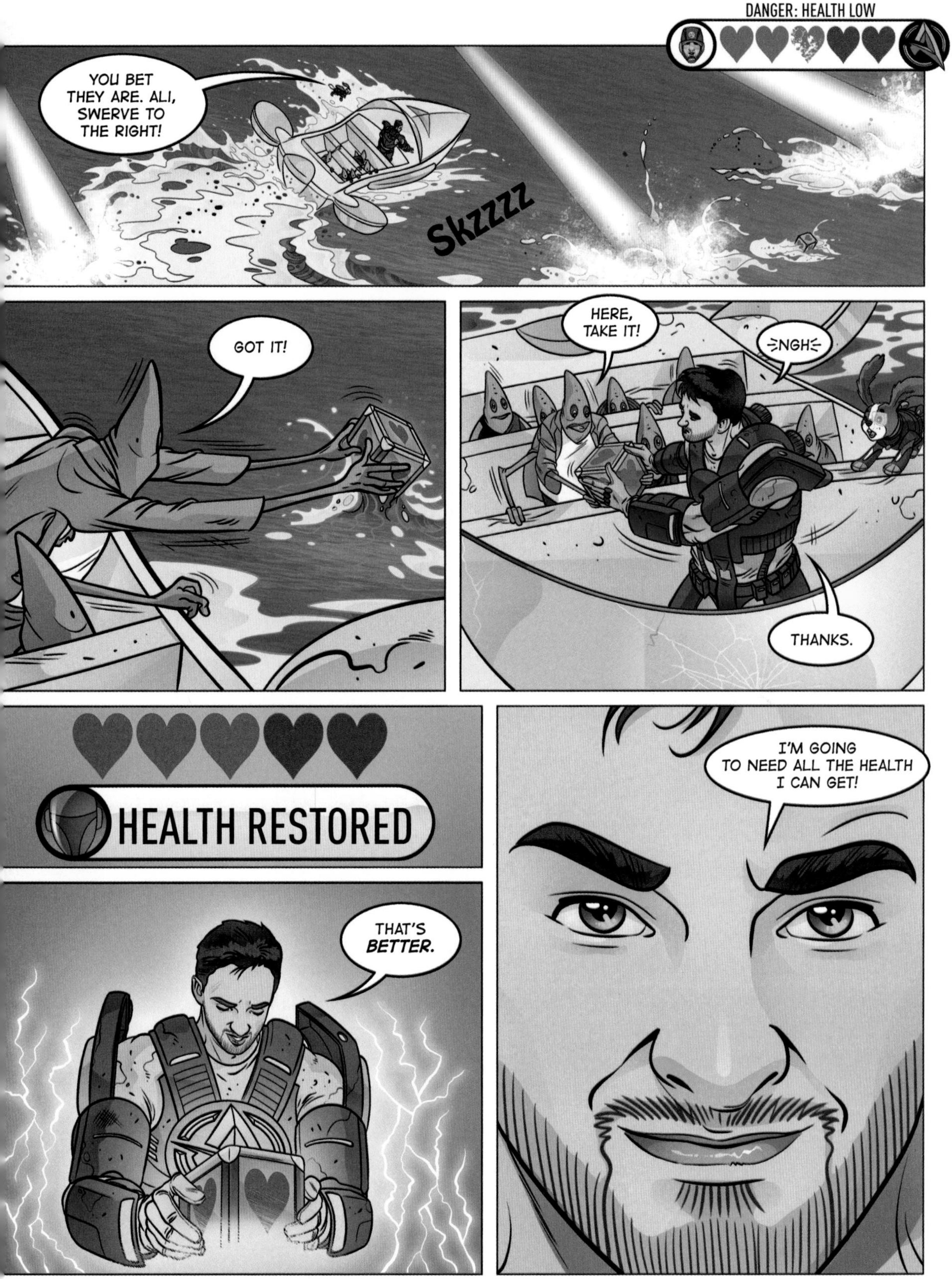

DANGER: HEALTH LOW
YOU BET THEY ARE. ALI, SWERVE TO THE RIGHT!
Skzzzz
GOT IT!
HERE, TAKE IT!
NGH
THANKS.
HEALTH RESTORED
THAT'S *BETTER.*
I'M GOING TO NEED ALL THE HEALTH I CAN GET!

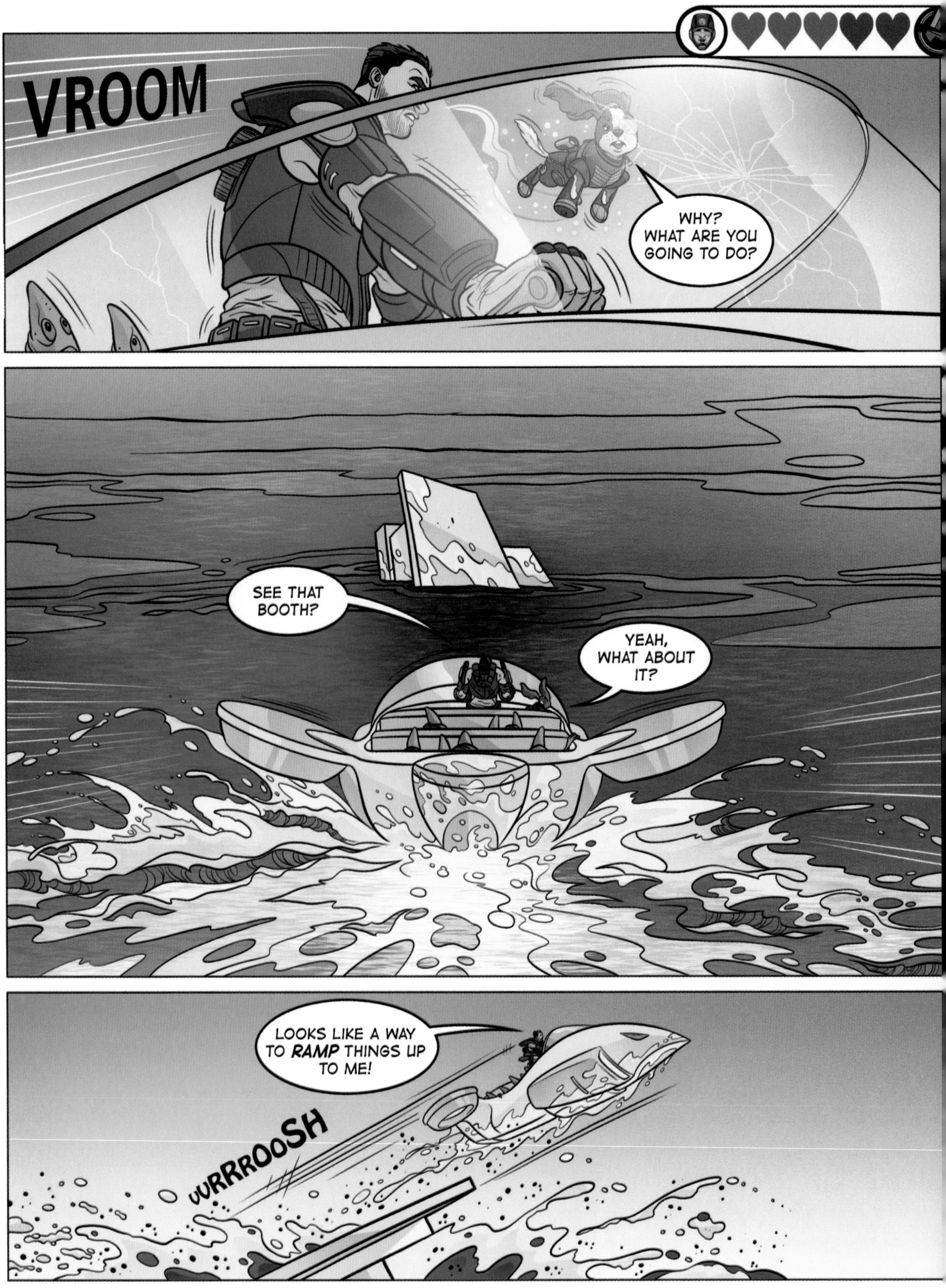
VROOM
WHY? WHAT ARE YOU GOING TO DO?
SEE THAT BOOTH?
YEAH, WHAT ABOUT IT?
LOOKS LIKE A WAY TO RAMP THINGS UP TO ME!
VRRROOSH

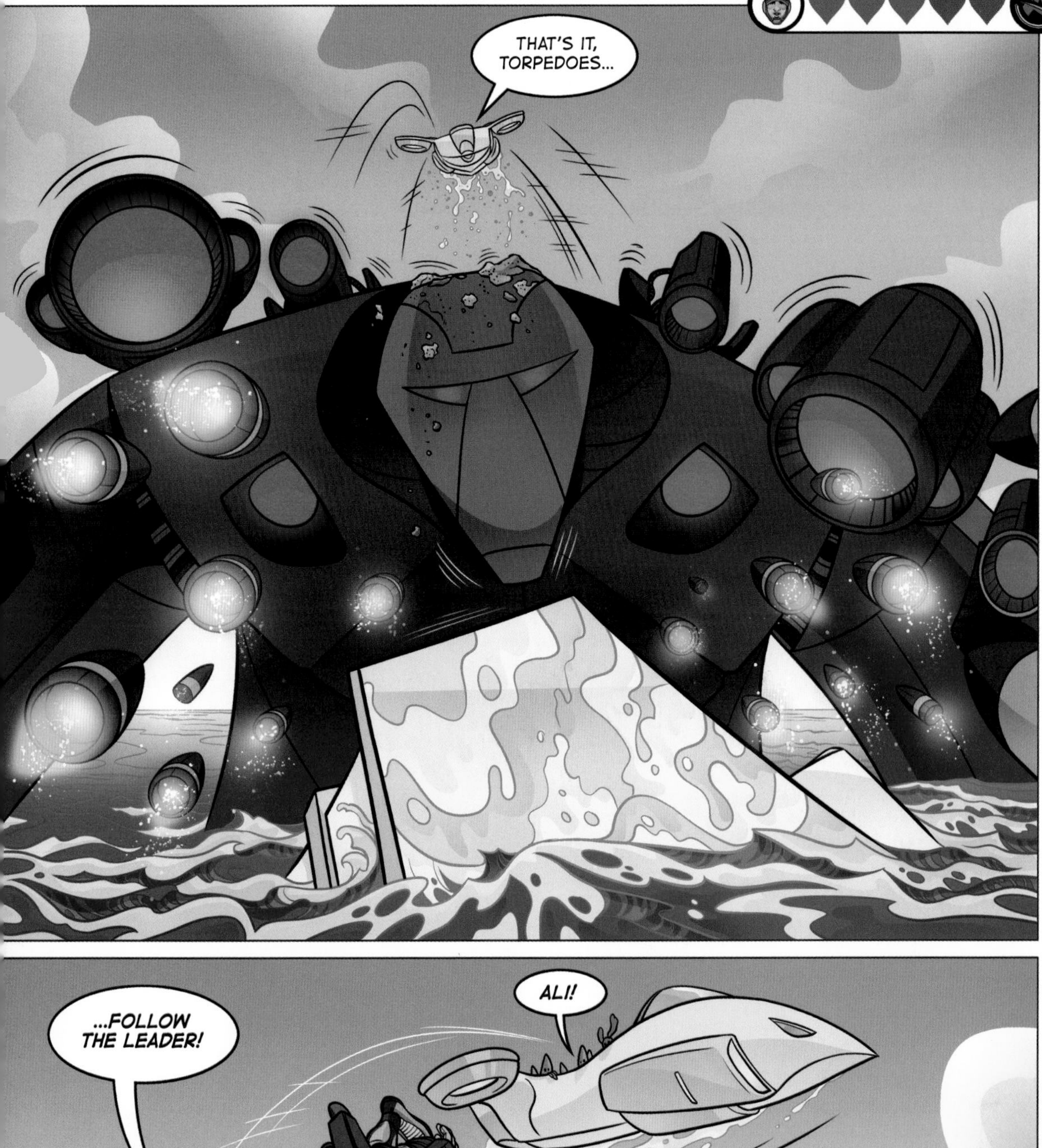
THAT'S IT, TORPEDOES...

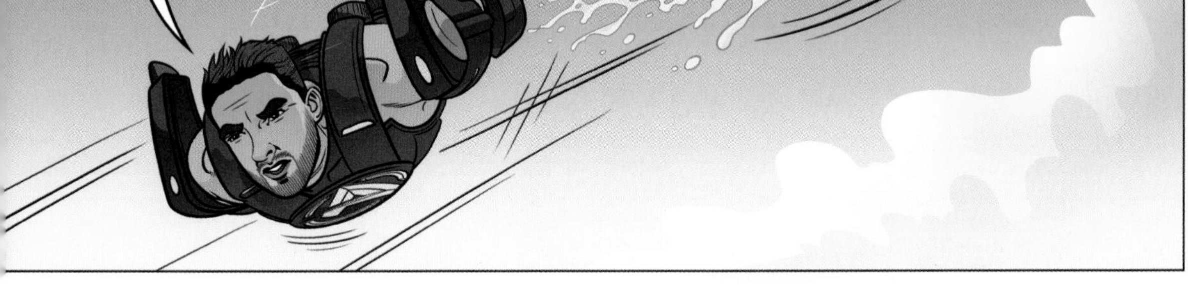
...FOLLOW THE LEADER!
ALI!

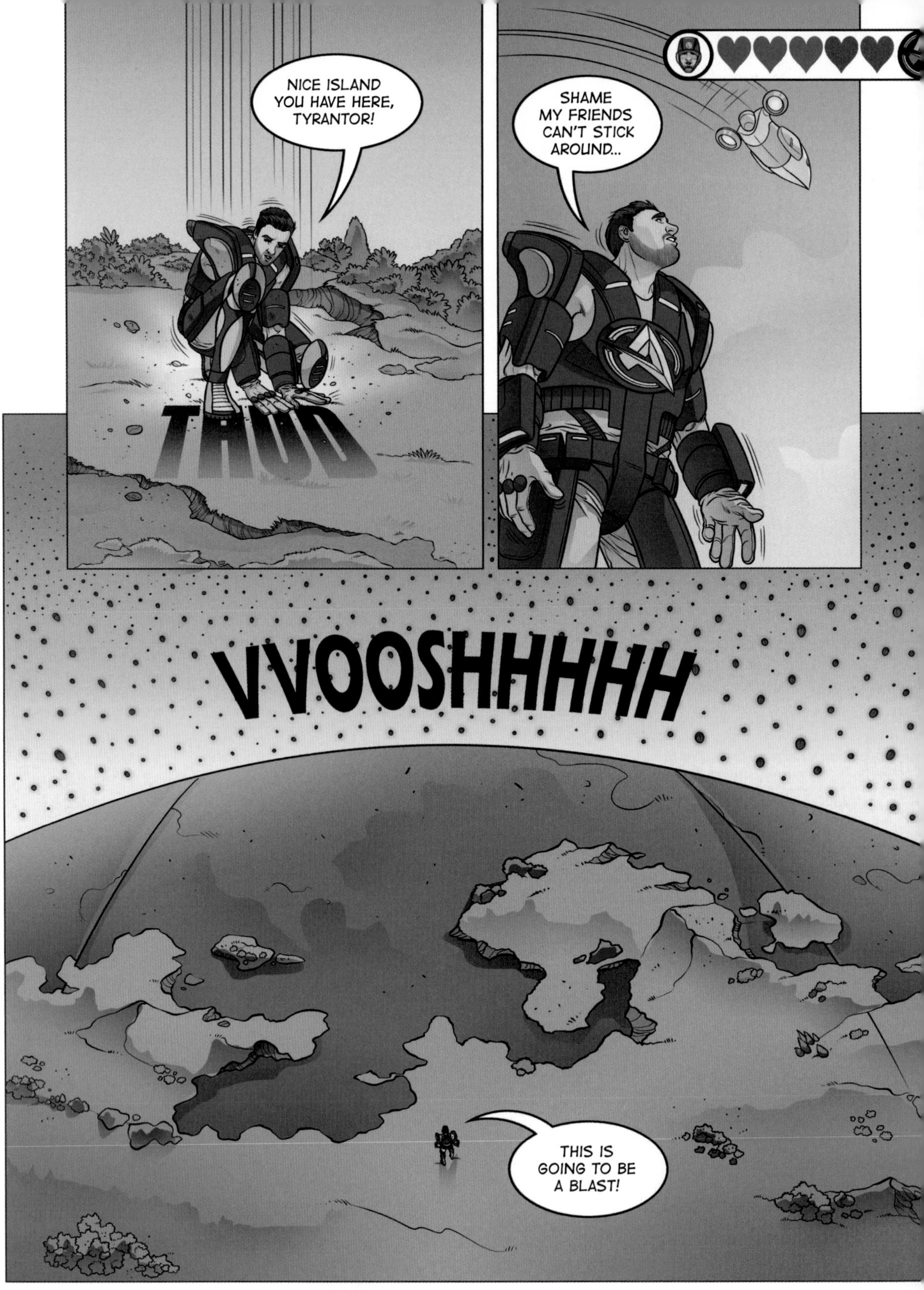
NICE ISLAND YOU HAVE HERE, TYRANTOR!
THUD
SHAME MY FRIENDS CAN'T STICK AROUND...
VVOOSHHHHH
THIS IS GOING TO BE A BLAST!

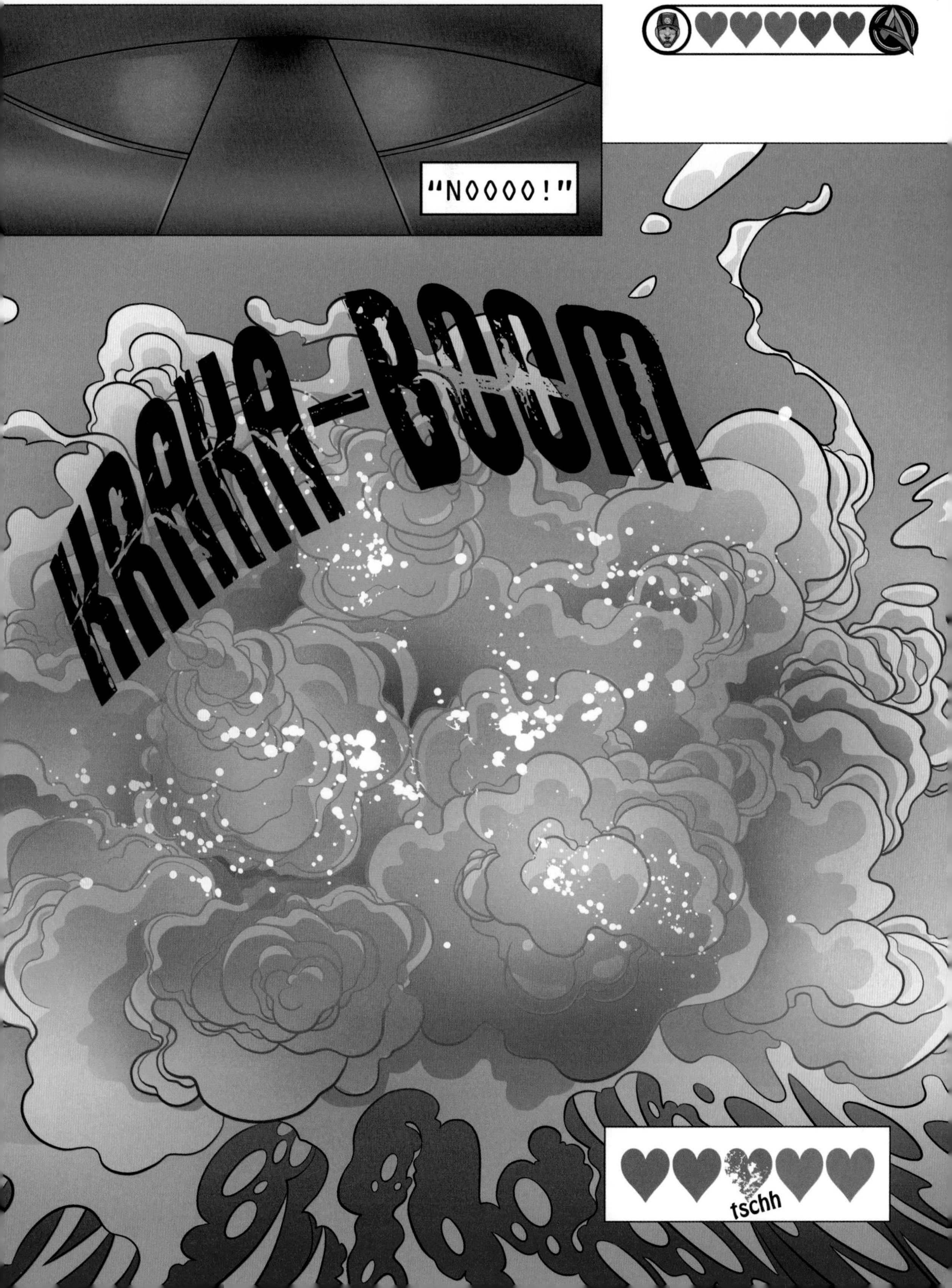
"NOOOO!"
KRAKKA-BOOM
tschh

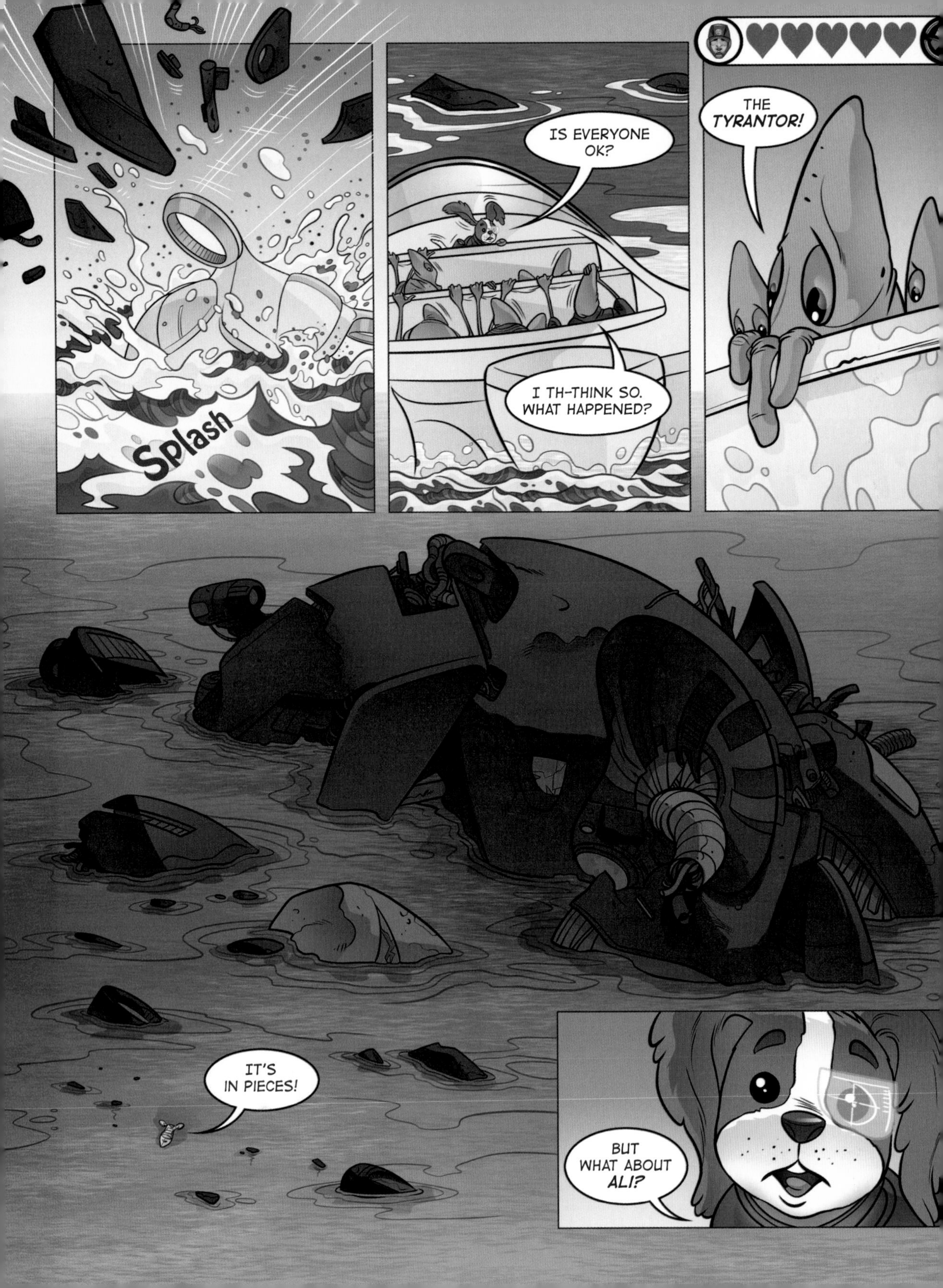
Splash
IS EVERYONE OK?
I TH-THINK SO. WHAT HAPPENED?
THE *TYRANTOR!*
IT'S IN PIECES!
BUT WHAT ABOUT *ALI?*

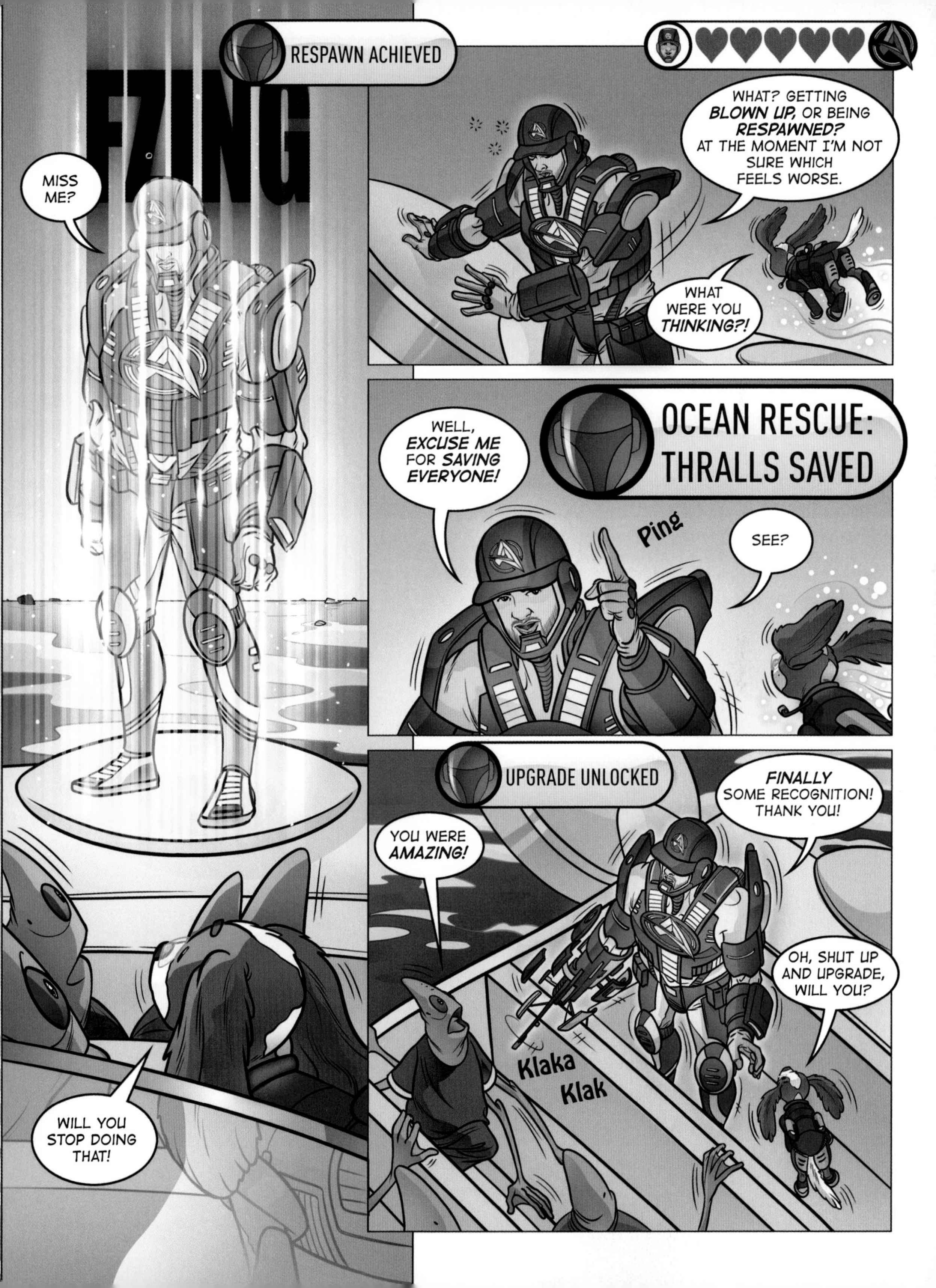
RESPAWN ACHIEVED
FZING
MISS ME?
WILL YOU STOP DOING THAT!
WHAT? GETTING BLOWN UP, OR BEING RESPAWNED? AT THE MOMENT I'M NOT SURE WHICH FEELS WORSE.
WHAT WERE YOU THINKING?!
OCEAN RESCUE: THRALLS SAVED
WELL, EXCUSE ME FOR SAVING EVERYONE!
Ping
SEE?
UPGRADE UNLOCKED
FINALLY SOME RECOGNITION! THANK YOU!
YOU WERE AMAZING!
OH, SHUT UP AND UPGRADE, WILL YOU?
Klaka Klak

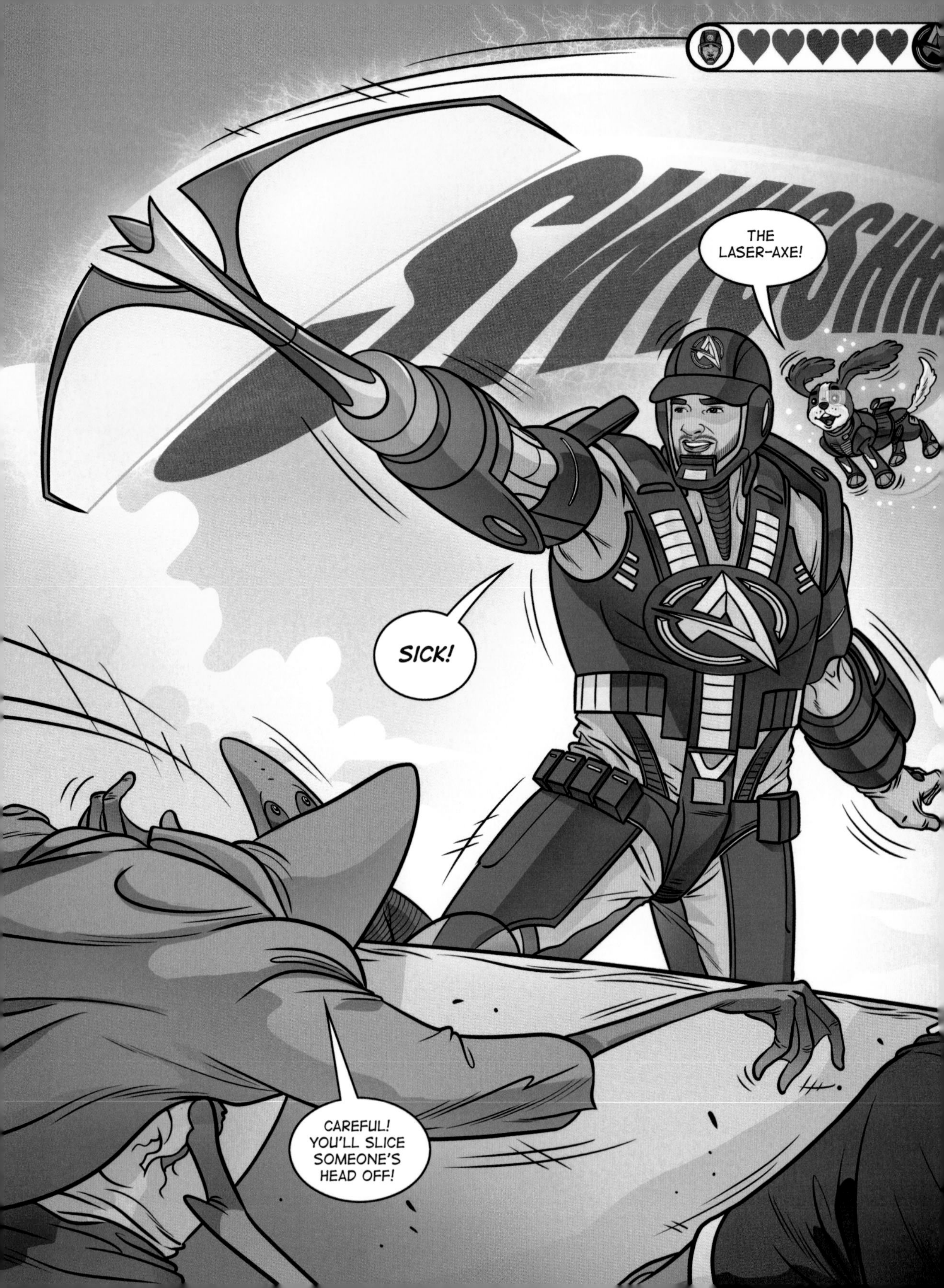
THE LASER-AXE!
SICK!
CAREFUL! YOU'LL SLICE SOMEONE'S HEAD OFF!

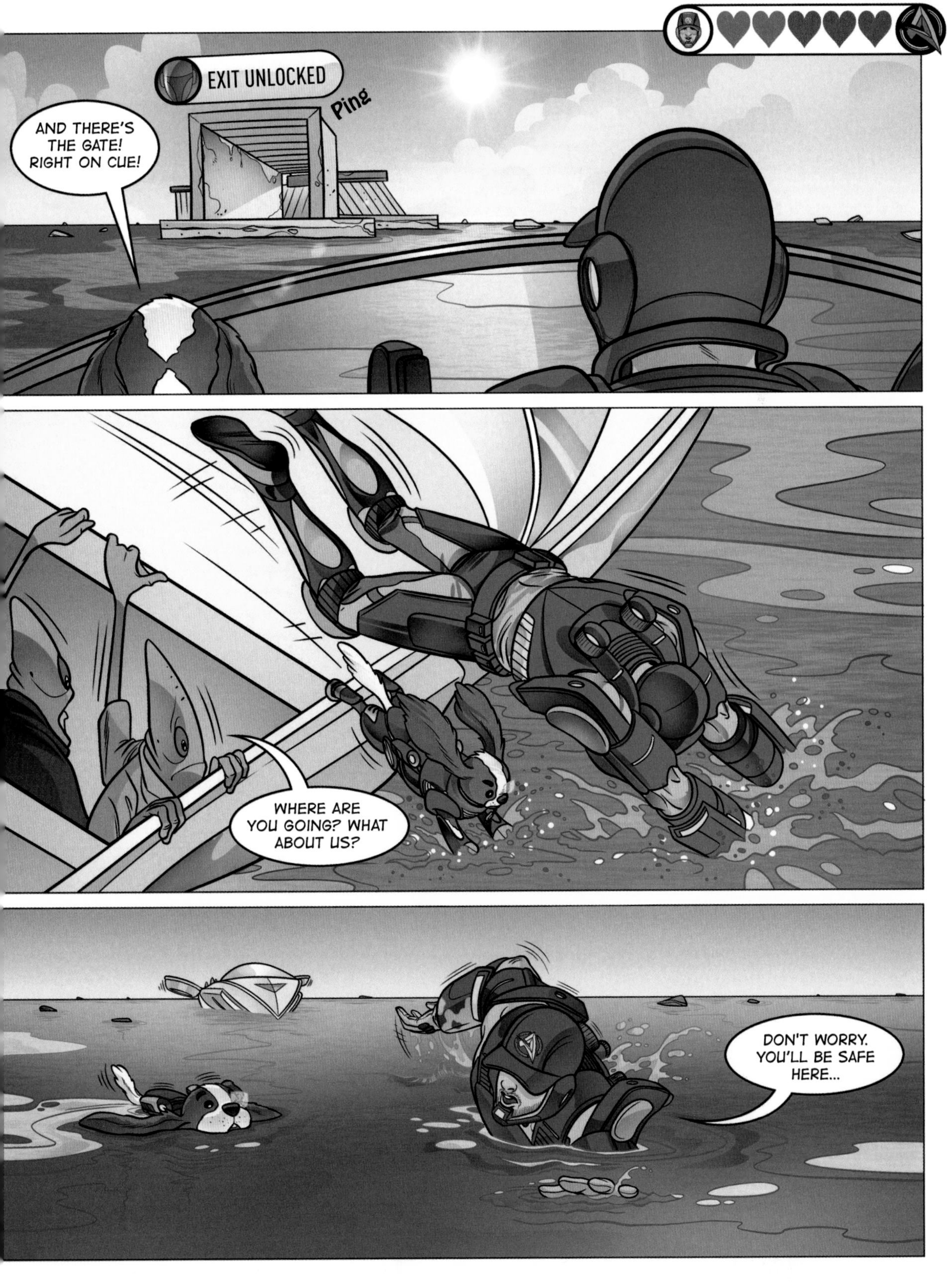
EXIT UNLOCKED
Ping
AND THERE'S THE GATE! RIGHT ON CUE!
WHERE ARE YOU GOING? WHAT ABOUT US?
DON'T WORRY. YOU'LL BE SAFE HERE...

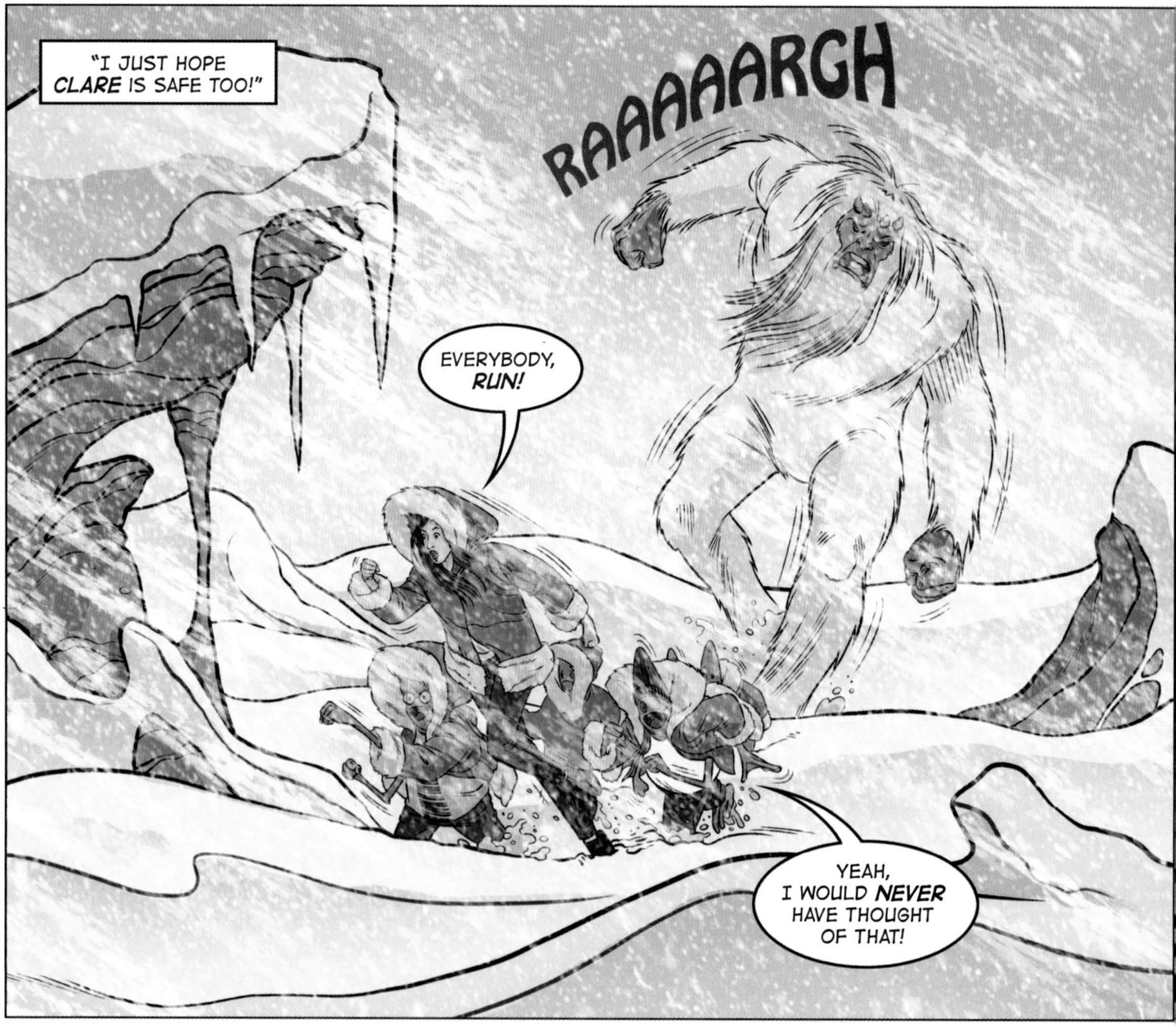
"I JUST HOPE CLARE IS SAFE TOO!"
RAAAAARGH
EVERYBODY, RUN!
YEAH, I WOULD NEVER HAVE THOUGHT OF THAT!
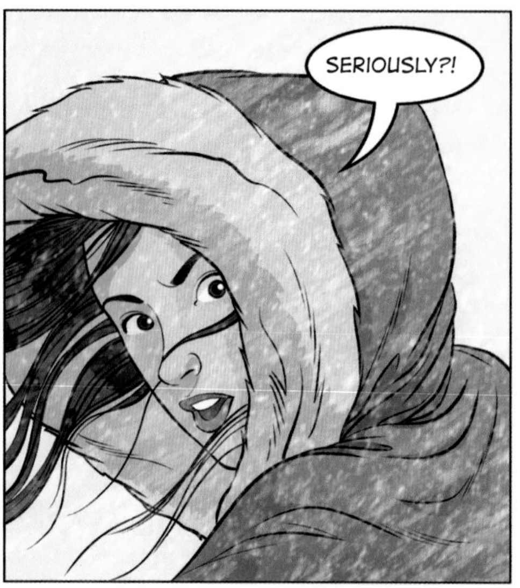
SERIOUSLY?!
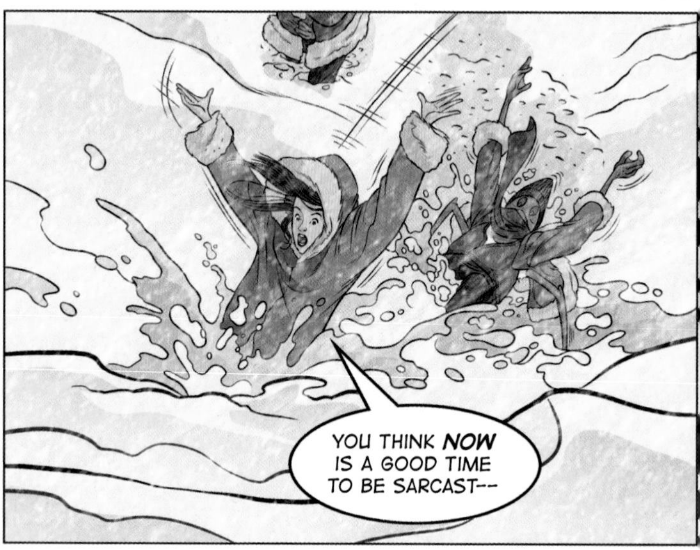
YOU THINK NOW IS A GOOD TIME TO BE SARCAST--

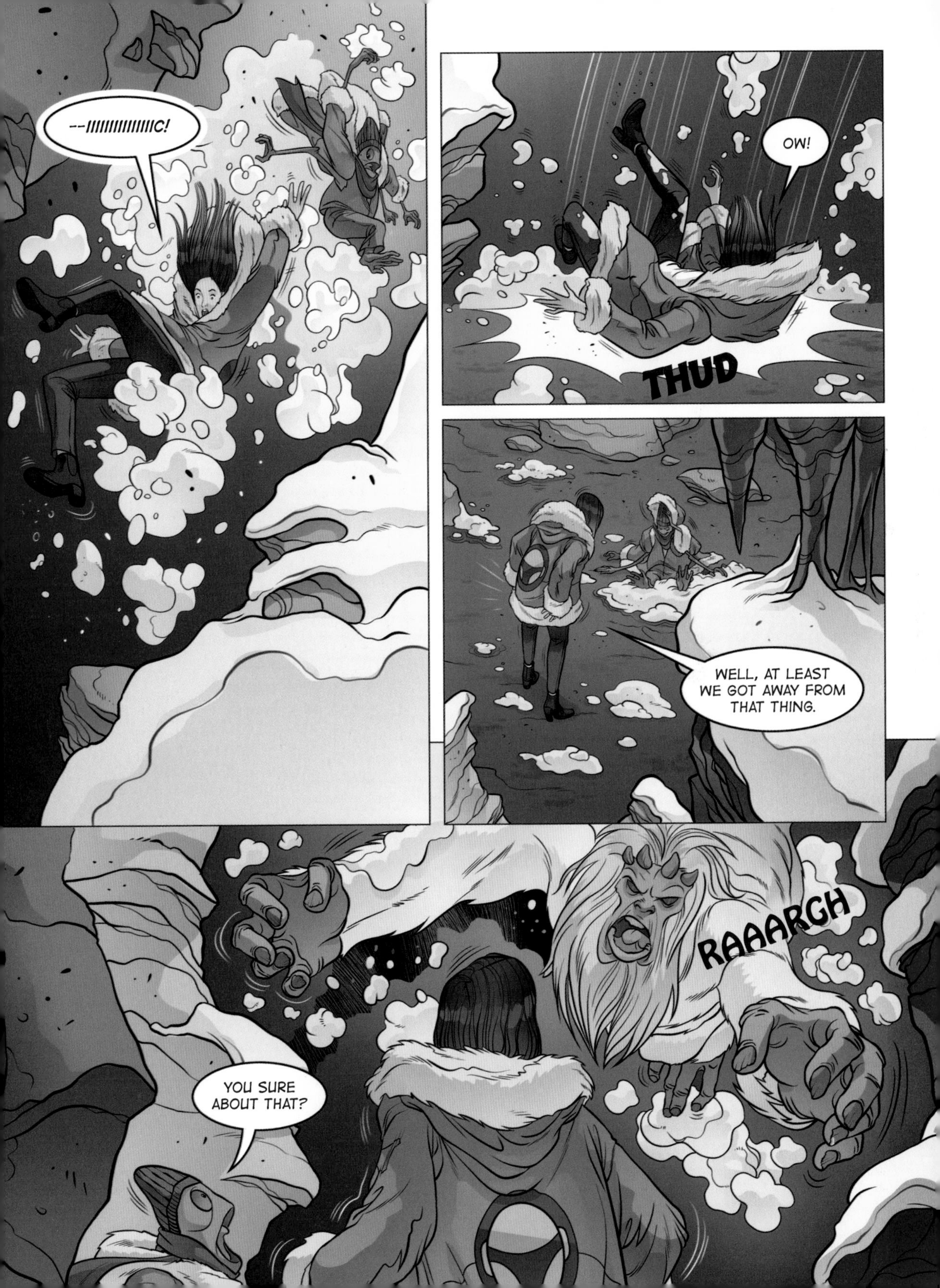
--IIIIIIIIIIIIIIIC!
OW!
THUD
WELL, AT LEAST WE GOT AWAY FROM THAT THING.
RAAARGH
YOU SURE ABOUT THAT?

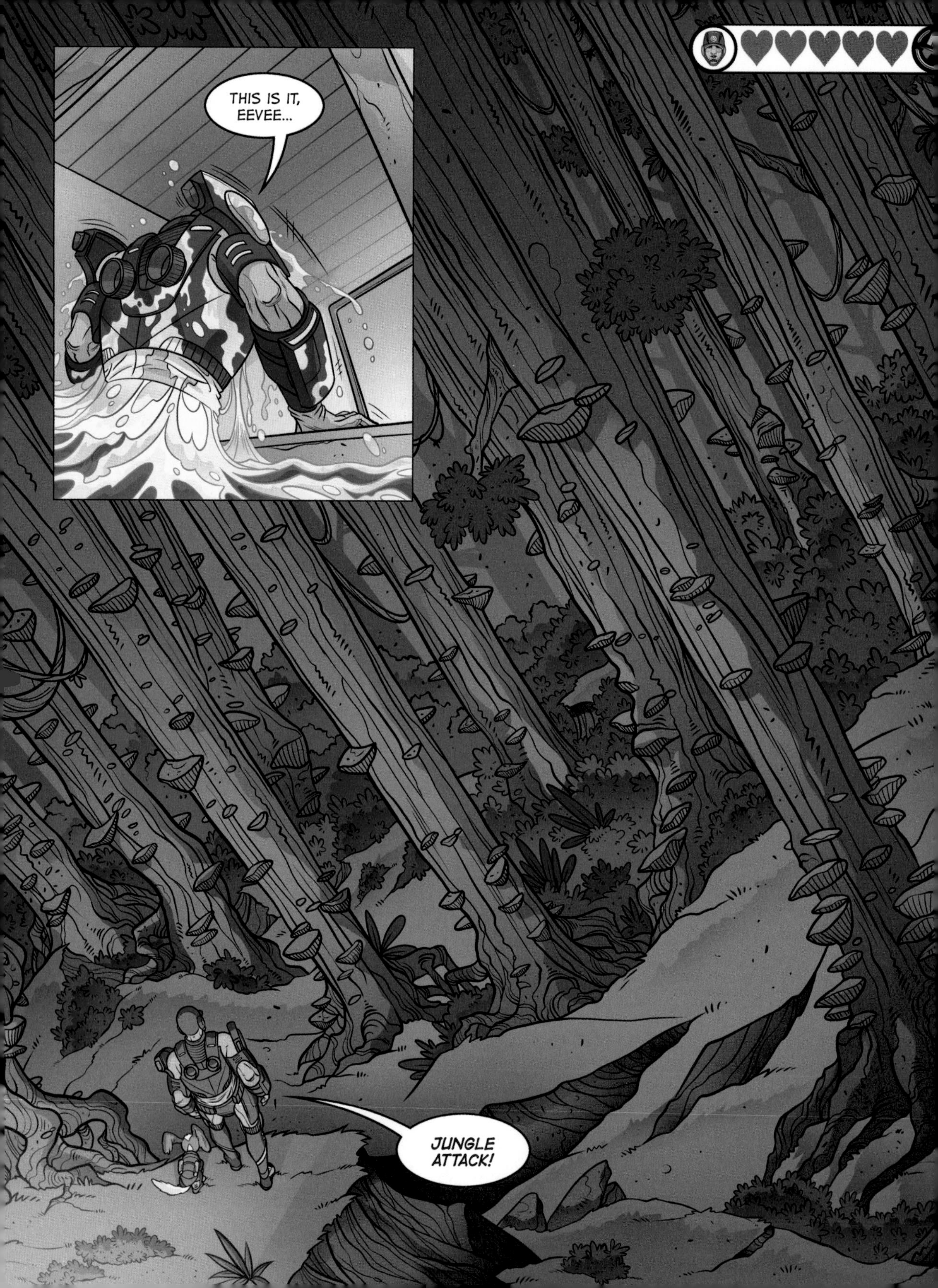
THIS IS IT, EEVEE...
JUNGLE ATTACK!

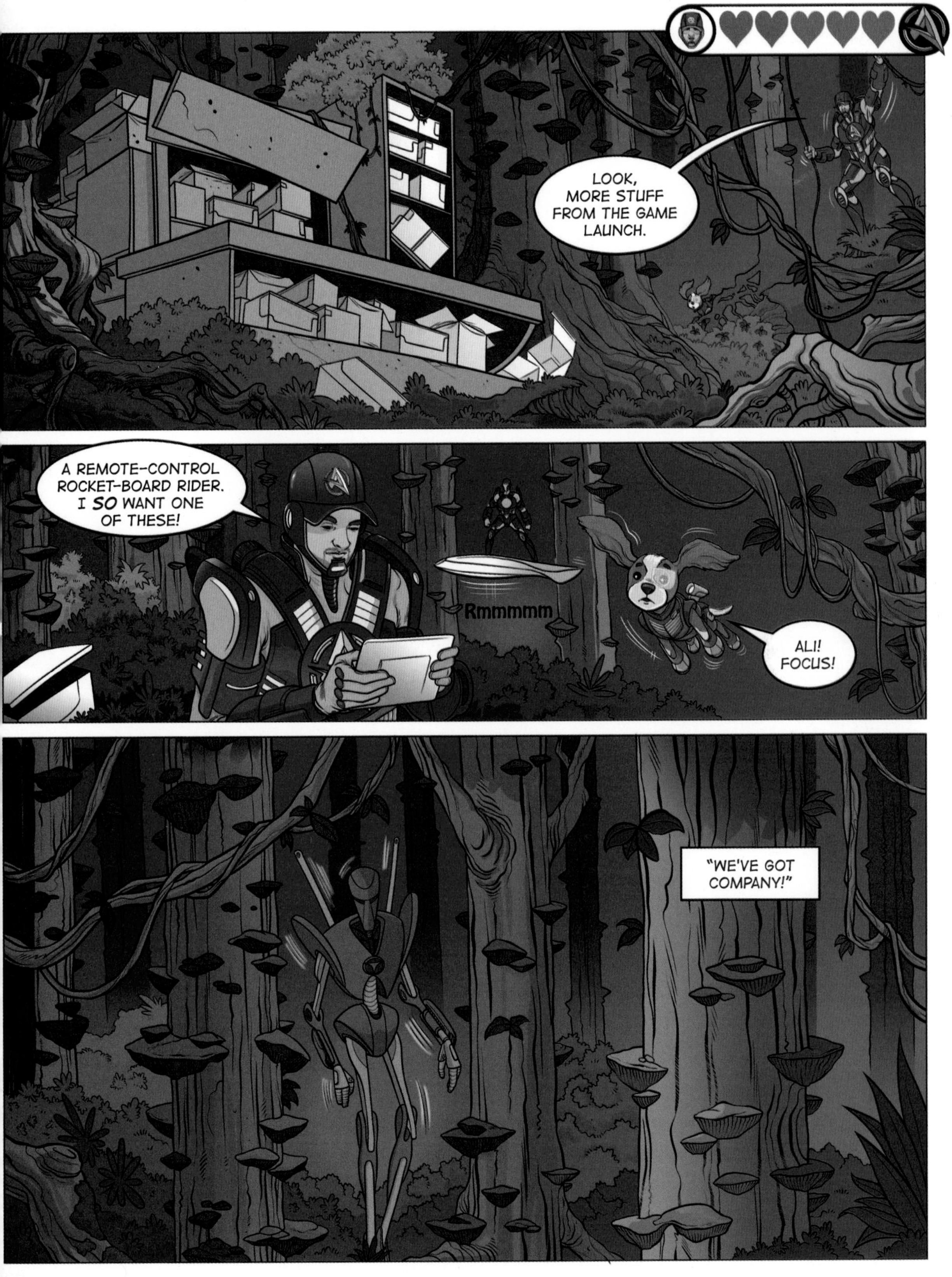
LOOK, MORE STUFF FROM THE GAME LAUNCH.
A REMOTE-CONTROL ROCKET-BOARD RIDER. I SO WANT ONE OF THESE!
Rmmmmm
ALI! FOCUS!
"WE'VE GOT COMPANY!"

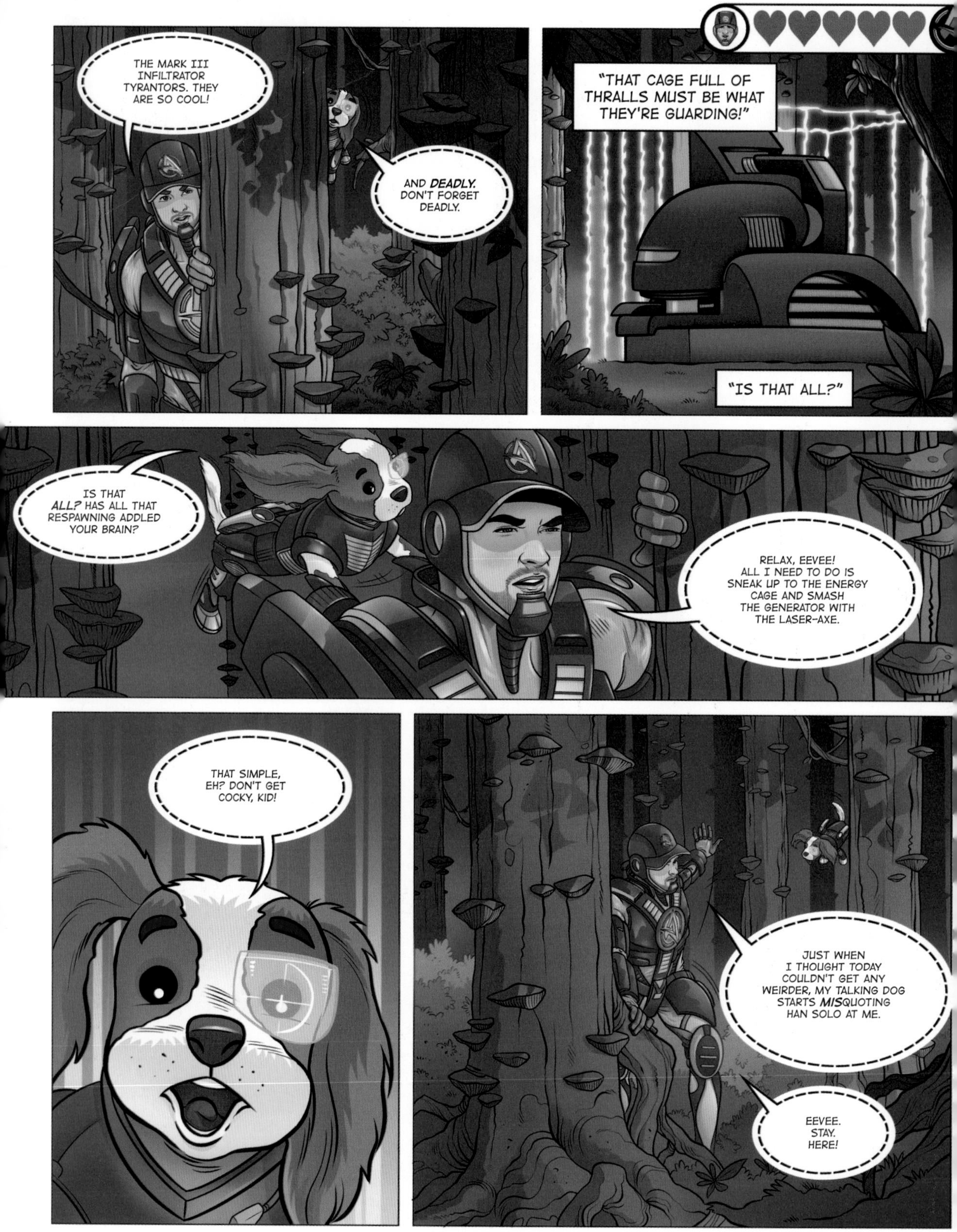

THE MARK III INFILTRATOR TYRANTORS. THEY ARE SO COOL!
AND ***DEADLY.*** DON'T FORGET DEADLY.
"THAT CAGE FULL OF THRALLS MUST BE WHAT THEY'RE GUARDING!"
"IS THAT ALL?"
IS THAT ***ALL?*** HAS ALL THAT RESPAWNING ADDLED YOUR BRAIN?
RELAX, EEVEE! ALL I NEED TO DO IS SNEAK UP TO THE ENERGY CAGE AND SMASH THE GENERATOR WITH THE LASER-AXE.
THAT SIMPLE, EH? DON'T GET COCKY, KID!
JUST WHEN I THOUGHT TODAY COULDN'T GET ANY WEIRDER, MY TALKING DOG STARTS ***MIS***QUOTING HAN SOLO AT ME.
EEVEE. STAY. HERE!

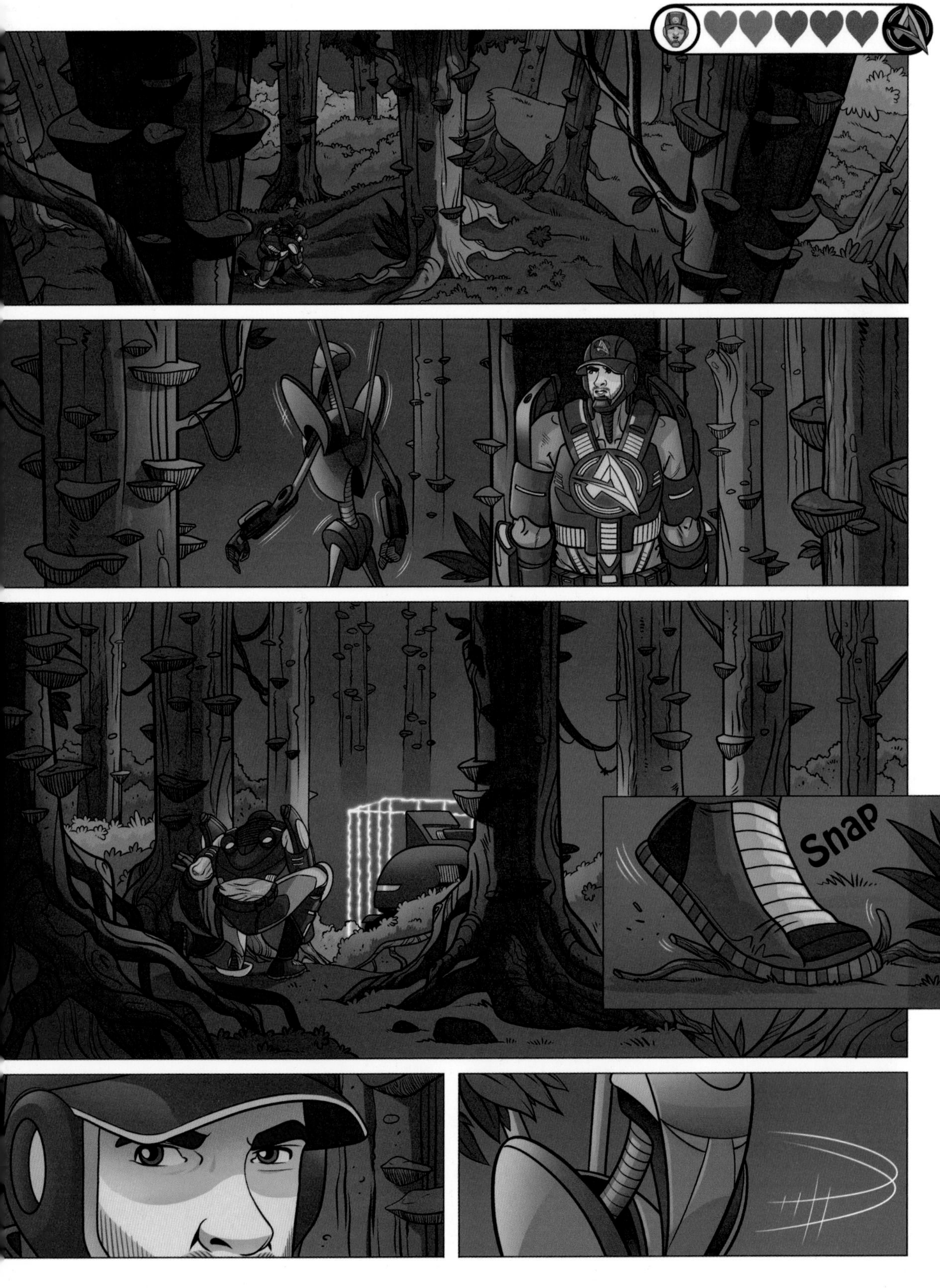
Snap

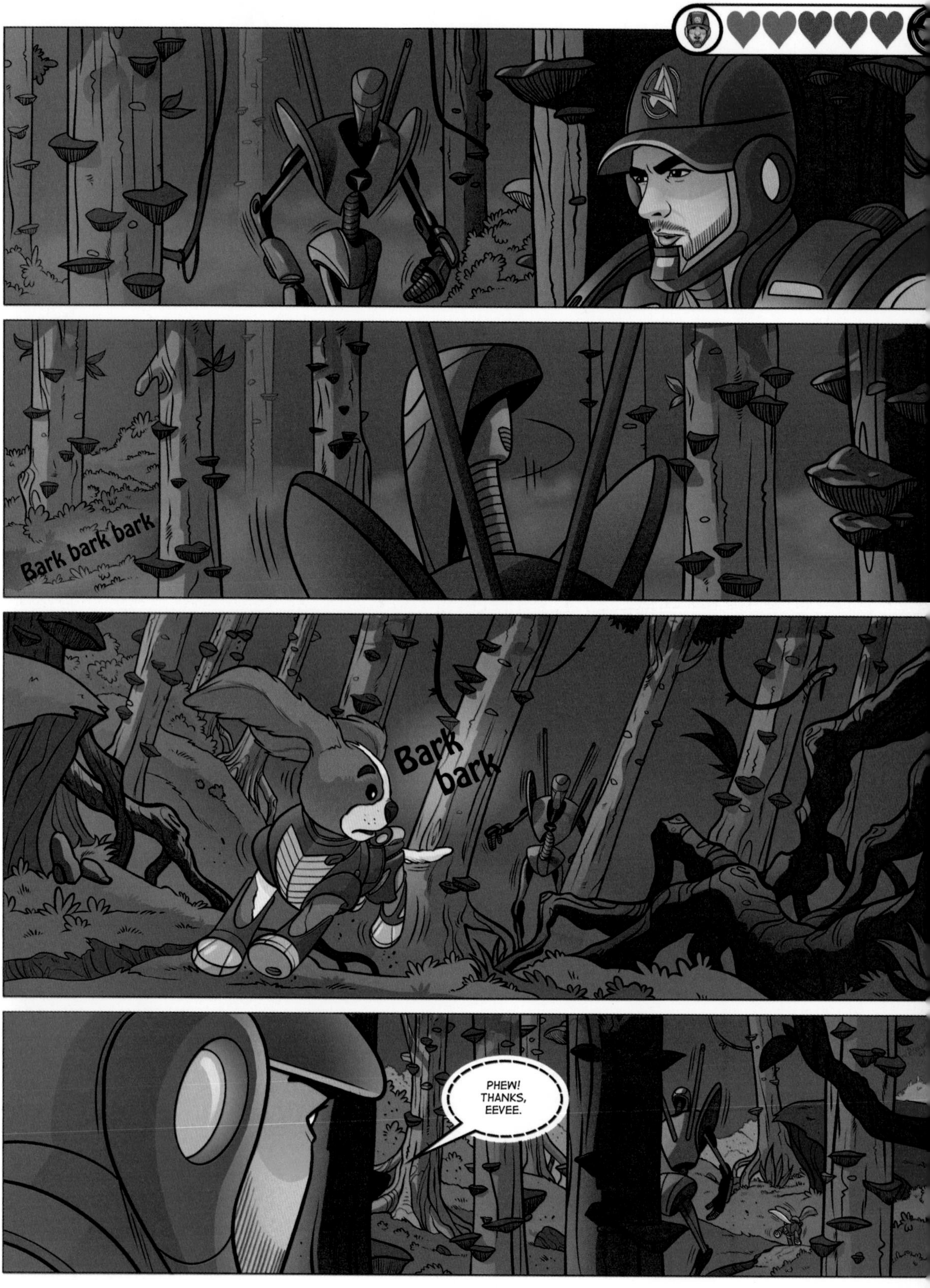
Bark bark bark
Bark bark
PHEW! THANKS, EEVEE.

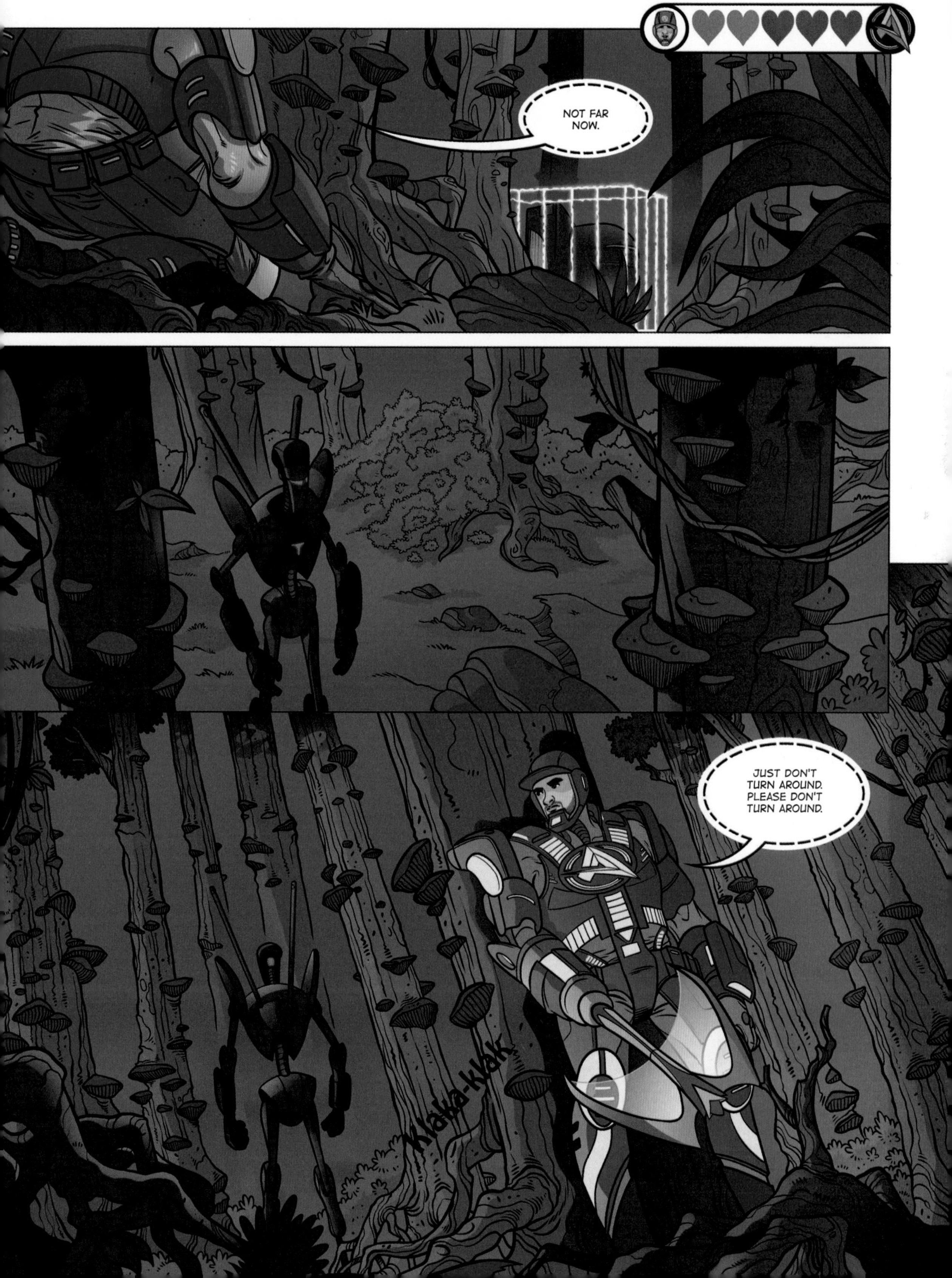
NOT FAR NOW.
JUST DON'T TURN AROUND. PLEASE DON'T TURN AROUND.
KLAKA-KLAK

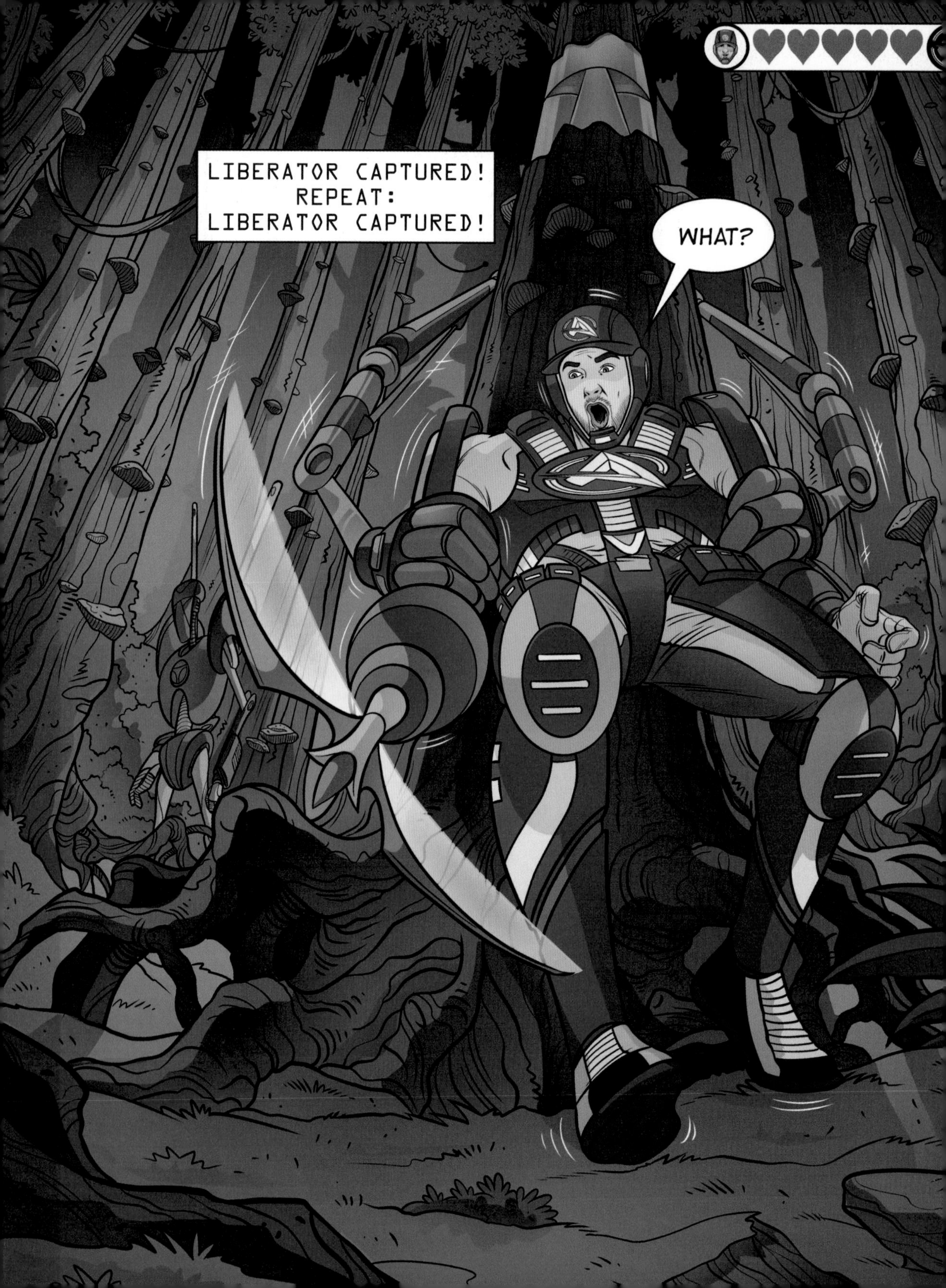
LIBERATOR CAPTURED!
REPEAT:
LIBERATOR CAPTURED!
WHAT?

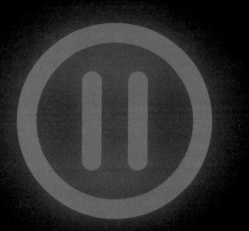

LEVEL SIX

6

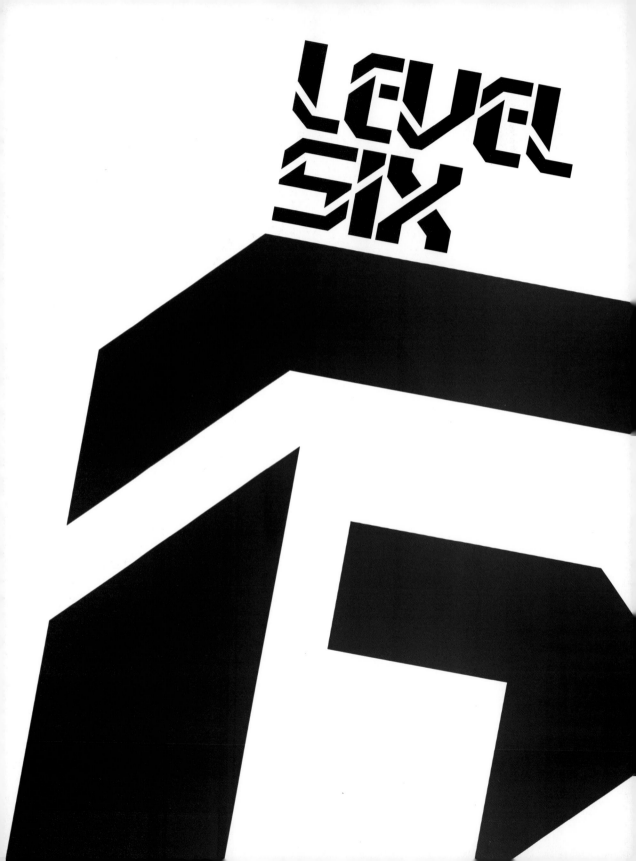

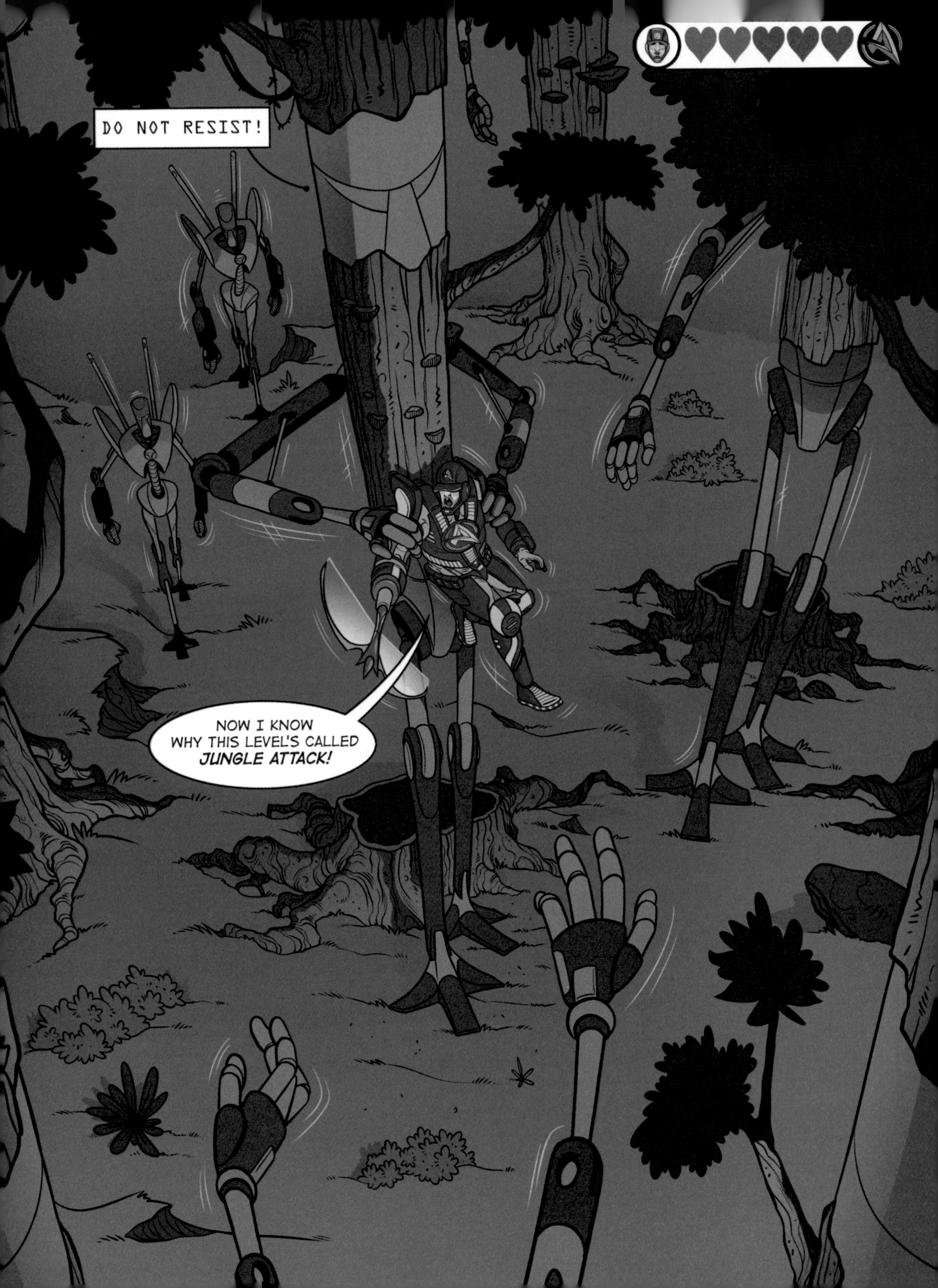
DO NOT RESIST!
NOW I KNOW WHY THIS LEVEL'S CALLED *JUNGLE ATTACK!*

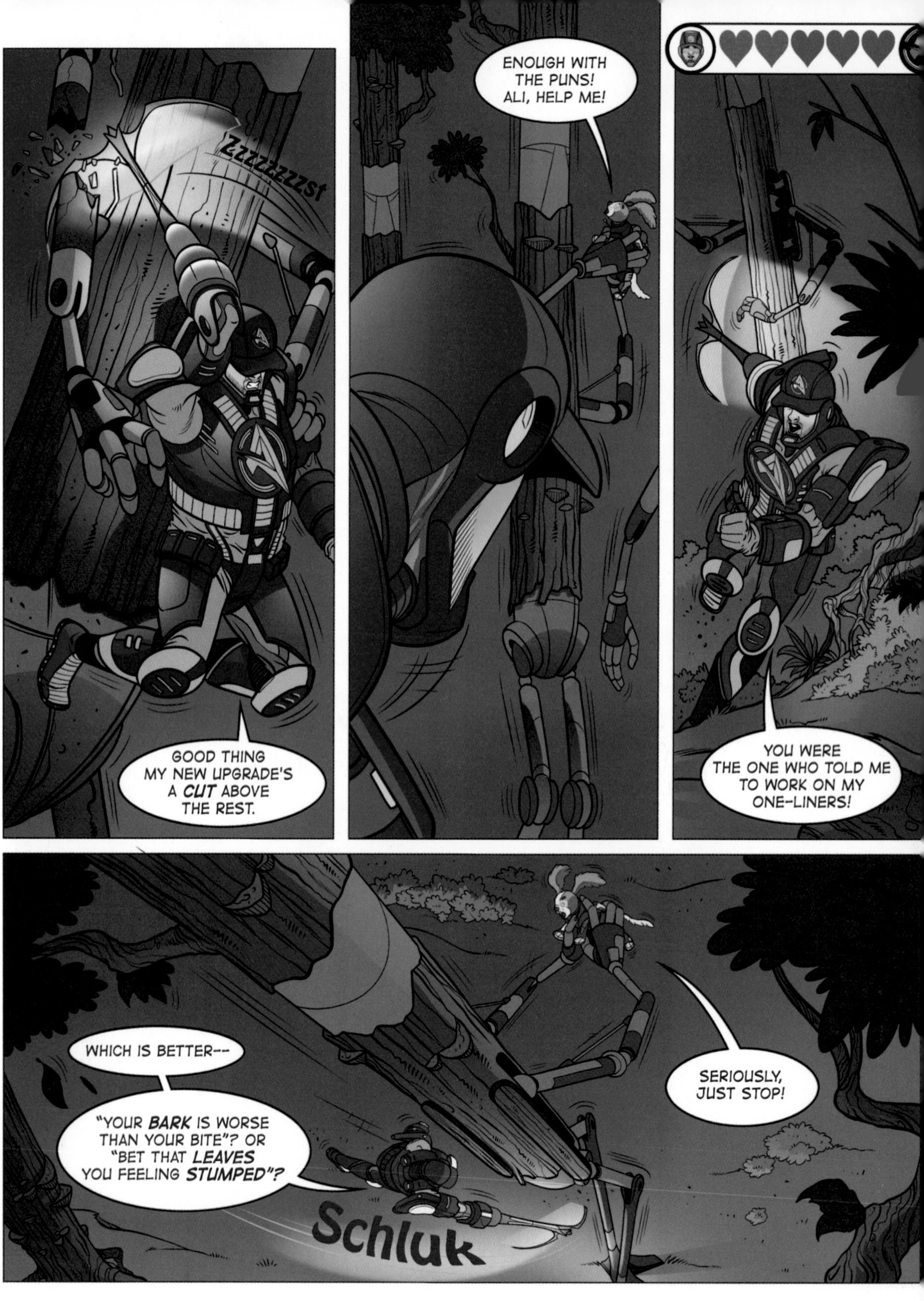
Zzzzzzzzzst
GOOD THING MY NEW UPGRADE'S A *CUT* ABOVE THE REST.
ENOUGH WITH THE PUNS! ALI, HELP ME!
YOU WERE THE ONE WHO TOLD ME TO WORK ON MY ONE-LINERS!
WHICH IS BETTER--
"YOUR *BARK* IS WORSE THAN YOUR BITE"? OR "BET THAT *LEAVES* YOU FEELING *STUMPED*"?
SERIOUSLY, JUST STOP!
Schluk

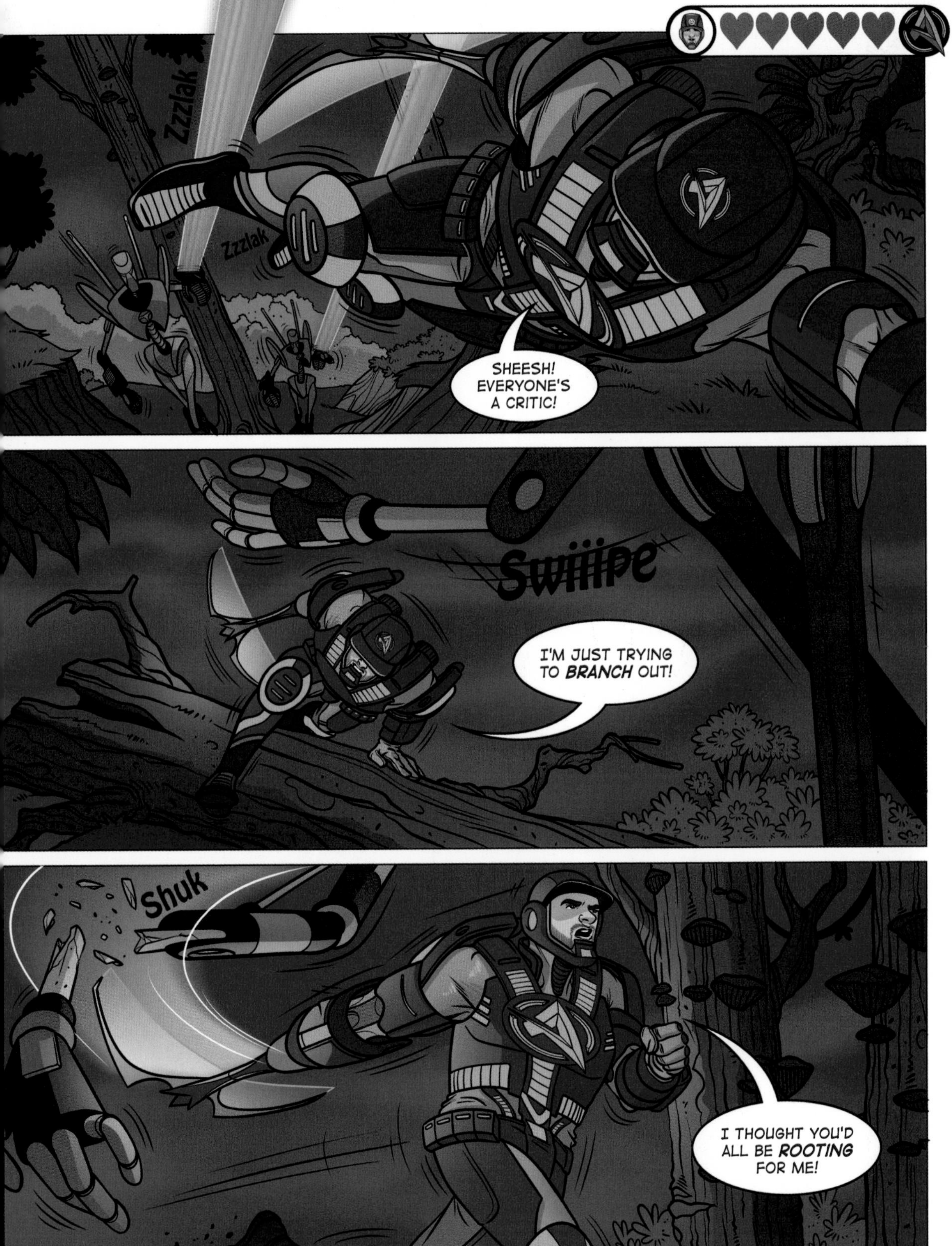
Zzzlak
Zzzlak
SHEESH! EVERYONE'S A CRITIC!
Swiiipe
I'M JUST TRYING TO BRANCH OUT!
Shuk
I THOUGHT YOU'D ALL BE ROOTING FOR ME!

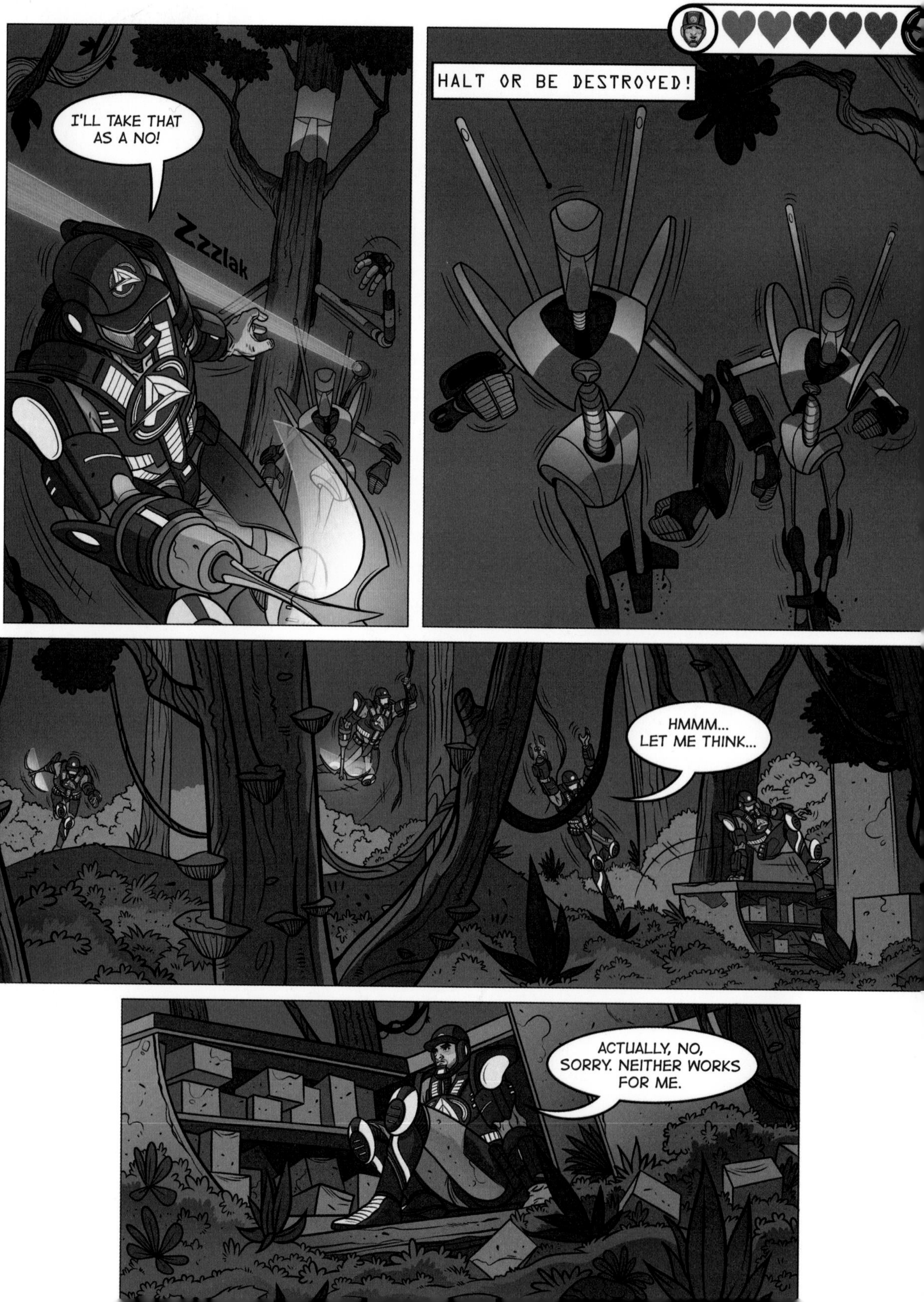
I'LL TAKE THAT AS A NO!
Zzzlak
HALT OR BE DESTROYED!
HMMM... LET ME THINK...
ACTUALLY, NO, SORRY. NEITHER WORKS FOR ME.

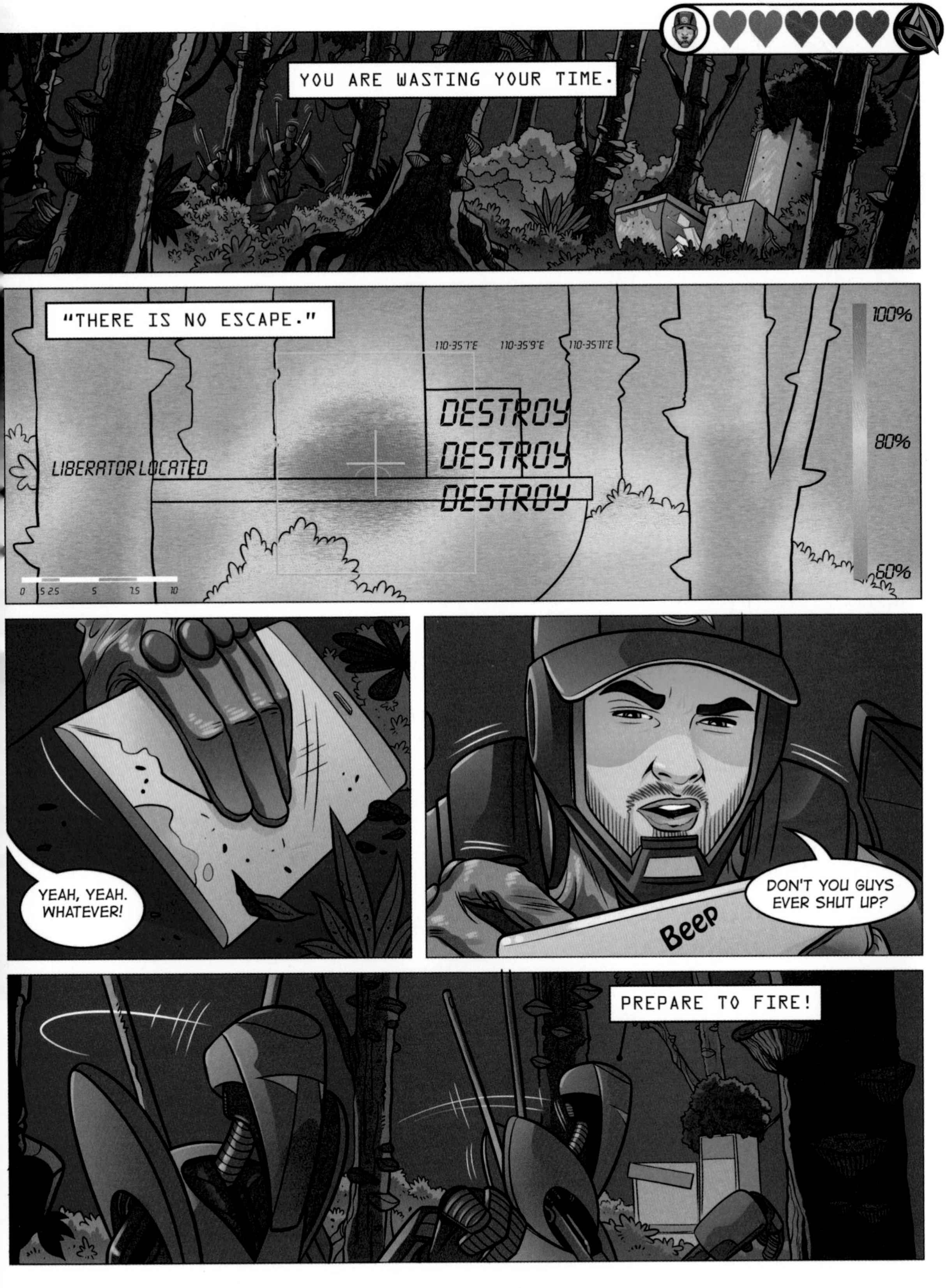
YOU ARE WASTING YOUR TIME.
"THERE IS NO ESCAPE."
110-35'7"E
110-35'9"E
110-35'11"E
100%
DESTROY
DESTROY
DESTROY
80%
LIBERATOR LOCATED
60%
0 .5 2.5 5 7.5 10
YEAH, YEAH. WHATEVER!
DON'T YOU GUYS EVER SHUT UP?
Beep
PREPARE TO FIRE!

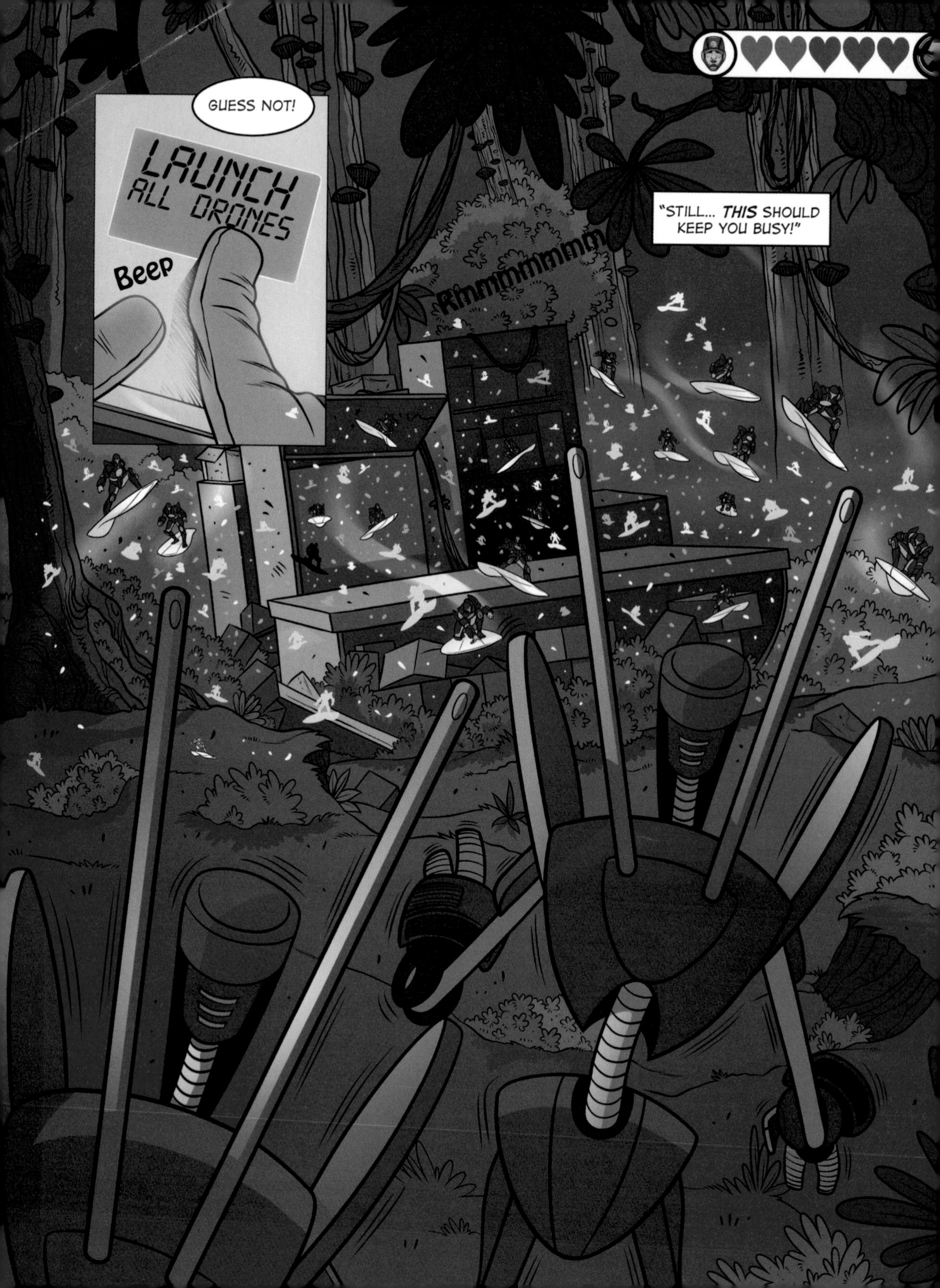
GUESS NOT!
LAUNCH ALL DRONES
Beep
"STILL... THIS SHOULD KEEP YOU BUSY!"
Rmmmmmmm

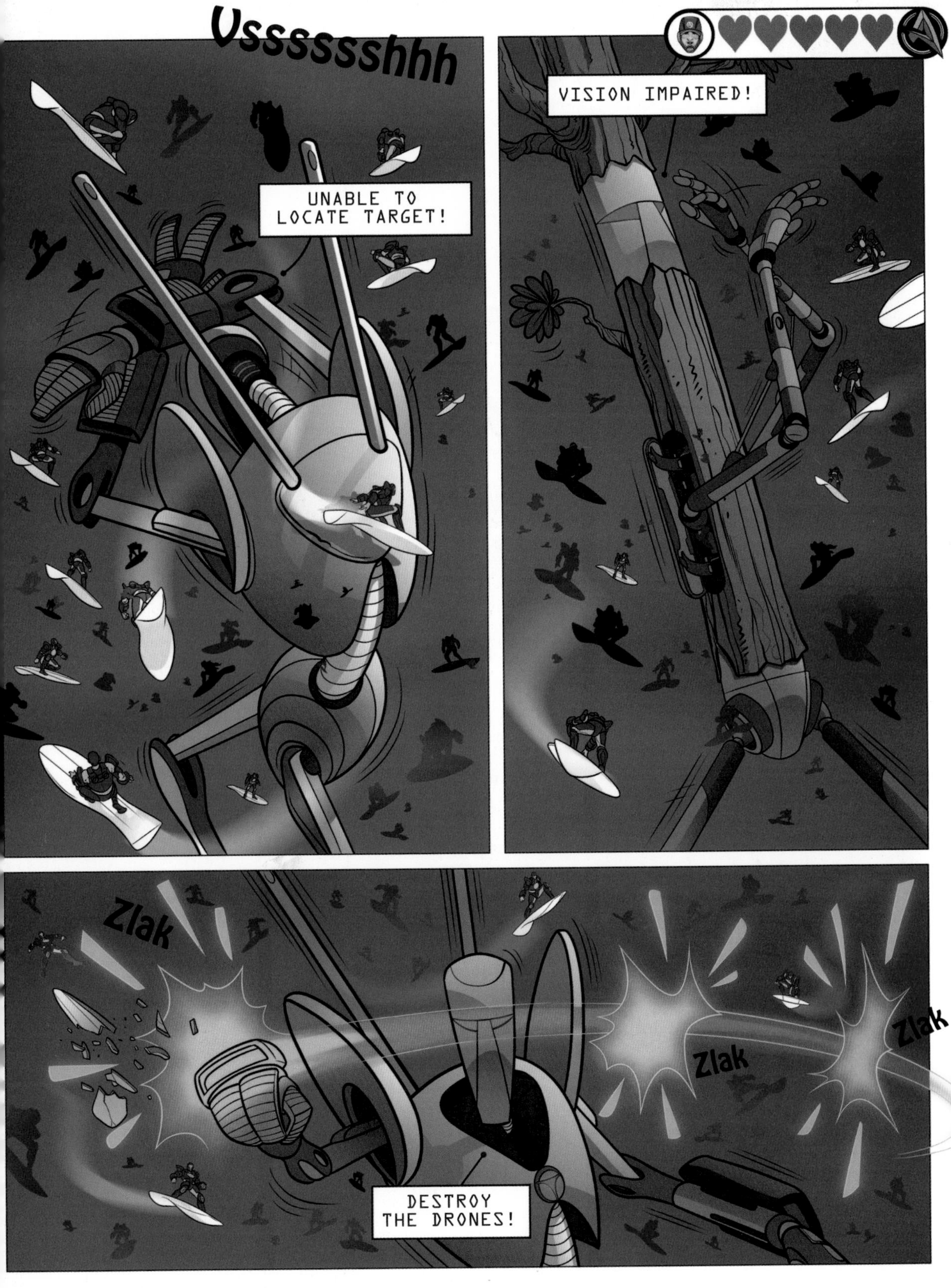
Vsssssshhh
UNABLE TO LOCATE TARGET!
VISION IMPAIRED!
Zlak
Zlak
Zlak
DESTROY THE DRONES!

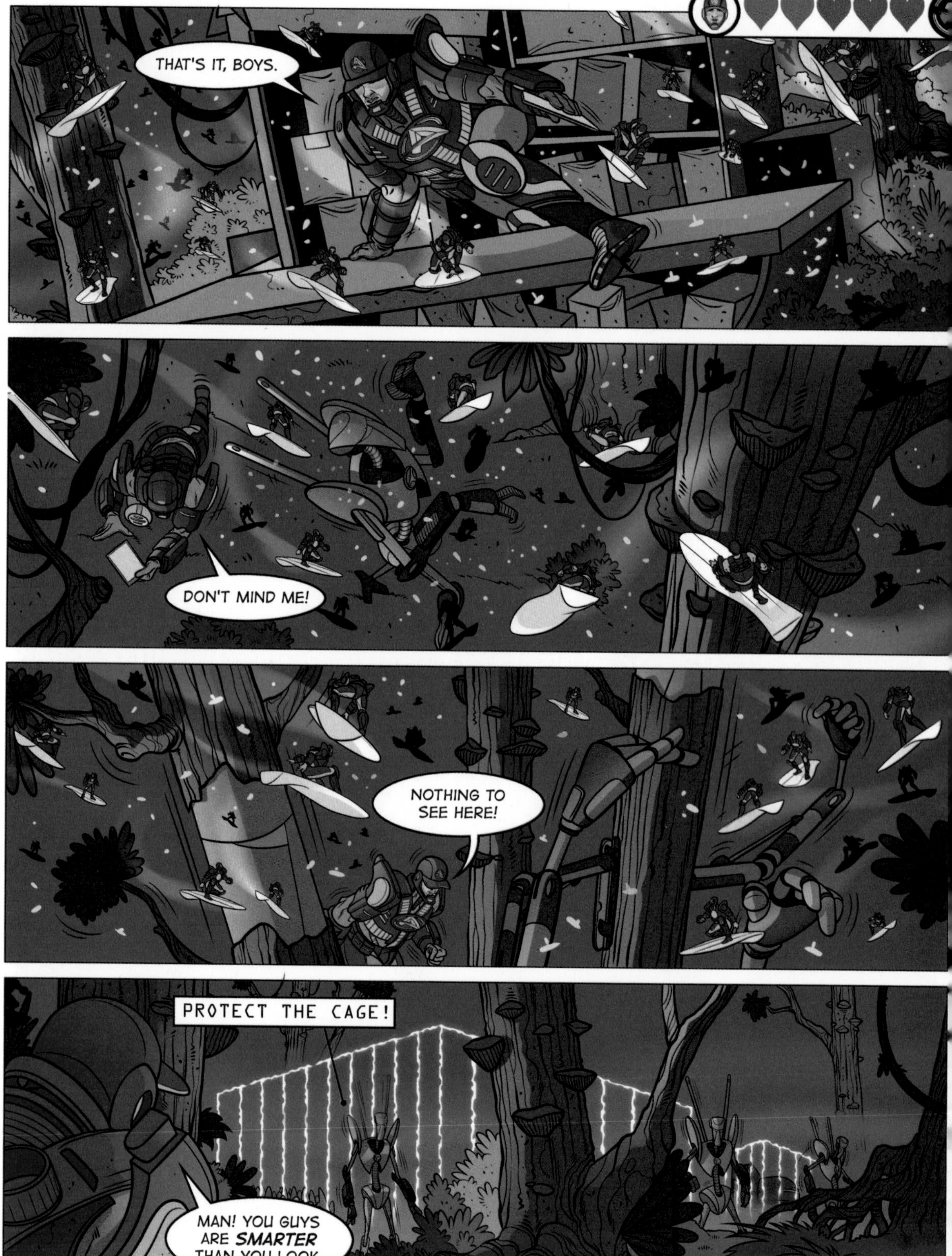
THAT'S IT, BOYS.
DON'T MIND ME!
NOTHING TO SEE HERE!
PROTECT THE CAGE!
MAN! YOU GUYS ARE **SMARTER** THAN YOU LOOK.

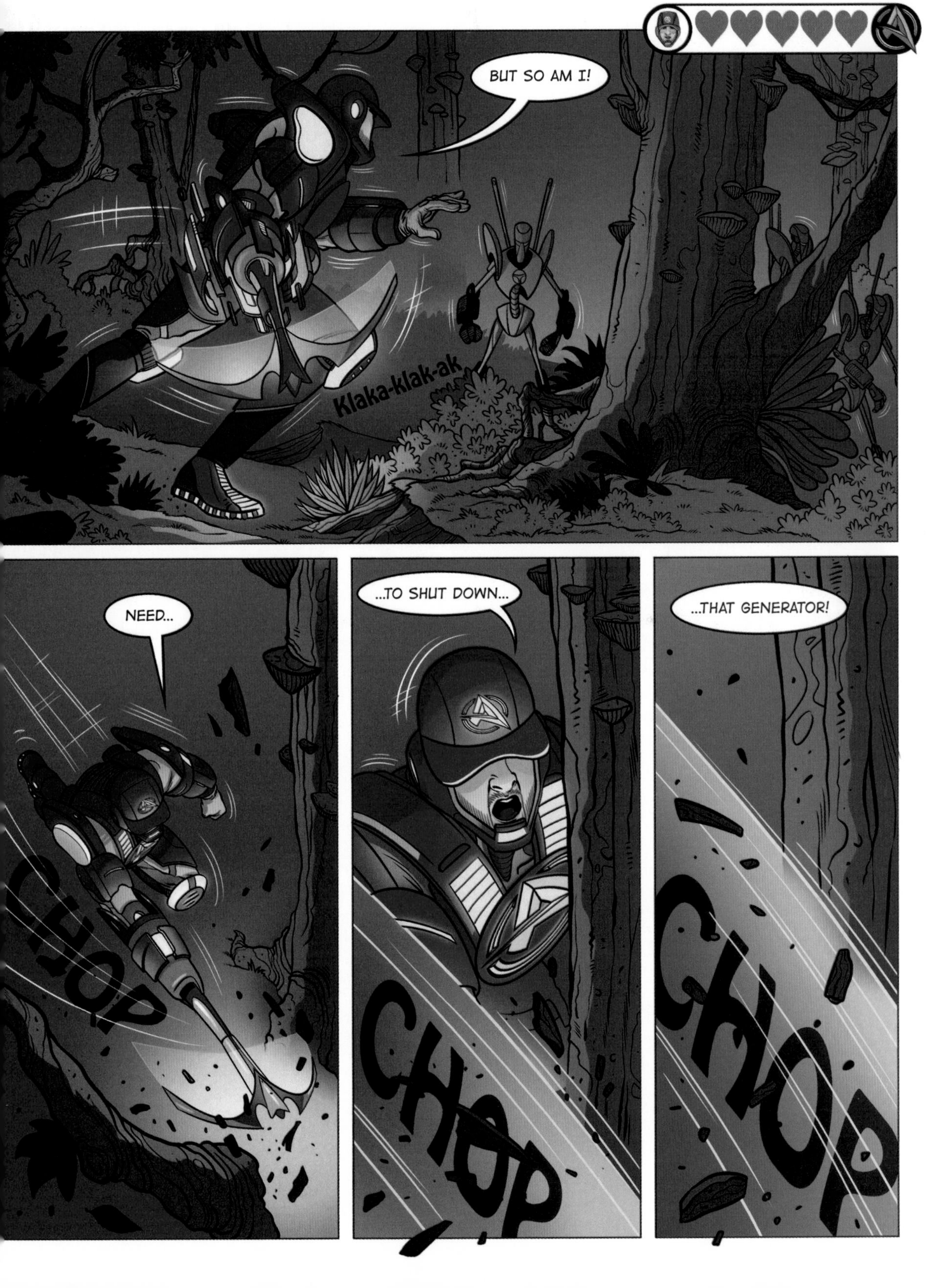
BUT SO AM I!
Klaka-klak-ak
NEED...
CHOP
...TO SHUT DOWN...
CHOP
...THAT GENERATOR!
CHOP

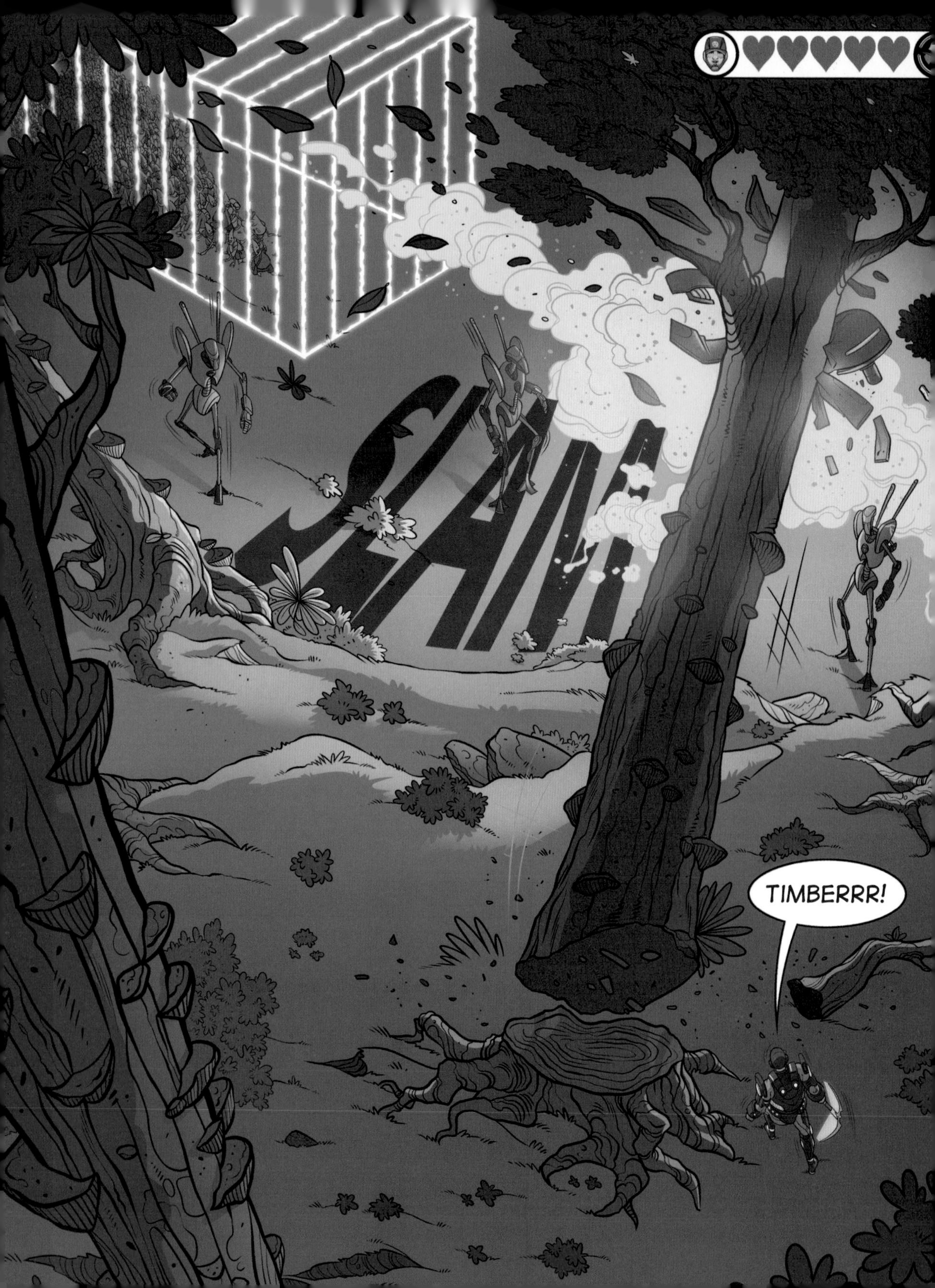
SLAM
TIMBERRR!

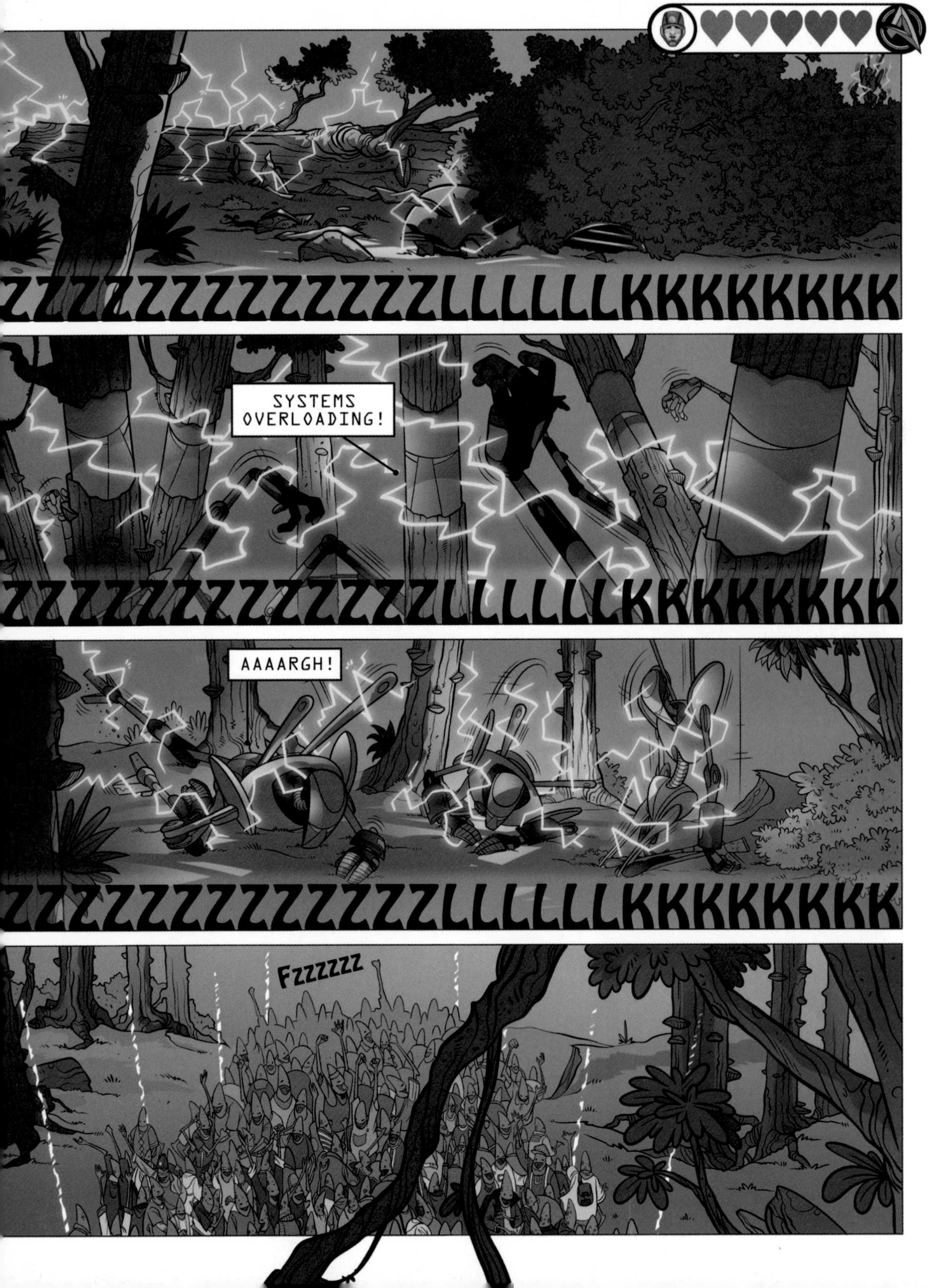
ZZZZZZZZZZZZZZZLLLLLLLKKKKKKKK
SYSTEMS OVERLOADING!
ZZZZZZZZZZZZZZZLLLLLLLKKKKKKKK
AAAARGH!
ZZZZZZZZZZZZZZZLLLLLLLKKKKKKKK
Fzzzzzz

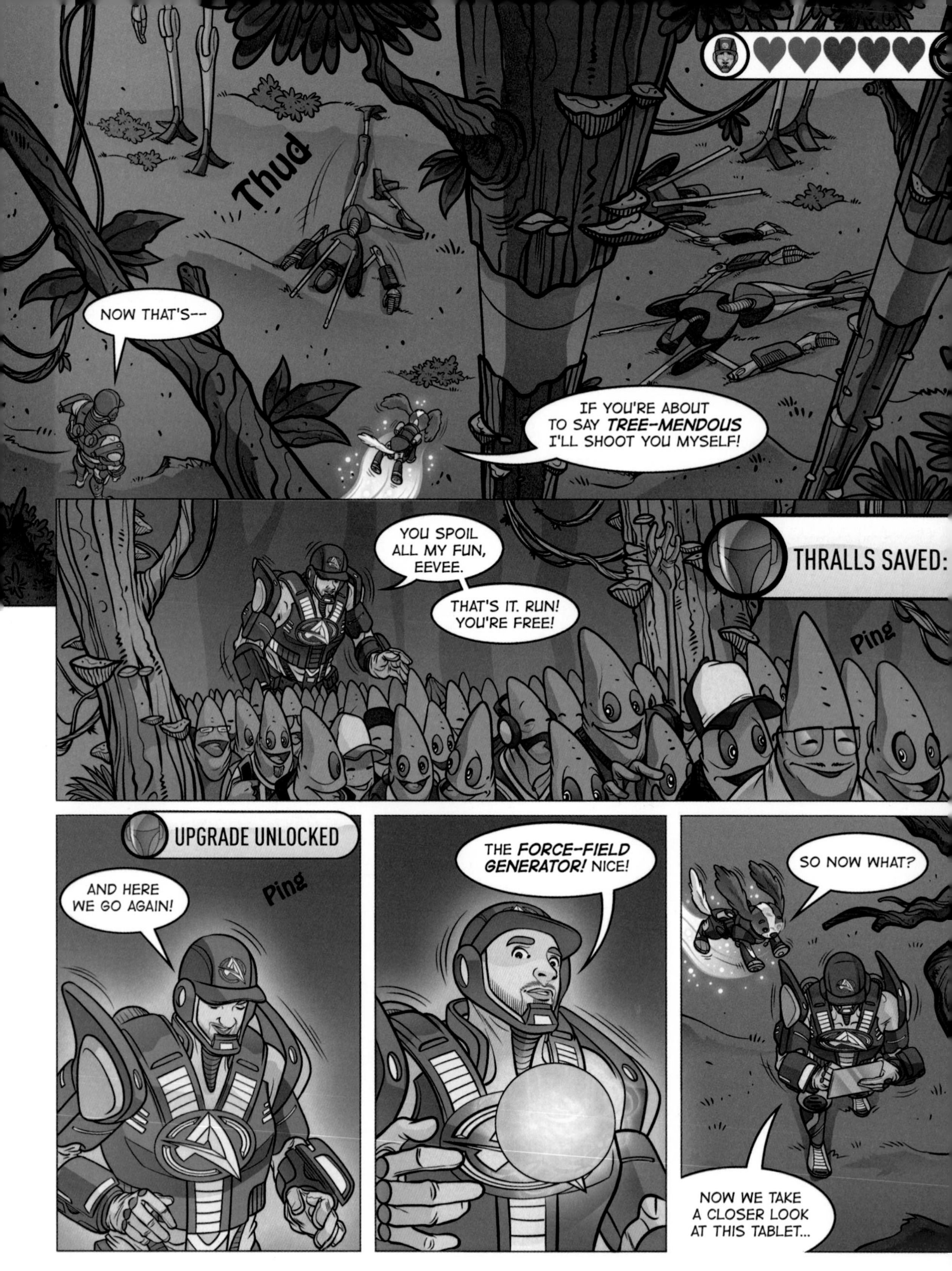
Thud
NOW THAT'S--
IF YOU'RE ABOUT TO SAY TREE-MENDOUS I'LL SHOOT YOU MYSELF!
THRALLS SAVED:
YOU SPOIL ALL MY FUN, EEVEE.
THAT'S IT. RUN! YOU'RE FREE!
Ping
UPGRADE UNLOCKED
AND HERE WE GO AGAIN!
Ping
THE FORCE-FIELD GENERATOR! NICE!
SO NOW WHAT?
NOW WE TAKE A CLOSER LOOK AT THIS TABLET...

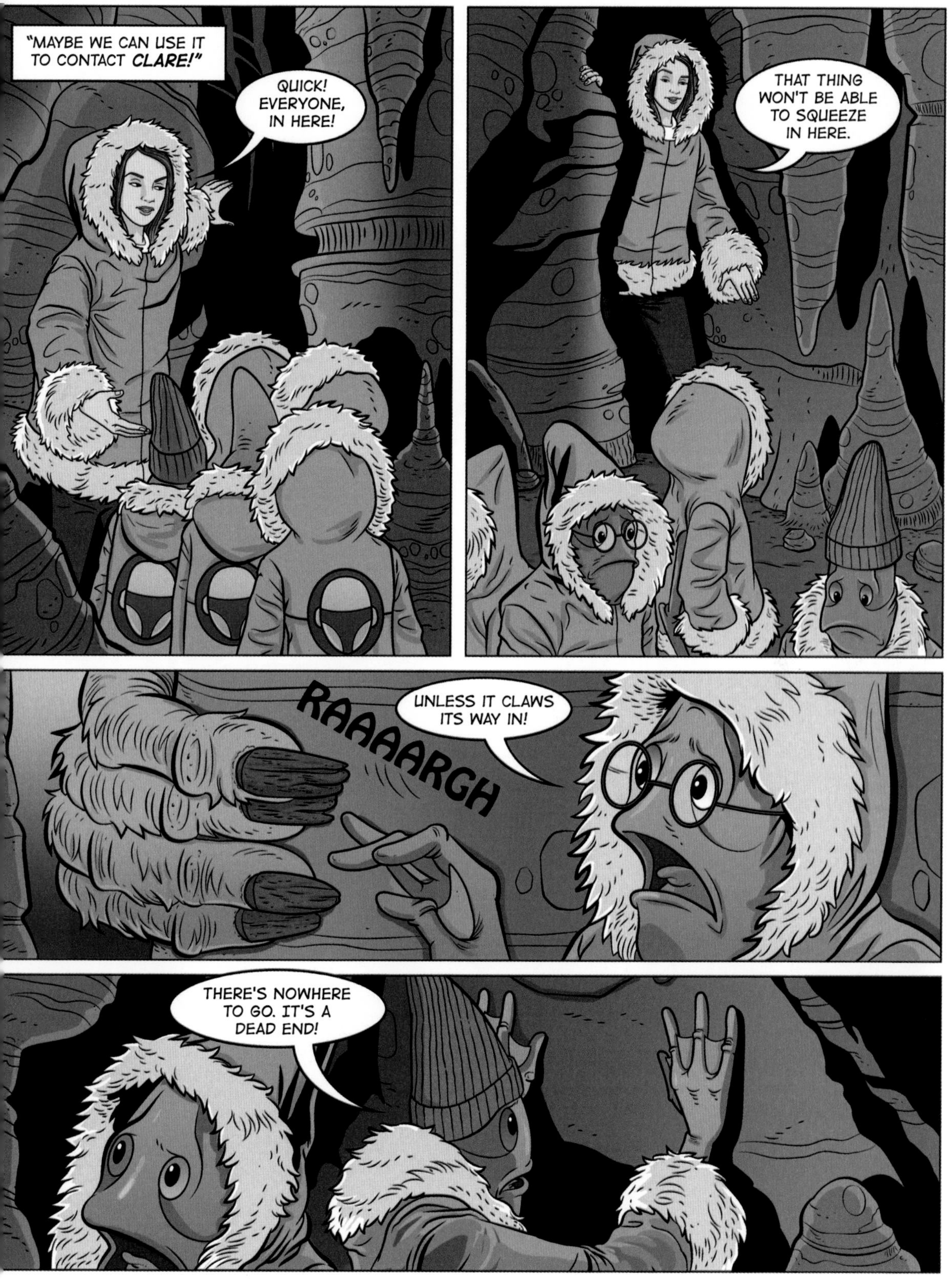
"MAYBE WE CAN USE IT TO CONTACT CLARE!"
QUICK! EVERYONE, IN HERE!
THAT THING WON'T BE ABLE TO SQUEEZE IN HERE.
RAAAAARGH
UNLESS IT CLAWS ITS WAY IN!
THERE'S NOWHERE TO GO. IT'S A DEAD END!

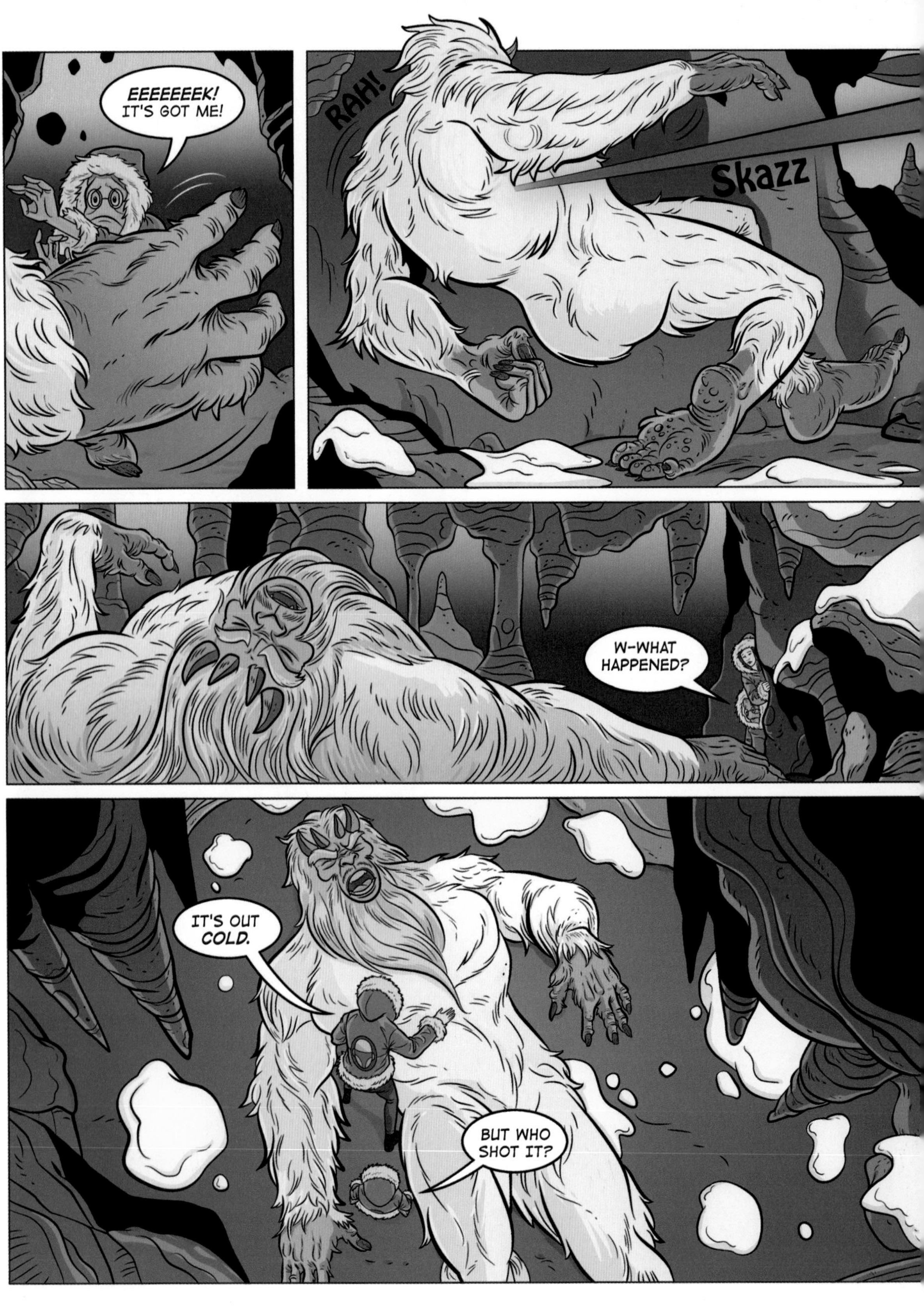
EEEEEEEK! IT'S GOT ME!
RAH!
Skazz
W-WHAT HAPPENED?
IT'S OUT COLD.
BUT WHO SHOT IT?

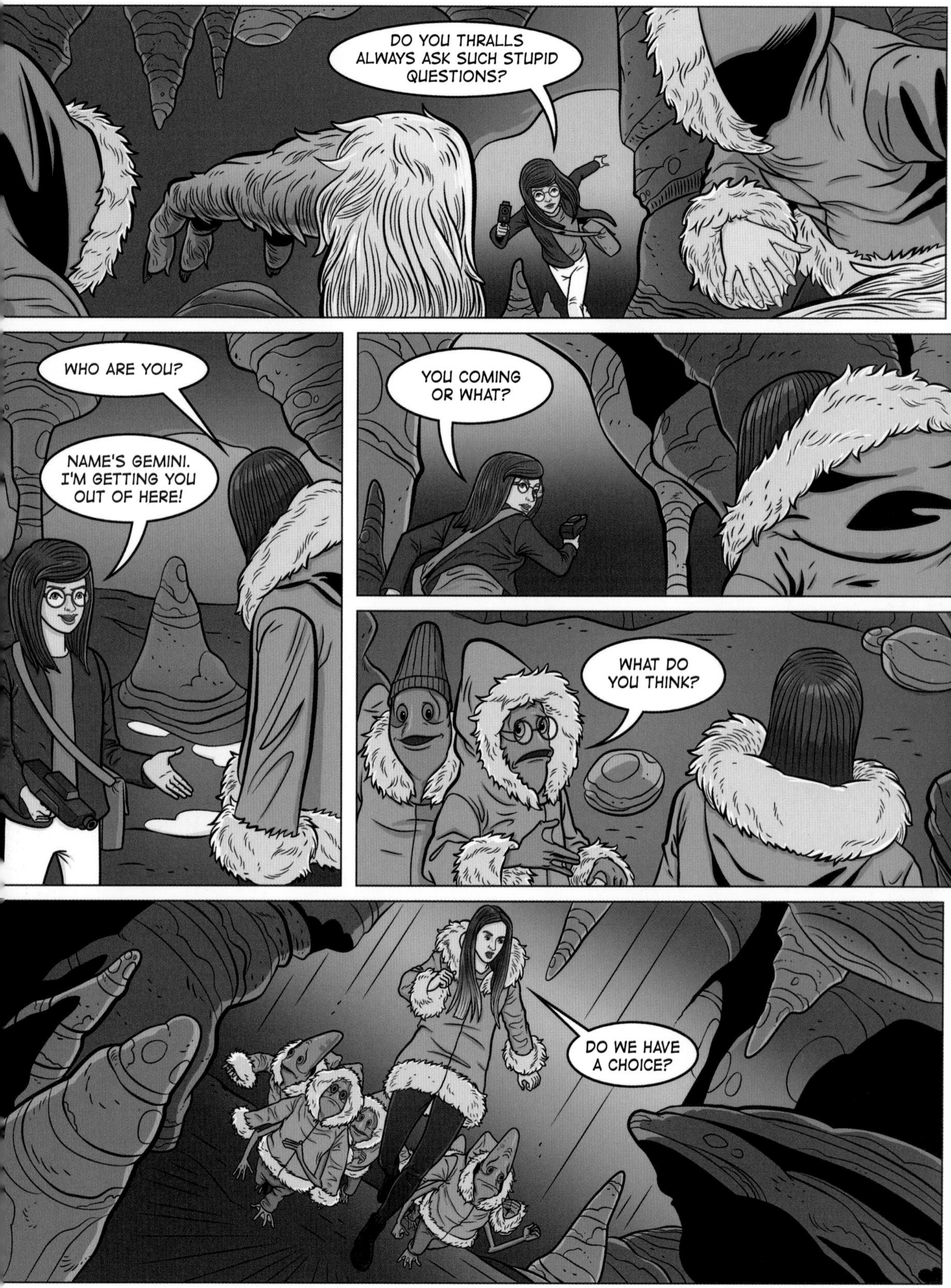
DO YOU THRALLS ALWAYS ASK SUCH STUPID QUESTIONS?
WHO ARE YOU?
NAME'S GEMINI. I'M GETTING YOU OUT OF HERE!
YOU COMING OR WHAT?
WHAT DO YOU THINK?
DO WE HAVE A CHOICE?

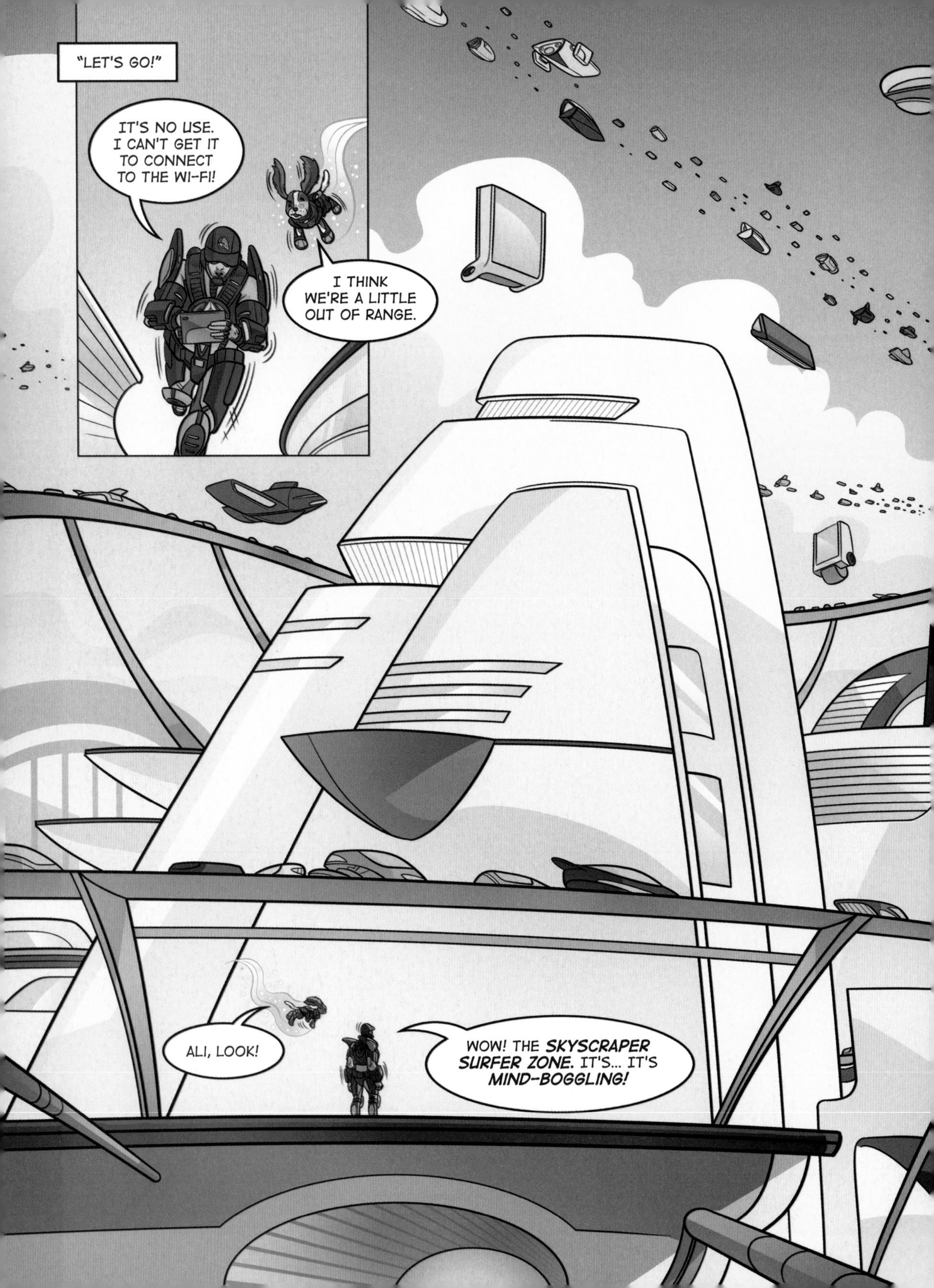
"LET'S GO!"
IT'S NO USE. I CAN'T GET IT TO CONNECT TO THE WI-FI!
I THINK WE'RE A LITTLE OUT OF RANGE.
ALI, LOOK!
WOW! THE *SKYSCRAPER SURFER ZONE.* IT'S... IT'S *MIND-BOGGLING!*

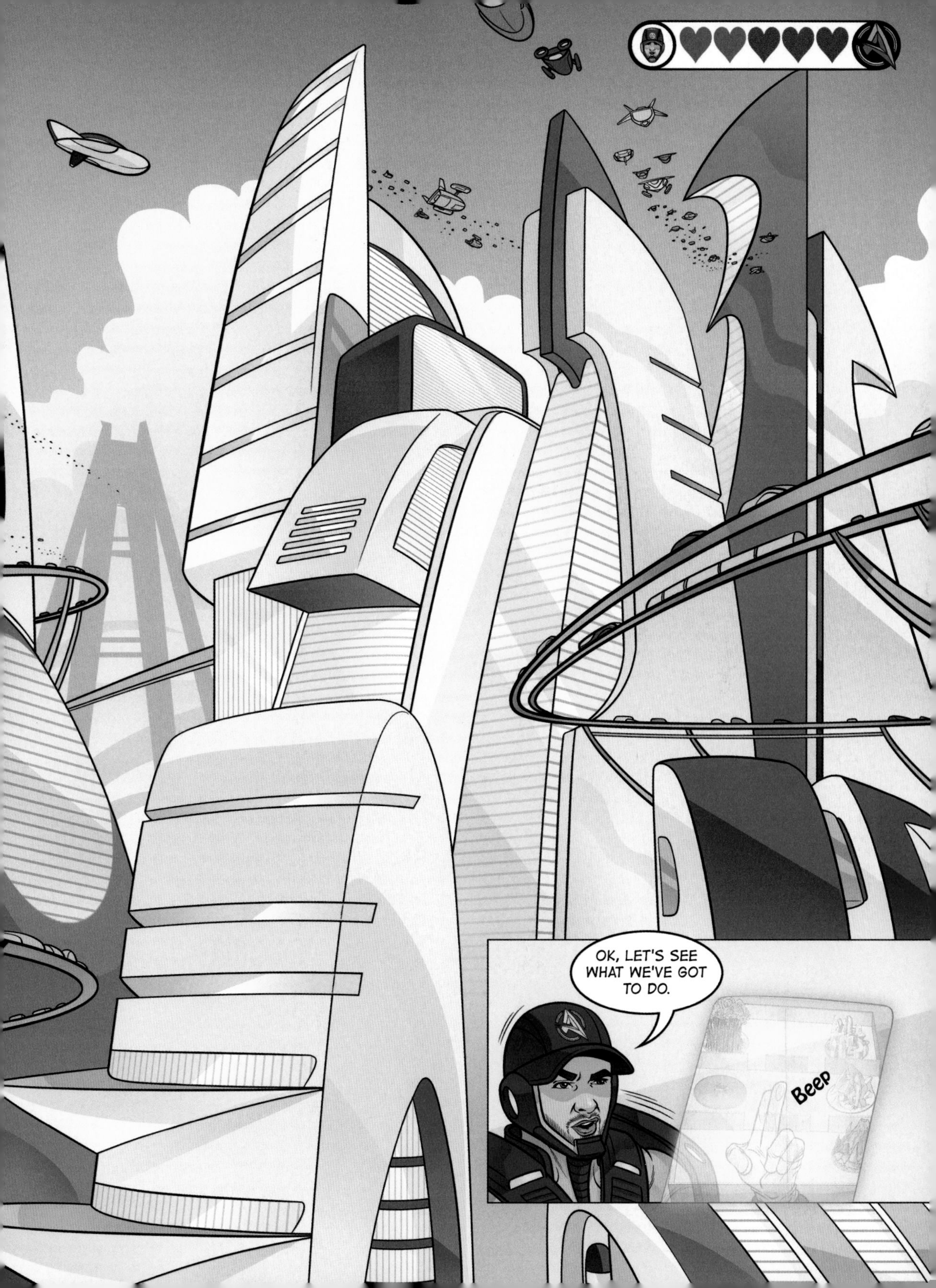
OK, LET'S SEE WHAT WE'VE GOT TO DO.
Beep

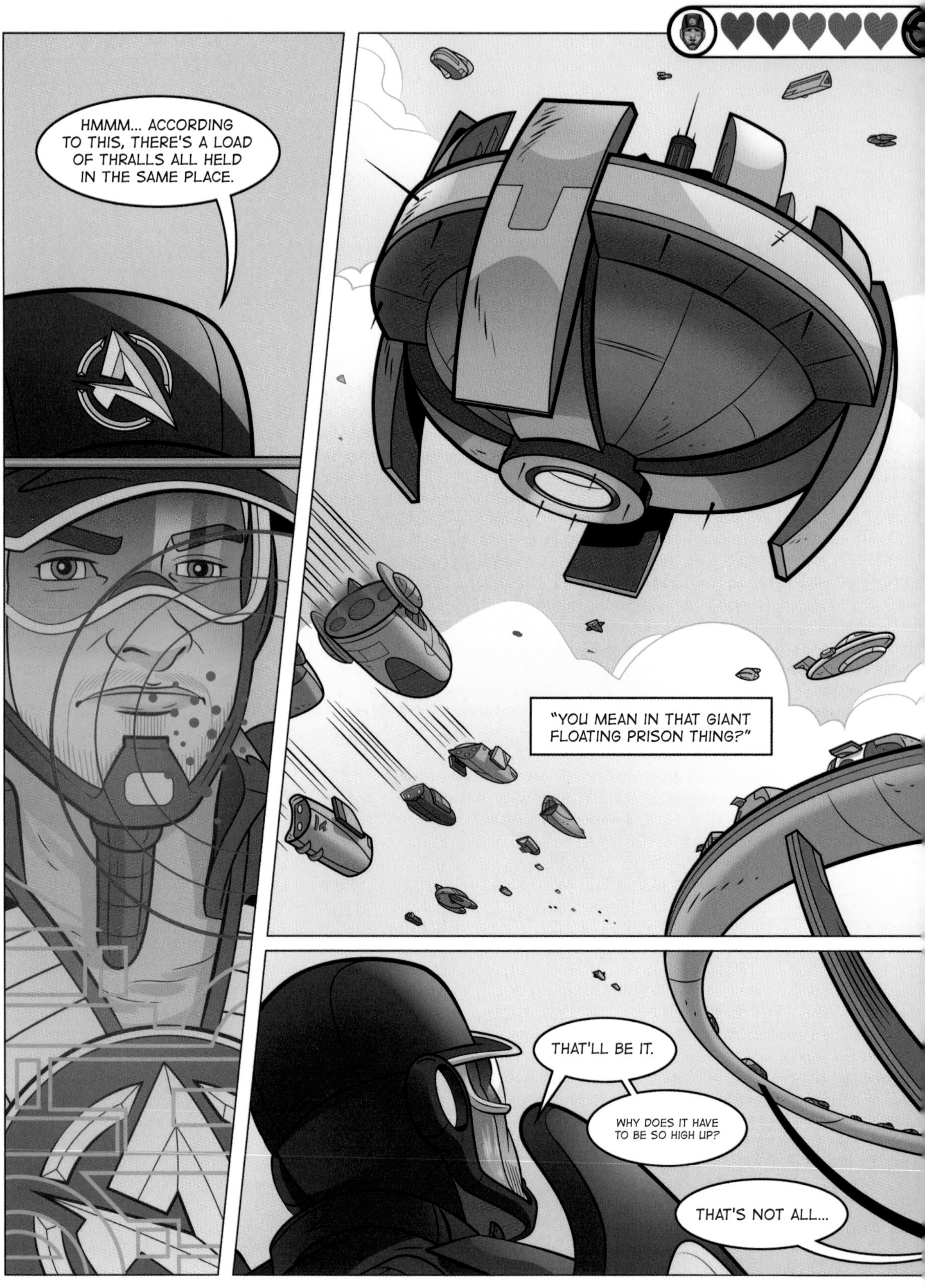
HMMM... ACCORDING TO THIS, THERE'S A LOAD OF THRALLS ALL HELD IN THE SAME PLACE.
"YOU MEAN IN THAT GIANT FLOATING PRISON THING?"
THAT'LL BE IT.
WHY DOES IT HAVE TO BE SO HIGH UP?
THAT'S NOT ALL...

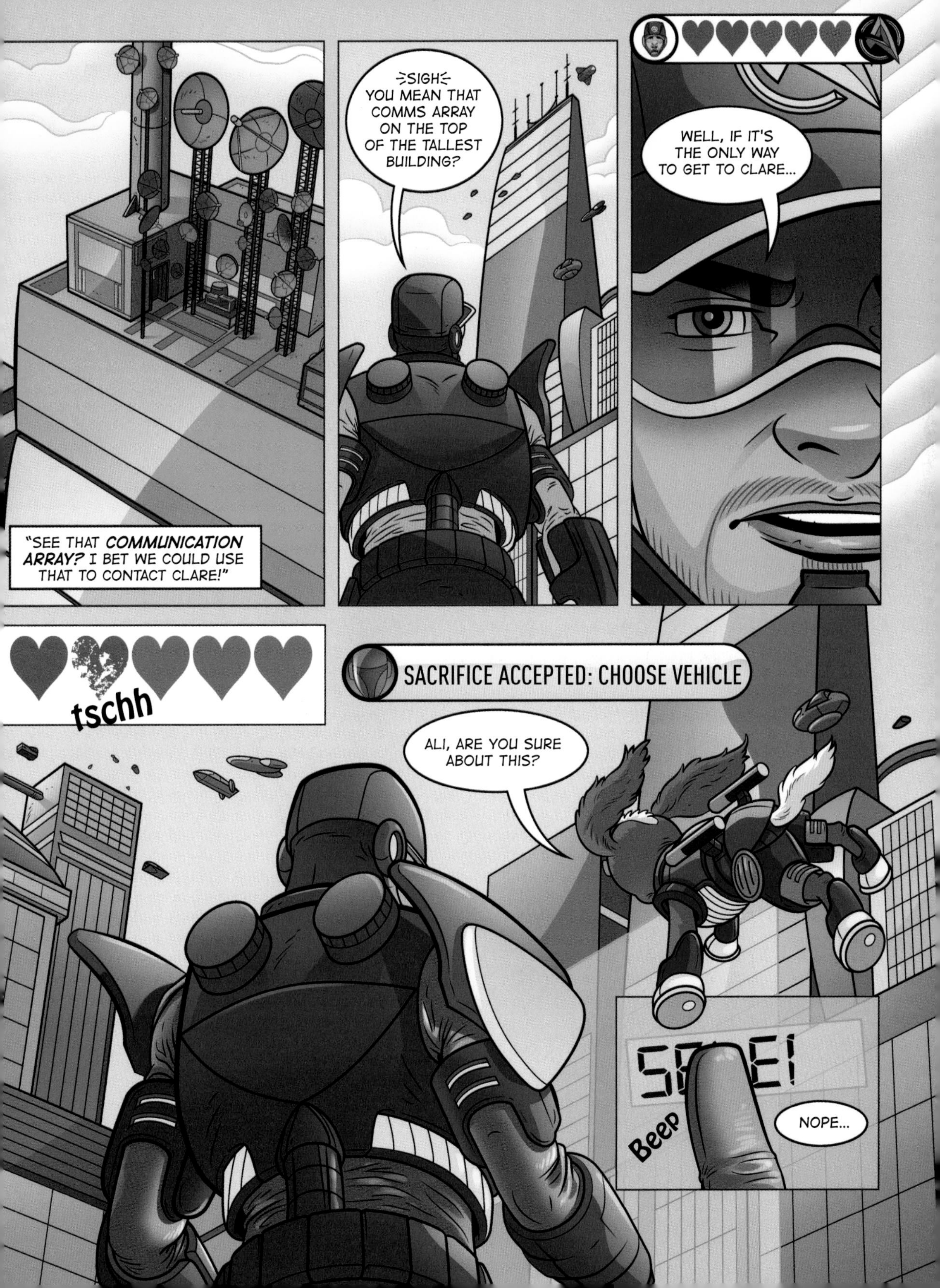
"SEE THAT *COMMUNICATION ARRAY?* I BET WE COULD USE THAT TO CONTACT CLARE!"
SIGH
YOU MEAN THAT COMMS ARRAY ON THE TOP OF THE TALLEST BUILDING?
WELL, IF IT'S THE ONLY WAY TO GET TO CLARE...
tschh
SACRIFICE ACCEPTED: CHOOSE VEHICLE
ALI, ARE YOU SURE ABOUT THIS?
Beep
NOPE...

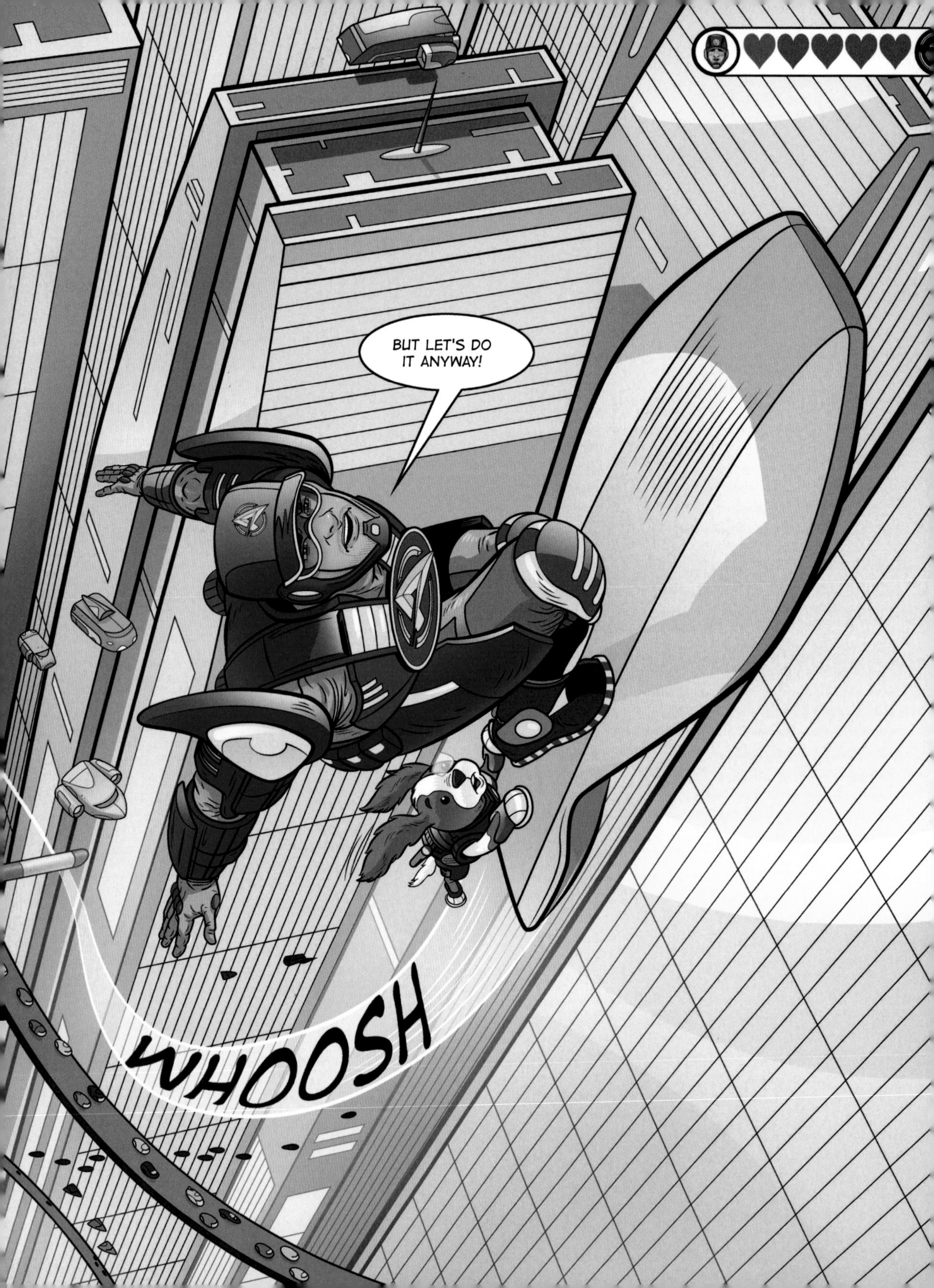
BUT LET'S DO IT ANYWAY!
WHOOSH

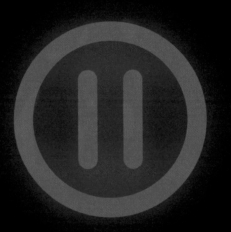

LEVEL SEVEN

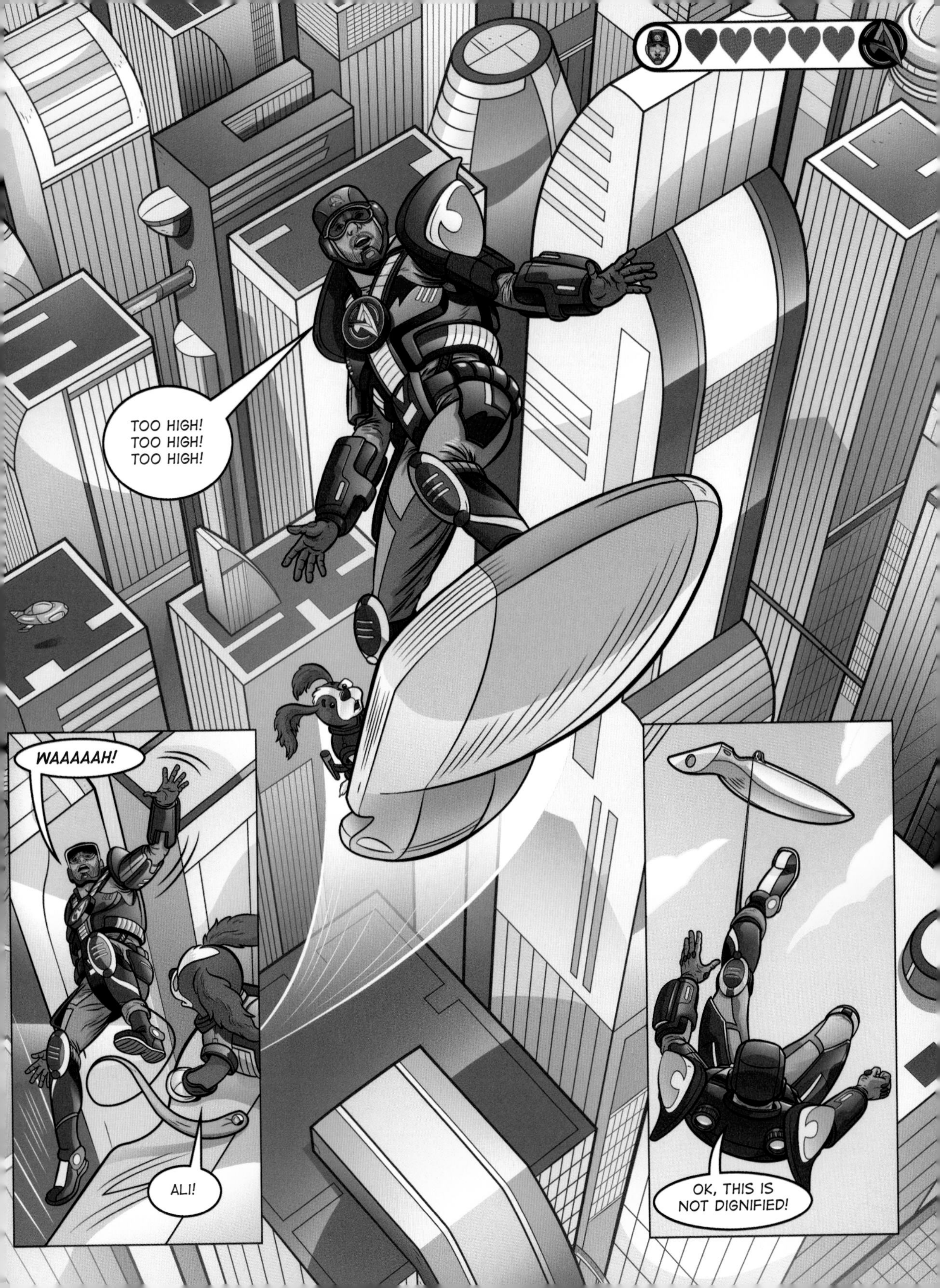
TOO HIGH! TOO HIGH! TOO HIGH!
WAAAAAH!
ALI!
OK, THIS IS NOT DIGNIFIED!

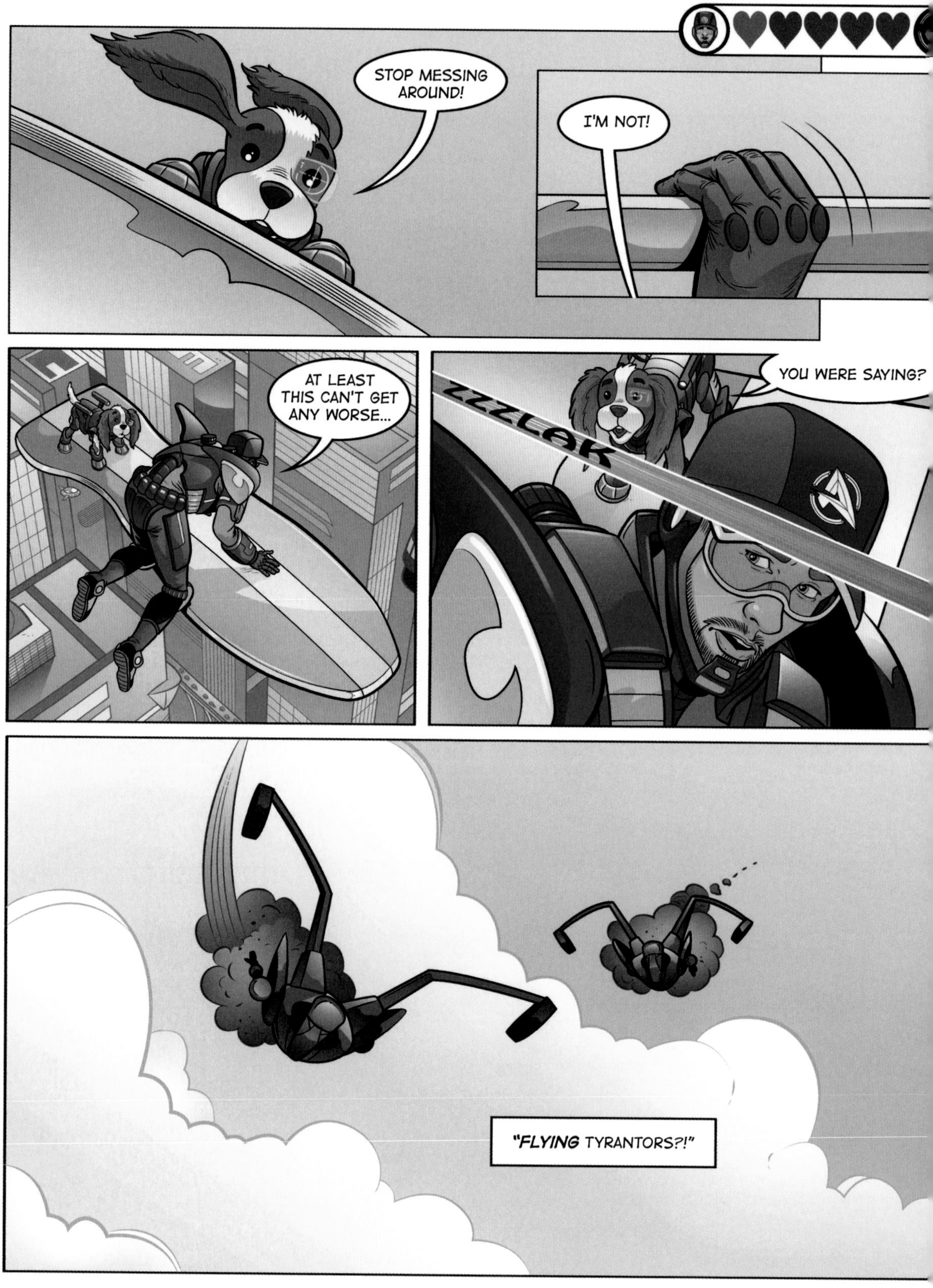
STOP MESSING AROUND!
I'M NOT!
AT LEAST THIS CAN'T GET ANY WORSE...
ZZZLAK
YOU WERE SAYING?
"FLYING TYRANTORS?!"

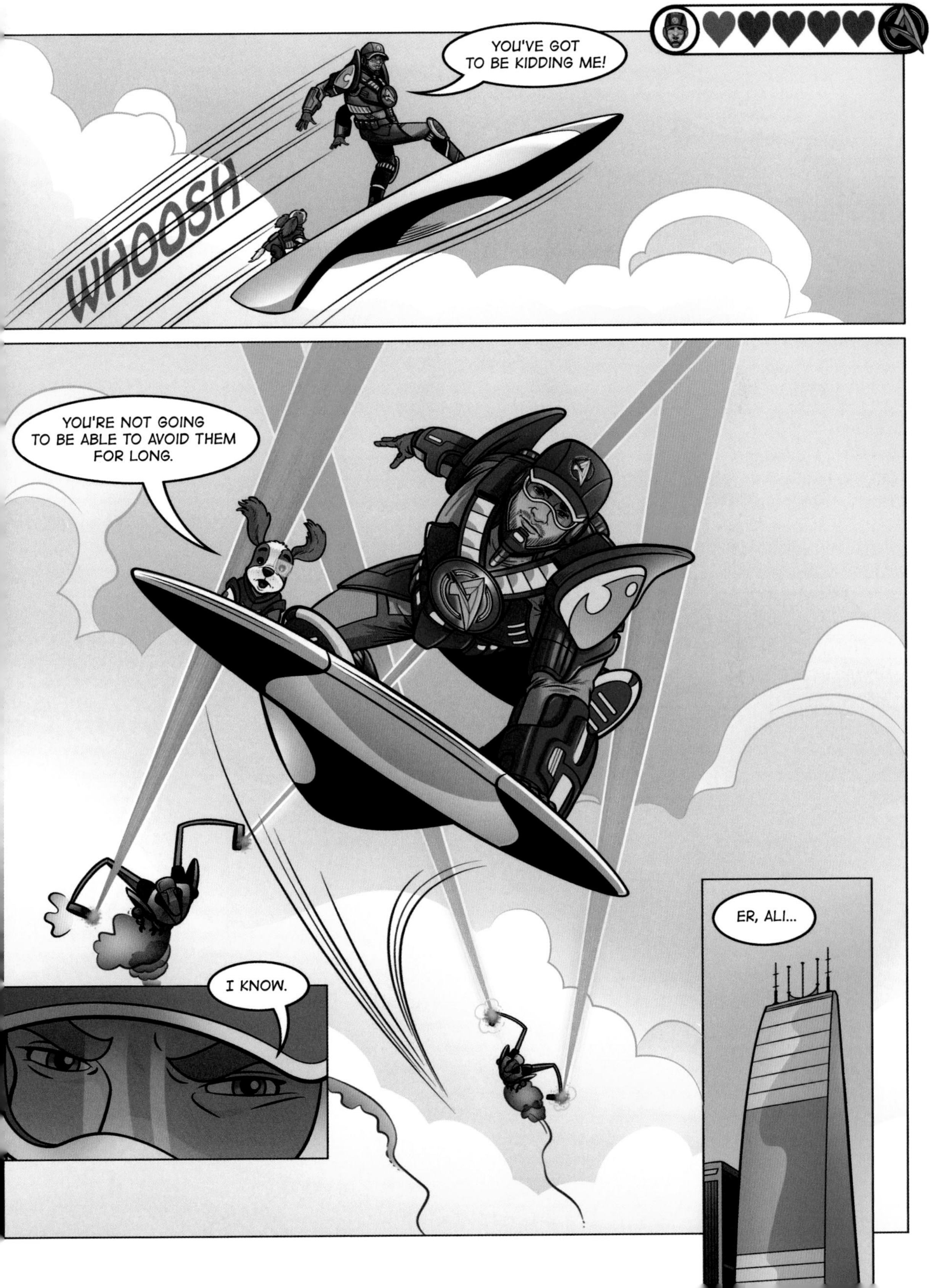
YOU'VE GOT TO BE KIDDING ME!
WHOOSH
YOU'RE NOT GOING TO BE ABLE TO AVOID THEM FOR LONG.
I KNOW.
ER, ALI...

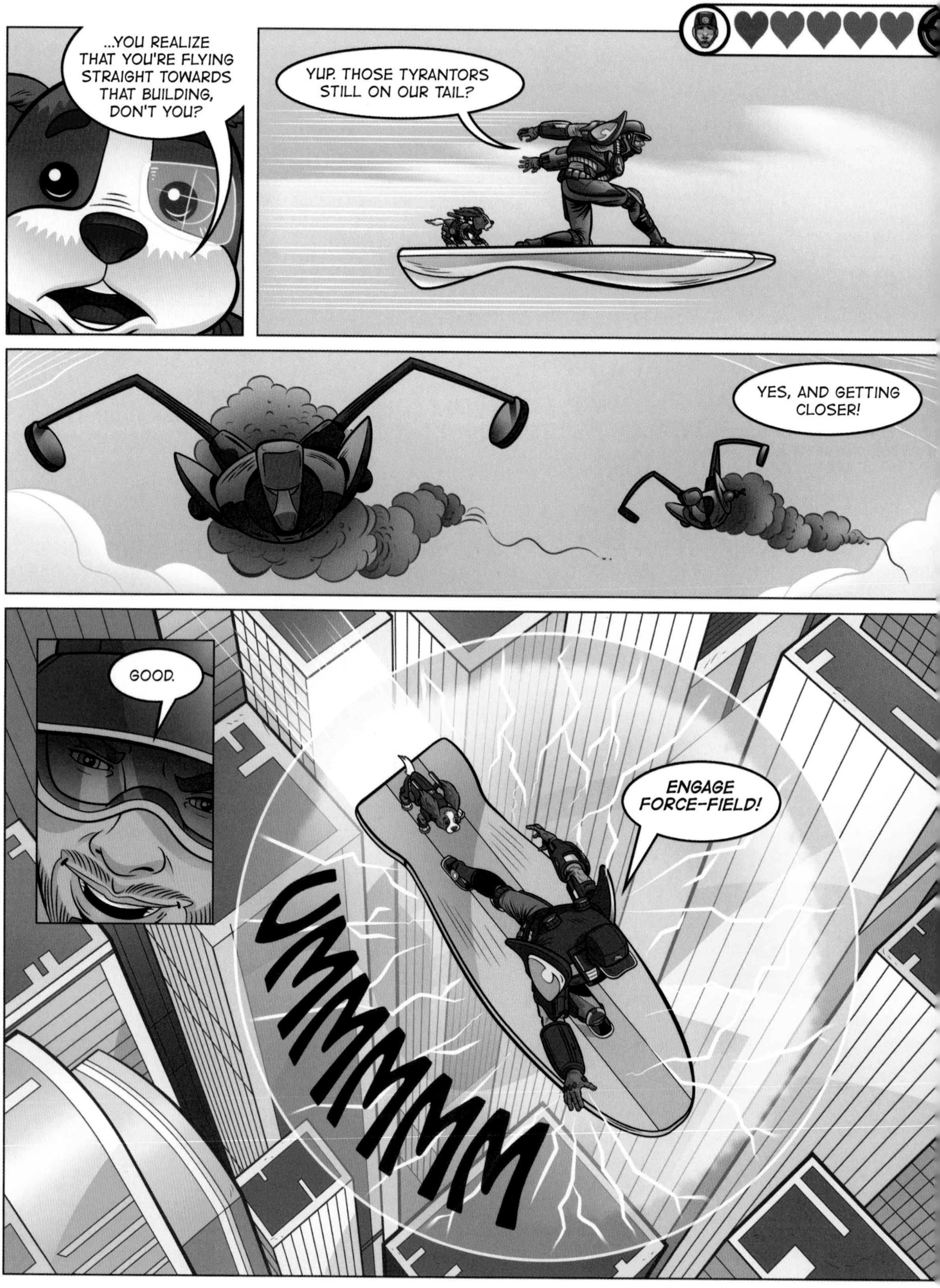
...YOU REALIZE THAT YOU'RE FLYING STRAIGHT TOWARDS THAT BUILDING, DON'T YOU?
YUP. THOSE TYRANTORS STILL ON OUR TAIL?
YES, AND GETTING CLOSER!
GOOD.
ENGAGE FORCE-FIELD!
UMMMMM

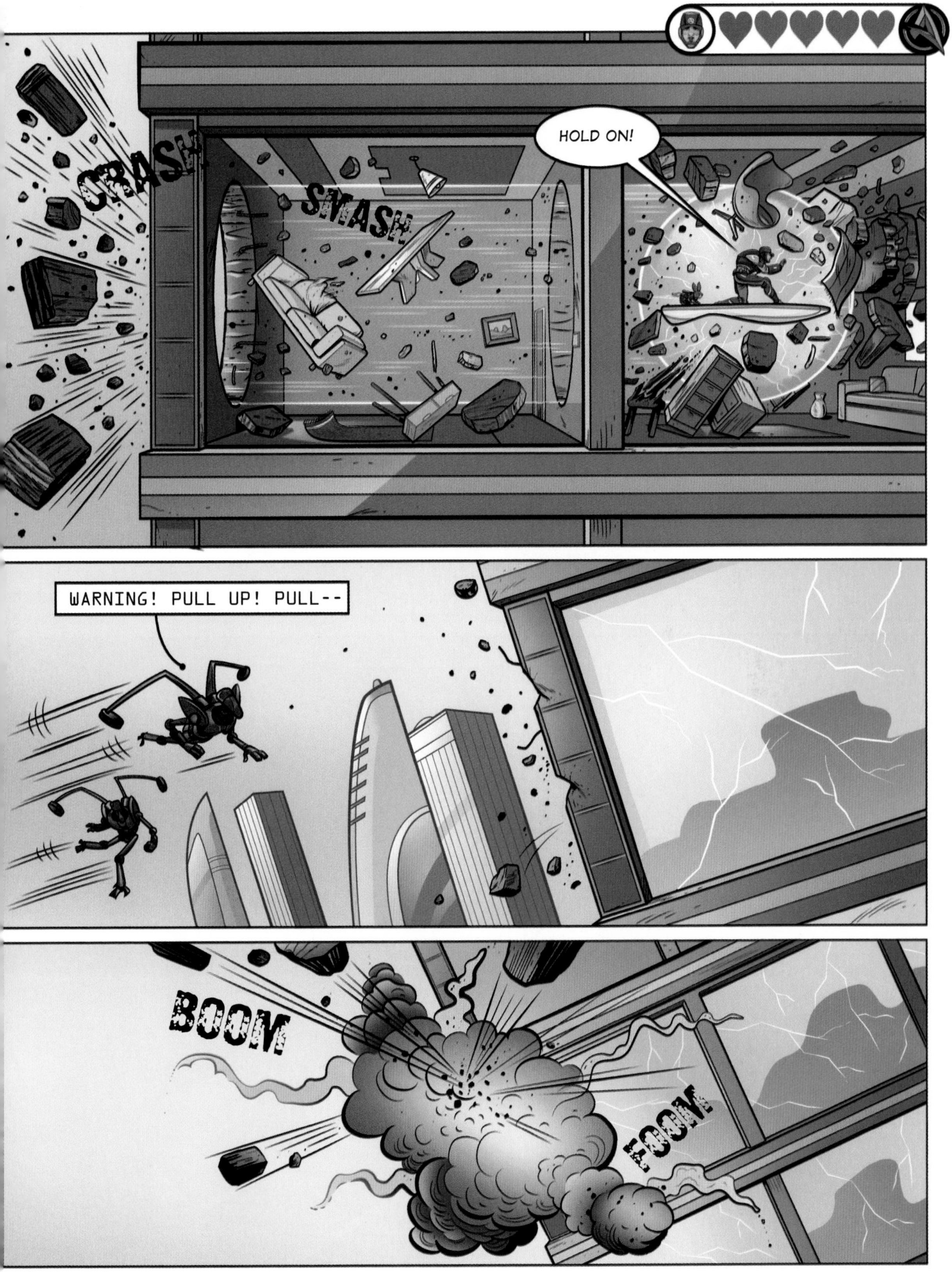
CRASH
SMASH
HOLD ON!
WARNING! PULL UP! PULL--
BOOM
BOOM

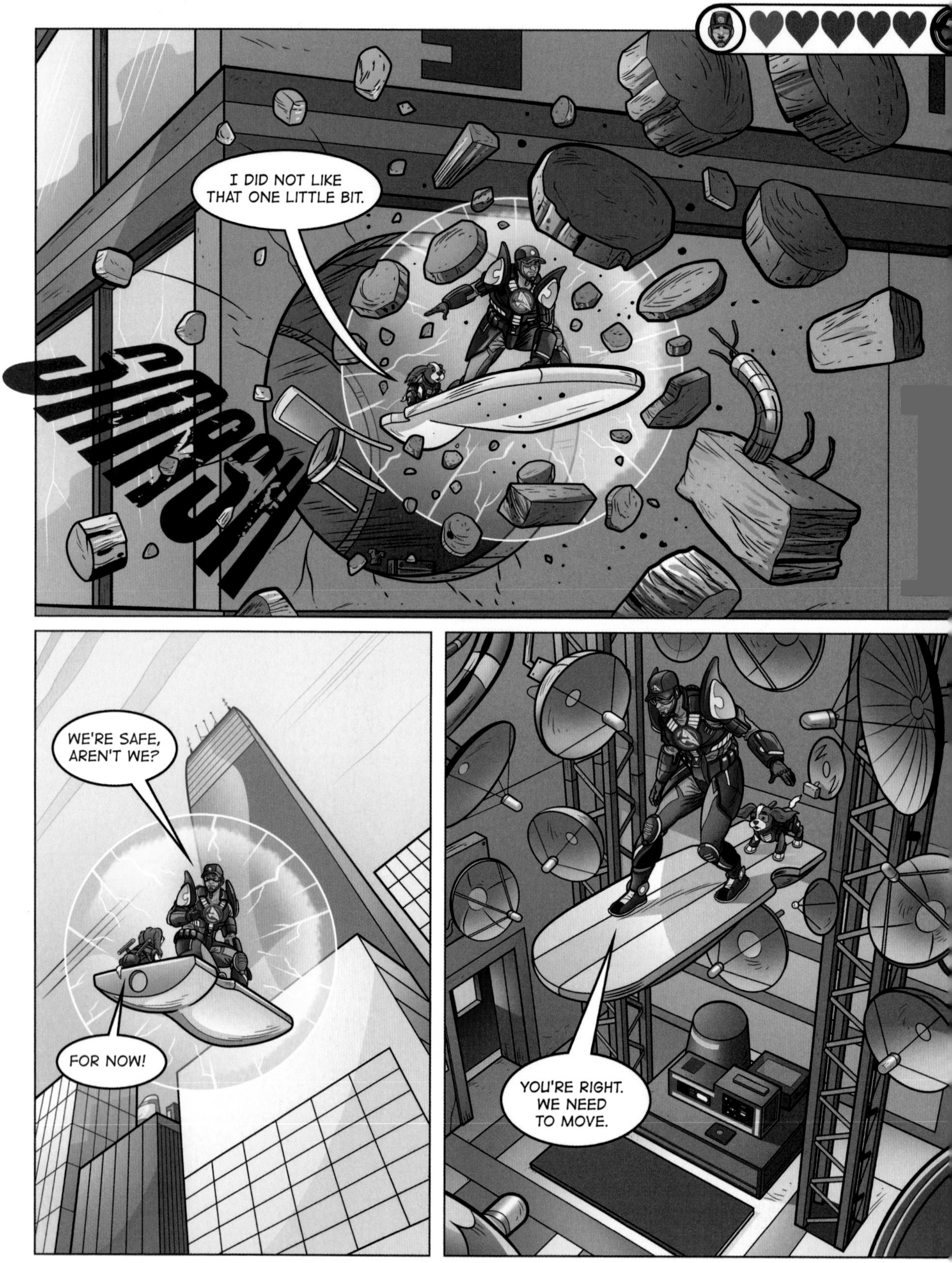
I DID NOT LIKE THAT ONE LITTLE BIT.
WE'RE SAFE, AREN'T WE?
FOR NOW!
YOU'RE RIGHT. WE NEED TO MOVE.

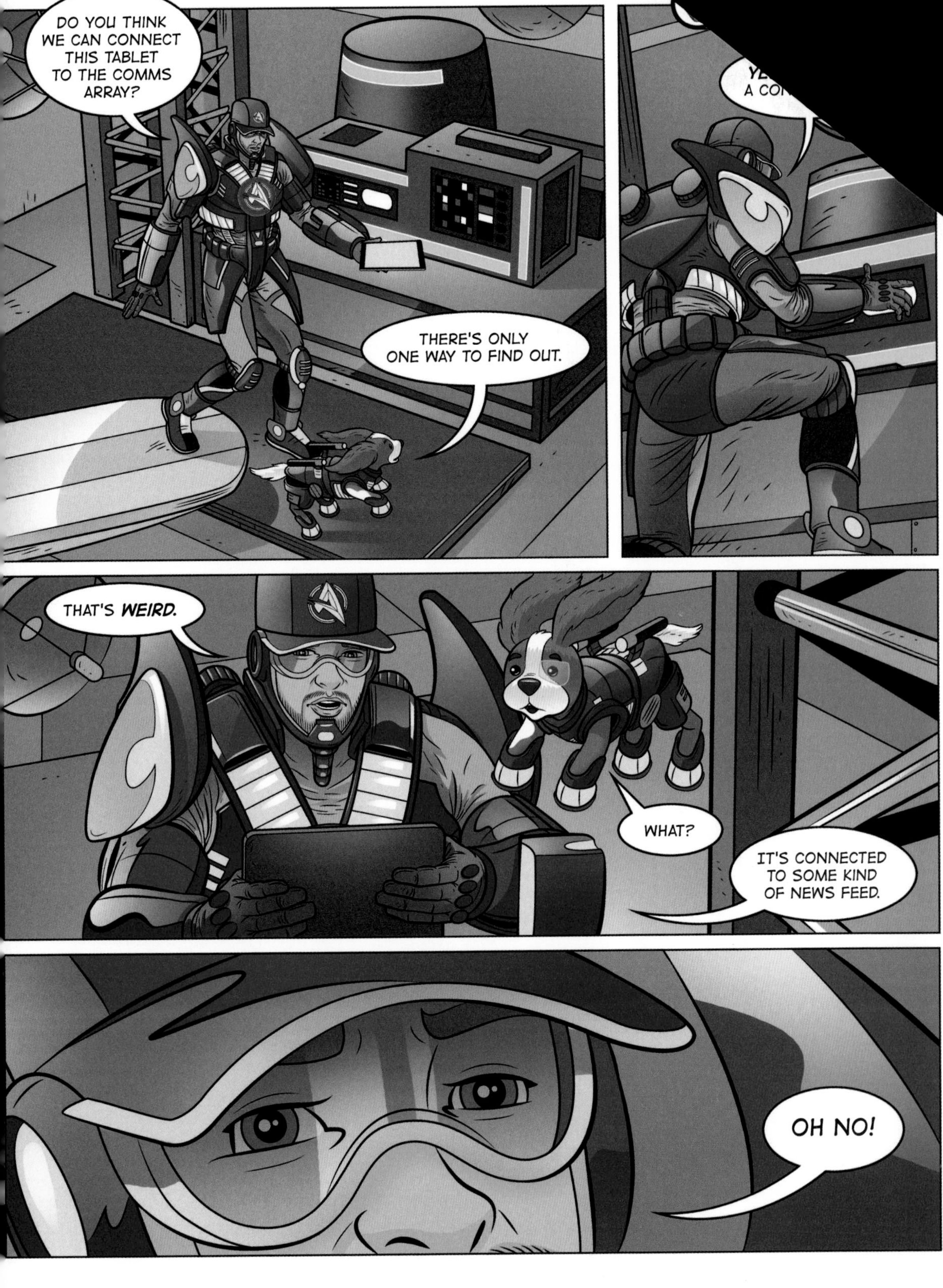
DO YOU THINK WE CAN CONNECT THIS TABLET TO THE COMMS ARRAY?
THERE'S ONLY ONE WAY TO FIND OUT.
THAT'S ***WEIRD.***
WHAT?
IT'S CONNECTED TO SOME KIND OF NEWS FEED.
OH NO!

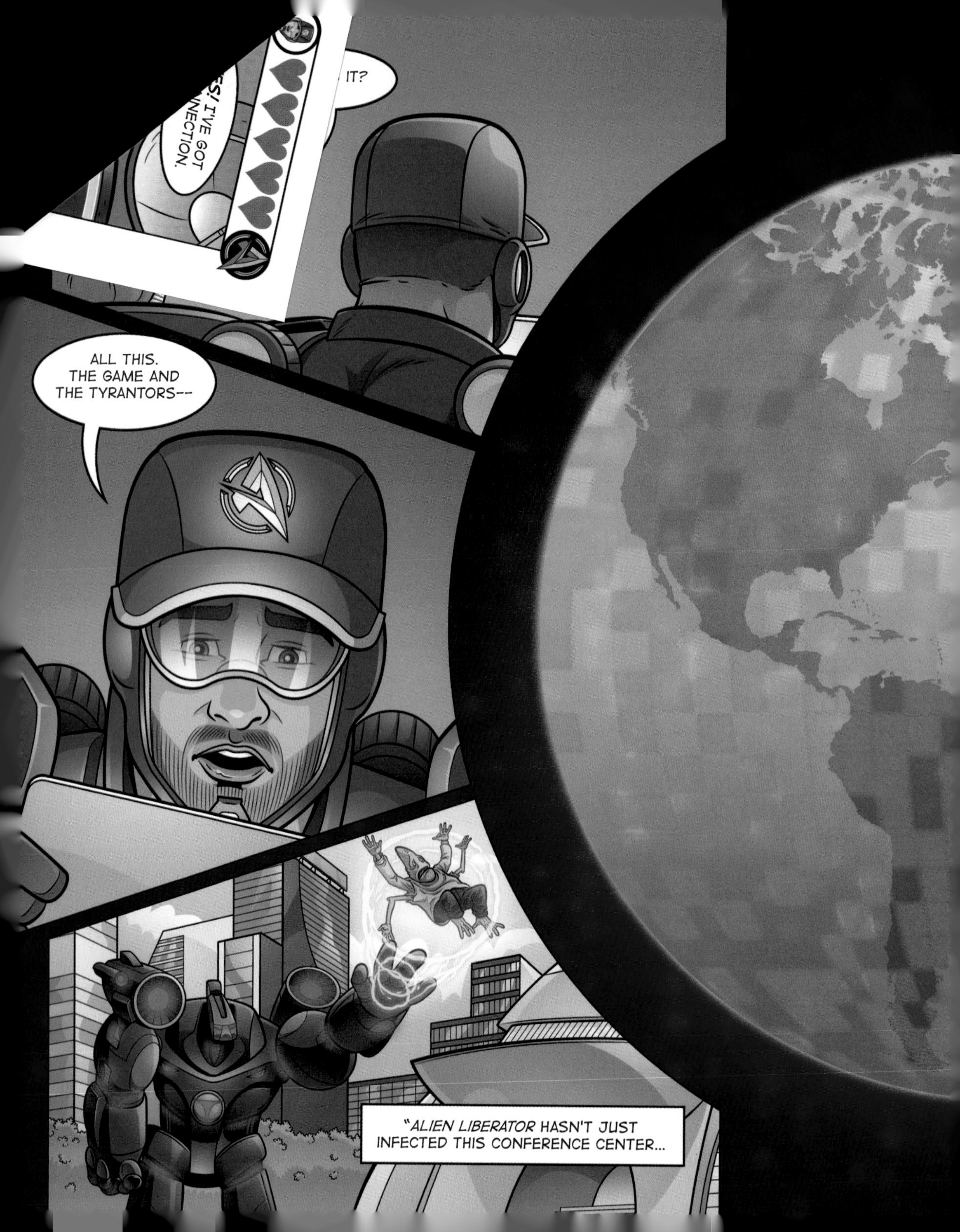
IT?
ALL THIS. THE GAME AND THE TYRANTORS--
"ALIEN LIBERATOR HASN'T JUST INFECTED THIS CONFERENCE CENTER...

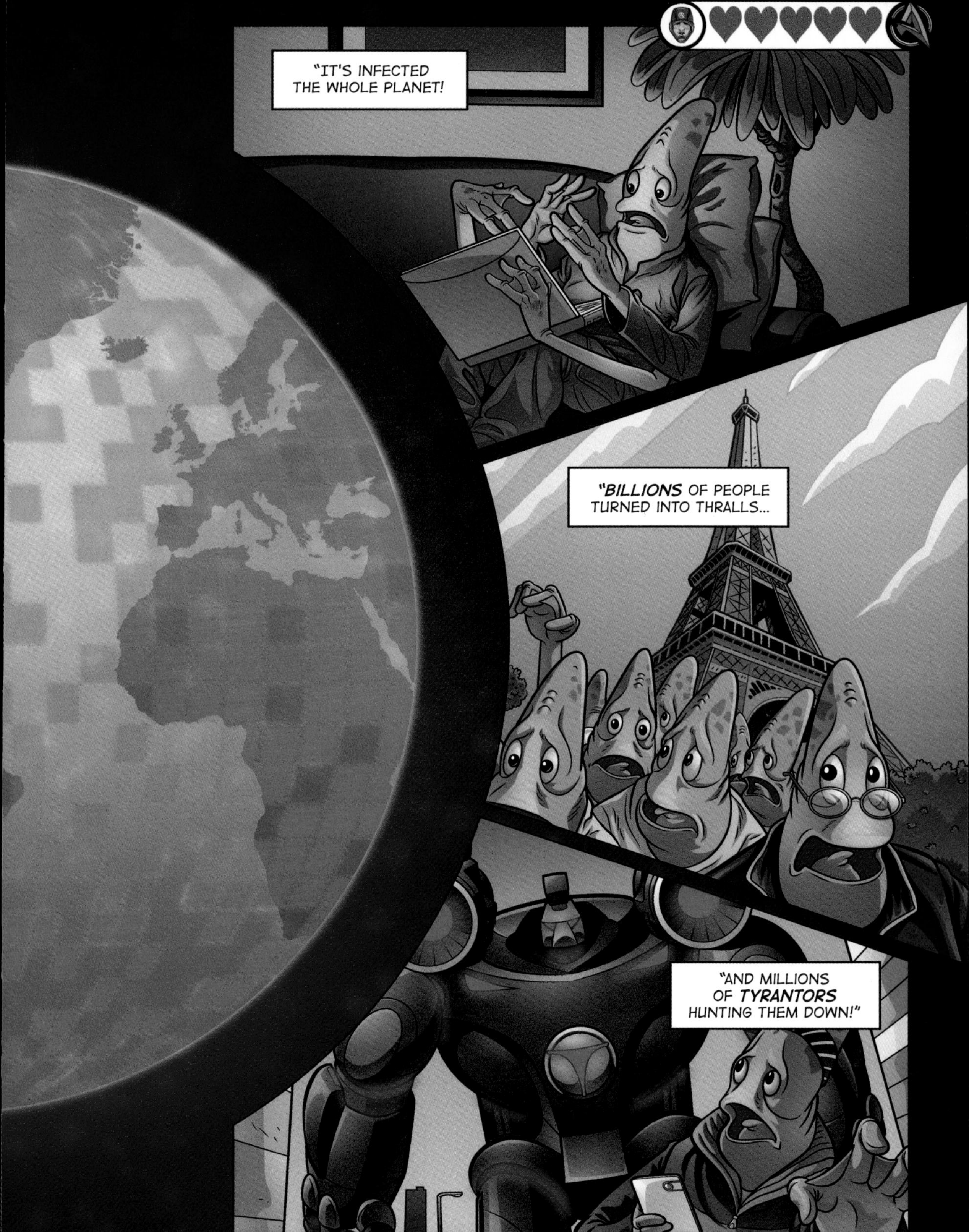
"IT'S INFECTED THE WHOLE PLANET!
"BILLIONS OF PEOPLE TURNED INTO THRALLS...
"AND MILLIONS OF TYRANTORS HUNTING THEM DOWN!"

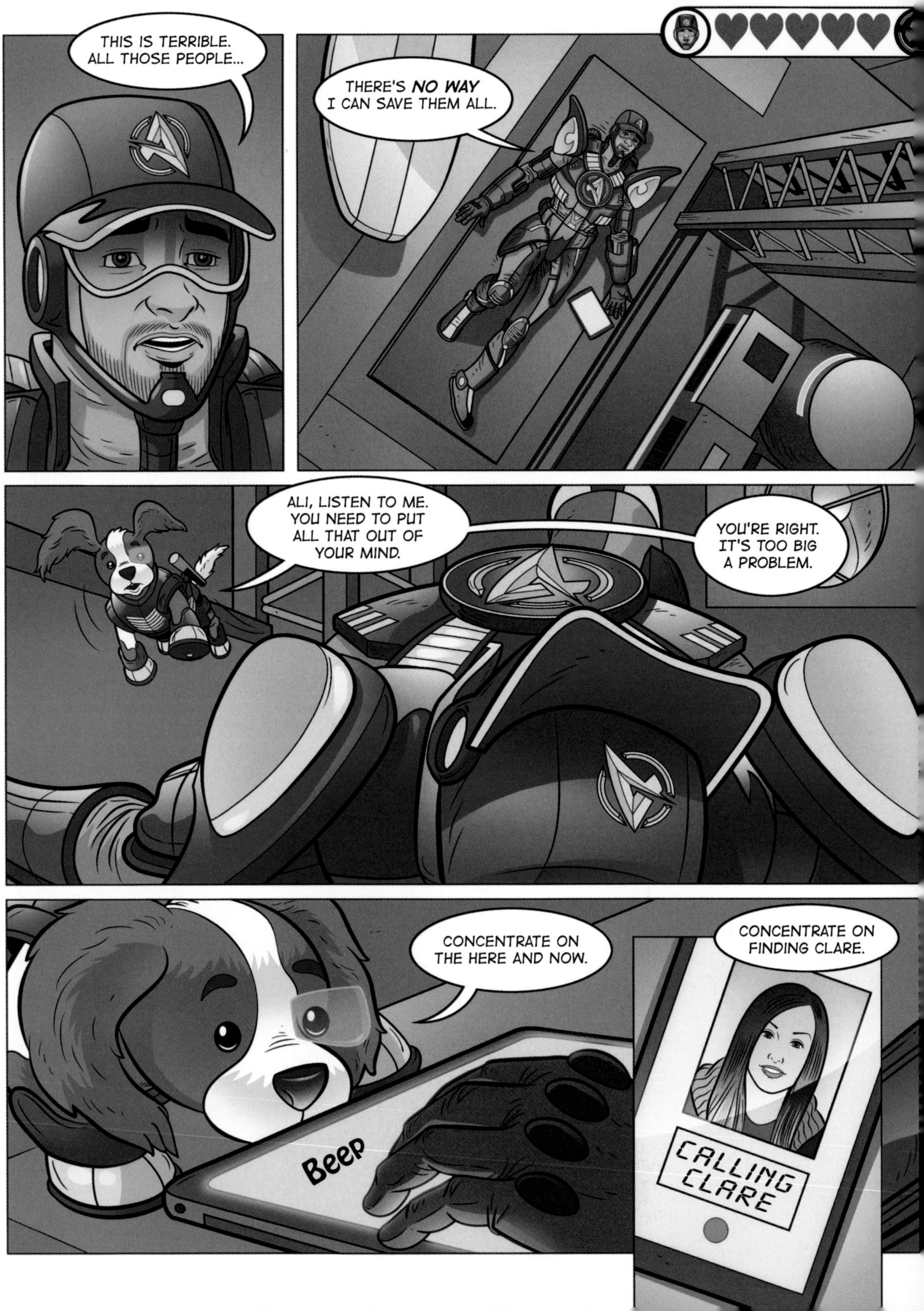
THIS IS TERRIBLE. ALL THOSE PEOPLE...
THERE'S NO WAY I CAN SAVE THEM ALL.
ALI, LISTEN TO ME. YOU NEED TO PUT ALL THAT OUT OF YOUR MIND.
YOU'RE RIGHT. IT'S TOO BIG A PROBLEM.
CONCENTRATE ON THE HERE AND NOW.
Beep
CONCENTRATE ON FINDING CLARE.
CALLING CLARE

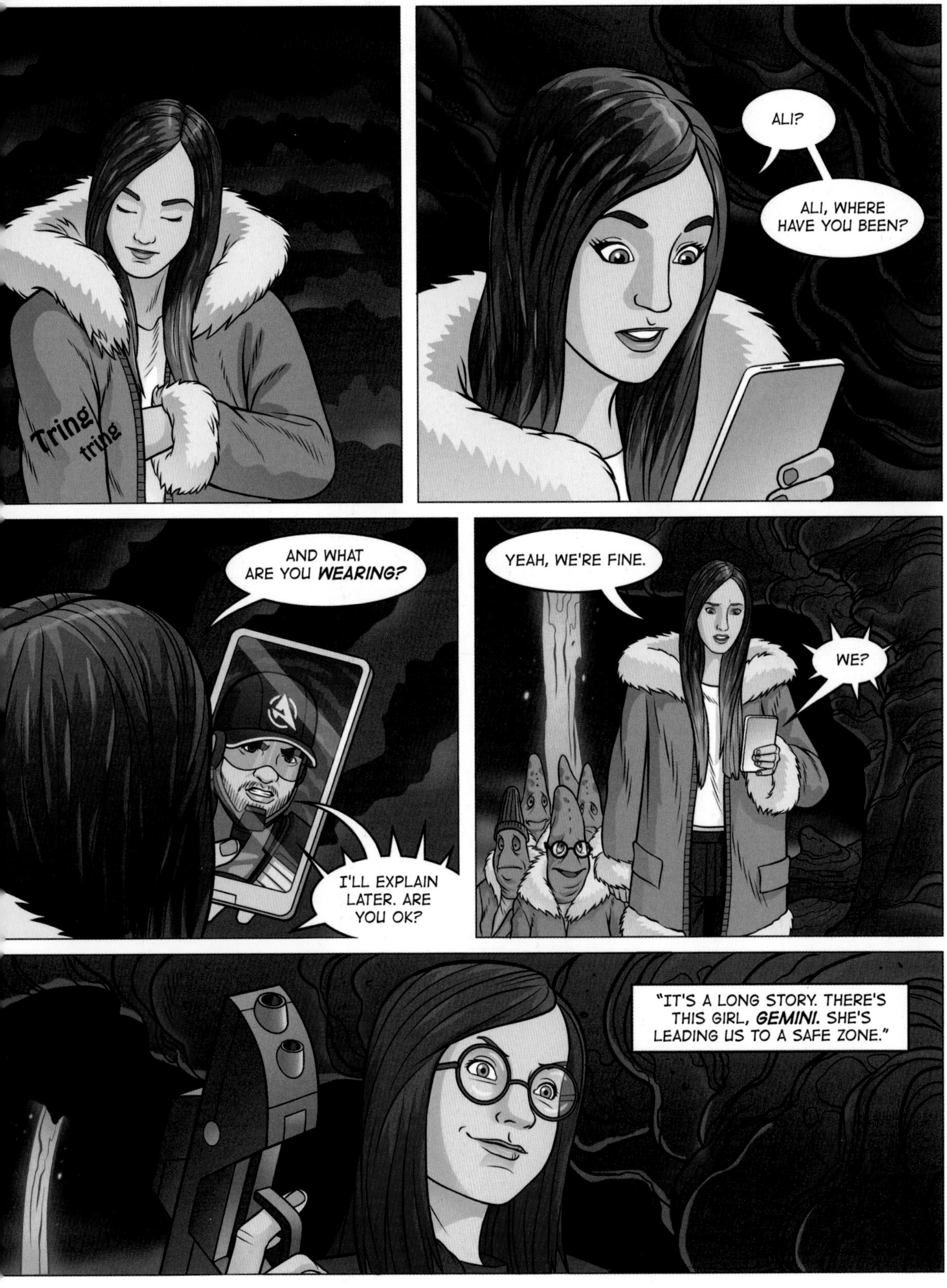
Tring
tring
ALI?
ALI, WHERE HAVE YOU BEEN?
AND WHAT ARE YOU *WEARING?*
I'LL EXPLAIN LATER. ARE YOU OK?
YEAH, WE'RE FINE.
WE?
"IT'S A LONG STORY. THERE'S THIS GIRL, *GEMINI.* SHE'S LEADING US TO A SAFE ZONE."

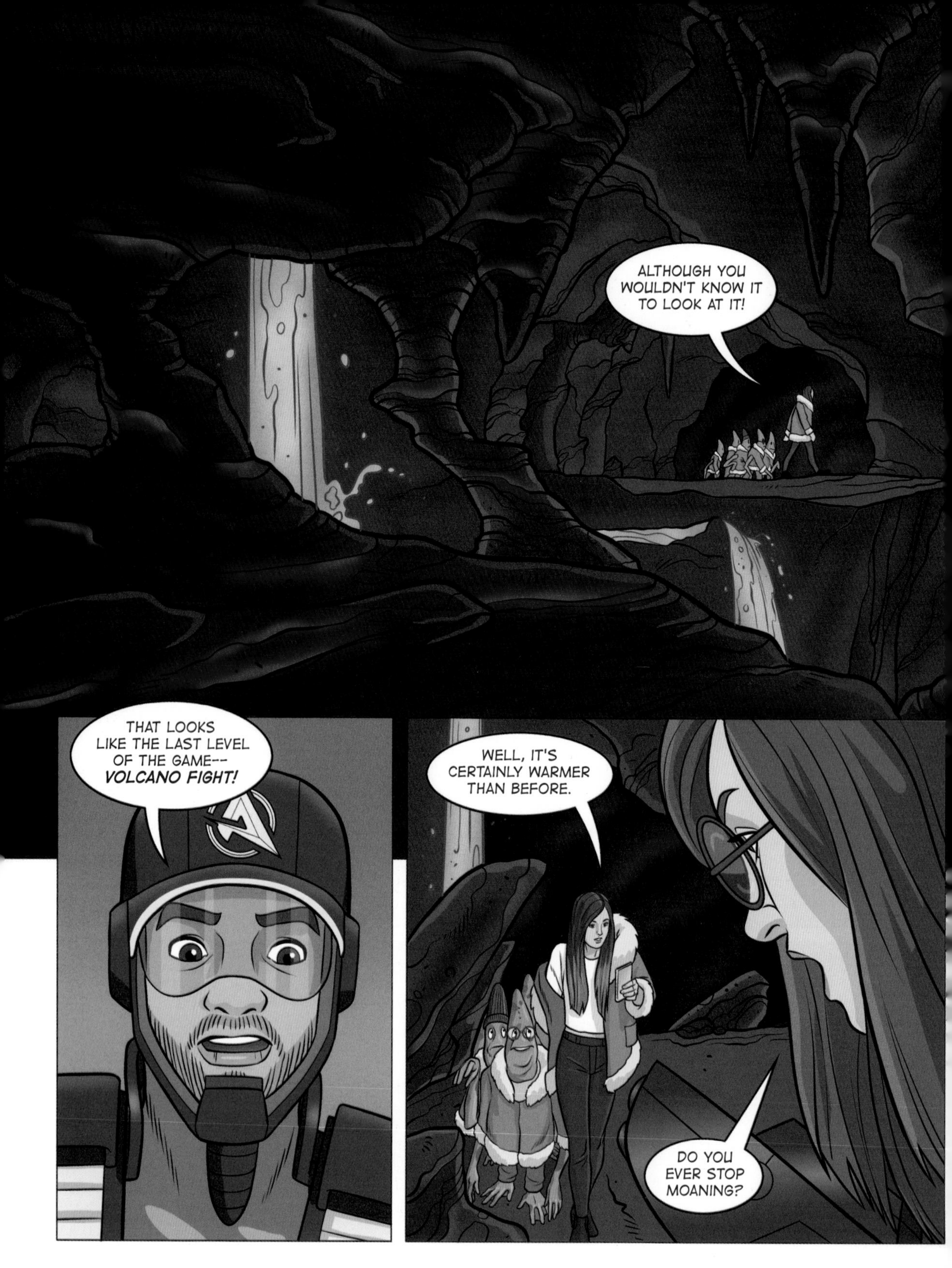
ALTHOUGH YOU WOULDN'T KNOW IT TO LOOK AT IT!
THAT LOOKS LIKE THE LAST LEVEL OF THE GAME-- *VOLCANO FIGHT!*
WELL, IT'S CERTAINLY WARMER THAN BEFORE.
DO YOU EVER STOP MOANING?

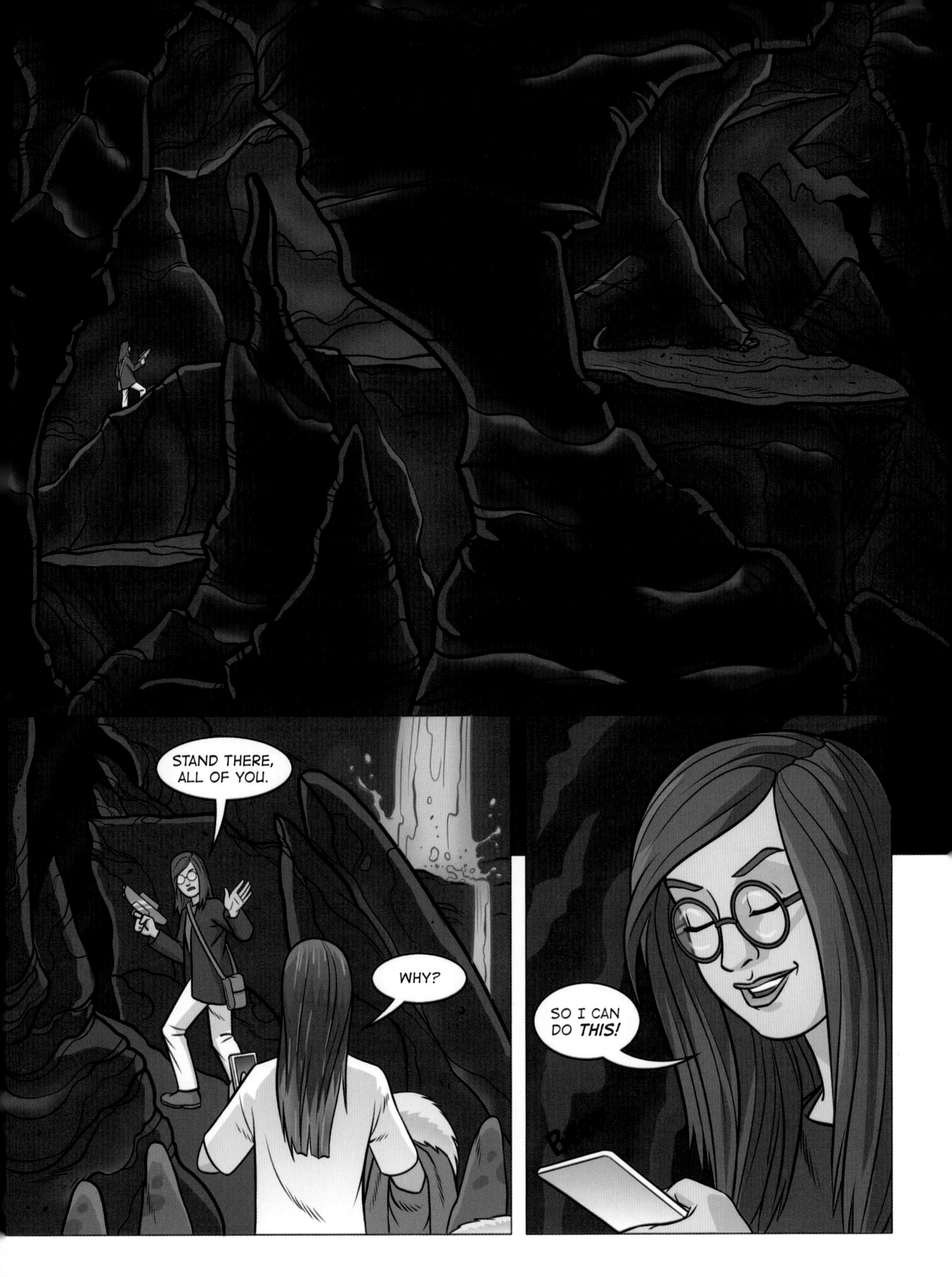
STAND THERE, ALL OF YOU.
WHY?
SO I CAN DO THIS!

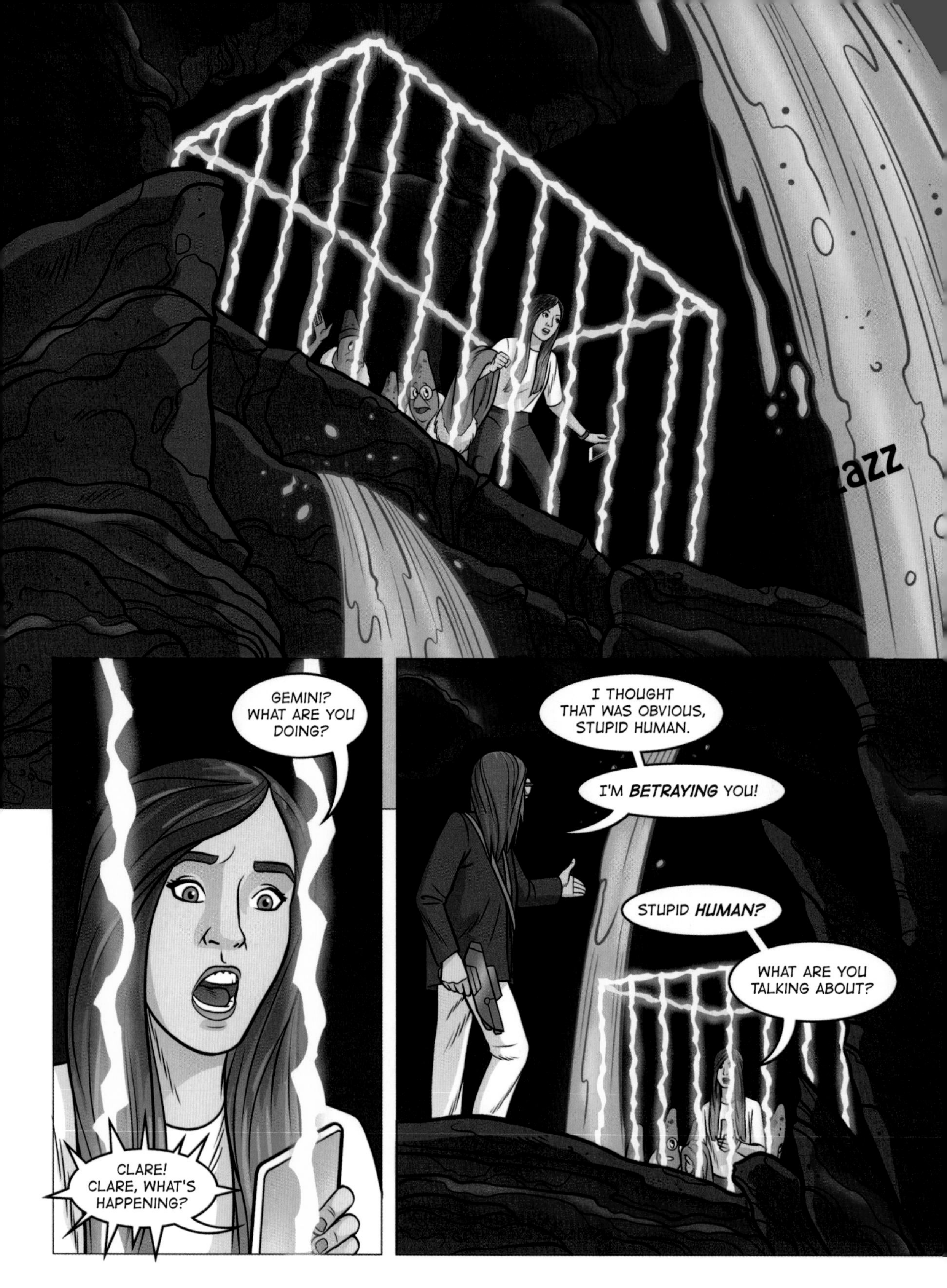
ZAZZ
GEMINI? WHAT ARE YOU DOING?
CLARE! CLARE, WHAT'S HAPPENING?
I THOUGHT THAT WAS OBVIOUS, STUPID HUMAN.
I'M **BETRAYING** YOU!
STUPID **HUMAN?**
WHAT ARE YOU TALKING ABOUT?

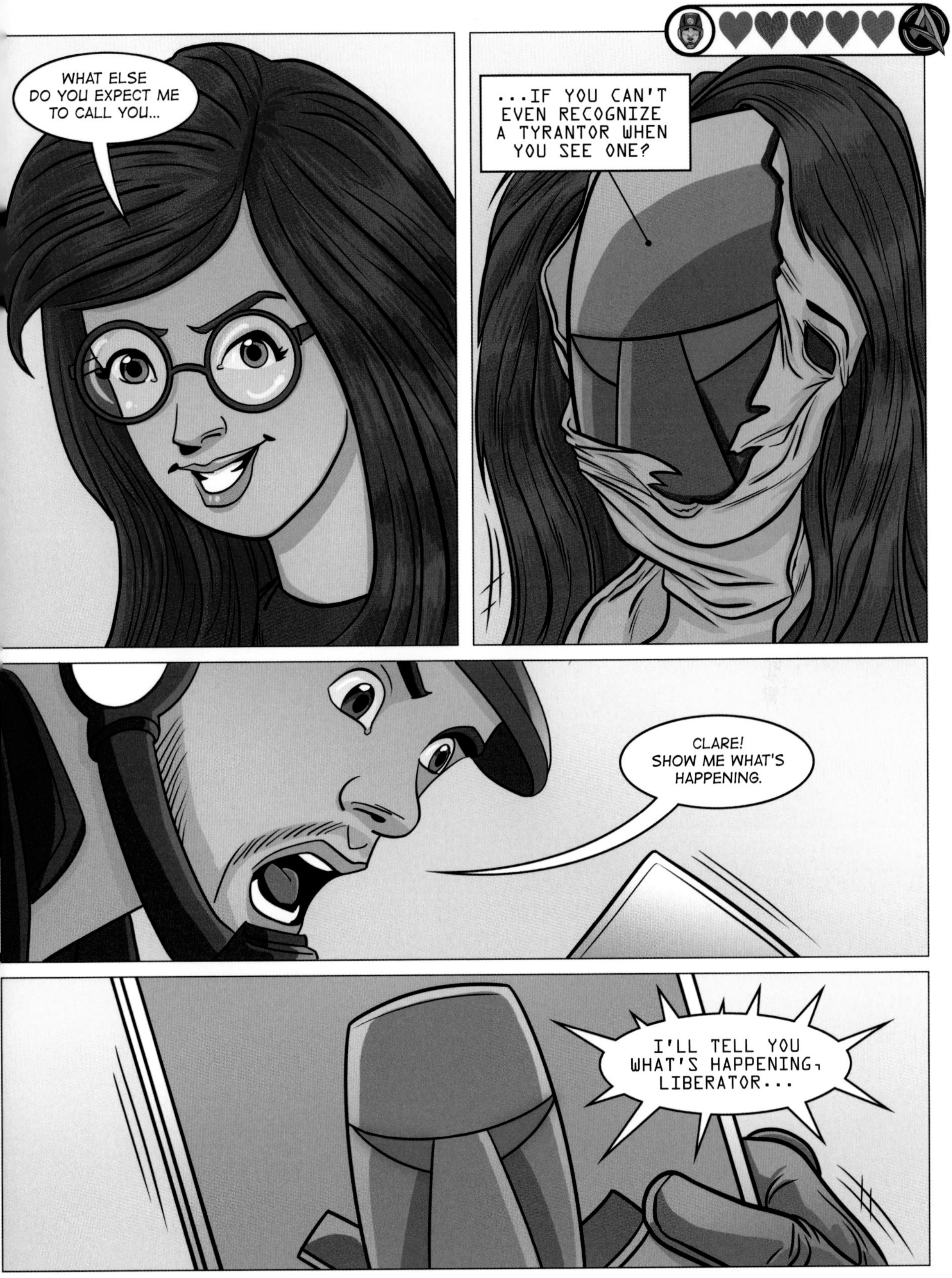
WHAT ELSE DO YOU EXPECT ME TO CALL YOU...
...IF YOU CAN'T EVEN RECOGNIZE A TYRANTOR WHEN YOU SEE ONE?
CLARE! SHOW ME WHAT'S HAPPENING.
I'LL TELL YOU WHAT'S HAPPENING, LIBERATOR...

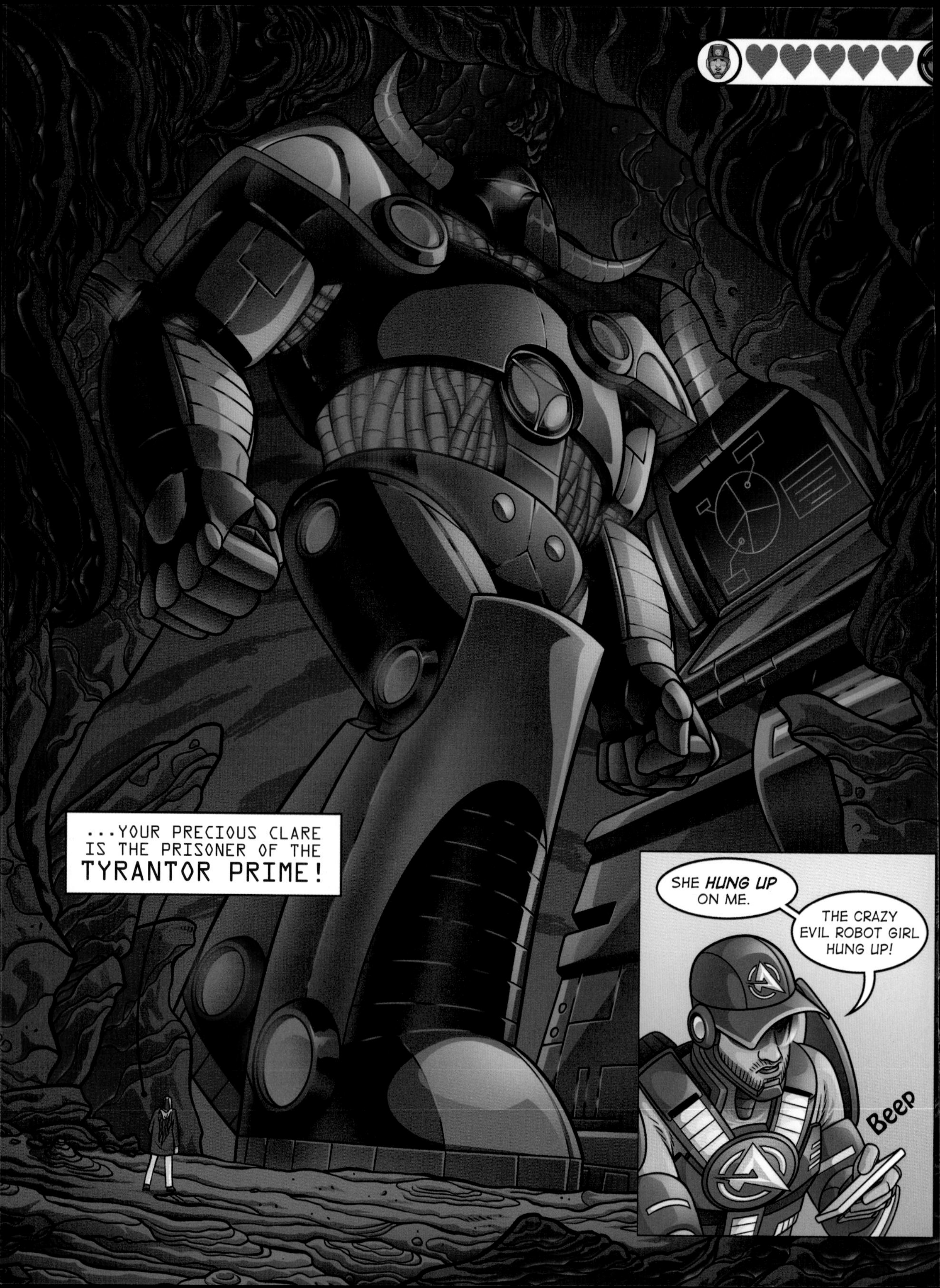
...YOUR PRECIOUS CLARE IS THE PRISONER OF THE TYRANTOR PRIME!
SHE HUNG UP ON ME.
THE CRAZY EVIL ROBOT GIRL HUNG UP!
Beep

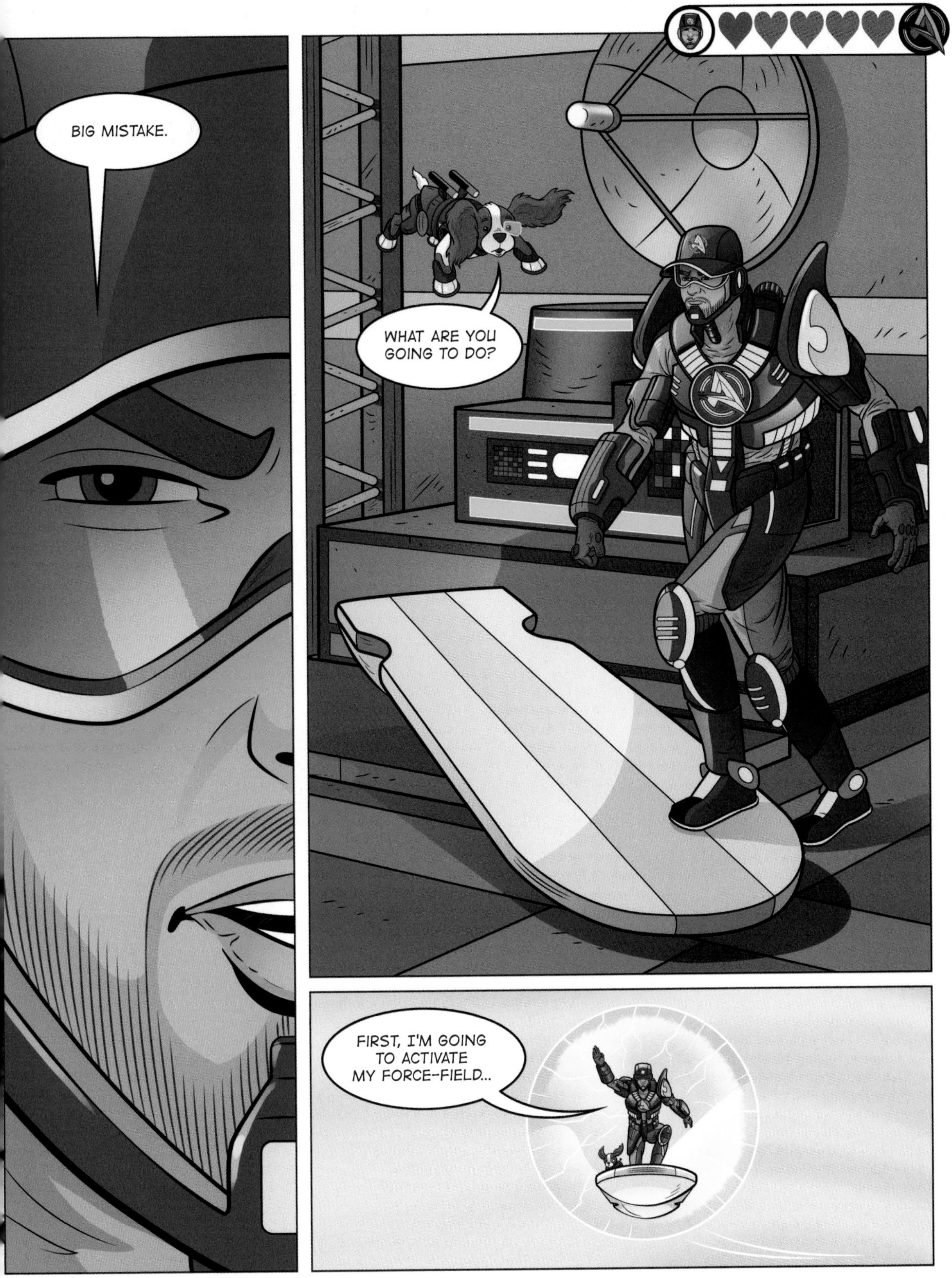
BIG MISTAKE.
WHAT ARE YOU GOING TO DO?
FIRST, I'M GOING TO ACTIVATE MY FORCE-FIELD...

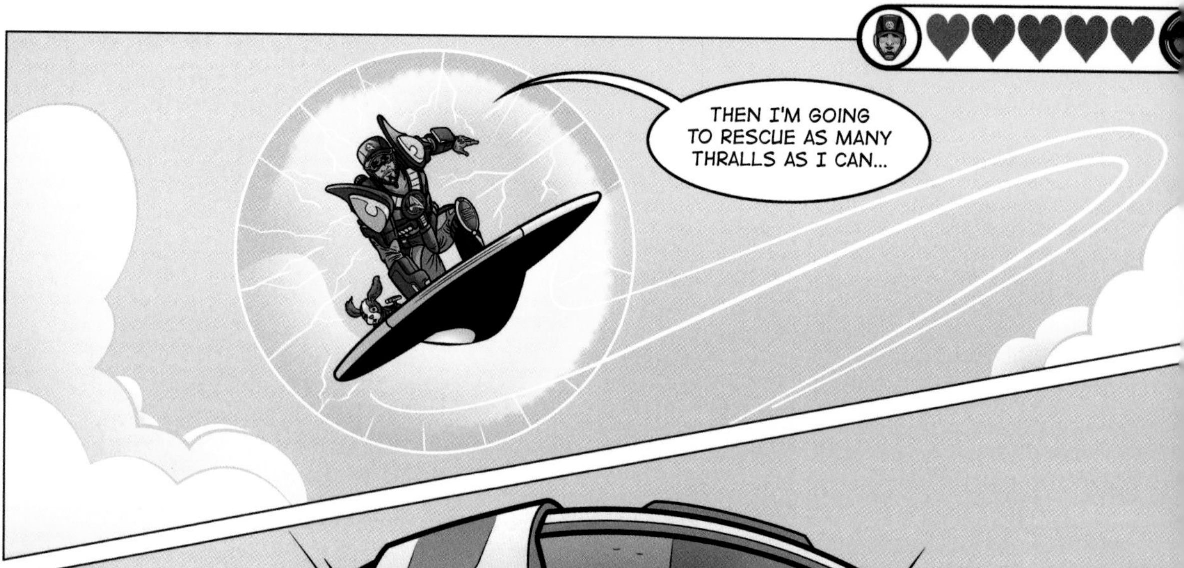
THEN I'M GOING
TO RESCUE AS MANY
THRALLS AS I CAN...

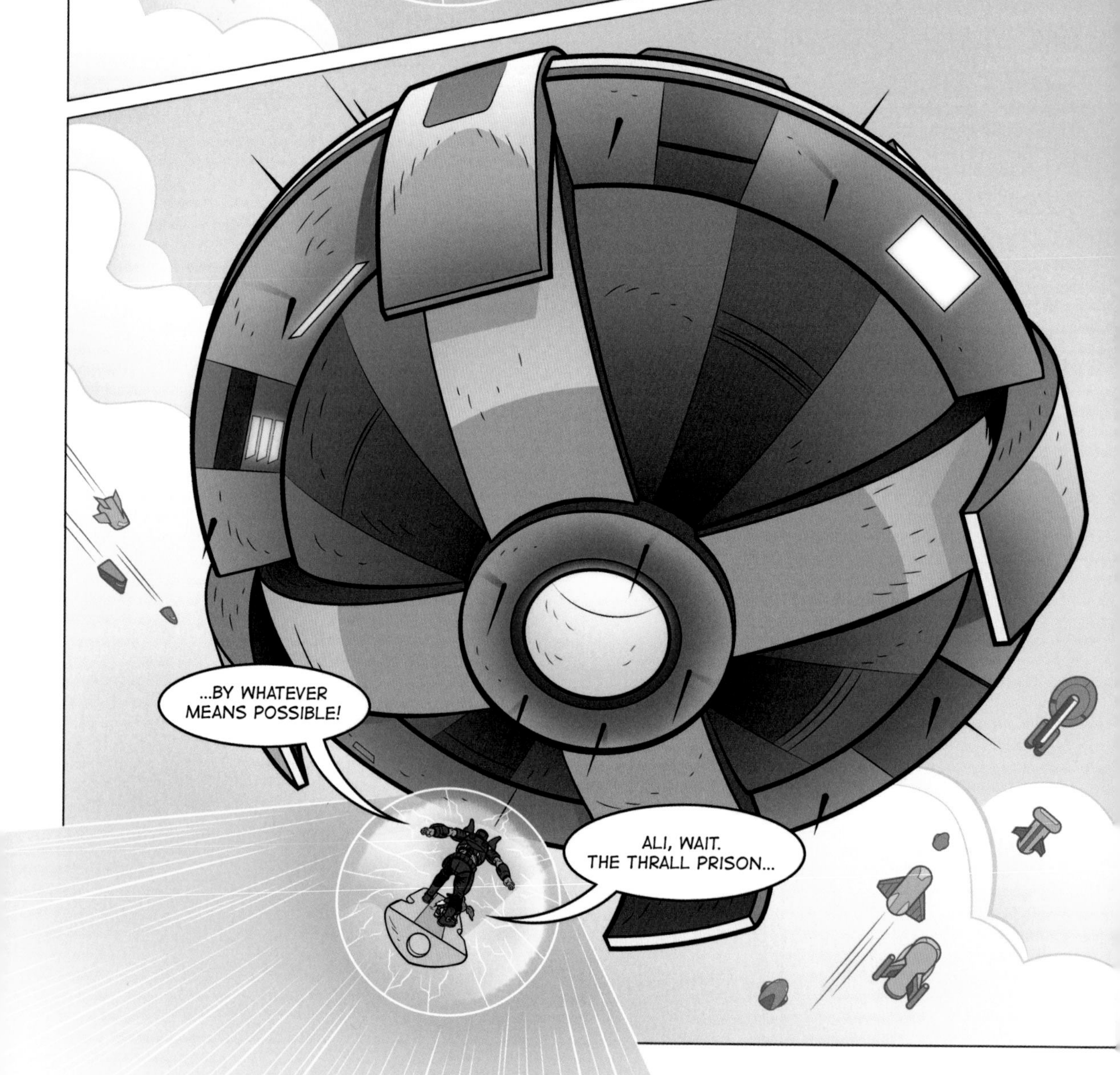
...BY WHATEVER
MEANS POSSIBLE!
ALI, WAIT.
THE THRALL PRISON...

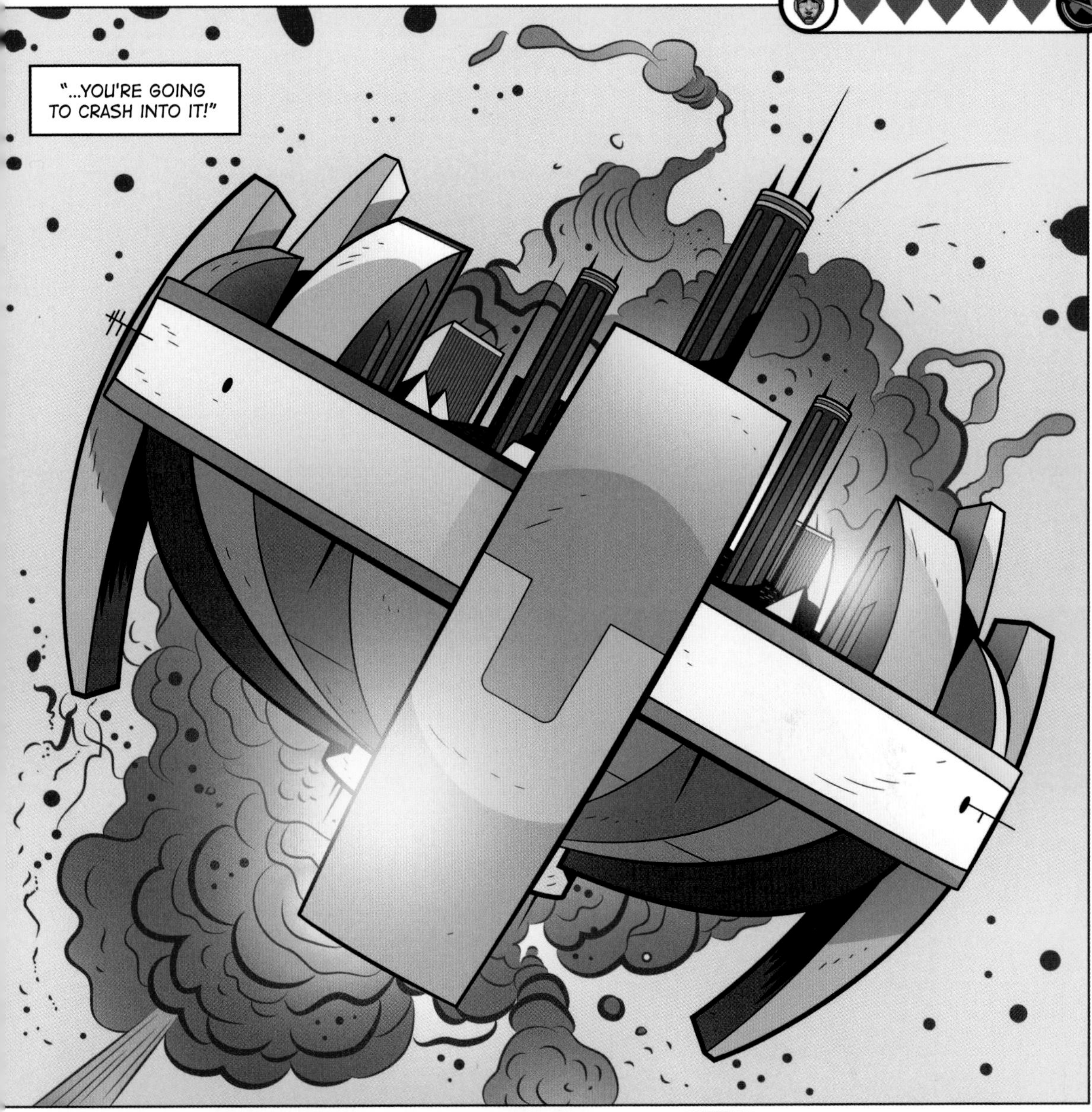
"...YOU'RE GOING TO CRASH INTO IT!"

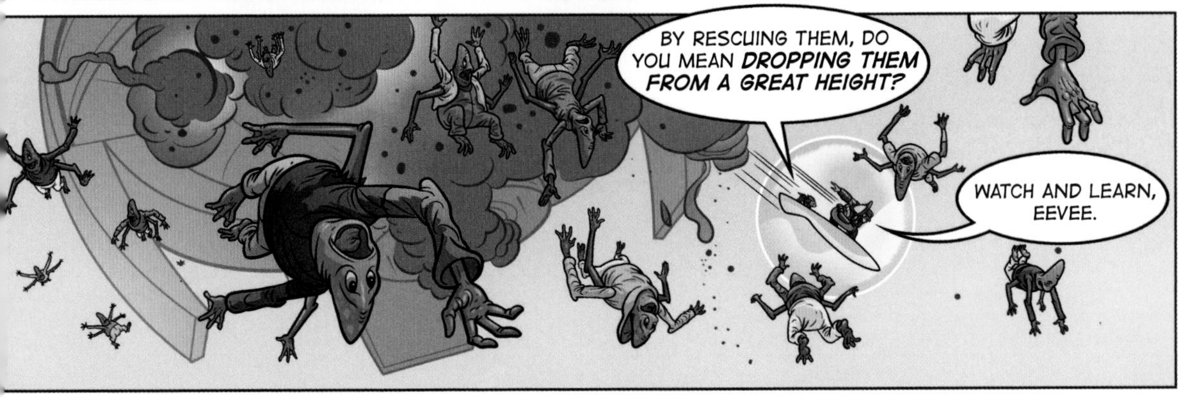
BY RESCUING THEM, DO YOU MEAN ***DROPPING THEM FROM A GREAT HEIGHT?***
WATCH AND LEARN, EEVEE.

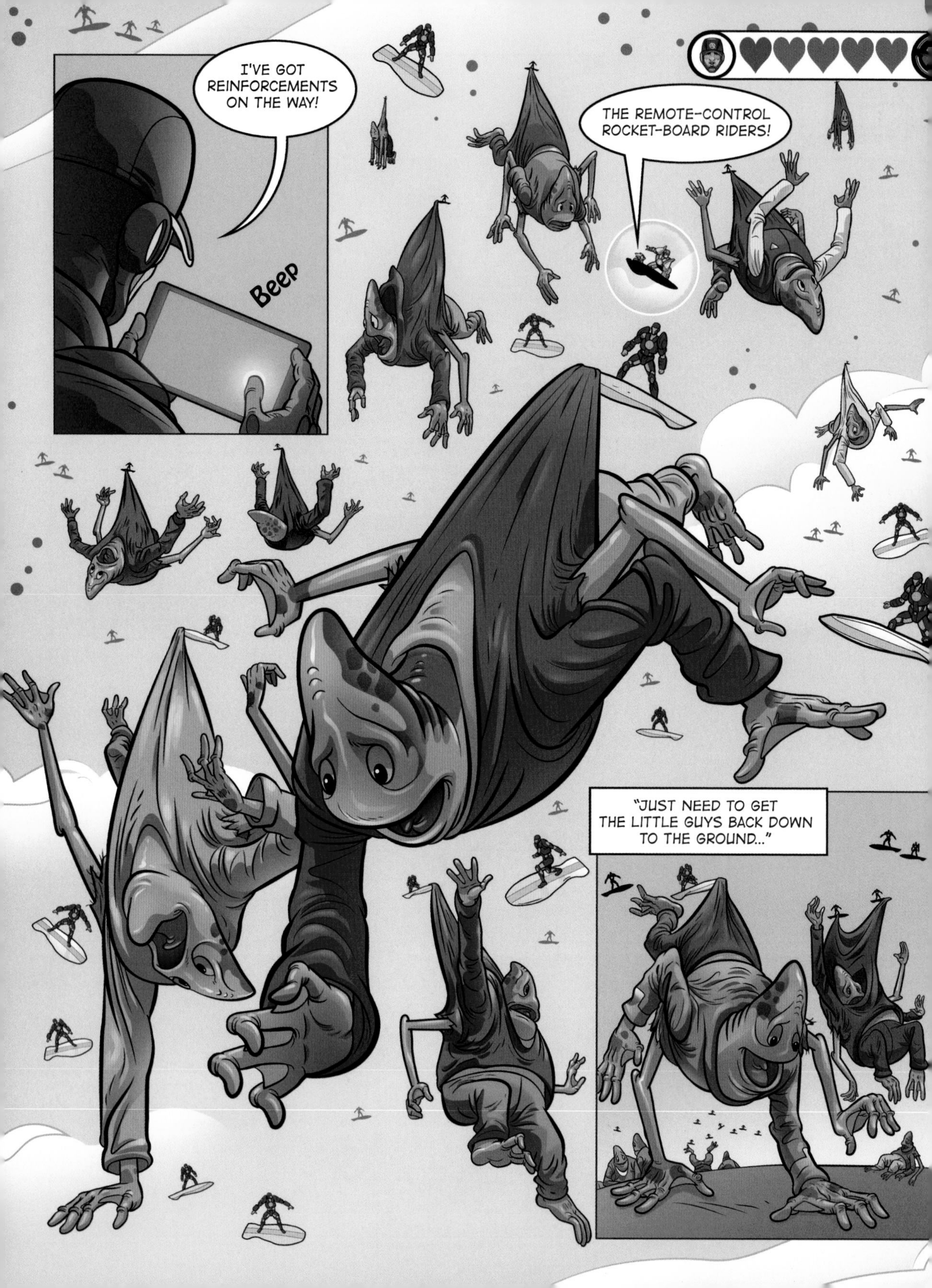
I'VE GOT REINFORCEMENTS ON THE WAY!
Beep
THE REMOTE-CONTROL ROCKET-BOARD RIDERS!
"JUST NEED TO GET THE LITTLE GUYS BACK DOWN TO THE GROUND..."

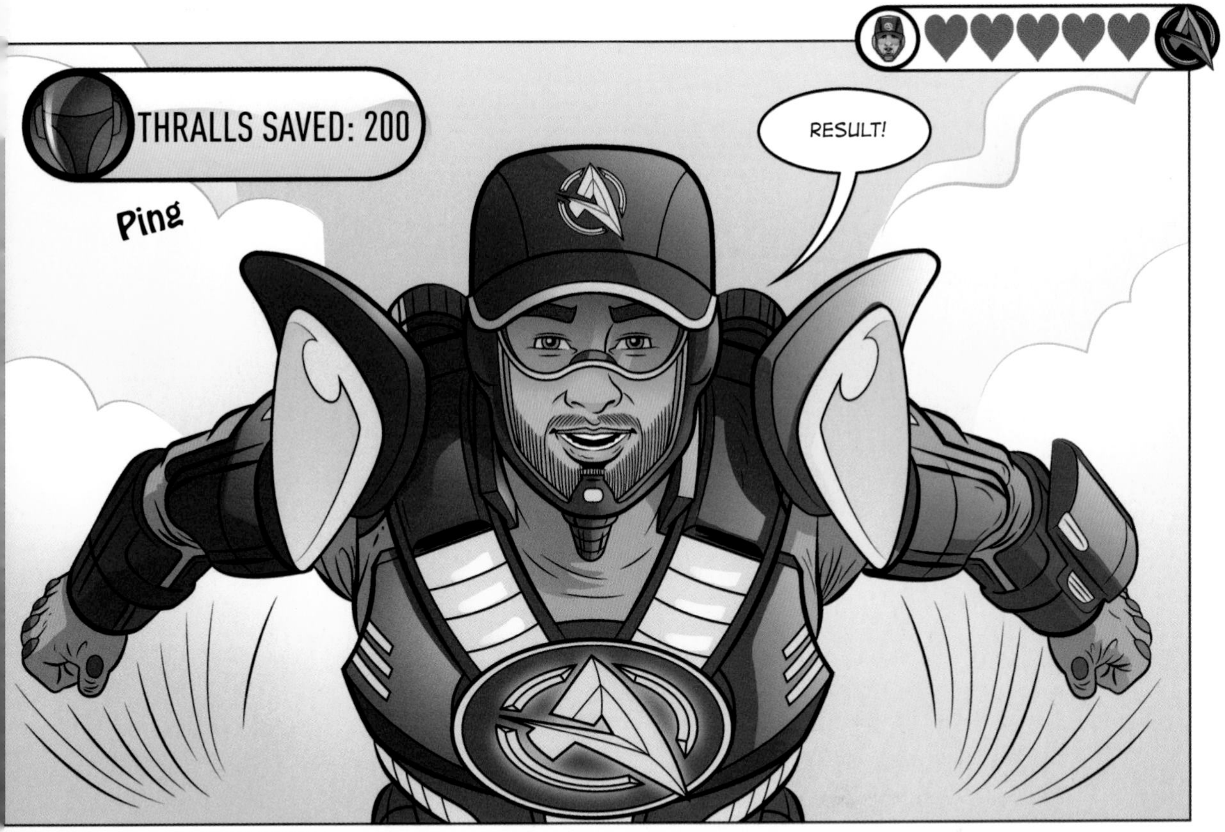
THRALLS SAVED: 200
Ping
RESULT!

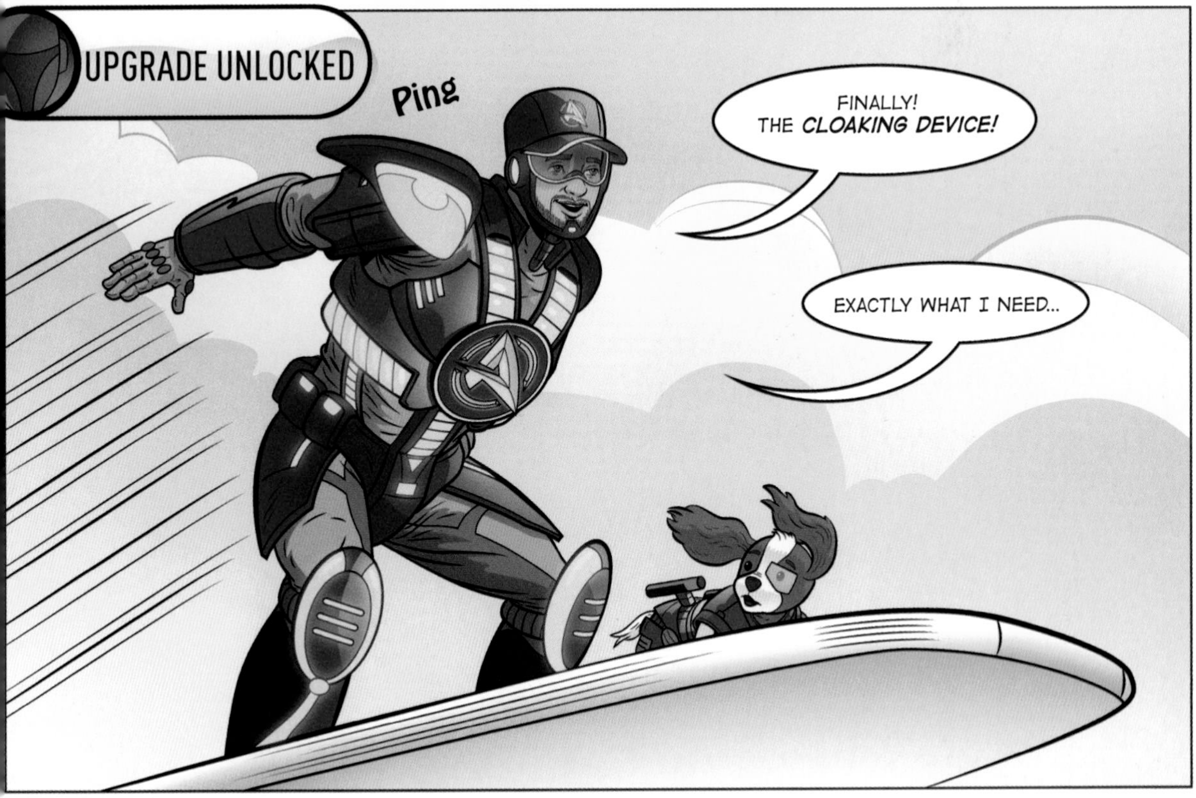
UPGRADE UNLOCKED
Ping
FINALLY! THE CLOAKING DEVICE!
EXACTLY WHAT I NEED...

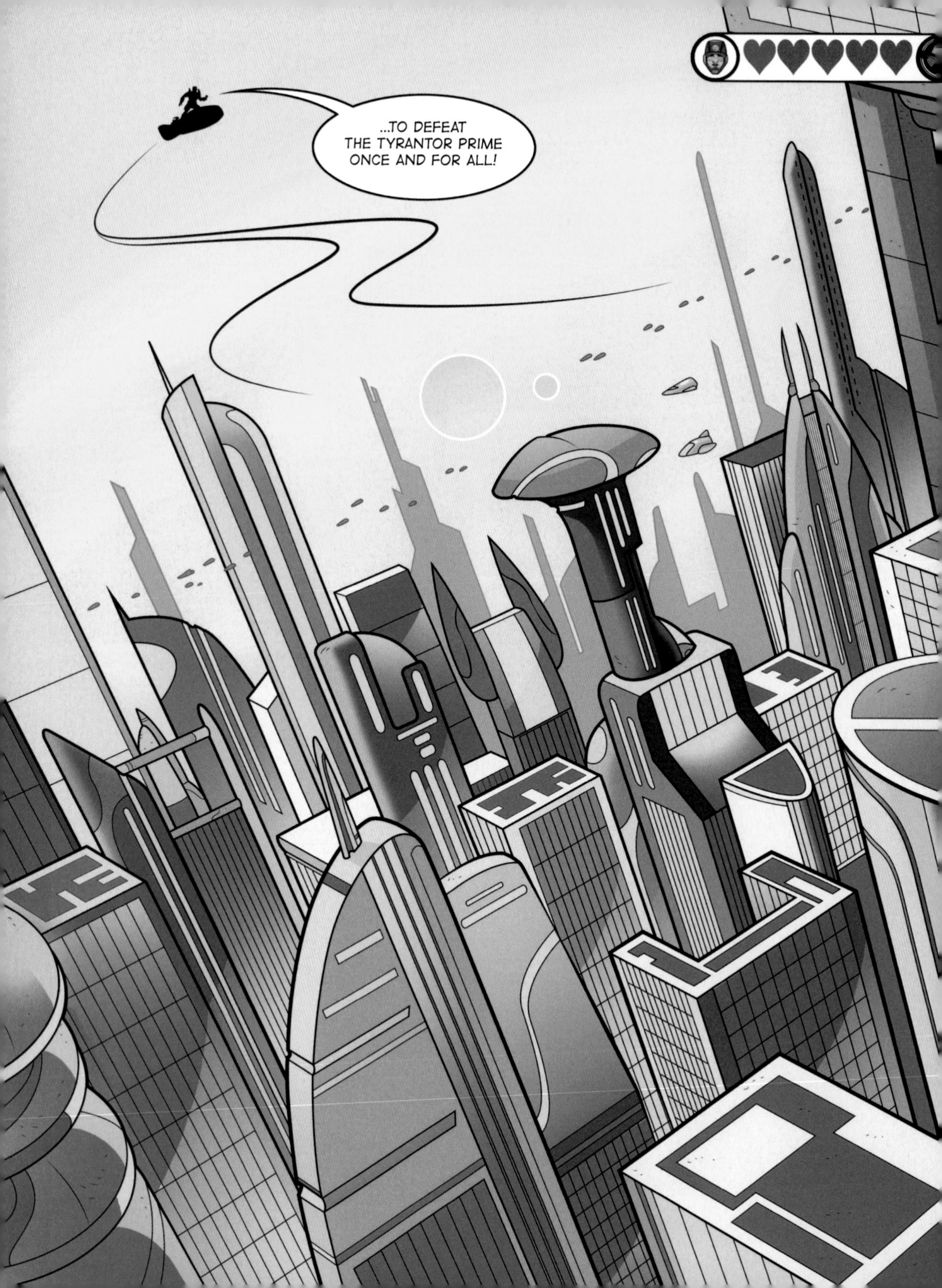
...TO DEFEAT THE TYRANTOR PRIME ONCE AND FOR ALL!

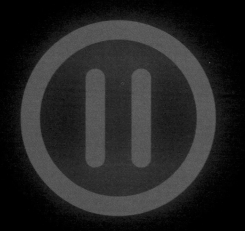

LEVEL EIGHT

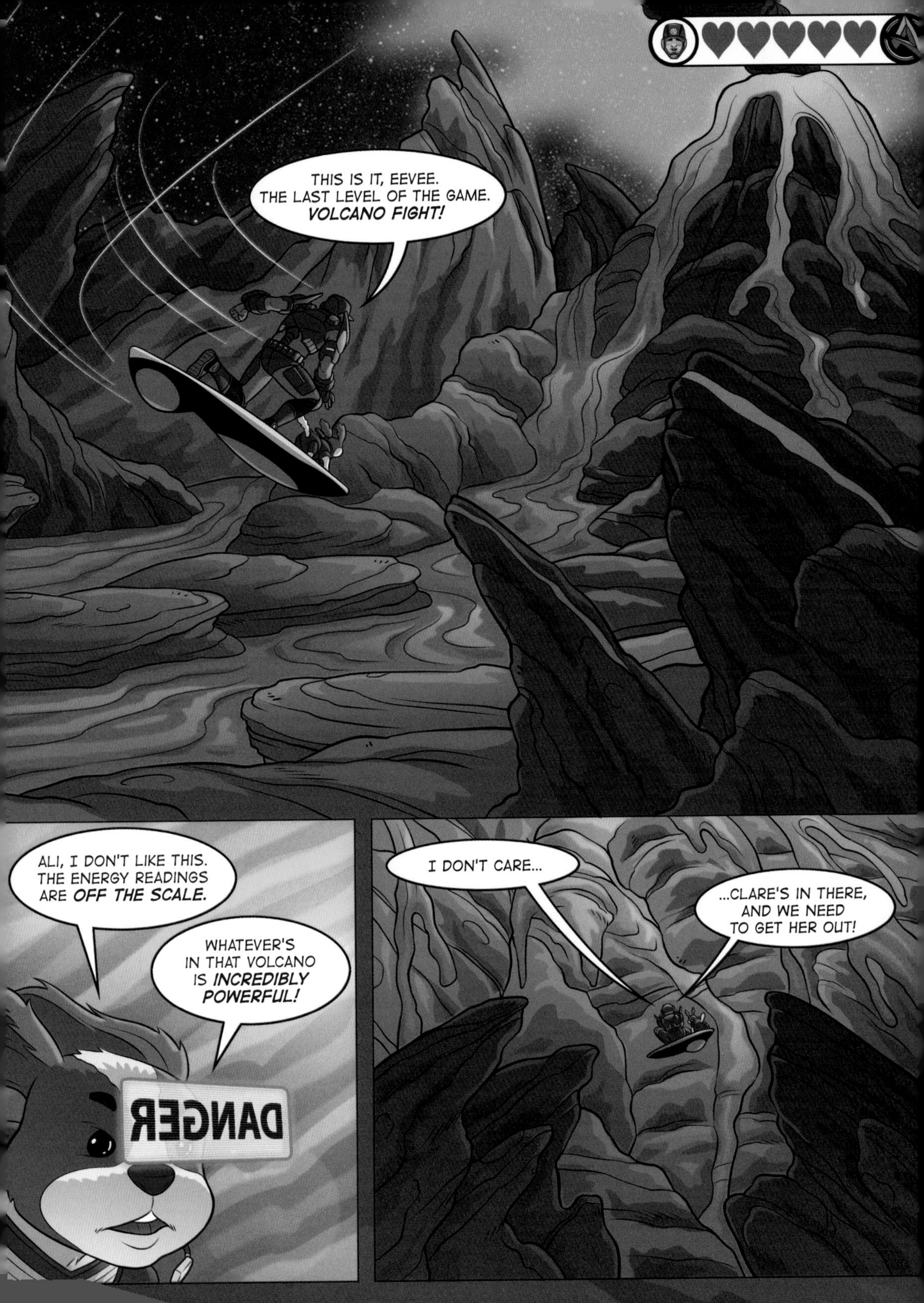
THIS IS IT, EEVEE. THE LAST LEVEL OF THE GAME. *VOLCANO FIGHT!*
ALI, I DON'T LIKE THIS. THE ENERGY READINGS ARE *OFF THE SCALE.*
WHATEVER'S IN THAT VOLCANO IS *INCREDIBLY POWERFUL!*
DANGER
I DON'T CARE...
...CLARE'S IN THERE, AND WE NEED TO GET HER OUT!

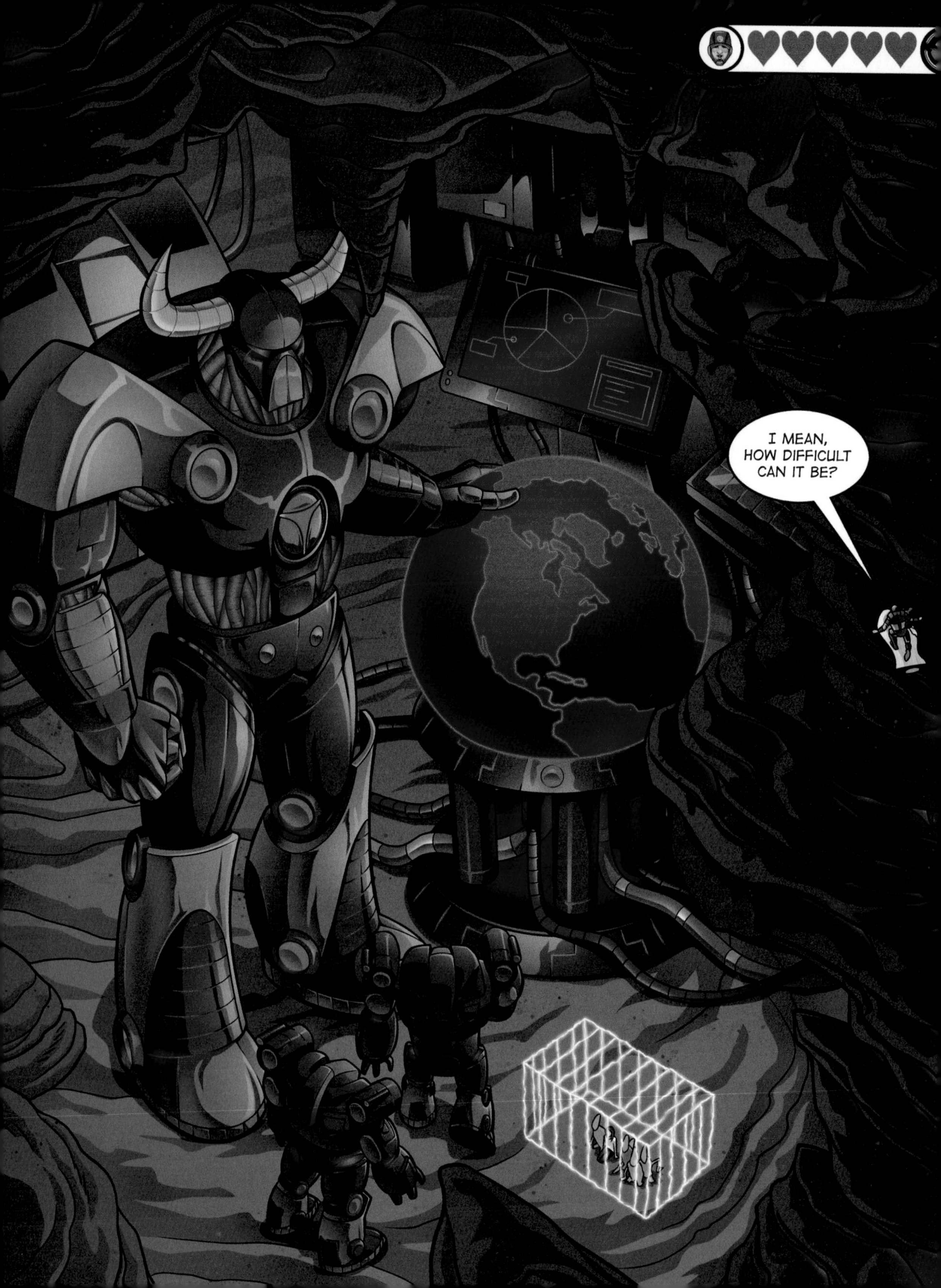
I MEAN, HOW DIFFICULT CAN IT BE?

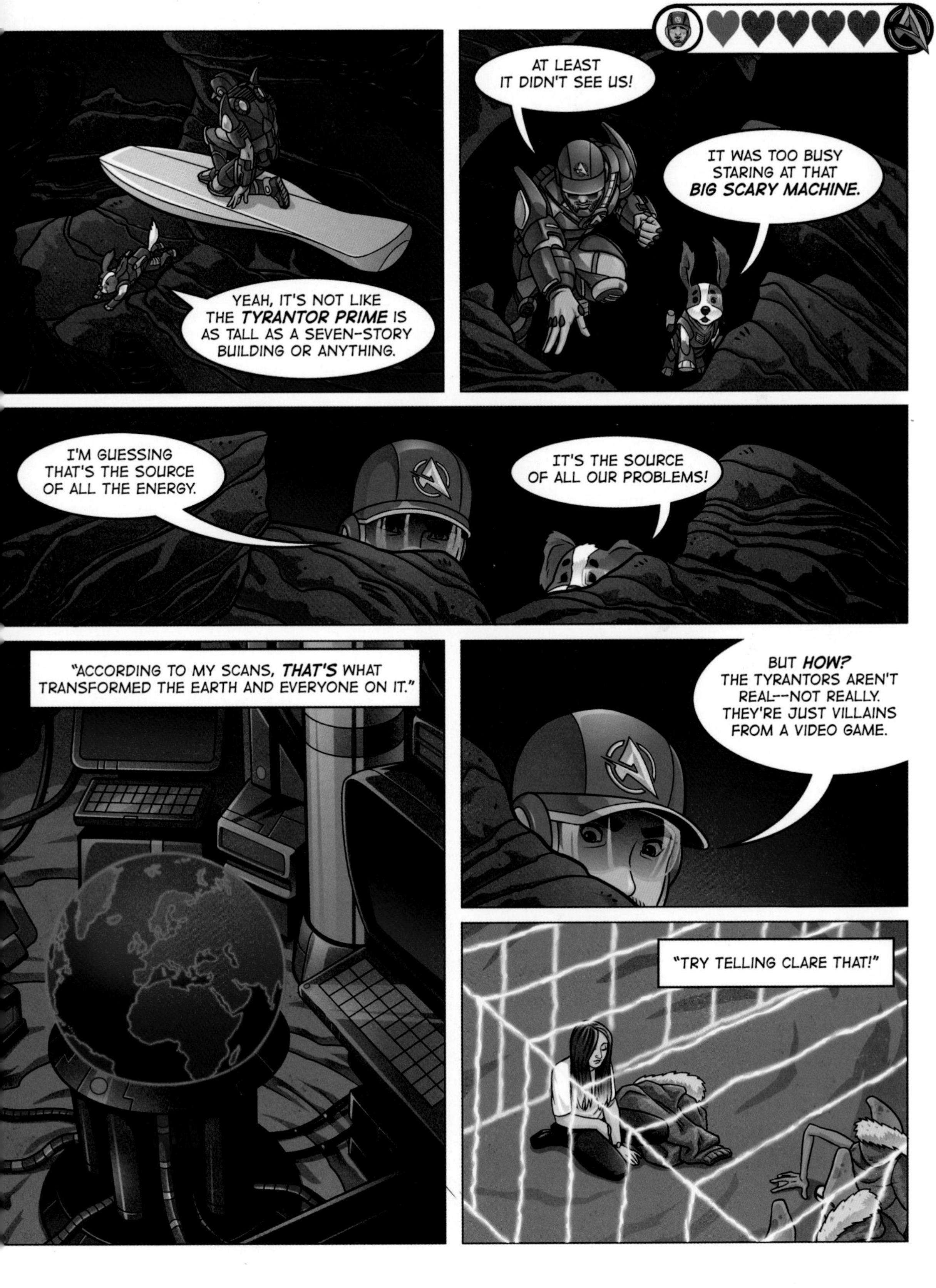
YEAH, IT'S NOT LIKE THE TYRANTOR PRIME IS AS TALL AS A SEVEN-STORY BUILDING OR ANYTHING.
AT LEAST IT DIDN'T SEE US!
IT WAS TOO BUSY STARING AT THAT BIG SCARY MACHINE.
I'M GUESSING THAT'S THE SOURCE OF ALL THE ENERGY.
IT'S THE SOURCE OF ALL OUR PROBLEMS!
"ACCORDING TO MY SCANS, THAT'S WHAT TRANSFORMED THE EARTH AND EVERYONE ON IT."
BUT HOW? THE TYRANTORS AREN'T REAL--NOT REALLY. THEY'RE JUST VILLAINS FROM A VIDEO GAME.
"TRY TELLING CLARE THAT!"

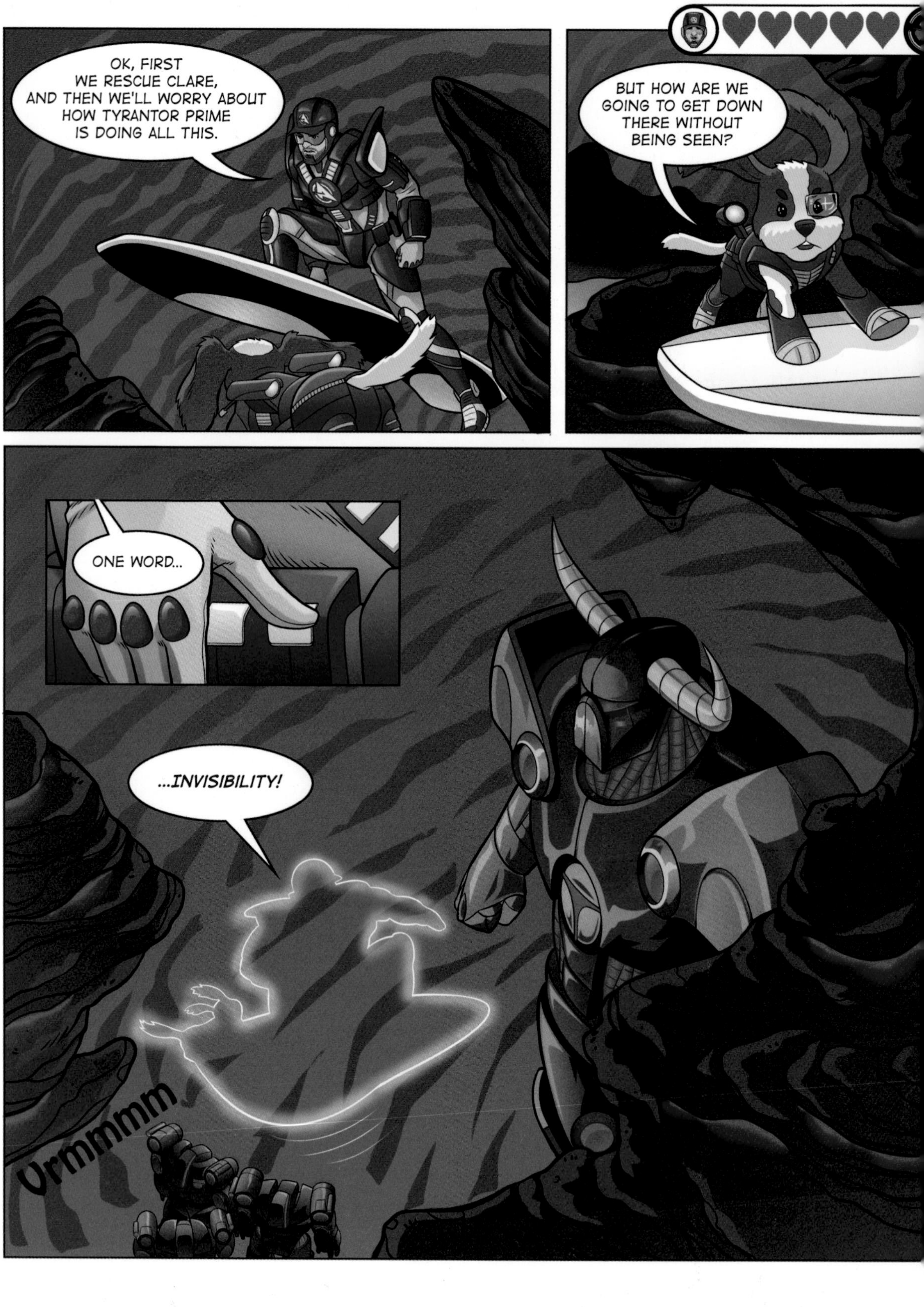
OK, FIRST WE RESCUE CLARE, AND THEN WE'LL WORRY ABOUT HOW TYRANTOR PRIME IS DOING ALL THIS.
BUT HOW ARE WE GOING TO GET DOWN THERE WITHOUT BEING SEEN?
ONE WORD...
...INVISIBILITY!
Vrmmmm

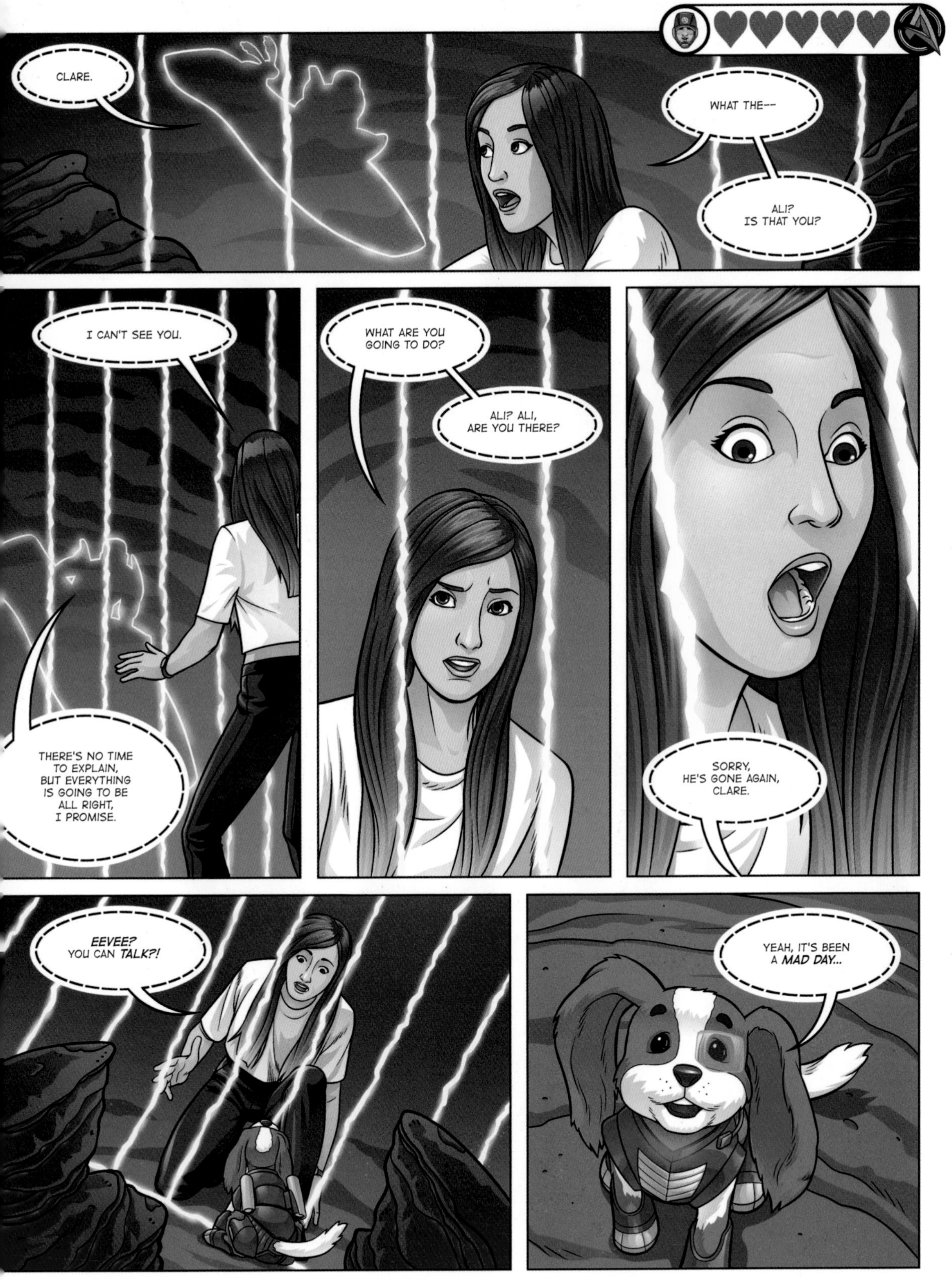
CLARE.
WHAT THE--
ALI?
IS THAT YOU?
I CAN'T SEE YOU.
THERE'S NO TIME
TO EXPLAIN,
BUT EVERYTHING
IS GOING TO BE
ALL RIGHT,
I PROMISE.
WHAT ARE YOU
GOING TO DO?
ALI? ALI,
ARE YOU THERE?
SORRY,
HE'S GONE AGAIN,
CLARE.
EEVEE?
YOU CAN *TALK?!*
YEAH, IT'S BEEN
A *MAD DAY...*

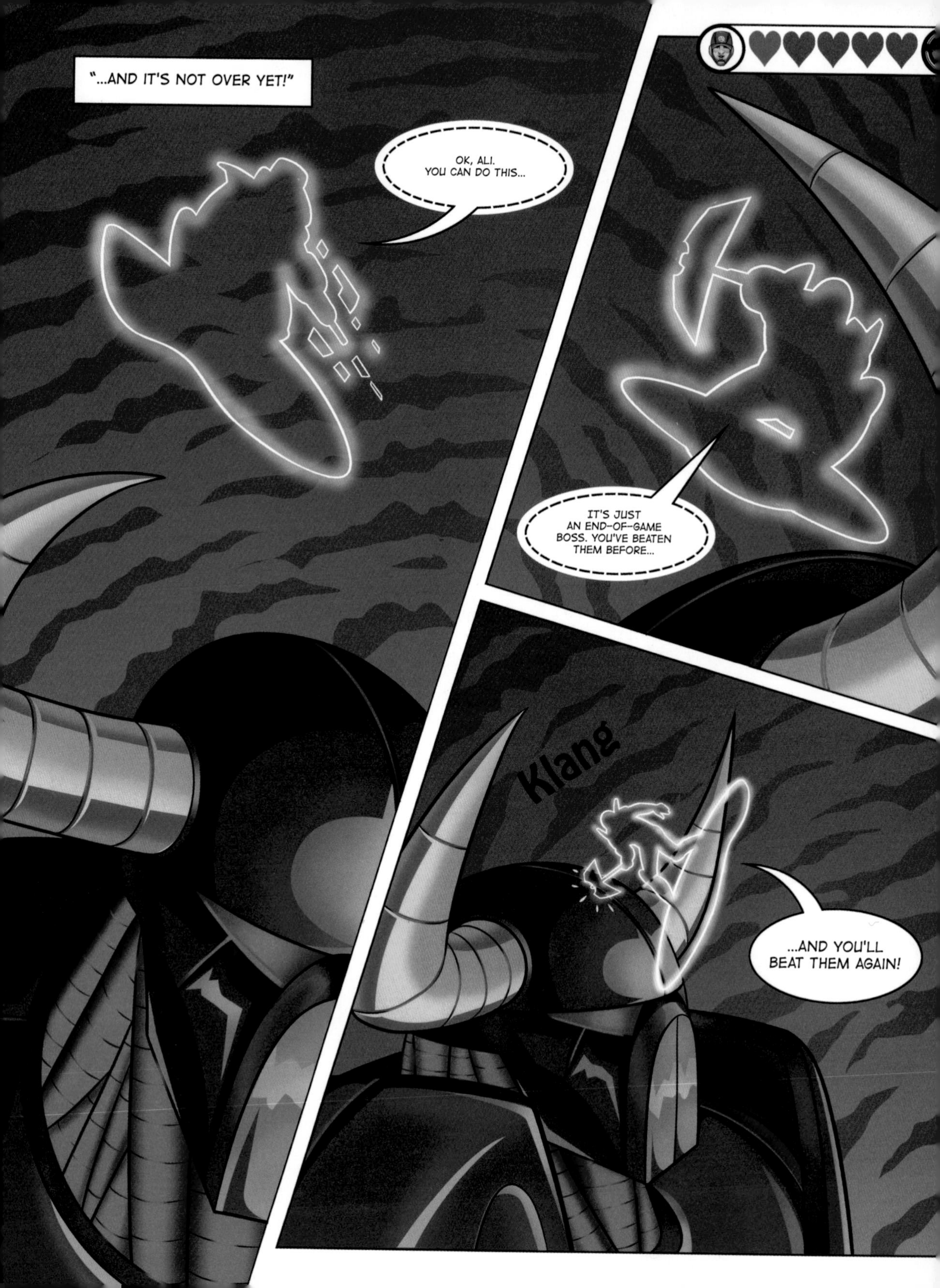
"...AND IT'S NOT OVER YET!"
OK, ALI. YOU CAN DO THIS...
IT'S JUST AN END-OF-GAME BOSS. YOU'VE BEATEN THEM BEFORE...
Klang
...AND YOU'LL BEAT THEM AGAIN!

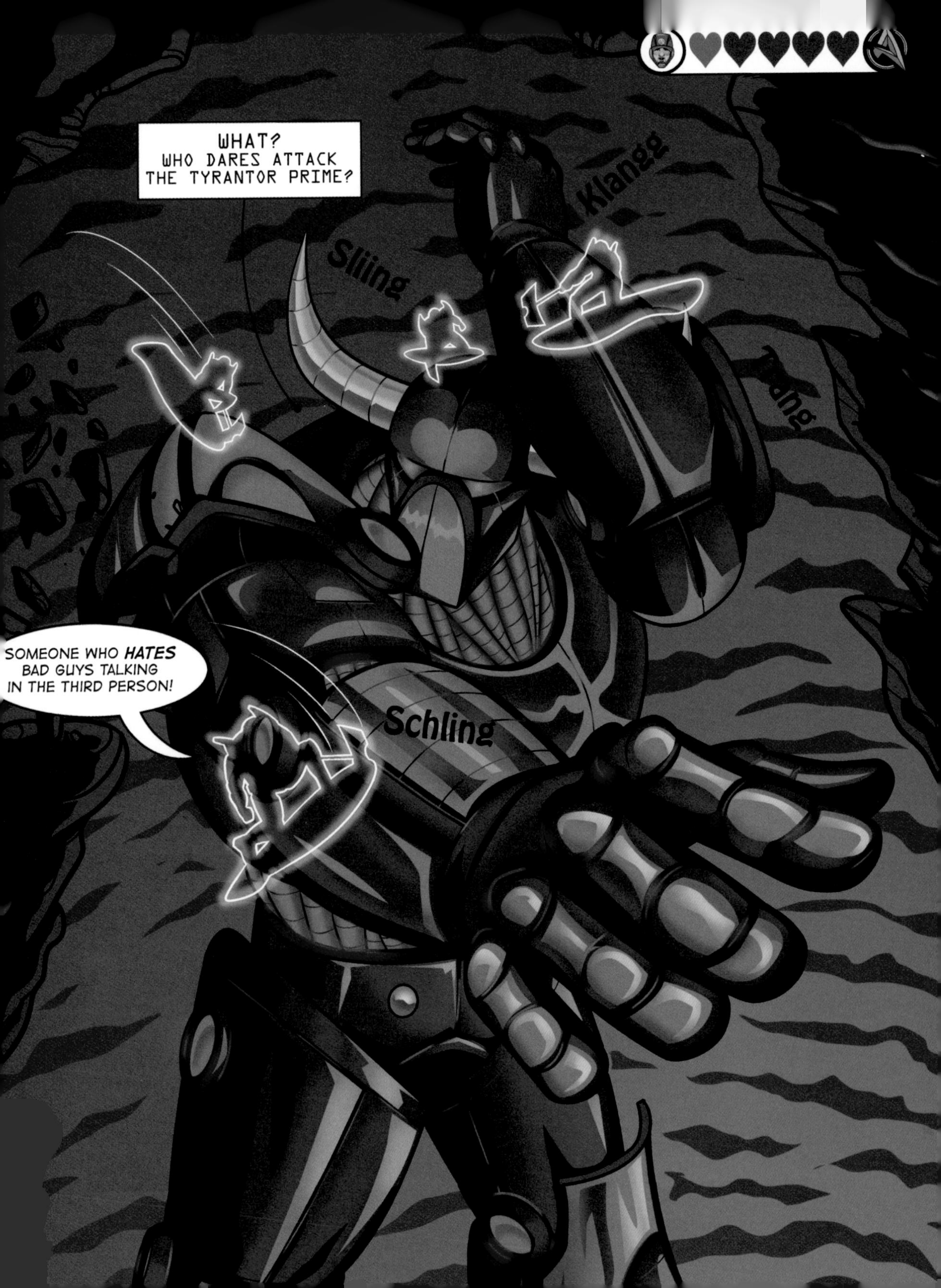
WHAT? WHO DARES ATTACK THE TYRANTOR PRIME?
Klangg
Sliing
Tang
SOMEONE WHO ***HATES*** BAD GUYS TALKING IN THE THIRD PERSON!
Schling

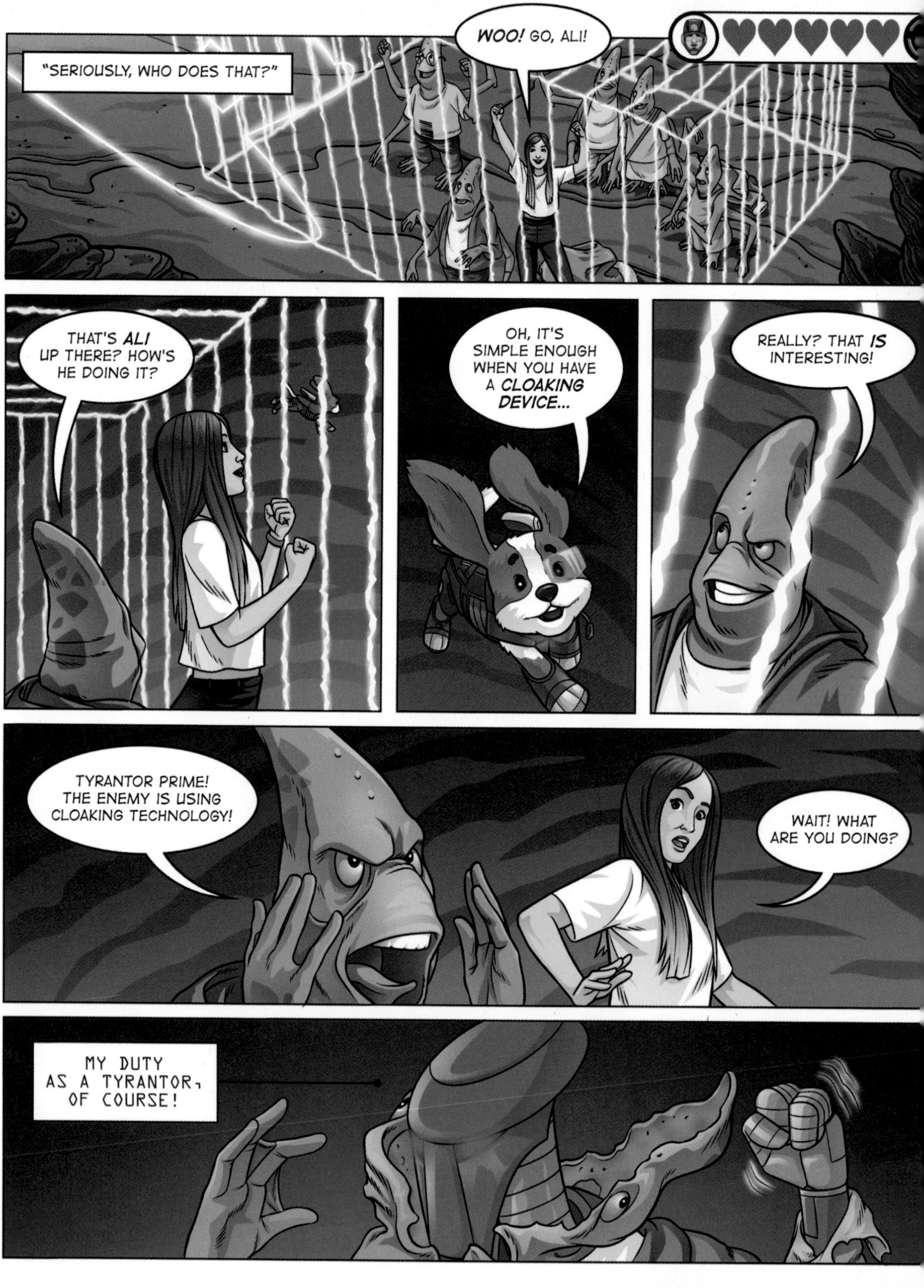
"SERIOUSLY, WHO DOES THAT?"
WOO! GO, ALI!
THAT'S ALI UP THERE? HOW'S HE DOING IT?
OH, IT'S SIMPLE ENOUGH WHEN YOU HAVE A CLOAKING DEVICE...
REALLY? THAT IS INTERESTING!
TYRANTOR PRIME! THE ENEMY IS USING CLOAKING TECHNOLOGY!
WAIT! WHAT ARE YOU DOING?
MY DUTY AS A TYRANTOR, OF COURSE!

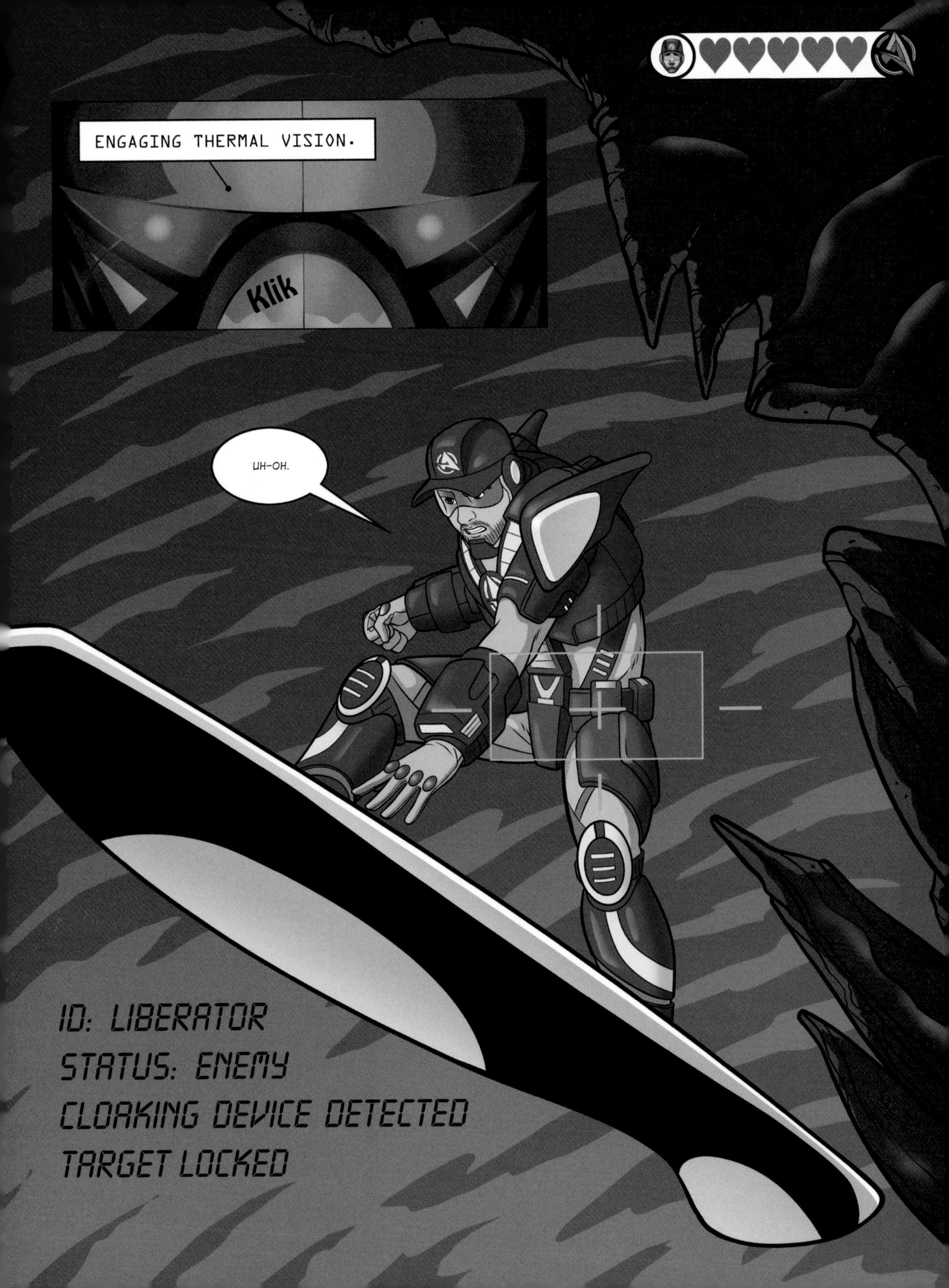
ENGAGING THERMAL VISION.
Klik
UH-OH.
ID: LIBERATOR
STATUS: ENEMY
CLOAKING DEVICE DETECTED
TARGET LOCKED

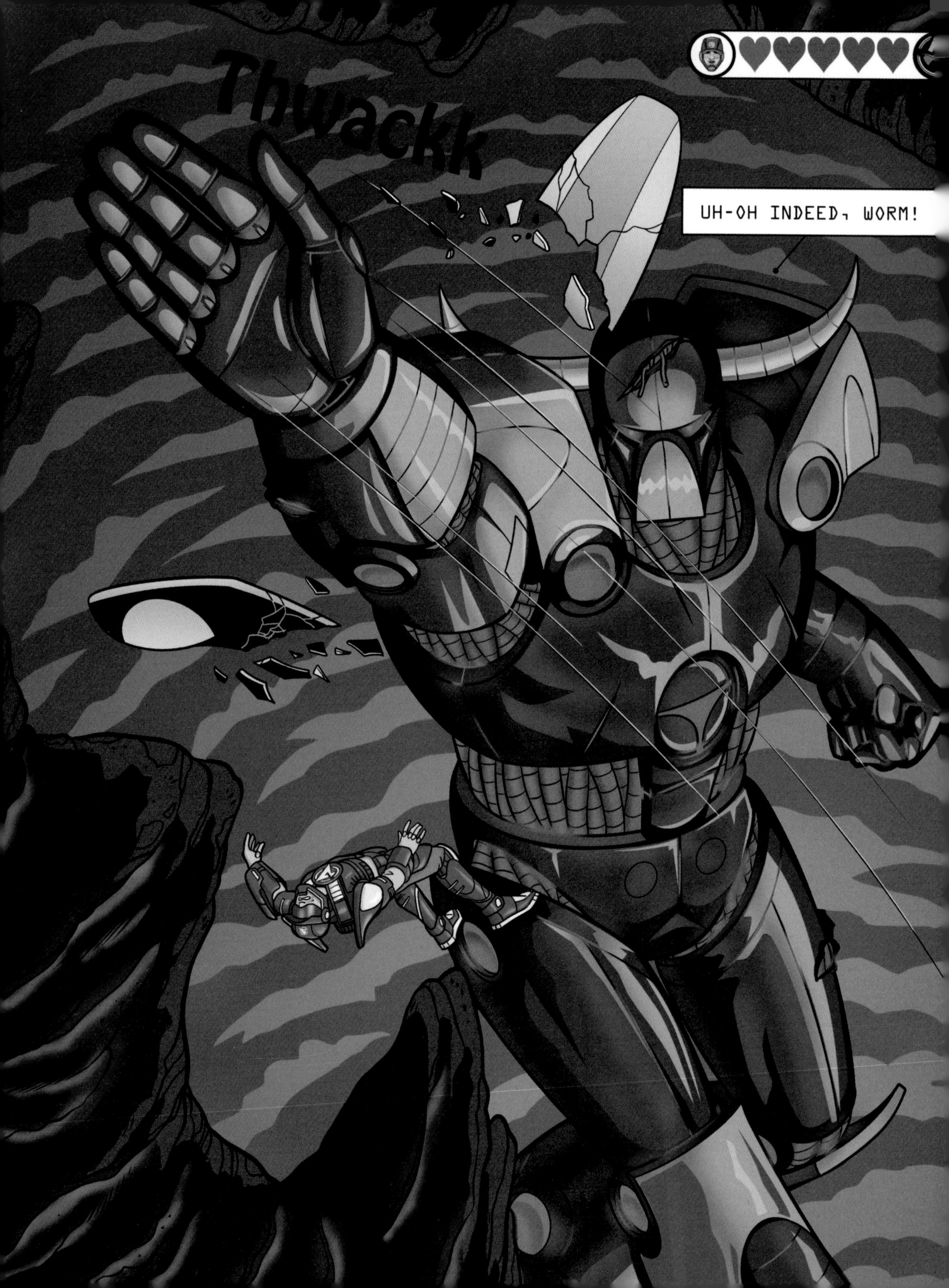
Thwackk
UH-OH INDEED, WORM!

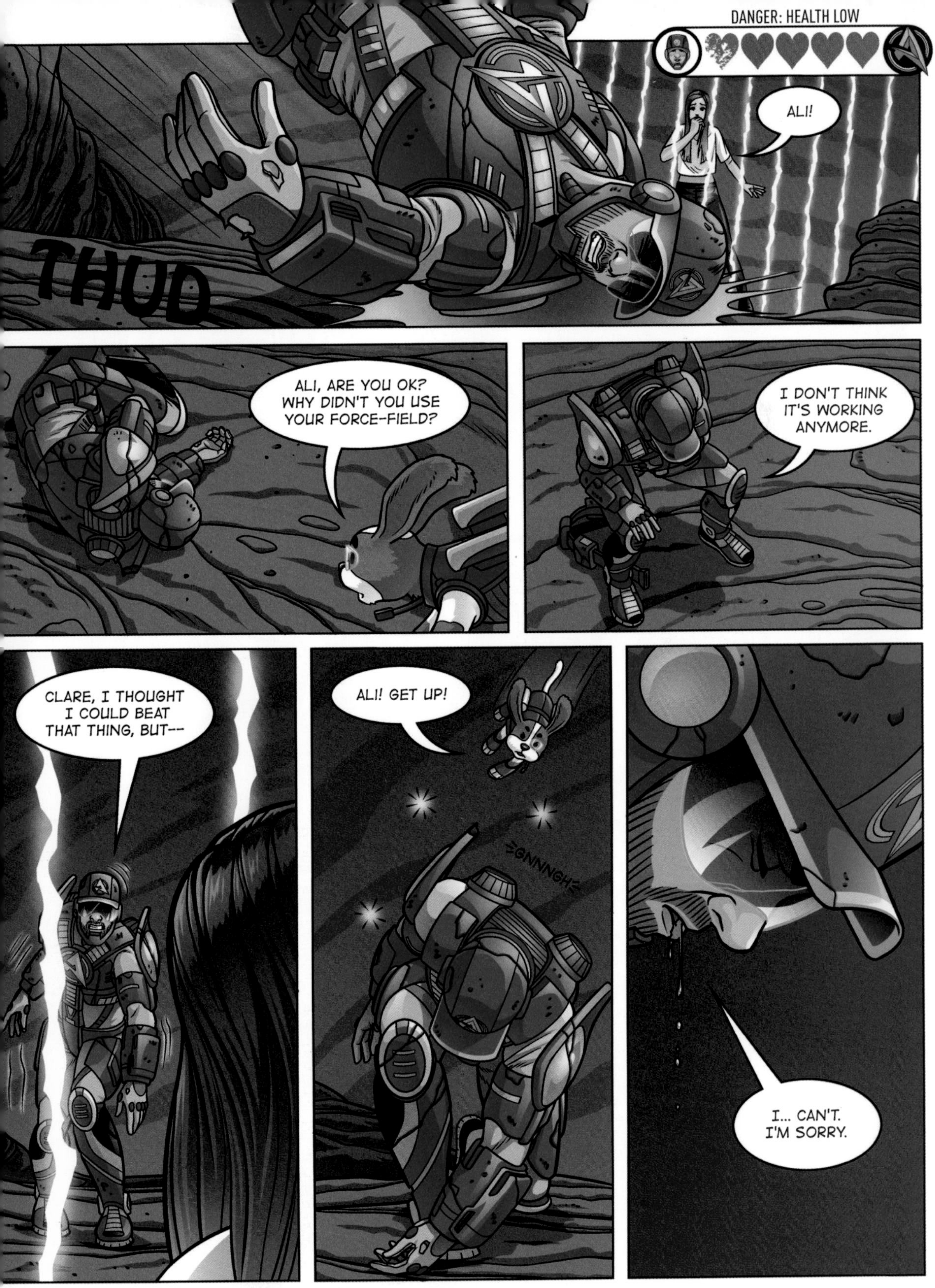
DANGER: HEALTH LOW
ALI!
THUD
ALI, ARE YOU OK? WHY DIDN'T YOU USE YOUR FORCE-FIELD?
I DON'T THINK IT'S WORKING ANYMORE.
CLARE, I THOUGHT I COULD BEAT THAT THING, BUT--
ALI! GET UP!
GNNNNGH
I... CAN'T. I'M SORRY.

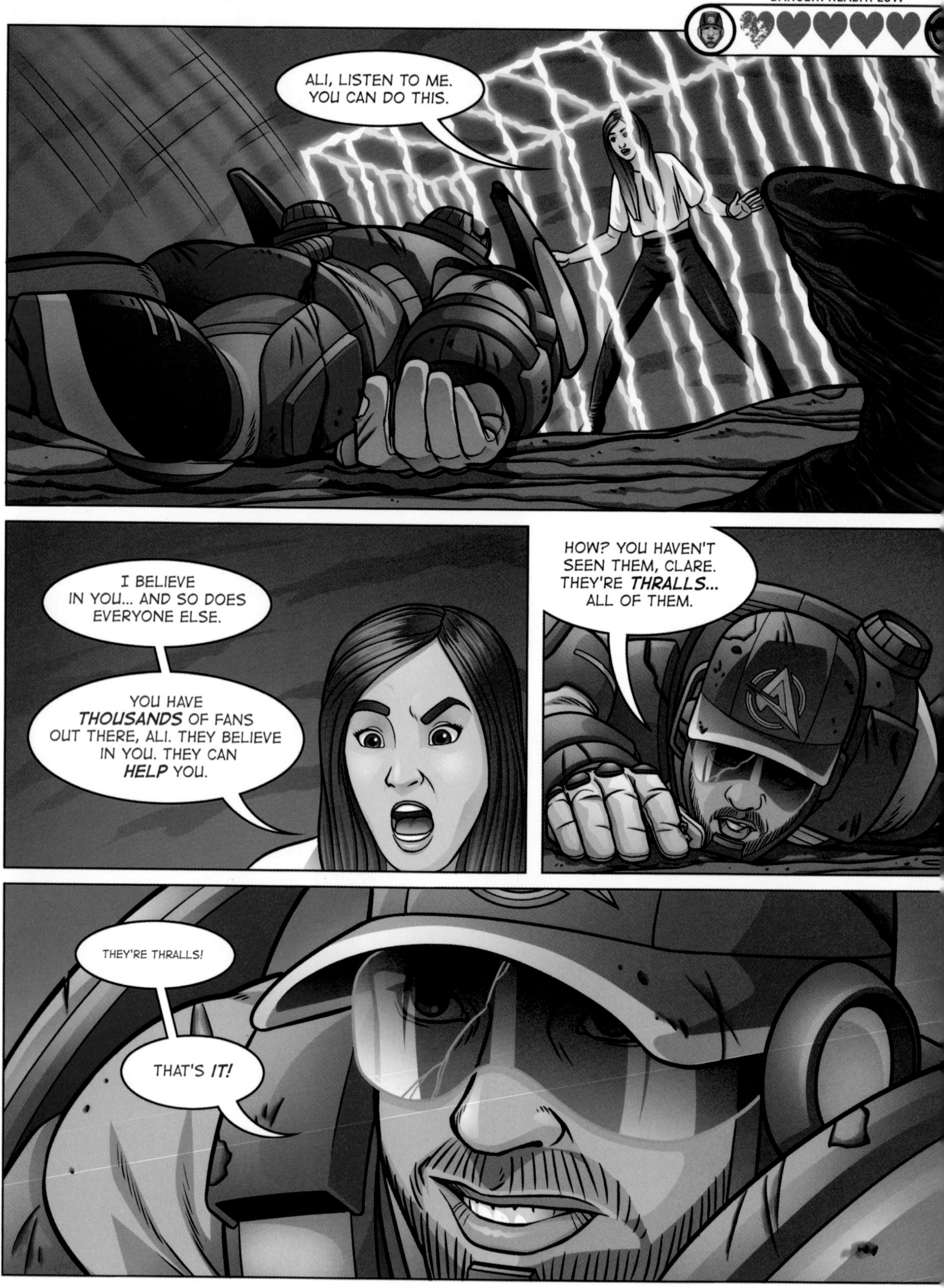
DANGER: HEALTH LOW
ALI, LISTEN TO ME. YOU CAN DO THIS.
I BELIEVE IN YOU... AND SO DOES EVERYONE ELSE.
YOU HAVE **THOUSANDS** OF FANS OUT THERE, ALI. THEY BELIEVE IN YOU. THEY CAN **HELP** YOU.
HOW? YOU HAVEN'T SEEN THEM, CLARE. THEY'RE **THRALLS...** ALL OF THEM.
THEY'RE THRALLS!
THAT'S *IT!*

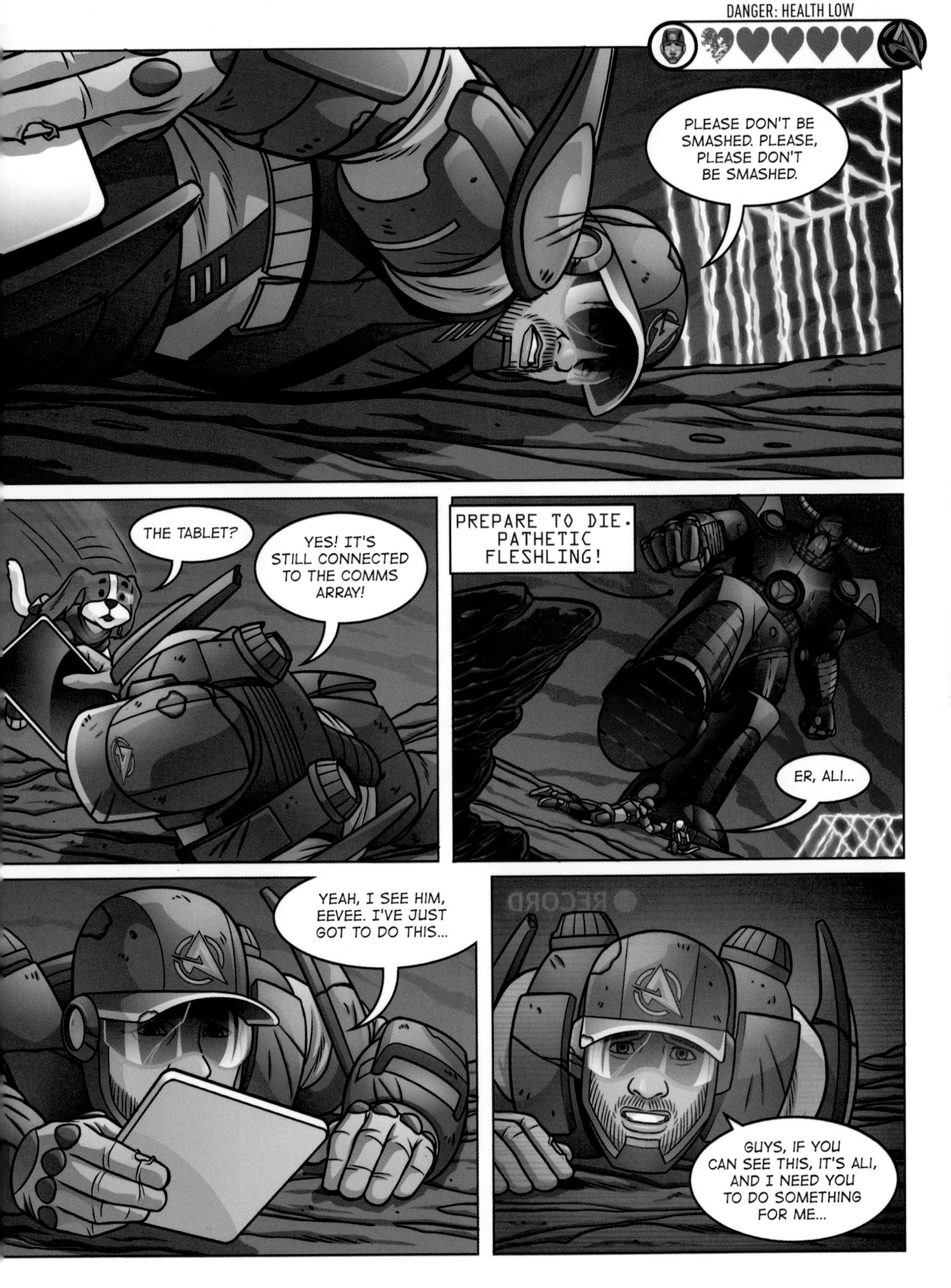
DANGER: HEALTH LOW
PLEASE DON'T BE SMASHED. PLEASE, PLEASE DON'T BE SMASHED.
THE TABLET?
YES! IT'S STILL CONNECTED TO THE COMMS ARRAY!
PREPARE TO DIE. PATHETIC FLESHLING!
ER, ALI...
YEAH, I SEE HIM, EEVEE. I'VE JUST GOT TO DO THIS...
RECORD
GUYS, IF YOU CAN SEE THIS, IT'S ALI, AND I NEED YOU TO DO SOMETHING FOR ME...

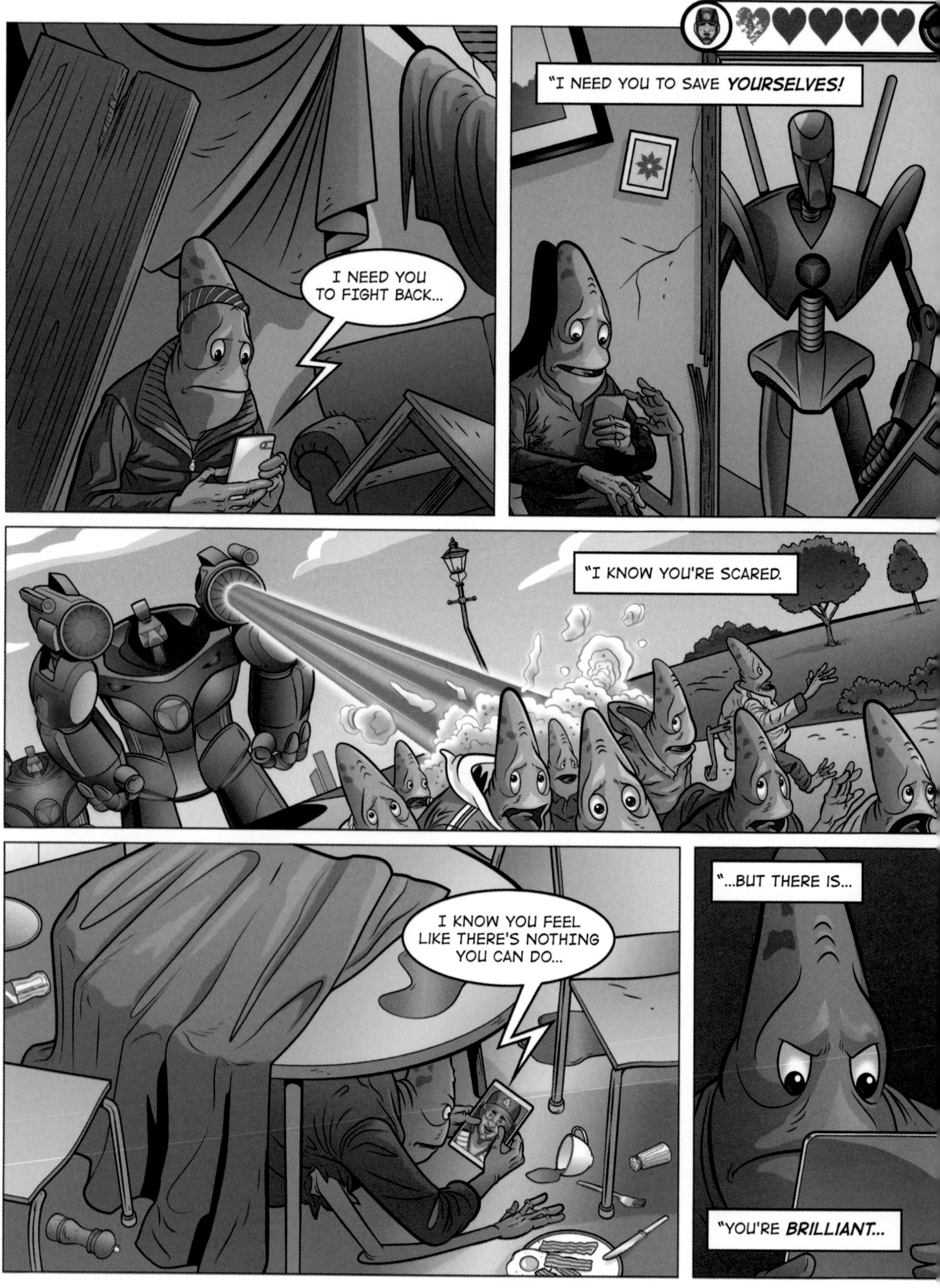
I NEED YOU
TO FIGHT BACK...
"I NEED YOU TO SAVE YOURSELVES!
"I KNOW YOU'RE SCARED.
I KNOW YOU FEEL LIKE THERE'S NOTHING YOU CAN DO...
"...BUT THERE IS...
"YOU'RE BRILLIANT...

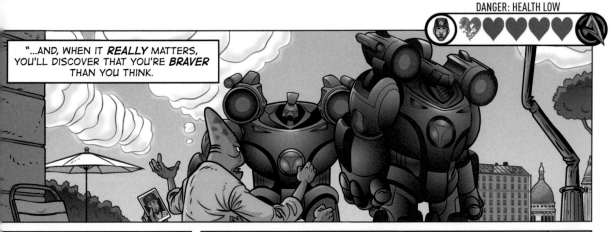

"...AND, WHEN IT **REALLY** MATTERS, YOU'LL DISCOVER THAT YOU'RE **BRAVER** THAN YOU THINK.

"TRUST ME--I KNOW!

"JUST REMEMBER, YOU'RE **NOT** ALONE.

"THERE ARE **MILLIONS** OF YOU OUT THERE WHO ALL FEEL THE SAME WAY.

"**BILLIONS** OF YOU.

"AND, WHEN YOU WORK TOGETHER...

"...THERE'S **NOTHING** YOU CAN'T DO!"

THAT'S ENOUGH SENTIMENTAL RUBBISH FOR ONE DAY, HUMAN!

HEY!

SO MUCH FOR ASKING FOR HELP.

Smash

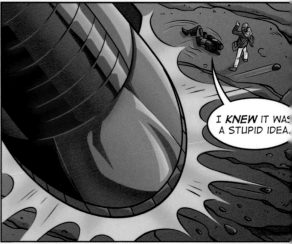

I *KNEW* IT WAS A STUPID IDEA.

NO. NO, IT WASN'T!

ALI, THIS IS *INCREDIBLE!* MILLIONS OF THRALLS ALL AROUND THE GLOBE ARE FIGHTING BACK.

AND IT'S ALL BECAUSE OF WHAT *YOU* SAID.

THIS IS GOING TO BE YOUR *BIGGEST UPGRADE* YET!

ALL THRALLS SAVED EVERYWHERE!

Ping

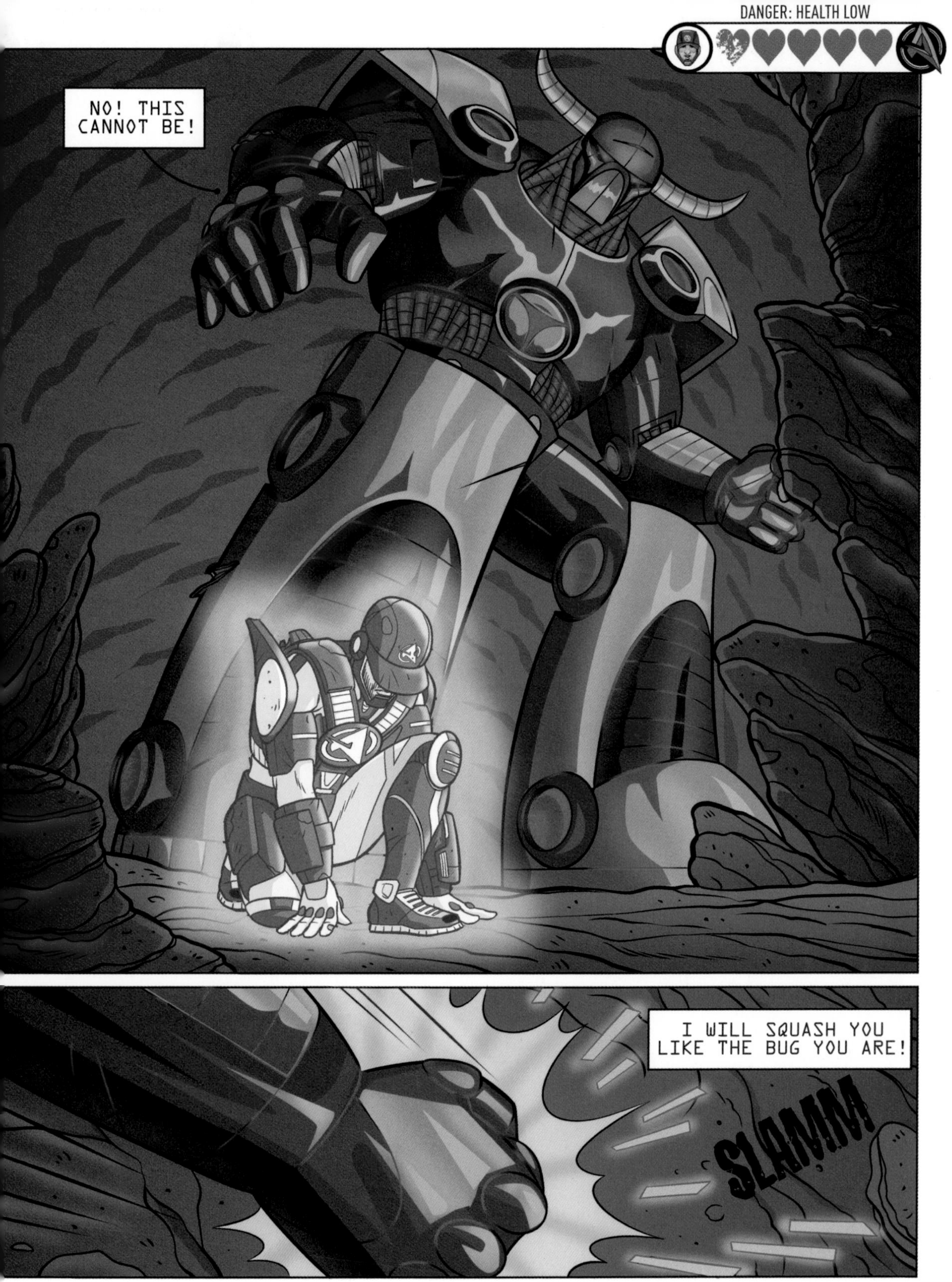
DANGER: HEALTH LOW
NO! THIS CANNOT BE!
I WILL SQUASH YOU LIKE THE BUG YOU ARE!
SLAMM

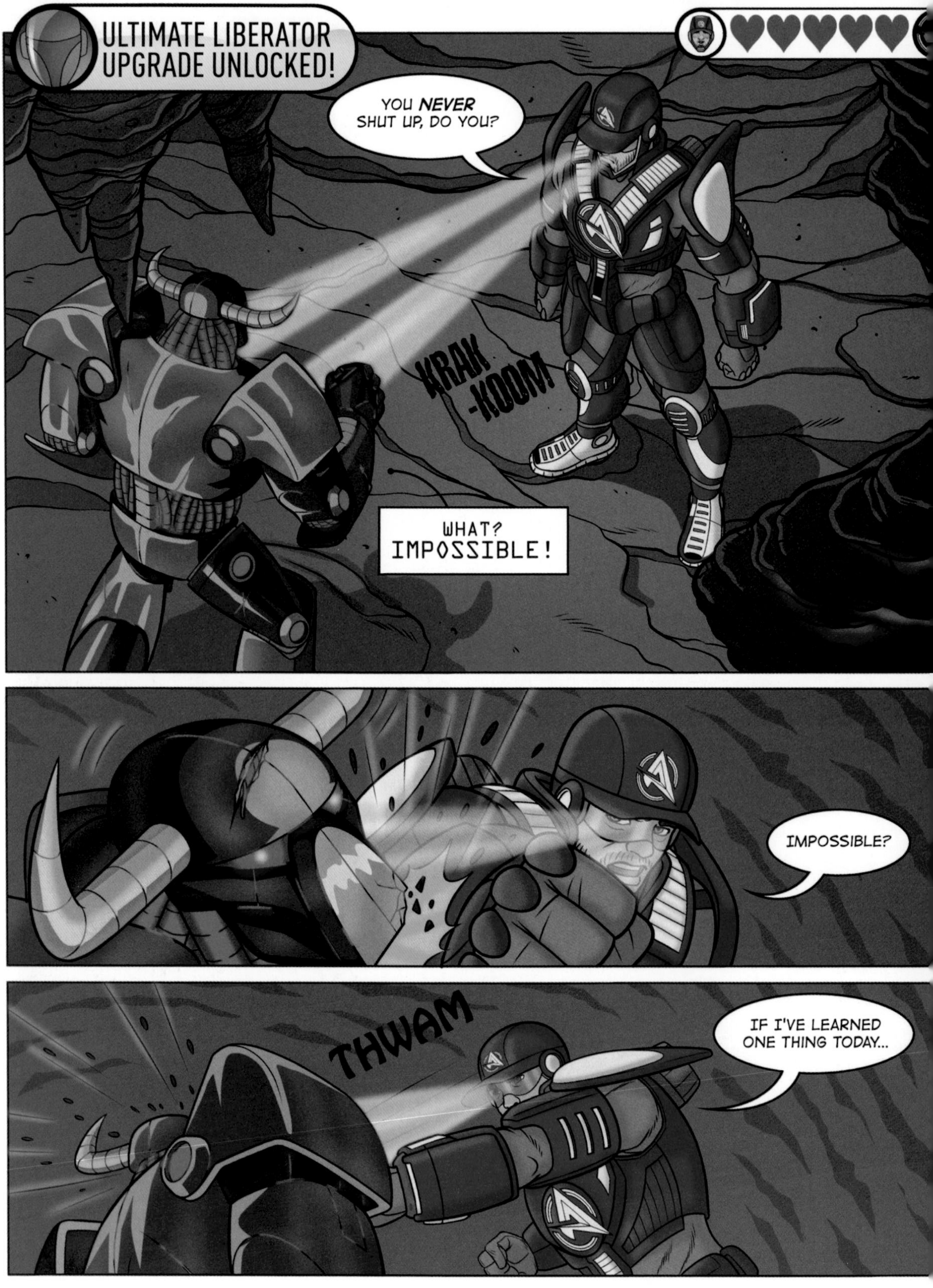
ULTIMATE LIBERATOR UPGRADE UNLOCKED!
YOU NEVER SHUT UP, DO YOU?
KRAK-KOOM
WHAT? IMPOSSIBLE!
IMPOSSIBLE?
THWAM
IF I'VE LEARNED ONE THING TODAY...

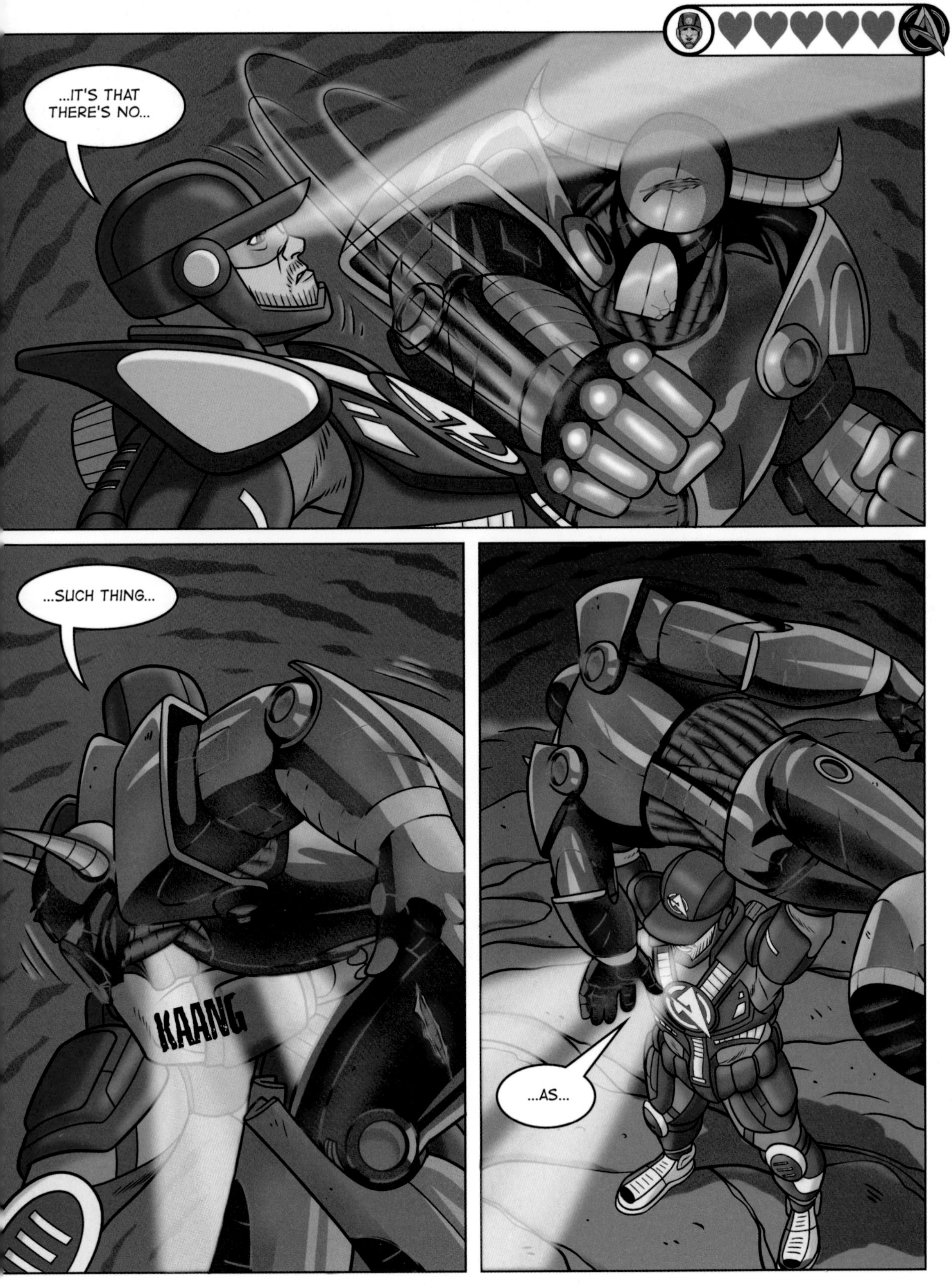

...IT'S THAT THERE'S NO...
...SUCH THING...
KAANG
...AS...

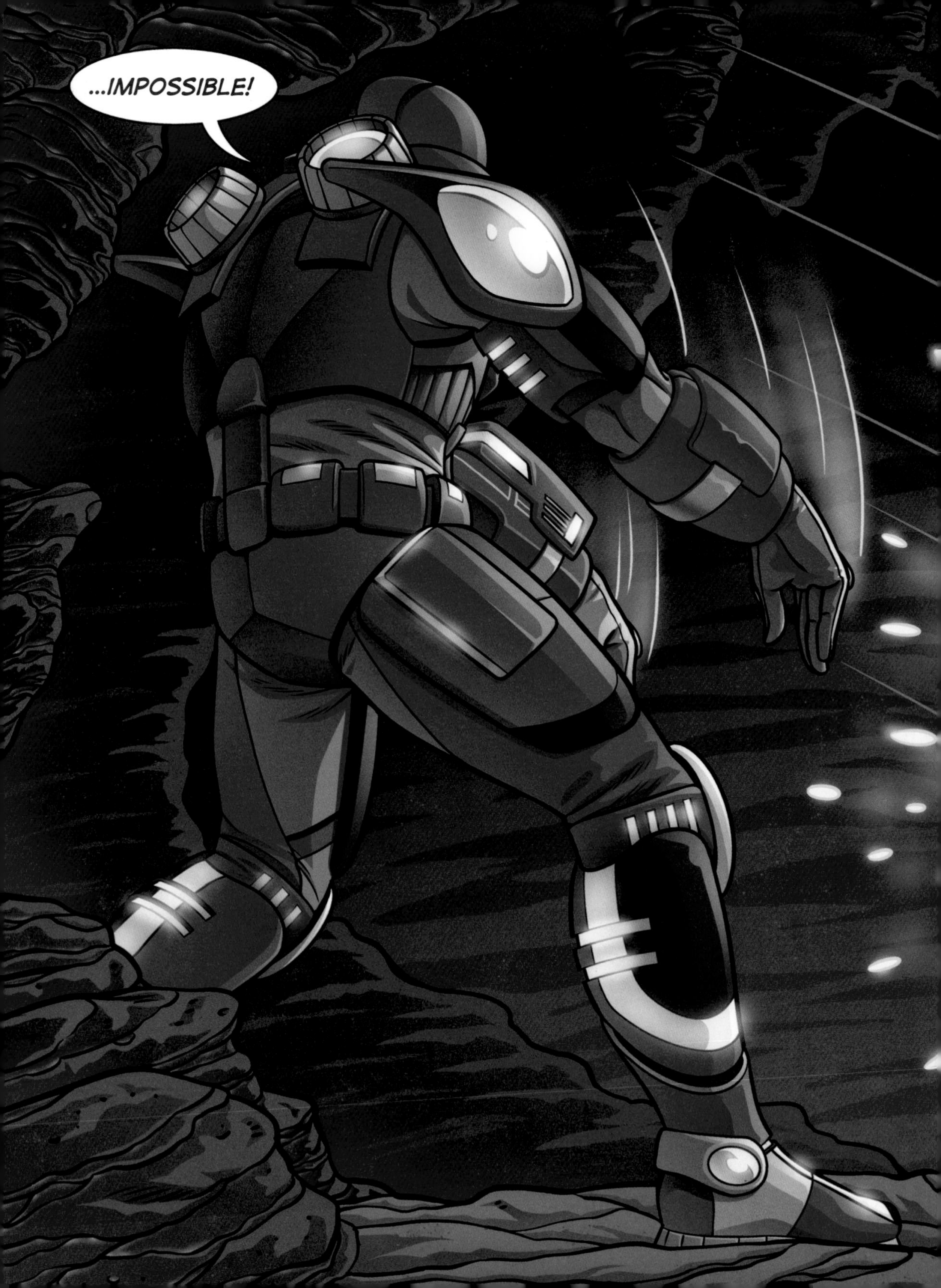
...IMPOSSIBLE!

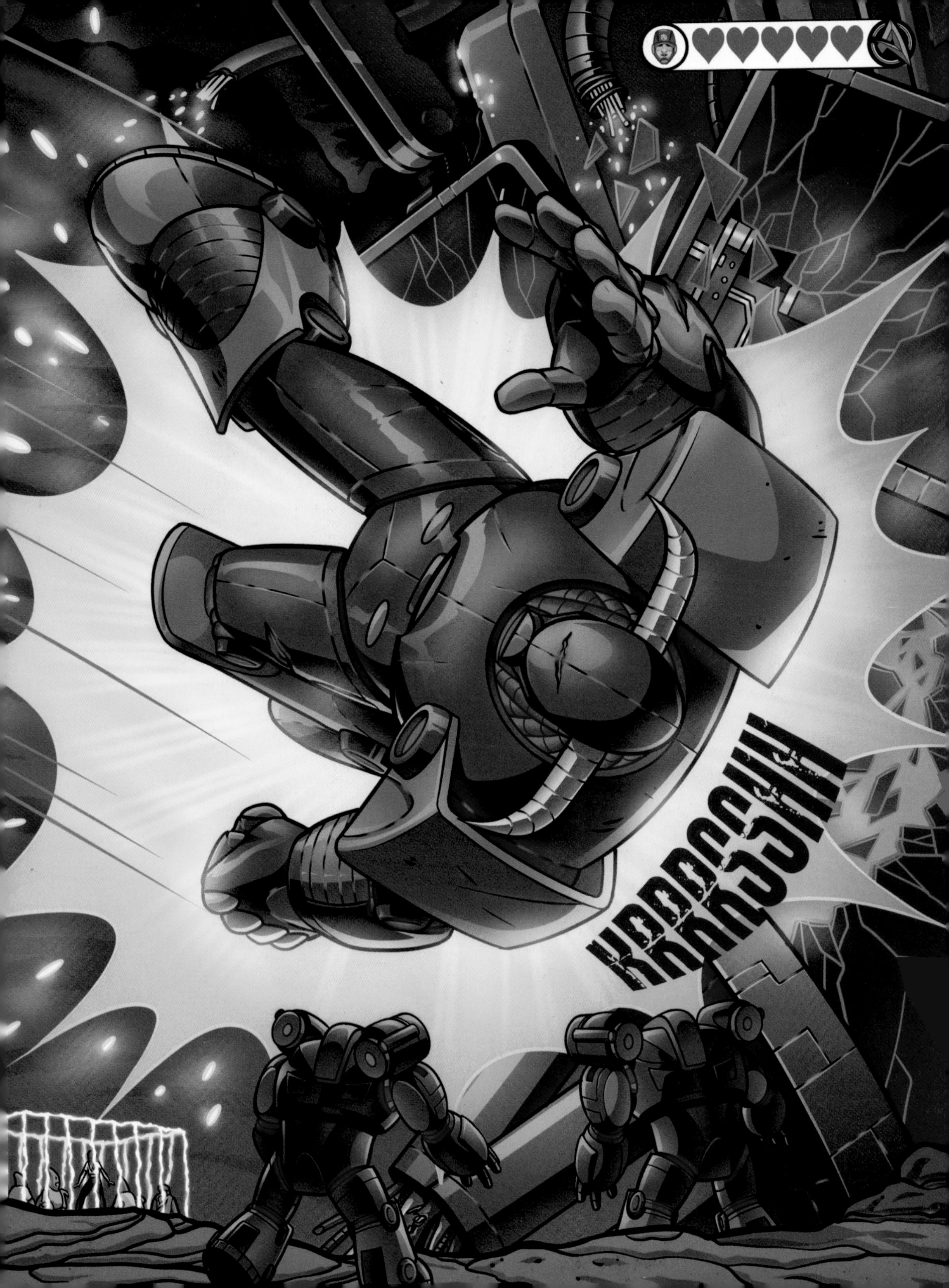
KRRRASSHH

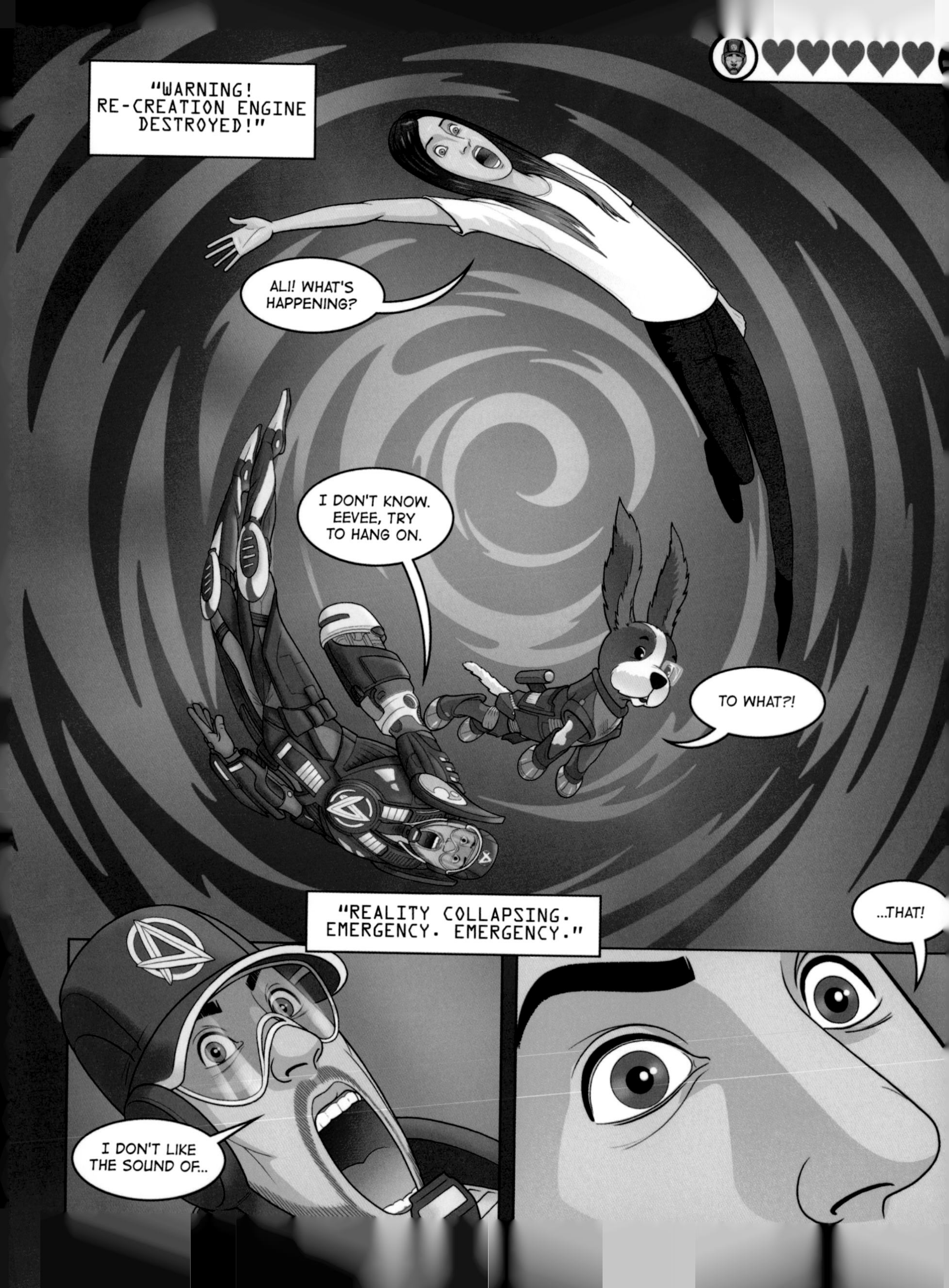
"WARNING! RE-CREATION ENGINE DESTROYED!"
ALI! WHAT'S HAPPENING?
I DON'T KNOW. EEVEE, TRY TO HANG ON.
TO WHAT?!
"REALITY COLLAPSING. EMERGENCY. EMERGENCY."
I DON'T LIKE THE SOUND OF...
...THAT!

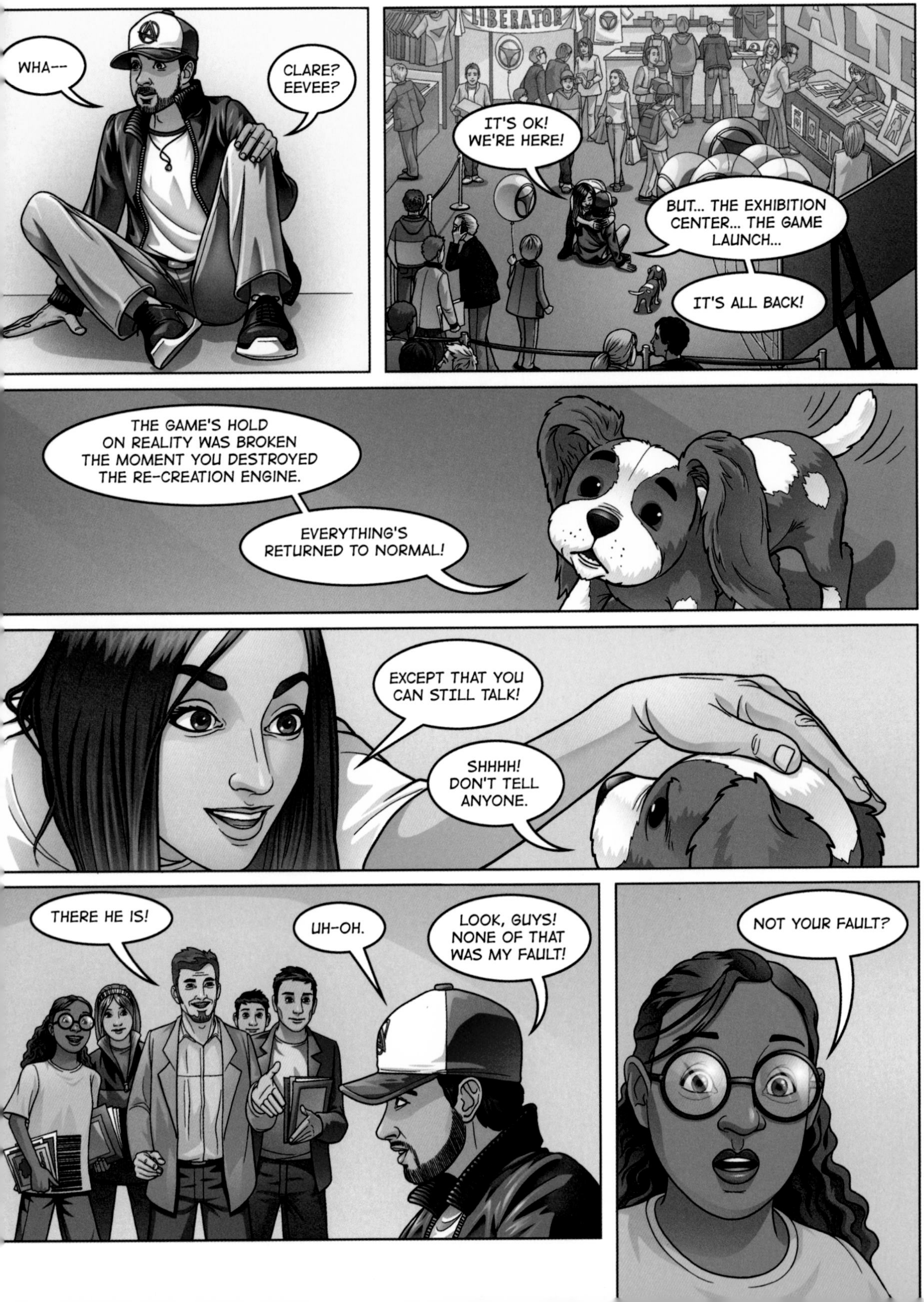
WHA--
CLARE? EEVEE?
LIBERATOR
IT'S OK! WE'RE HERE!
BUT... THE EXHIBITION CENTER... THE GAME LAUNCH...
IT'S ALL BACK!
THE GAME'S HOLD ON REALITY WAS BROKEN THE MOMENT YOU DESTROYED THE RE-CREATION ENGINE.
EVERYTHING'S RETURNED TO NORMAL!
EXCEPT THAT YOU CAN STILL TALK!
SHHHH! DON'T TELL ANYONE.
THERE HE IS!
UH-OH.
LOOK, GUYS! NONE OF THAT WAS MY FAULT!
NOT YOUR FAULT?

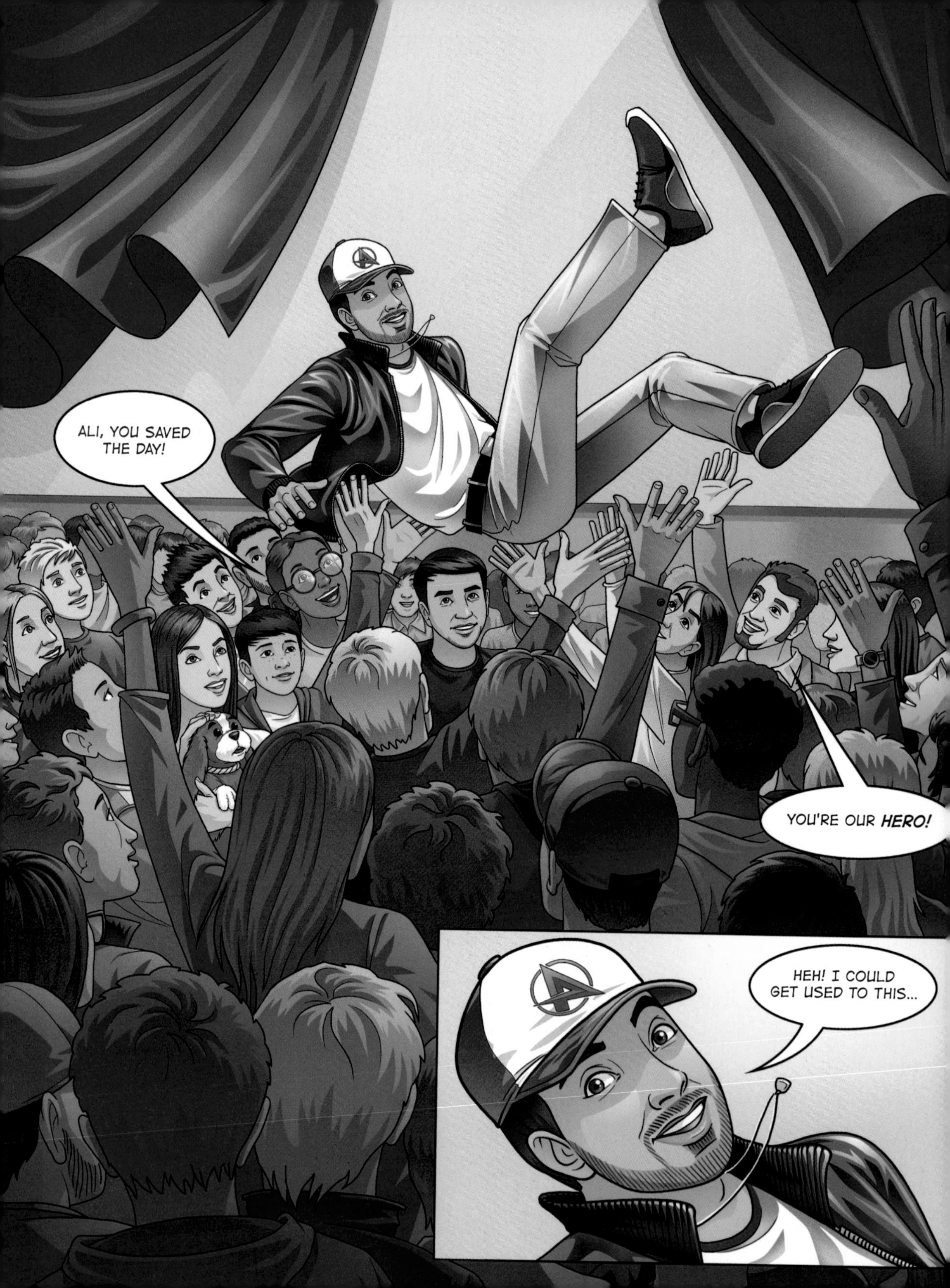
ALI, YOU SAVED THE DAY!
YOU'RE OUR HERO!
HEH! I COULD GET USED TO THIS...

STARRING	ALI-A
	CLARE SIOBHAN
	AND
	EEVEE
	AND INTRODUCING
	THOMAS CUSACK
STORY	ALI-A
	CAVAN SCOTT
ART	ALEK SOTIROVSKI
	MARTA MESAS
	DANIEL SANCHEZ LIMON
	PAUL MORAN
	GERGELY FÓRIZ
	JOHN BATTEN
	LEO CAMPOS
	MARTYN CAIN
	JANOS JANTNER
	KEVIN HOPGOOD

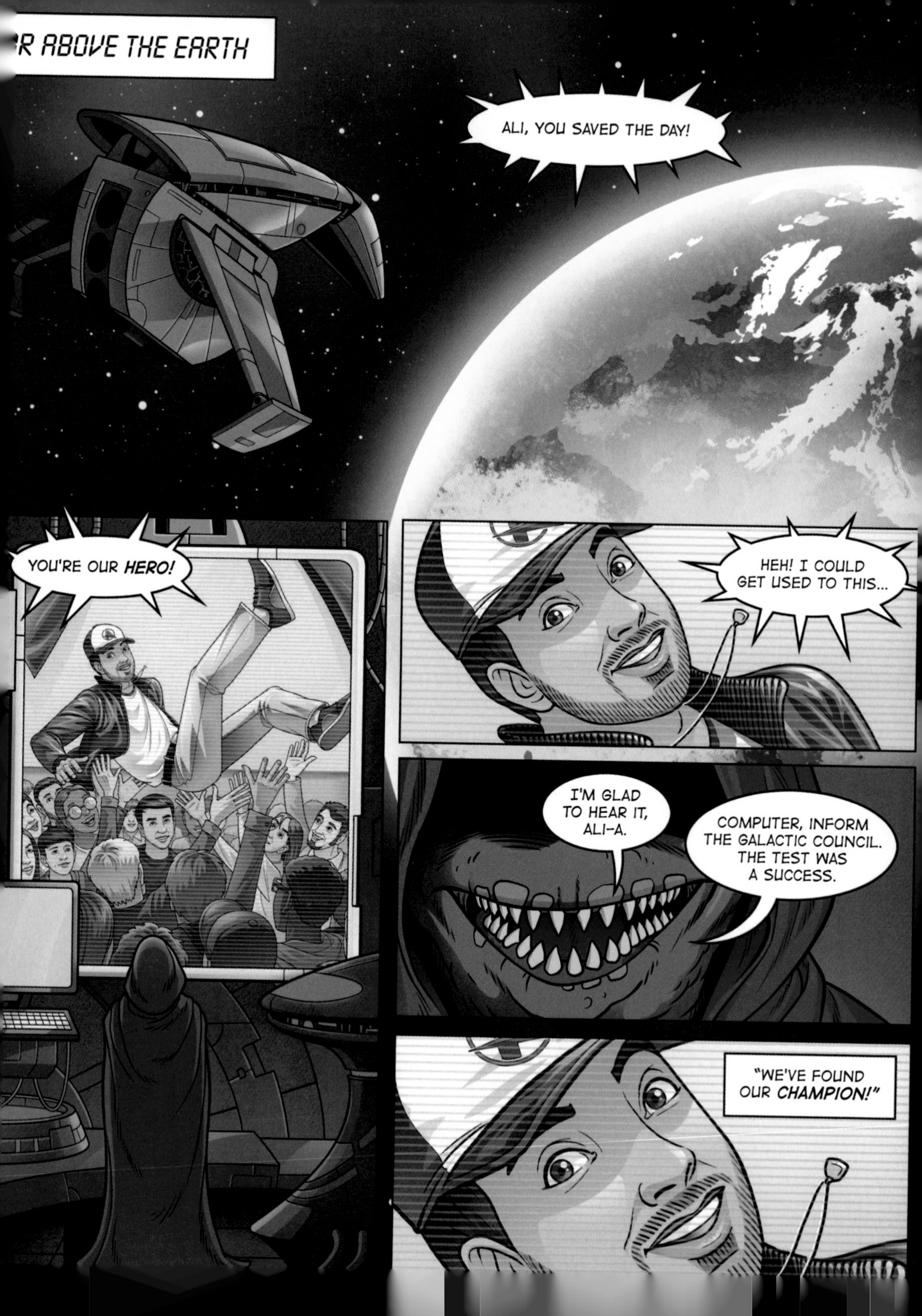
R ABOVE THE EARTH
ALI, YOU SAVED THE DAY!
YOU'RE OUR **HERO!**
HEH! I COULD GET USED TO THIS...
I'M GLAD TO HEAR IT, ALI-A.
COMPUTER, INFORM THE GALACTIC COUNCIL. THE TEST WAS A SUCCESS.
"WE'VE FOUND OUR **CHAMPION!**"

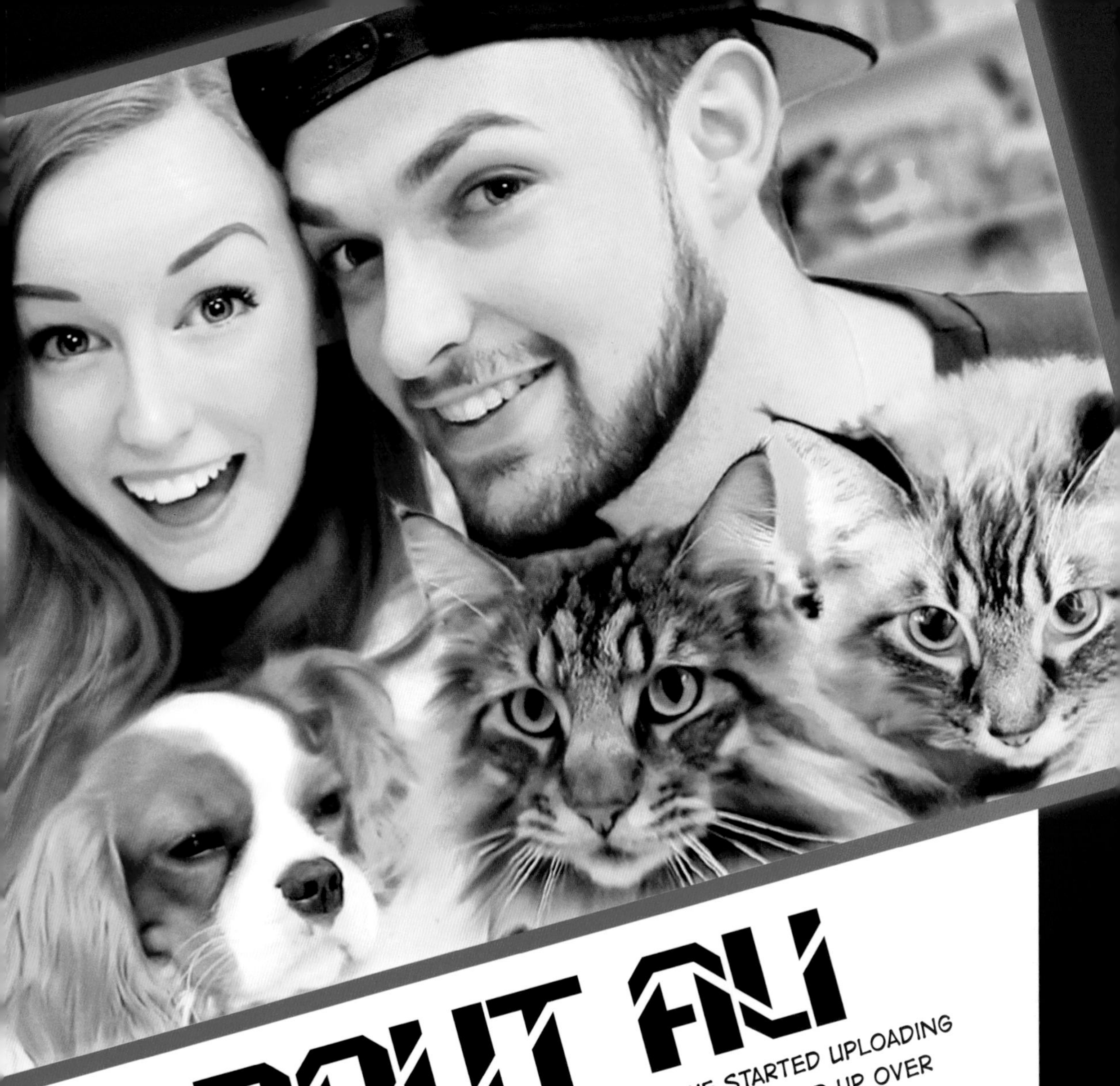

ABOUT ALI

ALI-A'S REAL ADVENTURE BEGAN IN 2009, WHEN HE STARTED UPLOADING SHORT GAMING CLIPS TO YOUTUBE. SINCE THEN, HE'S PICKED UP OVER 13 MILLION SUBSCRIBERS, ALL LOGGING IN REGULARLY TO CATCH HIS UNMISSABLE ***CALL OF DUTY*** AND ***POKÉMON GO*** VIDEOS.

TODAY, HIS CONTENT ISN'T JUST ABOUT GAMING, WITH HIS SECOND CHANNEL ALLOWING FANS A GLIMPSE OF HIS LIFE WITH HIS PARTNER, CLARE, AND HEROIC POOCH, EEVEE (WHO, AS FAR AS WE KNOW, CAN'T TALK IN REAL LIFE).

A FOR ACTION

ALI-A ON BECOMING AN ACTION HERO, FIGHTING GIANT ROBOTS ALONGSIDE CLARE AND EEVEE, AND THE FUTURE OF HIS GRAPHIC NOVEL ADVENTURES . . .

DID YOU EVER IMAGINE YOU'D BE INVOLVED IN CREATING A BOOK?

HONESTLY, IT WAS NEVER SOMETHING I EVEN CONSIDERED. I SAW A LOT OF YOUTUBERS DOING THEIR OWN BOOKS AND THOUGHT, *YOU KNOW WHAT, THAT'S PROBABLY SOMETHING I'LL LEAVE ALONE.* THEN, WHEN THE IDEA OF DOING AN ACTION-ADVENTURE WAS SUGGESTED, I REMEMBERED THE KIND OF STORIES I ENJOYED AS A KID, ABOUT HEROES GOING OFF ON ALL SORTS OF DANGEROUS MISSIONS. I THOUGHT DOING SOMETHING ON A SIMILAR SCALE WOULD BE REALLY EXCITING.

WAS IT ALWAYS GOING TO BE A GRAPHIC NOVEL?

NOT AT FIRST, BUT I WANTED THE STORY TO BE AS ACTION-PACKED AS POSSIBLE. PLUS, GAMES ARE OBVIOUSLY REALLY VISUAL, AND THE FANS WHO WATCH MY VIDEOS ARE USED TO SEEING ME ON-SCREEN, SO A GRAPHIC NOVEL MADE A LOT OF SENSE.

WHAT KIND OF COMICS DID YOU LIKE READING AS A KID?

I HAD A HUGE STACK OF COMICS LIKE THE *BEANO* THAT I'D PILE THROUGH, BUT THE ONE THAT REALLY STANDS OUT WAS *ASTERIX*. OH MAN, I USED TO GET REALLY SUCKED INTO THOSE STORIES. THEY WERE FILLED WITH ALL KINDS OF CRAZY ADVENTURES, AND THE CHARACTERS ALL HAD SUCH BIG PERSONALITIES. THEY REALLY INSPIRED *GAME ON!*

BUT THIS TIME THE MAIN CHARACTER IS YOU! WHAT WAS IT LIKE SEEING YOURSELF IN GRAPHIC-NOVEL FORM FOR THE FIRST TIME?

IT WAS SUPER-COOL, ESPECIALLY AS I KNEW I WOULD BE GIVEN ALL THESE AMAZING ABILITIES AND ARMOR UPGRADES. SEEING THE FIRST SKETCHES, IT REALLY HIT HOME HOW INCREDIBLE THIS WAS GOING TO BE. THE COMIC-BOOK ALI-A WOULD BE DOING THINGS THAT I'D NEVER BE ABLE TO DO IN REAL LIFE!

HOW DO YOU THINK THE REAL ALI WOULD COPE IF HE FOUND HIMSELF IN COMIC-BOOK ALI'S SHOES? COULD YOU SAVE THE EARTH FROM AN ALIEN INVASION?

I'D LIKE TO SAY THAT I'D STEP UP TO THE MARK, AND BE JUST AS EFFICIENT AT SAVING THE DAY. UNFORTUNATELY, I'M NOT SURE THAT WOULD ACTUALLY HAPPEN. I THINK THE COMIC-BOOK ALI IS WAY COOLER THAN THE REAL ME!

WHAT ABOUT EEVEE? SHE'D BE ABLE TO SAVE HELPLESS THRALLS FROM RAMPAGING ROBOTS, RIGHT?

OH, THOSE THRALLS WOULD HAVE NOTHING TO WORRY ABOUT. EEVEE WOULD BREEZE THROUGH EVERYTHING! CLARE TOO.

WAS CLARE EXCITED THE FIRST TIME SHE SAW HER ILLUSTRATIONS?

SHE WAS SUPER-EXCITED. IT MADE IT ALL SO REAL. SHE WAS GOING TO BE IN A BOOK! I KNEW FROM THE BEGINNING THAT I NEEDED BOTH CLARE AND EEVEE TO BE IN THE STORY. WE DO EVERYTHING TOGETHER, SO I COULDN'T GO ON AN ADVENTURE LIKE THIS AND NOT HAVE THEM ALONG. THE COMIC-BOOK ALI WOULD STRUGGLE IF CLARE AND EEVEE WEREN'T AROUND. HE NEEDS THEM BY HIS SIDE. THEY'RE A REAL TEAM.

WAS CREATING THE BOOK EVERYTHING YOU EXPECTED?

I'VE NEVER DONE ANYTHING LIKE THIS BEFORE. I THINK HAVING CAVAN FLESH OUT THE IDEA AND WRITE THE SCRIPT MADE IT EASIER TO VISUALIZE HOW EVERYTHING WOULD LOOK, MAKING SURE THAT THE ACTION WAS SPREAD THROUGHOUT THE BOOK TO KEEP PEOPLE TURNING THE PAGES. AND THEN SEEING THE SCRIPT COME TO LIFE WITH ALEKSANDAR AND THE TEAM'S INCREDIBLE ARTWORK HAS BEEN AN AMAZING EXPERIENCE. IT'S BEEN A LONG PROCESS, BUT EVERYONE HAS DONE SUCH A GREAT JOB. IT'S BEEN SO GOOD TO BE THERE FROM THE BEGINNING AND SEE IT ALL COME TOGETHER PIECE-BY-PIECE.

WERE YOU NERVOUS WHEN YOU FIRST ANNOUNCED THE BOOK?

DEFINITELY, BUT THE RESPONSE WAS GREAT. PEOPLE IMMEDIATELY STARTED TWEETING THAT THEY WERE LOOKING FORWARD TO READING IT. I WANT THEM TO HAVE THE SAME EXPERIENCE I HAD WHEN I WAS A KID--WANTING TO READ AS QUICKLY AS POSSIBLE TO FIND OUT WHAT HAPPENS NEXT, AND THEN GOING BACK TO READ IT ALL OVER AGAIN. I ALSO HOPE IT GETS PEOPLE READING WHO WOULDN'T NORMALLY PICK UP A BOOK. THAT WOULD BE AMAZING. AND, HEY, IF EVERYONE ENJOYS **GAME ON!** MAYBE WE CAN CREATE EVEN MORE ALI-A ADVENTURES DOWN THE LINE.

WHERE WOULD YOU LIKE TO SEE ALI-A GO NEXT?

THAT'S A TOUGH QUESTION. WE'VE SEEN HIM UP AGAINST ROBOTS, ALIENS, AND EVEN KILLER TREES, BUT THERE ARE SUBTLE HINTS TOWARDS THE END THAT SOMETHING ELSE IS COMING--SOMETHING BIGGER! THERE ARE SO MANY PLACES THAT ALI-A COULD GO IN THESE STORIES, MAYBE EVEN OUTER SPACE! WHO KNOWS?

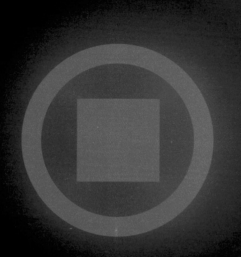

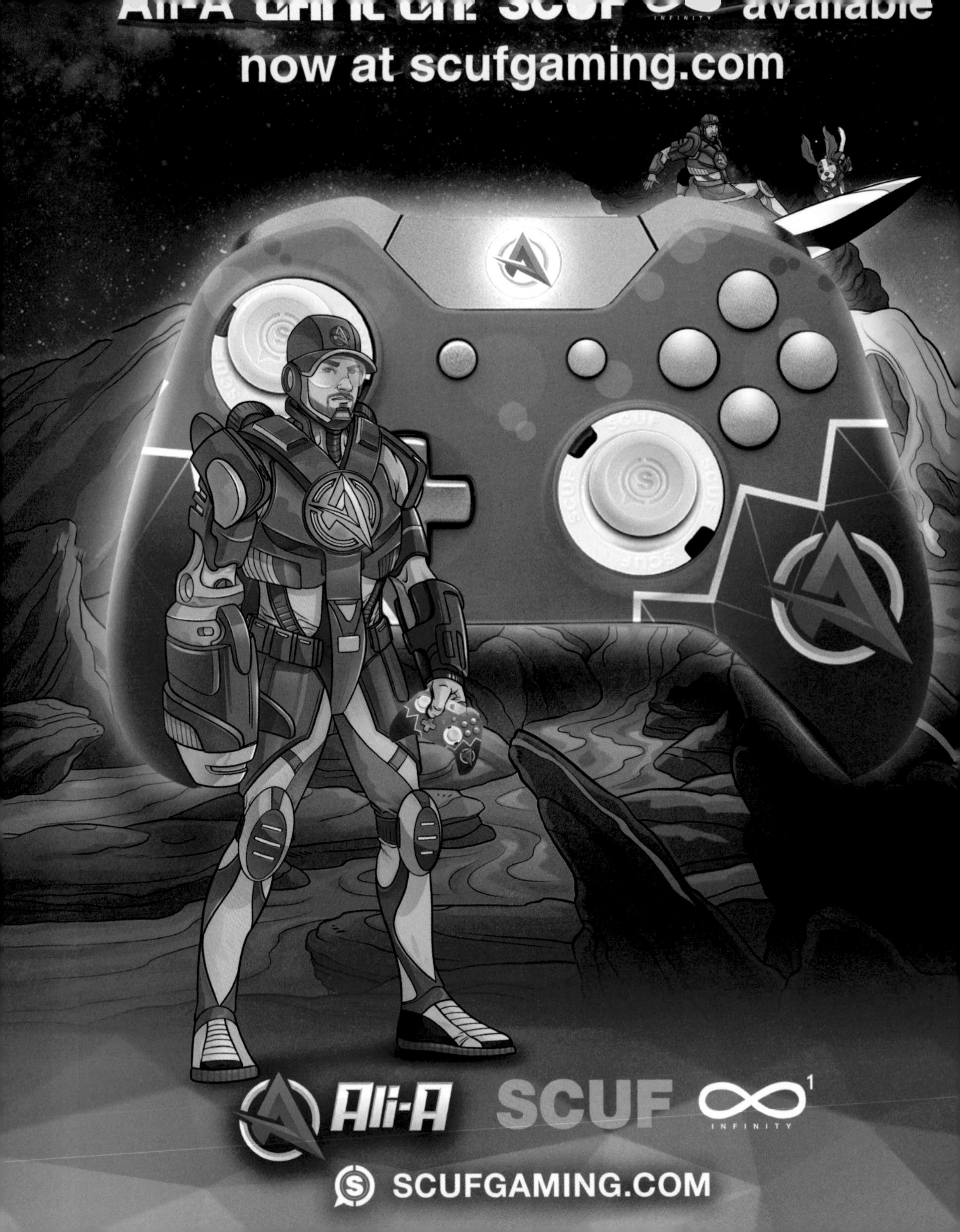
available
now at scufgaming.com
Ali-A
SCUF
INFINITY
SCUFGAMING.COM